The Singularity series:

Redshift
The Observer Effect
Uncertainty Principle
Quantum Entanglement
Event Horizon
Point Singularity

Prequel
Ani, or, the care and feeding of your great tree-
dwelling venomous tentacled land-devil

UNCERTAINTY PRINCIPLE

R.M. OLSON

ISBN-13: 978-1-990142-19-2

Cover by MiblArt

To Sara.
Thank you for believing in my two stupid scientists as much as I did.

" … and thus the uncertainty principle demonstrates the inherent limits of our ability to measure: we can know either the position of an electron, or its momentum, but never both. The more we strive to pinpoint with accuracy the one factor, the less accurate our knowledge of the other."

-From an introductory physic textbook, Sao Martim University, Vila Nova do Sol, Colorida

1

Aran

From his perch halfway up the tree, Aran glanced over at his best friend.

Istvay's dark hair, pulled back in its typical ponytail, glowed in the moonlight as they bent over the starchart they had pulled up in front of them. They had a sextant as well, and occasionally glanced up, taking measurements of the night sky. And for a moment, watching them, Aran felt a rush of fondness that was almost enough to make him dizzy.

The massive spider below him hissed, jolting him out of his reverie.

Well, it wasn't exactly a spider. To be honest, he had no idea what it was, and he'd never seen something quite like it before. But it had eight legs, a body multiple times Aran's size, and a very clear agenda that involved eating Aran, and probably Istvay as well.

"Easy there," he whispered, trying very hard not to allow his unease to show in his voice. "I'm—we're not a threat, neither of us are a threat."

The fact was, on this forsaken planet, there were very few places that were high enough out of the trees for Istvay to get a reading on the starchart. It just happened to be their bad luck that the one place that was happened to be the home of a—well, whatever the hell this thing was.

It was watching him, which, after all, was the point—they needed the readings, and Aran had agreed to keep the coast clear. And if Istvay still didn't actually know the full extent of what that currently entailed, it was just as well. They had to be able to focus on their work.

The spider hissed again and scuttled closer. On Aran's shoulder, Ani hissed in return. He was already holding her back with both hands to keep her from going after the thing.

"Easy there," he whispered again, trying to keep his voice steady. "Listen, this doesn't have to be a fight. Nobody here wants a fight, I don't think, and—"

The spider pounced. Aran scrambled backwards, clinging onto Ani's tentacles as hard as he could with one hand, while with the other, trying to catch himself on the slick branches of the tree. "No, it's fine, Ani, there's no need to—"

Ani wasn't listening. She made an abortive attempt to launch herself towards the beast, realized that Aran hadn't let go yet, and turned her snarl on him.

"Ani, listen, we don't just kill whatever—"

The spider recalibrated its aim and launched itself at Aran again.

"Hey now, it's alright, no one's trying to hurt you—" Aran managed to choke out.

The spider appeared extremely unconvinced.

Aran grabbed with both arms for a branch, swung himself up, and made a wild grab for Ani, who'd realized she was free and was attempting to fling herself at the spider again. "Ani, listen. It's not trying to hurt us—I mean, it is, but only because—" He jerked his leg out of the way as the spider's mandibles clamped shut right where his foot had been.

"Damn it to hell," he said through his teeth.

Istvay had glanced up from the nearby hilltop where they were making their measurements. "Is everything alright back there?" they whispered through the wavelink.

Aran ignored them. He could worry about reassuring Istvay after he'd gotten the hell out of here.

The spider's mandibles clicked shut again, catching the toe of Aran's boot and slicing through the thick leather upper as if it were paper. Aran swore again and kicked off, trying to one-handedly pull himself farther up the tree.

The branches were getting thinner, and he tried very hard to keep from thinking about the ever-growing distance between himself and the ground.

Although, as much as he hated heights, he was a little preoccupied with more urgent things at present.

"Aran? Aran, listen, I'm getting close to done here. I don't want to interrupt you in the middle of something, but can you please just let me know if you need help?"

There was a studied calm to Istvay's voice, and Aran groaned internally. "I'm fine," he hissed, squeezing his hand to activate his wavelink. "Can't talk right now. Be ready to run."

There was a moment of silence, which probably meant Istvay understood both what Aran was trying to tell them, and a handful of things he was very desperately trying not to tell them.

The branches under his hands were getting noticeably thinner as he scrambled higher. It wouldn't be long before they wouldn't hold his weight anymore, and Ani had almost wriggled free of his grip.

On the bright side, the thinness of the branches meant that the spider couldn't actually follow him up the tree, considering it outweighed him by several hundred kilos.

He glanced down, and wished, desperately, that he hadn't.

"Ani," he whispered, squeezing his eyes shut. "Don't worry, Ani, we'll be fine."

Ani didn't seem particularly worried about whether or not she'd be fine—she seemed much more focused on ensuring that the spider would not be.

"Ani, listen. If you just behave for a few more minutes, I'll get you a treat as soon as we get down. Okay?"

She was hissing a challenge to the spider below them, and the spider seemed more than willing to take her up on the offer.

Aran could just let her go—he'd encountered very few creatures that could hurt Ani, and she was eminently capable of taking care of herself—but it hardly seemed fair that the spider, whose territory they had invaded without an invitation, should pay the price of their adventure. Besides, for all he knew, this was an endangered species. He already felt a little sick whenever he thought about what Ani must have done to the ecosystem on the last planet they'd visited.

He yanked a retractable line from his supplies pouch, and, swallowing hard, he stepped carefully along the branch he was standing on, making his way out over the forest floor. The branch dipped alarmingly at his weight, and his feet slipped once, almost making him lose his balance. He had to pause for a moment, eyes closed, heart pounding, trying to get his terror under control.

And then, at last, he managed to reach up and slip the retractable line over the branch above him, far enough out that he might be able to let himself down without impaling himself on another branch.

The line caught with a soft *ting*, and Aran breathed a sigh of relief.

Then he glanced down, and swore.

At the soft sound, the creature below him had reared up, snapping its mandibles together in fury. With a movement that was almost too rapid for Aran's eyes to follow, it spat.

He just had time to catch a glimpse of a white blur shooting out towards him, then something sticky and strong surrounded him, catching his arms and binding them against his body.

"Damn it to hell," he choked, and then had to clamp his mouth shut to hold back the nausea as his feet fumbled for purchase on the branch. He tried to catch his balance, but without the use of his arms, there was nothing he could do.

He swore once more, helplessly, as his feet slipped and he plummeted towards the forest floor below.

The shock of the fall pulled the breath from his lungs, and he could feel Ani scrabbling against his shoulder where she, too, had been trapped by the web. And then the line he'd thrown over the branch caught with an impact that knocked the breath from his lungs, then gave, then caught again, tumbling him over and over in short, jerky starts and stops. Finally he came up short, swinging helplessly a few metres above the jungle floor.

He had one brief, shocked moment to take stock of how incredibly lucky he'd been—the thick webbing the spider had spat had caught the line as well as his arms, absorbing enough of the impact that he hadn't broken any bones or wrenched his arms from their sockets—before he glanced up.

The spider was already on its way down towards him. He twisted frantically, trying to get a hand free. He managed to free his fingers for long enough to squeeze his fist, activating the wavelink.

"Pishti," he gasped, "how close to done are you?"

He yanked desperately at his bindings, and his hand slid free, just enough that he could hit the light on his palm screen. It shot a brilliant beam of light towards the spider, and the creature flailed back. Aran gulped in a short breath of relief.

"Aran? What the hell are you—" Istvay seemed to think better of the question. "Yes. I got the last measurement I need, I'm just noting it down and I'm done." There was a note of grimness to their voice, and Aran couldn't exactly blame them.

They cared about him. Maybe not in the way he wished they would, but they cared about him, deeply.

And he'd learned thoroughly and effectively over the last few weeks that if there was one thing that was as important to him as saving Istvay's damn, stubborn life, it was—

Well, it was seeing Istvay happy.

Which meant paying attention to the things that were important to them, which apparently involved Aran not getting eaten by giant spiders.

Because yes, finding the cure for the genetic defect that was slowly killing his best friend was unutterably important. Yes, it was the thing that Aran had basically spent his life searching for, and would spend the rest of his life searching for until he found it.

But he'd also seen what happened when he hurt Istvay. When he ignored what they wanted in his effort to give them what he was certain they needed. And he wasn't going to do it again, not for himself, not to make himself happy, not to fix Istvay regardless of the outcome. They were a team, and he wasn't going to ruin things again.

"Good," he grunted.

He'd almost worked himself free of the spider's web, at least, enough to be able to cut himself loose to drop the remaining distance to the ground. Ani, however, had almost done the same.

With the final wrench, he tore one arm free, yanked the bush-blade out of his pouch, and slashed at the remainder of the sticky strands. The spider above him was hesitating, clearly not appreciating the light from his palmscreen, but the light wouldn't hold it off forever.

The thick strands resisted his knife, but he sawed away frantically.

"Listen, Pishti, I'm going to be heading over there in just a second, and—" he glanced up again.

The spider above him was a dark shape, multiple eyes glowing in the light of his palmscreen.

"And, it's—possible I might have company."

"I'm not even going to ask," said Istvay, their voice going even more grim. "Just get back here alive, and we can figure the rest out." There was a momentary pause. "There. I'm finished. What do you need?"

The last of the web split with the sticky tearing sound, and Aran fell the last few metres, landing heavily on the forest floor. Ani gave an undignified squawk of protest, and he barely managed to catch her again before she launched herself at her antagonist.

"Ani, it's fine, it's—"

The spider was descending the tree at speed.

Aran groaned, scrambled to his feet, and started off at a dead run. "If you've got a light tube, it might be helpful," he panted. "It doesn't seem to like anything too bright. And as long as we don't expose it to the light for too long—"

"For hell's sake, please stop worrying about the damn thing's light sensitivities! I'm sure it'll be fine. Which can't be said for you if whatever it is eats you!"

Aran sighed, glancing over his shoulder.

Istvay did have a point.

"Tell me where you are, I'll come find you." Istvay's voice was tight with worry.

"Um, no need." He could see his friend through a break in the trees ahead of him, and a moment later, he crashed through the branches practically on top of them.

Istvay swore and caught him, steadying him on his feet. "Aran, what the actual—"

"Light," Aran gasped. Istvay swore again, yanking a light tube out of their pouch. They swung it up, igniting it as the spider burst through the trees after Aran.

It gave a high-pitched squeal, shying back.

"This way." Istvay yanked Aran down a narrow trail.

The spider was still behind them, mandibles clicking angrily.

On the positive side, the light had stopped the creature from actually eating them.

On the negative side, it had made it very, very angry.

"In here," Istvay panted, and shoved Aran into a narrow opening between two tree roots. Aran scrambled inside, and Istvay tumbled in after him, landing practically on top of him.

For a few moments the two of them simply lay there, gasping for breath as the spider prowled outside.

"Are you hurt?" Istvay's voice carried its typical mixture of concern, alarm, and mild exasperation. They rolled up on one elbow beside Aran, their face centimetres from his, their brown eyes scanning him for injury.

"No," Aran panted. "No, I'm fine. I'm—"

He trailed off.

Damn it to hell. Damn it to actual hell. That was the thing about adventuring with Istvay.

He was in love with them.

He had been, for as long as he could remember. And for as long as he could remember, he'd pushed it away, because Istvay had made it very clear that, while they cared for Aran, they didn't have any interest in a relationship. But in the back of his mind, the traitorous thought was always there: that perhaps one day Istvay would change their mind. Return his feelings.

But if the last few weeks had taught him anything at all—and he hoped they had—it was that he needed, more than anything else in the universe, for his friend to be happy. That seeing Istvay sad was like stabbing a knife through his own chest and watching himself bleed out. And nothing—no subtle hope, no longing wish—was worth that.

He could still hear Istvay's drunken confession of a few days previous: *"I know what you want me to be, Aran. I know how you feel. And I wish I could be that for you, but … I can't."*

Istvay trusted him. The very least Aran could do was be the kind of person Istvay could trust, and stop waiting for things they'd made it clear they didn't want.

He drew in a long breath and let it out again, then sat up. Istvay was shoved up against him, their body pressed against his, their breath warm on his skin, but—

Well, it was funny. Now that he'd decided, finally, that this was over, it was funny how much easier it made things.

"Well," he said, grinning at his friend. "That was exciting. Just like old times, right?"

Istvay blinked and scooted back, although in the confined space it was difficult. "Yeah," they said, clearing their throat. "Yeah, just like old times." Their voice was rough, and Aran peered at them more closely.

"Are—you alright? Because if—"

"I'm fine," said Istvay irritably. "I was just—I'm fine. Listen, I think it's gone."

Aran watched his friend curiously for a moment, then shrugged and turned to the glimmer of starlight from outside.

Cautiously, he poked his head out of the small opening.

When nothing pounced on him, and Ani's grumbling growl remained steady, he turned back. "I think you're right. It's gone. Let's get back to the pod."

Istvay nodded, and the two of them scrambled out of the narrow space.

Aran cast a quick glance at his friend as the two of them walked.

Istvay was staring fixedly ahead, their jaw set.

Aran sighed.

Istvay had been behaving oddly since their and Aran's escape a few days previous from the aliens who'd taken the two of them, along with the rest of the human survivors of the diplomatic ship, captive when they arrived in the system, but he hadn't been able to put his finger on why.

"Look, Pishti," he said after a moment. "Do you—want to talk about anything?"

Istvay blinked up, startled. "What?"

Aran shook his head. "Never mind."

The two of them reached the clearing where they'd put down the pod, and for moment Aran stood staring up at the stars.

The horizon to the east was grey with the promise of a sunrise, but the sky was still dark, and stunningly beautiful. The stars overhead made patterns that were entirely unfamiliar, forming constellations that Aran had never seen, but something about the cool of the night air, the way the stars burned pinpricks through the blue-black of the sky, somehow felt like home.

"I think I got enough of a reading," said Istvay quietly next to his ear, and he turned, startled.

His friend was watching him with their usual fond smile, the moonlight catching on their sharp cheekbones and prominent nose and softening the five o'clock shadow along their jawline. "Now I just need to sit down and make the calculations, and then we should be able to fill in the missing section of the map."

The map that would lead the two of them to the raiders. Lead them, if everything went well and they were incredibly lucky, to a cure for the sickness that had been slowly killing Istvay for years now.

Aran closed his eyes, his muscles shakier than they should be.

This had to work. It had to.

Istvay paused a moment. "Should I even ask what happened back there?"

Aran opened his eyes and managed a grin. "I'm not completely sure you want to know."

Istvay sighed. "I'm not completely sure I want to either," they muttered. They stepped back, looking Aran over critically. "You've got spider gunk all over you. Why don't you go rinse off while I work on the calculations? I'll holler if I need help."

"You were always better at maths than I was," said Aran. "If you call for me, I'll know you're desperate."

Istvay chuckled and shoved him. "Go on, you stink."

There was a small stream just out of sight of the clearing. It was cold, but not unbearably so, and Aran shucked off his filthy, spider-web-covered shirt and trousers and dived in. The shock of the cold on his skin took his breath away, but the sharp burn of it on his tired muscles and the feeling of clean water washing away the sweat and grime was infinitely enjoyable.

The spider web took some time to scrub from his skin and hair and short beard, and by the time he'd finished and climbed out of the stream, shivering, the sun was peeking over the horizon in a brilliant blaze of orange.

The planet they were on now was about three days' travel from the one where they'd been captured and almost killed by the yibo. It was as far as their incomplete map had been able to take them, without a halt to do some readings. Still—Aran glanced around him.

They had to be getting close.

This planet had either been terraformed, or was yet another planet with naturally occurring oxygen, which seemed unlikely. Either way, it had clearly been abandoned. They'd scanned the entire planet as they approached, and hadn't come across a single sign of a settlement. Which, considering the reputation of the aliens they were trying to contact, almost certainly meant they were getting close.

He had a feeling that these raiders were the land-devil equivalents in this system.

He pulled on his trousers and slung his shirt over one shoulder, letting the fresh morning breeze dry the dampness from his skin. When he stepped through into the clearing where Istvay was bent over their calculations, the rising sun had bathed the entire clearing in an orange glow. He shook the water from his hair and turned, closing his eyes and basking in the warmth of the rays on his skin.

"Aran? Are you—" Istvay broke off with a strangled sound.

Aran opened his eyes quickly, turning to his friend in concern.

Istvay was staring at him, and he frowned. "Pishti?"

Istvay looked a little like they'd been hit upside the head.

"Istvay?" He felt a sudden twinge of worry as he crossed quickly over to his friend. "Pishti, are you alright? Did something—"

He paused to blink away the water that had pooled on his

eyelashes.

"No," mumbled Istvay, looking away hurriedly. "No, no, I'm—" they cleared their throat. "I'll grab you a towel."

Aran laughed and dropped to the ground cross-legged beside his friend. "What is this, the edge of the northern Rim Mountains? It's not like I'm going to catch a cold out here."

Istvay cleared their throat again and glared down at their palmscreen, where they'd clearly been hard at work scribbling calculations. "Um. I just. Look, I don't want you getting sick or something."

Aran put his hands on the ground behind him and stretched out, closing his eyes and tipping his head back, letting the sun play over his bare chest and face. "Fine, I'll just do this until I'm dry, then. Happy?"

Istvay made another slightly strangled sound.

Aran cracked his eyes open a slit, blinking back the water that had dripped to pool on his lashes again. "What?"

"I said, that's a good idea," said Istvay through their teeth, looking fixedly in the other direction.

Aran sighed and closed his eyes again.

Two weeks ago, he would have been going halfway crazy wondering what Istvay was upset about. But—well, but this was the nice thing about the fact he'd finally realized it wasn't all about him. Istvay could be as cranky as they wanted, and there was no lingering sense of awkwardness like there always had been before, when he'd refused to respect his friend's boundaries.

He leaned back, a small smile playing on his lips.

It still hurt, a little. It would probably always hurt somewhere deep inside him. You couldn't love someone like this and know they'd never love you back, at least not in the same way, and not have it hurt. But in the end, the comfort of finally having certainty after years of being on edge was a relief in and of itself.

"Um," said Istvay at last, clearing their throat.

Aran blinked his eyes open.

Istvay was still staring down at their palmscreen. "I—think I've got it," they said quietly.

Aran sat up and leaned to look over their shoulder.

The partial map that Istvay had copied glittered on their tiny, glitchy palmscreen.

"If my calculations are correct, this should be the planet we're on, right here." Istvay's finger touched a glowing speck on the map.

Aran stared down at it, his heart beating faster.

The place Istvay had touched was right across from the red blinking point in the centre that indicated their goal.

"That means—" he breathed, barely able even to say the words.

This time Istvay did look up, their brown eyes dark with a mixture of concern and excitement. "Yes," they said quietly. "We're only one planet away. We could be there in a matter of hours."

2

Savina

"So, Savina," said Joska, looking up from the control panels of the ship. "Here we are." The worry-creases in the pilot's tawny-brown face were deeper than they had been when Savina had first met her, but her gaze was as perceptive as ever, a hint of good humour lurking in her eyes despite the circumstances.

Savina nodded brusquely, trying not to let her unease show.

'Here' was the remote alien planet Chief Justice Alba Espina had pointed out on a starmap as inhabited, with a settlement large enough that there would likely be medical facilities.

After almost being murdered by the yibo, this system's sapient inhabitants, just over two days ago, Savina hadn't exactly relished the idea of showing up on the yibo's doorstep a second time, but honestly, they hadn't had much of a choice. The diplomatic party they'd picked up on their way out of the yibo city they'd been fleeing from was in bad shape. And although Savina would have happily let them burn, one look at Joska, or at her little brother's mulish expression, told her that if she voiced this opinion, she'd be dealing with a mutiny.

And Rafel, too, the *Dolphin's* lone crew besides Joska—for all his bluster, there was a sick look to his face that told Savina his injury was worse than he wanted to admit.

Not that she cared. Whatever Joska might think, Savina had pulled the man out of the way of the alien weapons-fire out of pure self-interest. To keep him from slowing them down, and to keep Joska from losing her damn mind when she found her friend had been left behind.

But she couldn't hide, even from herself, the pinch of worry that came every time she looked at Rafel's wan face, pallor turning his already pasty complexion sickly.

"I'm going to get my weapons," she snapped, unstrapping herself from the copilot's seat. It was Rafel's usual position, but right now, sitting upright in his cot seemed the extent of his strength.

Joska nodded. "May not be a bad idea. But—" she added, holding up a finger in warning. "We're depending on the yibo's goodwill to keep ourselves, and everyone here who's injured, alive. So we can't afford to antagonize them. Do you understand that, Savina?"

Savina scowled at her. "I've somehow managed to keep myself and Beni alive for twenty-seven years," she snapped. "You don't have to treat me like—"

"I'm well aware of your competence," said Joska dryly. "However, I have a much lower tolerance for intentional homicide than you do."

Savina rolled her eyes, but the tension that had settled in a sick knot in her stomach was enough to stop her from any additional retort.

She blew out a long breath as she strode back along the ship's corridors.

As much as she hated to admit it, Joska was right. The last few weeks had, if nothing else, taught her that there were things in this galaxy the likes of which she'd never dealt with, and had no desire to.

She finished strapping on her assorted weaponry and stepped out of the small cabin she and her sibling Beni had shared, before the ship was so crowded with refugees that there was hardly room to move, to find Nicolau standing next to the makeshift sick bay, deep in conversation with Joska.

It didn't escape Savina's notice that her little brother stood suspiciously close to Ines, the young linguist from the Chief Justice's diplomatic mission, or the fact that his hand was slipped, inconspicuously, around the girl's waist.

Or the fact that Ines didn't seem to mind this in the slightest, her hand resting on top of his, the light olive colour of his skin contrasting with the dark umber of hers.

Savina sighed to herself, torn between irritation and amusement.

Still, she could hardly blame him—if you were stranded on an alien planet, with no idea how much longer you had to live and no way home, a lengthy courtship seemed excessive.

"Savina!" Nicolau called, catching sight of her. "Come, we need your opinion."

From the wry look on Joska's face, Nicolau was the only one of the party who seemed to feel the absolute necessity of Savina's opinion. Savina smiled to herself as she came over.

"What is it?" she asked, making her words brusque.

Nicolau gestured at the crowded mess of what had once been the clean, quiet main deck of the *Dolphin*. "We were just trying to figure out how we're going to manage this. The Chief Justice won't be able to walk—Ines says she's essentially delirious at this point, which, considering what she's been through, probably isn't all that unexpected." There was a note of worry in his tone that had Savina biting back an exasperated sigh. "And Rafel isn't doing well either. That leaves us—you, me, Beni, and Joska—and what's left of the diplomatic mission: Ines, Yosip, and Feliu. With the shape Feliu's in, he's certainly not going to be carrying anyone, and I doubt Yosip will be carrying anyone either." He glanced over at the old diplomatic aide, whose weathered brown face wore a twinkly, good-natured smile that seemed entirely at odds with their current situation.

"I wish I could contradict you," the man said, "but I'm afraid I'm not as young as I was. I can help with the supplies, though, at least, and swap one of you off in an emergency."

"How far are we from the yibo settlement?" Savina asked, turning to Joska.

Joska sighed, concern and exhaustion mingled in her expression. "If the map is correct, we're only a couple kilometres from the village."

Savina gave a brusque nod. "Good. Then listen. We're all going together." She held up her hand as Nicolau opened his mouth to protest. "I quite frankly don't care if you disagree. We'll drag the cots behind us if we need to. But we're not splitting up, not in this hellscape of a system where everything we meet wants to kill us."

Joska shook her head wearily. "I can't argue with that. Well then, I guess we'd best pack up. We'll make up litters for the injured so we can carry them, and we'll need some of the knapsacks for supplies."

The others nodded, and turned to their assigned tasks.

"Savina?" whispered Beni when the captain had left. "Are you sure this is a good idea?"

Savina closed her eyes and sighed. "Beni," she said, trying to keep her voice patient. "Like Joska said—we don't have a better option right now."

"I—I know," said Beni, their voice soft. "I just—it's just, the last time—"

"Beni, can I touch you?" she asked, and when her sibling nodded, Savina put a hand on their arm. "Listen to me. It's going to be alright. I've … been thinking about this. Maybe it's for the best. Maybe being here—I mean, if we can find a place that doesn't know anything about us … we can get Nicolau and the others home. But maybe we—maybe we don't need to go back. Maybe we can find a place—"

Find a place we'll be safe, she wanted to say.

But she wasn't sure there was a place that was safe. And perhaps Beni's blindness meant they wouldn't see the lie in Savina's face, but she knew very well her sibling would hear it in her voice.

Beni didn't answer, just nodded and turned away.

Savina cursed silently.

Damn those bastards to hell. Damn those yibo bastards to hell, and—she glanced towards the old woman lying semiconscious on her cot, her dark skin sunken against the bones of her face, her elegant white hair filthy and damp with sweat.

Damn Alba Espina.

This had been Alba's fault, all of it. And the woman bloody well deserved to die for it.

That was something that could be arranged, as soon as Savina had the leisure.

It didn't take long for them to get ready—there really wasn't much to prepare. The supplies in the ship were still mostly salvageable, but it would be a stretch to call them anything other than the barest minimum. The makeshift litters, Nicolau constructed with Ines's help. When Savina asked him where he'd learned it, he shrugged and said his father had brought him with when they were bringing their produce to market, and they carried it like this when the drones broke down.

And then he'd gone suddenly quiet, a sad, faraway look to his face that made Savina's stomach twist.

Weeks ago, he'd considered the people who'd raised him as his parents—at least, she assumed he must have learned at some point that he was adopted, but with no knowledge of where he'd come from, they were his parents.

And now, faced with siblings who were brutal murders, and who'd dragged him away from his friends and everything familiar to supposed safety from a dying ship without his consent, and into situations he'd never have dreamed of—

He'd taken it with an impressive amount of equanimity. But she could tell that under his brave exterior, he was on the verge of falling apart.

"Alright then," said Joska, surveying the scene. "I suppose we'd best get moving."

The climate where they'd put down on this new planet was not the wet, sticky jungle heat of the one they'd fled. Instead, it was a dry, windy grassland. There were no trees, but the rolling hills in all directions, framing the horizon, made the apparent openness something of a deception.

At least, thought Savina as they stumbled over the rough ground, the litters bumping painfully between them, they weren't trying to push their way through the jungle. At least there was that. And open as the prairies were, they should be able to see any potential threat coming—

Nicolau shouted in alarm, and Savina spun to see a massive, reptilian beast with a long, blunt snout, its body low-slung and heavy but its speed deceptive for its bulk, loping in a strange, waddling gait across the plains towards them.

Savina took two quick steps almost on instinct, placing herself in front of Beni and Joska, who were hampered by the litter, and grabbed for her pulse pistol and stolen yibo atomizer gun. Nicolau had laid down his end of the other litter to snatch his own gun, but Ines was quicker. As Savina watched, the timid girl yanked out her pulse pistol with the air of someone who knew how to use it, and fired directly down the beast's yawning gullet. It stumbled, but kept coming, and she fired again. Nicolau fired as well, and the thing collapsed in a steaming heap less than a metre away from the two of them.

Savina barely had time for a quick gasp of relief before Beni hissed, "Vina!"

Savina didn't even have to look at her sibling to know what was coming next.

"My—my echolocator is picking up … something. Around us," they said.

Slowly, Savina turned. She heard, behind her, Nicolau's muttered curse, followed almost immediately by an embarrassed apology that must have been directed at Ines.

Desperate as the situation was, Savina couldn't stop herself from rolling her eyes

Then she sucked in a quick breath, fighting back a swell of panic.

They were surrounded.

Poking from the grass, she could see countless glittering eyes. The beasts were squat and wider than they were tall, their bulky bodies large and covered with a sort of scaly armour, their legs short and bent. They had long snouts full of sharp teeth, similar to the crocodilos back on Colorida, but where crocodilos were clearly adapted to water, these were land creatures—their legs set more firmly under their bodies, their thick tails dragging through the grass behind them.

Joska laid Rafel's litter on the ground and straightened, her pulse pistol drawn, to stand beside Savina and Beni, placing herself between the beasts and the injured man, and Rafel was trying to sit up, fumbling weakly for his own weapon. Yosip's and Feliu's weapons were out as well, although of the two of them, only Yosip looked comfortable with his, and Nicolau and Ines were checking their own pistols, having stepped back from the dead creature at their feet.

It wasn't going to be enough. There was no way it was going to be enough.

Savina found herself biting back what could have almost been tears of frustration.

She'd just wanted to keep Nicolau safe. That was all. She'd just wanted to keep her baby brother safe, and every damn time she turned around in this damn system—

"Savina," said Joska quietly. "How many of them do you think you can take?"

"Not enough," snapped Savina. "What, you think I'd stay here while the rest of you got away?"

"That's—not exactly what I was thinking," said Joska quietly. "But I thought maybe between the two of us—"

Savina shook her head sharply. "If you can get my idiot baby brother to run, maybe he and Ines could make it. But if you can do that, you could probably talk these stupid scavengers into turning vegetarian and guiding us to the village themselves."

Joska gave a dry chuckle, and for a moment Savina wondered how and when that sound had become so familiar and comforting, even in a situation like this one. "If that scientist were here, I've no doubt he'd say something about, if we're all going to die anyway, we may as well leave the poor beasts alone."

"If that damn scientist were here," said Savina through her teeth, "his damn tentacled nightmare-pet would have made this all unnecessary."

Joska chuckled again.

The beasts were creeping closer.

"Shoot at anything that gets too close," called Savina over her shoulder. "We'll take as many of the bastards down as we can. Maybe if we kill enough of them, they'll find an easier meal."

There wasn't really any hope of that. They were all going to die. And she could tell, from the grim nods of the others, that they knew it as well as she did.

Suddenly, one of the beasts on the outskirts raised its head and gave a strange, chirping call.

As quickly as they'd come, the animals faded back into the long grass, leaving nothing behind but the limp body of their dead companion.

Savina turned to stare at Joska.

The woman's expression echoed Savina's confusion.

"What—" Nicolau began.

And then, through the grasses, Savina saw familiar shapes that made her heart beat faster with something she wasn't sure was relief, or terror—petite, bipedal, lemur-like creatures, a little shorter than a human, with long, prehensile tails and large eyes made larger by the dark fur surrounding them.

The group of yibo approaching through the long grass were dressed differently from the ones in the city they'd left, their tunics a similar style, but made of a thick, heavy material clearly built to withstand the wind and the chill, with warm trousers underneath. But they appeared no more willing to take chances with strangers.

The leader had a drawn weapon, and was approaching them cautiously.

"Savina," said Joska under her breath, warning in her voice. Savina glowered at her.

As much as she'd love to, she wasn't going to shoot their only chance to get the hell out of this feeding-ground. At least, not yet.

The yibo who seemed to be in charge stared at them for a moment, then made a brusque gesture for them to drop their weapons.

"No way in hell am I going to—" Savina began, but Joska leaned down to place her own weapon in the grass.

"I know you, Savina," she muttered as she straightened. "And I'd bet my ship and my next ten cargo hauls that that's not the only weapon you're carrying."

Savina glared at the woman, but—she was right.

"It looks like we found our settlement, anyways," said Joska. "Or rather," she added, "they found us."

3

Alba

Alba heard dimly, from the part of her mind that wasn't so fogged by pain that it still could piece together what was happening around her, voices arguing in accented yibo tones, followed by the calm, matter-of-fact voice of the ship's captain, Joska.

Alba should be … doing something. Helping, somehow. She was the ambassador, and this was her responsibility, her problem. She'd brought them to this planet, and it was her duty to ensure that whatever happened here would not end in such a spectacular failure as their last attempt at diplomacy had.

She moaned, trying to force her brain back into full consciousness by sheer willpower, and then she felt a warm hand on her arm.

"Alba," said Yosip quietly. "It's alright. They've brought us to their village, and Joska's taking care of things. Just rest now."

Somehow, the sound of his familiar voice, the kindness in his tone, defused the panic, and she let herself slump back and her eyes fall closed.

The rest of what happened was something of a blur—yibo voices chattering around her, the AI program in her wavelink that Ines had created translating their words, but her exhausted brain unable to make sense of them. The sensation of movement, the sharp, overwhelming jolt of pain as she was transferred onto a cot, warmer and much more comfortable than whatever she'd been lying on before. Then there was the sting of a needle in the soft skin of her forearm, and she knew nothing more.

When she woke again at last, it was to a scene that was utterly unfamiliar. She blinked, gazing around her and waiting for the rest of her brain to catch up, and wondered, somewhere in the back of her mind, if she was still dreaming.

She was in a clean, sterile building, awash with sharp chemical scents that, as unfamiliar as they were, still evoked the image of a hospital.

She tried to move, then groaned as her entire body protested.

And then she recognized the absence of pain in her knee, something at once so overwhelming and so expected that she found herself almost nonplussed at its absence.

"This one's awake," the cheerful AI voice translated in her ear, and it was only then that she realized that the odd background noise she been hearing was the chattering speech of the yibo.

Yibo.

Her brain was slowly piecing together the events of the past few days. The reason why the sound of that language left the sharp, bitter taste of panic in the back of her throat.

The yibo. The diplomatic mission.

General Cavaco's people, negotiating with the humans' yibo captors. Promising them humans to use as cannon-fodder in exchange for the yibo's help in Cavaco's planned military coup back in their home system. Her flight from the city with the tiny remnants of her diplomatic corps, the strange, terrifying aliens, raiders, who had come after them, the hunger and the viciousness in those blood-red eyes.

The people she'd left behind.

It was the first time she'd allowed herself to think of it. Had she been in full possession of her faculties, even now, she would have stopped the thought before it had begun.

But the thought had already insinuated itself into her brain, and it was too late to push it back.

She'd abandoned them. There had been people inside the yibo government compound, the survivors of the diplomatic ship, people who were looking to her to save them. And she'd fled, and left them there, because there was something that she had to do that was more important than their lives. Something that would cost them their lives.

Because the alternative was to sacrifice the lives of everyone in the Joias System.

The humans' only way home was back through the portal. The only way for the yibo to destroy their entire system, for General Cavaco to use his alien allies to take full control of the Joias System government, was back through the portal. And Alba had the map that told her the portal mechanism was on this planet.

The portal mechanism she would have to destroy.

The thought sat sick and heavy in her stomach.

She was not accustomed to losing. She was not accustomed to playing a game where she didn't know the rules, and there was no way to win.

But she was playing this game, whether she wanted to or not. She'd brought those people through the portal. They'd come because they believed in her ability to make things right. And she could still save them. But she wouldn't, not at that price.

She took a deep breath.

As a judge, and then as Chief Justice and Head of the Judicial Council of the Joias System, every decision she'd made over the past four decades had been a decision that would shape people's lives. And perhaps she hadn't been as aware then as she was now of the immediate and long-term effects of those decisions. But she'd made them, nonetheless. Just as she'd made the decision to do all in her power to destroy the portal. And she'd never been the type to have sympathy for someone who moaned about a situation that they themselves had brought about.

"How are you feeling?" asked an accented voice in Common Dialect.

Alba looked up to see someone who must be a yibo medic standing at her bedside. They were looking through a chart, glancing at the sensors above her bed.

"I'm doing well enough, thank you," she said, trying to calm her nerves. "Thank you for your care."

The yibo nodded. "I'm glad to hear it. We've put some boneset on your knee, which should speed the healing significantly. It is a difficult break, and your body is old and not able to renew itself at the speed which it might if you were a younger person. But despite that, I have high hopes for your full recovery."

"I am very aware of my age," said Alba tartly.

The medic hesitated. "We understand that you are the leader of the humans in your … band. The mayor of our town, I think you'd say, would like to speak with you. Are you feeling well enough?"

Alba closed her eyes for a moment.

Her head still ached dully, and the thought of speaking with some self-important rural yibo villager with delusions of grandeur was vaguely horrifying. But she and the rest of the diplomatic corps, to say nothing of the ship's captain Joska and her crew, were at the yibos' mercy for the foreseeable future.

Best get it over with.

"Of course," she said, opening her eyes again. "You may tell your mayor I would be happy to meet with them at their convenience."

"Good, good," said the medic, nodding. "She will come shortly, as this is a matter of some urgency." He turned to the readout on the machine over her bed, made a quick note on his pad, and turned to the next patient, leaving Alba to her uncomfortable thoughts.

It couldn't have been more than half an hour before the mayor arrived. She was tall for a yibo, with fur of a light tan, the circles around her eyes a soft brown. Her clothing was fine—a tunic and trousers of thin, delicate fabric, decorated with intricate patterns of a much brighter colour than Alba had seen in the yibo city they'd left —and she strutted into the room with all the pompous self-assurance of a Rim Mountain village major-domo who thought their village was the crown jewel of the known world, and they the ruler of it. She examined Alba with an imperious expression, then pulled a seat out from the wall and sat haughtily.

Alba grimaced and pushed herself into a sitting position. The movement made her head swim, and she had to grab for the headboard to steady herself before she could do any more.

The yibo woman watched her impassively, and Alba gritted her teeth, trying to wrestle a pillow into position behind her so she could lean back.

By the time she turned back to the mayor, she was already exhausted, her temper fraying at the edges. But she was a politician, and at the least, she had a lifetime of training in acting polite to people she despised.

"You asked to see me," she said, keeping her tone carefully

neutral.

"Yes," said the mayor in a heavy accent. "I did." She made a brusque gesture with the tip of her tail. "Your people were wandering out on the plains, and we saved you from being attacked by the gorrum. We brought you to our village, and gave you food and medicine and shelter." She leaned forward. "And now we will have to discuss the price."

Alba bit back her instinctive sharp response.

"We are not unappreciative," she said at last. "But you must see that at the moment, we have very little to bargain with."

The mayor sat back, still watching her. "Your ship's captain, Joska, offered her ship as collateral when you first arrived, as security on your debt," she said. "I have heard other voices, though, reminding me that there are still places in the system that traffic in humans. You yourself may not bring much, but there are some healthy young ones in your party who might be worth something. Unless you have something more interesting to bargain with."

Alba straightened, her stomach tightening with remembered terror. "Surely you have some moral code that would prevent you selling people who come to you injured and asking for aid?" Her voice was sharp, and she sucked in a calming breath.

She had dealt with people in her political career on a regular basis who thought they could take advantage of a situation by offering threats. This was nothing new. But the odd tremor in her hands, the knot of fear that tightened her throat, was.

"Madam Mayor," she said, her voice a little steadier. "If Joska pledged her ship, and you accepted the offer, certainly your laws don't allow you to then go back on your bargain and demand a different price. Or are yibo laws so much different than human laws that they have no regard for basic principles of negotiation?"

The woman was silent, but Alba noted the hint of irritation in her expression.

"That cannot reflect well on your reputation," Alba continued. Her mind was grasping to recall every overheard conversation in the yibo government buildings. "If word spreads that your village is one to accept a bargain, and then change the terms when you find something more profitable …" She spread her hands.

"I should be concerned about our reputation as an easy target for freeloaders," the mayor snapped. "I'm only asking what is due us."

"You accepted an offer," said Alba. "You accepted the terms. Taking a ship as collateral is hardly taking in freeloaders. And if you're selling humans off—there are enough yibo who speak our language that rumours will certainly spread."

She wasn't positive of the veracity of her last statement, but experience seemed to suggest it was correct enough.

The mayor was scowling. "Don't forget yourself. I will make the final decision."

"Of course," said Alba. "However, I'm certain there are people in the village who might have something to say about your leadership, should the market for their products begin to dry up."

"Are you threatening me?" the mayor snapped, standing abruptly.

"Heaven forbid," said Alba dryly. She paused, closing her eyes for a moment against the pounding in her head. "I will speak with my friends, and I'm certain we will find a way to work off the inconvenience we have posed to your village. And," she added, "I'm sure that between us, we will be able to find a good-faith and accurate amount. Since extortion of injured guests to your village would be a shameful thing indeed, I'm certain you'd intend no such thing."

"Of course not," said the mayor. Her eyes were narrowed. "But you'll not be permitted to leave the village until your debt is paid. Collateral or no."

She turned away, noticeably omitting the respectful head-tip that Alba had grown used to in the government buildings in the yibo city, and strode out of the room.

Alba dropped back against the pillow, closing her eyes.

Prisoners, again.

She didn't have time for this. Somehow, they had to find the portal mechanism and shut it down, and time was already sliding through her fingers like water. Surely it wouldn't take the yibo head of government Kachik and his people long to figure out where she'd gone to ground, and if he didn't know her plans, he knew, at least, that she would be working against him if she possibly could.

He'd be after her. And Captain Mattin worked with Cavaco. He'd see Alba as an existential threat, one that had to be eliminated at all cost.

In the council chambers of Vila Nova do Sol, this would be a challenge she'd meet with head high—her position as one of the three Joint Heads of Government, her connections, her legal acumen, her reputation as harsh, but fair, would give her a weight of moral authority that would be difficult to confront. But here ... what did she have left? No knowledge of the language, the customs, the legal systems, except what little she'd gleaned from observation in Kachik's halls. No reputation, certainly, no connections—at least, none that didn't wish her dead—

She closed her eyes, trying to keep from thinking of the hopelessness of the situation.

She was startled out of her reverie by a familiar voice that spoke without a trace of yibo accent.

"Madam?"

She turned. It was Feliu, Yosip standing close behind him.

"Madam, how—how are you feeling?"

She was horrified to see the hint of tears in her clerk's eyes.

"I'm quite well, Feliu," she said, in the sharpest voice she could muster. "I'm not quite as fragile as all that."

Feliu closed his eyes for a moment, and she could see his relief by the way his posture slumped, some colour returning to his normally pink face. It sent a feeling half of desperate gratitude, half of supreme discomfort, through her.

"That is quite enough of that," she said. "We have things to deal with at present that are slightly more urgent than a broken kneecap. We are, it appears, prisoners here in all but name."

Feliu's posture straightened at once, his expression becoming once more businesslike. "I apologize, Madam," he said stiffly.

"No apology necessary," she said, her tone softening. "I … appreciate the concern."

Yosip was watching them, smiling, and at her words, his habitual smile widened. "From what I hear, we could have been much worse off than simply prisoners. Word is, the mayor insisted on negotiating with you rather than Joska, because she assumed that someone who'd barely regained consciousness after an injury would be more pliable to deal with. You appear to have disabused her of that notion."

She sighed, and lowered her voice. "The problem is, Yosip, we don't have time to spare dealing with this. We have to find the portal mechanism, and we have to find a way to destroy it. How long do you think before soldiers appear at the village walls to hunt us down?" She gestured down at the medical cot in disgust. "I can't even walk. We won't stand a chance against a company of soldiers."

Yosip pulled up a stool and dropped down into it. "That's … what

I meant to talk to you about," he said quietly. "Beni was able to increase the signals on the wavelinks so they can reach through the forcefield, and I've been in contact with some of the crew back in the yibo city." He paused, glancing at her. "I'm sorry, Alba, I should have begun with this—they're unharmed, as of the moment. It appears that as long as the humans are giving the yibo government what it wants, the yibo have no particular motive to kill the rest of the crew. And Captain Mattin, for all his faults, is giving the yibo what they want."

Alba nodded, trying not to let the sick relief show on her face.

She knew better. She knew better than to allow considerations such as that to influence her decisions, but—but after everything that had happened, the thought that perhaps the people she'd left behind were safe, at least for the moment, was a relief that was almost visceral.

"That's excellent news, I'm sure," she said brusquely, once she'd recovered herself. "But I hardly see how—"

"That's not all." There was a grave note to his voice. "My friends say negotiations are proceeding quickly. And considering one of the prerequisites of the deal was proof of your death, I'm afraid you're right to be worried."

Alba sank back on her cot.

She was so tired. She was so, so tired, and it had been so long since she'd been able to rest.

"Very well," she said. "Then we simply need to find the location of the portal mechanism from a group of rural yibo who are all but outright hostile, escape from our apparent prison sentence, travel Mystery-knows-how-far, and shut down the mechanism under the very noses of the yibo soldiers I am certain are guarding it, all before we're hunted down and murdered. Correct?"

"Alba …" said Yosip quietly, and the sympathy and the sheer, unearned kindness in his tone was almost enough to break her.

She closed her eyes. "What do we do now?" she whispered. "What in the Mystery's holy name are we going to do now?"

There was a small noise, and she opened her eyes, turning her head quickly.

Across the narrow room from her was the bed where Rafel, Joska's injured crewmember, lay.

And standing beside the bed was that innocent-looking, unassuming young woman, with her wide green eyes and round cheeks and dark hair with the hint of auburn at the roots, the colour incongruous against the light brown of her skin. The one who, Alba was almost certain, was none other than Savina Moya, the ruthless assassin Alba had put out a warrant for, light-years away and lifetimes ago.

For just a moment, the girl's eyes met Alba's. And for just a moment, Alba caught a flash of pure, unadulterated hatred in that glare.

Then the girl smiled her dimpled, innocent smile, and turned to leave. But something about that smile left shards of ice in Alba's veins.

"Alba?" asked Yosip quietly.

She dragged her gaze away. "It's nothing."

How much had the girl overheard?

Perhaps their time was even shorter than she had imagined.

4

Aran

Aran stared at his friend for a moment, then leapt to his feet, shrugging his shirt back on. "What are you waiting for? Let's go!" He strode over to their makeshift camp and dropped to his knees, shoving equipment into battered cases with shaking hands.

His chest was tight, a mixture of desperate hope and existential terror that had grown stronger and stronger the closer they got to their goal. Because what if he was wrong? What if this whole thing was fake? What if they found the person who'd sent the blood sample through the portal to the Joias System, only to realize that there was no cure—that something had happened to the sample on its way through the portal, or their DNA tests hadn't accurately read the alien DNA? That there was no way to save Istvay's life?

He shouldered one of the knapsacks and grabbed as many of the cases as he could hold, striding over to where they'd left the pod. He ducked inside, glancing around quickly, and began shoving the equipment into whatever open spaces he could find, hardly caring what the results of his packing looked like.

Istvay arrived a few moments later and bent beside Aran, packing the scientific instruments carefully away, tucking them into a blanket for extra padding.

Aran glanced over at them as he finished. They were folding the blanket carefully, smoothing each crease with their fingers before making the next fold. Their hands trembled, making the folds ever so slightly uneven.

He closed his eyes for a moment as he turned away, ducking back out of the pod and starting back across the clearing.

Istvay was dying. It was becoming clearer every day. He could see it in the growing hollows under their eyes, the way it took them longer than usual to wake in the mornings, their frequent pauses to rest. That had been why, although neither of them said it out loud, Aran had been the one distracting the spider while Istvay worked out the starcharts. And yes, they'd both pretended it was because Istvay was better at that sort of thing, and Istvay was, but—

That hadn't been the reason. They'd both known, without having to say it, that Istvay wouldn't be strong enough.

The effects of the genetic defect were gradual, at first—deeper hollows under your eyes, losing weight no matter how much food you ate. The slow onset of weakness. And then at some point it would reach a tipping point, and the symptoms would speed up. You could go from healthy, if gaunt, one day, to two months later hardly able to sit up on your bed. It didn't take long, once it started.

It had already started. There was no turning back the clock. He found a cure for Istvay within the next few weeks, or it would be too late.

And he could see, looking at them, that they knew it as well as he did.

It only took a few minutes to finish gathering up their few remaining supplies. Istvay joined him when he was almost finished, their jaw clenched.

"Well," said Aran, trying to smile. "I think that's it. I'll bring the last load over to the pod, then we can—"

From overhead, there was a noise a little like thunder, and when he looked up, he had to shield his face against the brilliance of whatever it was.

Istvay swore. "It's a ship." Their voice was grim. "I don't know about you, but there are very few people in this system with a ship that I want to see right now." They grabbed Aran's arm and dragged him after them into the woods.

The two of them crouched in the undergrowth, watching the craft descend.

It was a craft—that much became obvious after only a few moments. But it wasn't until it had landed, steaming and hissing, in the large clearing next to their pod that Aran was able to make out the shape of it. It was large and sleek, built for speed both in-atmosphere and out. The design was spiky and angular, the colours red on black. Looking at it, Aran shivered despite himself.

There was something about the ship that looked—aggressive. Frightening.

"Aran," said Istvay quietly. "Do you have any idea who that is?"

On Aran's shoulder, Ani was muttering a low growl.

"I didn't see many of the yibo ships," Aran whispered. "But this doesn't look like—"

The hatch slid open, and a moment later, a figure stepped out.

Aran sucked in a sharp breath, and beside him, Istvay did the same.

Aran had never seen a creature like this one. But he knew, immediately, what it was.

The newcomer was tall, taller than a human by a good half-metre.

She—at least, Aran guessed it was a female, although at this point it was only conjecture—wore an outfit of something that moved and rippled like cloth, but was likely armoured. The charcoal-grey colour would blend easily with shadows, but the camouflage effect was ruined by the bright red cloak the creature had flung over her shoulder. Her eyes, too, were blood-red, her features disturbingly human, but with sharp incisors visible at the edges of a vicious smile. Long black hair hung almost to the creature's knees, pulled into a half ponytail but otherwise loose, and a scarlet ribbon was woven through the tresses, the colours of it hypnotizing against the shiny black. The alien's skin was pale, an almost translucent shade of ivory, her body muscular, her movements smooth.

She surveyed the clearing and paused for a moment, closing her eyes and raising her head as if—well, as if she were a predator scenting out its prey. Then she turned and said something back into the ship.

A moment later, half-a-dozen more of the creatures emerged. All of them were smiling, small, hungry smiles.

"Well," Istvay whispered, their voice barely audible in Aran's ear. "I guess I know why the yibo are frightened of raiders."

Aran nodded, hardly able to take his eyes off the raider captain. She glanced around the clearing, once, then her eyes came to rest on the spot where he and Istvay were hiding.

"Hello, humans," she purred in Common Dialect. "You may as well come out."

Aran took a deep breath, holding the still-growling Ani firmly onto his shoulder. "I—guess we don't need to go looking for them after all," he whispered to Istvay.

Istvay's eyes went wide. "Aran, no, wait—"

Aran had already got to his feet and stepped out into the clearing.

Like the raider captain said—no point in hiding anymore.

The captain smiled as Aran emerged, and for a moment he had the same sensation that he got back on Colorida, staring into the eyes of a mottled land-shark—a mix of exhilaration and pure animal terror.

He swallowed hard. Ani tightened her grip on his shoulder, clearly almost out of patience after the day she'd had.

"Ani, be nice," he whispered. "These are friends." He glanced up at the raider captain. "I think," he amended.

"You may as well tell your friend to come out as well." The raiders' voice was deeper than a human's, and cut with amusement. She had a strange accent, different than the yibos'. "We'll kill both of you either way, but this will be easier on all of us."

Aran cleared his throat. "Listen. I—I think you sent a box through the portal to our home world. I'm just trying to figure out—"

The raider captain stared at him for a moment. Then she threw back her head and laughed.

"Aran! What the hell—" Istvay's voice hissed through his wavelink.

"One of your human friends lured one of my people into the yibo city and shot him in the face. And while she was getting away, she shot more of my people. I lost four of my crew to her. We lost her trail, worse luck, but I thought at the very least we could take back from her crew what she took from ours. There's only two of you, I see, but that's enough for a start. We'll find the rest soon enough."

"Aran! Get to the pod! They clearly aren't here to talk!" Istvay's voice had taken on a familiar frantic tone.

Ani was hissing like an angry cat, her eye-pouches bulging.

"No, Ani!" Aran whispered. "We can't make enemies!" He turned back to the raider, who was now looking slightly puzzled.

"Look," he said shortly, trying to keep hold of Ani. "I'm really sorry about—about whatever happened back in the city. But this is actually kind of important—"

"Aran, for hell's sake!"

Ani pulled one of her tentacles free of his grip, spiking him in the process. He yelped and let go, grabbing for her again as she made an abortive launch from his shoulder towards the raider captain's face.

"Kill him," the captain snapped, and two of her crew started around the edges of the clearing, like he'd seen crested gaterlings do when they were stalking a helpless fawn.

Ani yanked another tentacle free. Aran grabbed for her again and missed, and she flung herself in a tentacled mass of pent-up irritation towards the raider captain just as one of the other raiders leapt towards Aran. Aran dived out of the way, and the creature's clasping hands caught the edge of his trouser leg. The raider jerked him towards them, and Aran yanked at his trapped leg desperately. "Ani!" he shouted, looking wildly around the clearing.

The raider captain had jumped out of the way, and Ani had landed on the raider behind her. She was biting down with her beak, every tentacle-spike fastened into the raider's body. The raider was covered in armour, but Ani's gnawing was clearly making a dent—Aran could see the telltale convulsions beginning.

He cursed under his breath. "Ani!"

Damn it to hell, if the raiders were upset before, the chances of having a civil conversation with them after this would be—well, he wasn't sure what they would be, but a hell of a lot less than they had been. And that wasn't saying much.

Ani turned at his voice, and she leapt from her victim, soaring half-way across the clearing before she caught herself with one tentacle on the shoulder of another of the raiders, then landing firmly on the face of the raider who had their clawed fingers around Aran's ankle.

"No, Ani, dammit—" Aran gasped, yanking his foot free.

Another raider was sprinting towards them, and Aran grabbed the first thing he could find in his supplies pouch—a retractable cord—and shot it off into the creature's face. The raider jumped back, scrabbling at their eyes, and Aran grabbed a flare and shot it off at another raider, who must have seen what was happening and was on their way over.

Ani had apparently finished with her victim, because he could hear in the back of his mind the sound of the raider's body landing hard on the forest floor. Then she was boiling across the ground towards the raider Aran had pushed back with the flare.

There was the unmistakable throb of a pulse weapon, and a raider dropped, clutching at their shoulder.

"Aran, get in the damn—" Istvay's voice cut off in a muttered curse. The clearing was by now a scene of utter chaos, and it took Aran a moment to even spot his friend. They were standing on the edge of the clearing, a pulse weapon in their hand and a grim look on their face.

"No!" he shouted. "No, Pishti, you can't. I'm fine, I've got Ani, just—" he scrambled to his feet and dodged out of the way of the grasping fingers of another raider. Ani was attacking two raiders at once now, her body a flurry of lime-green tentacles and ear-piercing hissing.

"Look," Aran panted, trying to catch the eye of the raider captain. "Look, sorry for the—for the misunderstanding, but I just really need to know—"

Istvay swore. "Fine, just hold on for two seconds, then," they snapped through the wavelink.

The raider captain's head was turning in Istvay's direction, and Aran leapt forward, plowing directly into her. She turned in shock, then grabbed him by the front of the shirt, her face a snarl of fury.

"How dare you—" she began.

"Listen," said Aran. "I just—I'm not trying to make trouble, we just really need to know—"

"Need to know what?" she snarled, her fingers closing on the shirt hard enough that her blunt claws tore through the fabric.

"That box that you sent through the portal," he gasped. "I need some information."

Ani, apparently realizing that Aran was now no longer where she'd left him, was hurtling across the clearing towards them.

"Please, it's important," he said frantically, half-turning in the captain's grip to try to catch Ani on her way past.

The captain was simply staring at him.

Then there was the distinct, whining hum of the escape pod powering up, and both of their heads turned in time to see the craft lift a few centimetres off the ground, then careen towards the centre of the clearing.

"Aran, get the hell down," Istvay snapped through Aran's wavelink.

Aran wrenched himself out of the raider captain's grip, leaving a handful of his thin shirt behind, and flung himself to the ground as the pod plowed through the clearing like a heavy-ball in a game of pins. He reached out, catching the tip of one of Ani's tentacles as she boiled past him, and she turned in irritation, then the hatch was down and Istvay was out of the pod, grabbing him by the arm and yanking him up.

"Come on!" they grunted, and he scrambled to his feet and followed them inside, hitting the hatch lock the moment he and Ani were in.

Istvay was already in the pilot seat, their fingers dancing over the controls, and the pod lifted and shot towards the horizon.

Aran managed a quick glance back, and for a split second he caught a glimpse of the raiders scrambling to their feet and running for their own craft before they were too high up to see.

But a moment later, he could make out the bright starburst of a ship launching towards the atmosphere.

He turned to Istvay, and the two of them exchanged glances.

"Well," said Istvay grimly. "That could have gone better." They paused, glancing at their screen, which showed the alien craft rising after theirs at a disturbing speed. "Doesn't look like they've given up, either." They glanced at Aran with an attempt at humour. "I guess changing our minds about finding the raiders isn't an option anymore."

"On the bright side," said Aran, trying to distract himself from the sickening anxiety welling in his stomach that came every time he was on a ship headed out of atmosphere, "I would never have agreed to it anyways."

5

Savina

Savina was dizzy with fury as she strode through the potholed streets of the yibo village and back to the small, cramped outbuilding that the yibo had turned into temporary accommodations for the humans.

So that was why that bastard Alba had asked them to come here. To shut down the portal, and ensure they'd be stranded here permanently.

She took a deep breath.

It was fine. It would be fine. She'd been looking for an excuse to kill Alba for a long time. Even Joska couldn't argue with this.

"Savina?"

She glanced up, startled out of her thoughts. Nicolau stood at the edge of the dirt path leading to their temporary quarters, grinning at her, Ines beside him. "How's Rafel? Joska said you went to see him."

Savina smiled a wide, innocent smile, and was rewarded by a quick flash of alarm in her little brother's face.

"He's healing well. The doctors say he'll be able to leave the hospital within a day or two. Apparently, the yibo medicine is effective even for humans."

Nicolau made no attempt to hide the relief in his face. "Thank the Holy Mystery for that. I've been worried about him. Thanks for checking on him, Vina." He paused. "Do you want dinner? Ines brought some food back, and we were just about to eat."

Savina hesitated, then nodded, settling herself on the rough grass beside them.

Ines was, after all, one of Alba's people. It was possible she'd know more about what Savina had overheard.

"I was—I was just telling Ines about—we were just talking about our families," Nicolau said apologetically as he dished out the bland-looking boiled yibo food. He seemed to feel awkward that Savina hadn't been part of the conversation, although in fairness, she had no desire to be. "She grew up in the Rim Mountains too, until—well, until she was twelve. Then she got—she came to do Sol."

He stumbled on the words, and Savina eyed the girl more closely. "Are you one of the kids that got taken into do Sol for schooling?" she asked.

Nicolau turned to glower at Savina, but Ines cleared her throat, looking down. "I—yes," she said in a soft voice. "I was."

"Funny, isn't it?" Savina said lightly. "And now here you are working for Alba Espina, who voted for that proposal."

The shot hit home, she could tell by the way the girl's shoulders stiffened.

"I imagine you're very grateful that you can pay back the person who gave you such an opportunity," she continued, her tone still light.

Ines was staring at the ground. Nicolau looked like he wanted to strangle Savina with his bare hands.

"I—I guess I don't exactly think about it like that," said Ines at last, quietly. "They needed someone who was good at linguistics, and I—I guess they thought I could—"

Nicolau covered her hand in his and squeezed it gently. "Ines is incredibly talented." There was an anger in his voice that he was making no effort to disguise. "Listen, Savina—"

"It's alright," said Ines, looking up at him with a small weary smile. "It's a fair question." She turned back to Savina. "I guess I should hate her, probably. But—" she shrugged, dropping her gaze again. "Don't they say that peace comes when you surrender your will to the Mystery? Anyway, this isn't about me. It isn't about Alba, either, or any of us. It's—I have family back in the Rim Mountains. I used to send money home. Well, I guess I still do, they're supposed to be paying my salary to my parents while I'm gone. And I don't know if I'll see them again." Her voice cracked. "But at least I can make sure they're alright. It doesn't really matter what I have to deal with, as long as I can—as long as I can make it better for them."

Nicolau was watching Ines, his face an odd mixture of concern, and care, and a hint of residual anger that Savina knew very well was directed at her.

"Ines," he said, squeezing her hand tighter. "It's alright. I understand. I feel the same way. I haven't seen my—" he tripped over the words a moment. "My adoptive parents for a long time. But as long as they're safe—" His voice choked a little, and Ines looked up at him, and for a moment, the two of them looked utterly lost in each other's gaze.

Savina sighed in irritation. From the look of things, she wouldn't get anything more out of either of them, at least not anything useful.

She stood and strode into the building behind them.

They hardly seemed to notice she'd left.

Once inside, she sank down on her cot, closing her eyes against the late afternoon light that danced uneven and overly bright through the translucent walls, and dropped her head into her hands.

Damn Alba to hell. Damn her to the Void. She was planning to trap all of them behind the portal, and that pathetic, sappy little interpreter her baby brother had gone stupid over didn't even seem to care.

She yanked one of the knives out of her belt, turning it over and over between her fingers.

It should be easy enough to sneak into the hospital. There were a hundred ways Savina could kill Alba, but she wanted to watch the woman die slowly. Wanted to see the fear in her face as the life drained out of her.

The bed creaked, and she looked up with a start to see Joska sitting beside her.

"Savina. I got permission to go check on the ship, gather our things," the woman said. "I was hoping you'd come with me. We'll need two of us to carry things, and Beni is about asleep on their feet. The yibo told me that as long as we don't travel in a large group, and we keep to the paths as much as possible, we shouldn't be a target for the creatures we ran into last time."

Savina scowled, shoving the knife back into its hidden holster in her belt. "Fine," she said shortly.

She needed some fresh air anyway. And she was too angry to sit still any longer.

They reached the edge of the village, where Joska had a quiet conversation with two of the yibo guards. At last, the yibo stepped aside to let them pass, but two of them followed after Joska and Savina as they ducked through the opening in the force-field. Savina scowled at them, but they stayed a polite distance back.

"Nicolau told me where to find you," Joska said quietly as they walked. "He said you seemed upset."

Savina fought down the sudden surge of fury. "Alba lied to us," she said flatly, when she had her voice under control. "She didn't choose this planet because it had medical facilities. This must be where the equipment to open the portal is located. She wants to destroy it. She wants to stop any of us from getting home."

Joska was quiet.

"Well?" Savina snapped at last, irritably. "Are you going to actually say something?"

"Do you know why she's doing this?" asked Joska after a few moments.

Savina glared at the woman. "Why the hell does it matter?"

Joska chuckled wryly, and didn't answer.

"I guess you know why, don't you?" said Savina. "Were you planning on telling me at some point?"

Joska was silent a while longer. At last, she glanced over at Savina. "I've spoken with Feliu and Yosip," she said. "I think I can make a fairly good guess." She paused. "While they were in the government compound, it seems they found that the yibo intended to go through the portal and—well, I'm not completely clear on the details. But the sum of it was, the people back home would be conscripted as cannon fodder in an alien war, and Cavaco would end up in charge of the government. I—" she shook her head. "I can't say I love everything our Chief Justice has done. But I can at least give the woman her due—she's not one to shirk from something she considers her duty. So if, as you say, she intends to sabotage the portal, my guess is that she sees this as the only way to stop that from happening."

Savina stopped walking, staring at Joska. "And you—you're fine with that? With being trapped behind the portal, never getting home again?"

Joska paused a moment, then sighed. "Savina," she said at last. "I've known since the moment we came through that portal that our chances of getting back alive were slim. If—" Her words choked off, and Savina blinked at her.

She'd never seen Joska break down before.

Joska took a deep breath. "My life hasn't been the luckiest." Her voice was thick, and Savina felt that unconscious, unwelcome twist of guilt that she'd been feeling more and more often around Joska.

The woman shrugged. "I don't have much family back there—a niece, down on Colorida. She got into trouble a couple of times, but she's out of prison now, cleaned herself up a bit. I stop by there when I can. And—" she drew in another deep breath, as if speaking was more difficult than she'd imagined.

"And if I'm trapped here in exchange for keeping her alive? Giving her a chance at a life that I never quite got, as much as I tried for it?" She shook her head. "Like I said—I don't think all that much of some of the decisions the Chief Justice has made. She's too arrogant by half. But this one? I hope I'd be brave enough to do the same thing myself, in her position."

Savina stared at Joska for a long, long moment.

She hadn't said it. She could have. She could have rubbed in Savina's face the fact that the only reason she was here was Savina. That just as she'd been on the verge of finally climbing out of the hole she'd been thrown into by the solar storm that wrecked her ship, Savina had come in and taken it all away. She could have said that, and she would have been within her every right to.

But she hadn't.

And somehow, that made it worse.

They walked the rest of the way to the ship in silence.

When they reached it, it took only a few minutes to gather the remainder of their meagre possessions and pack them into the battered knapsacks Joska dug up from the ship's supply storage. Savina slung one of the bags over her shoulder, scowling at their yibo guards, who were still keeping a respectful distance.

"You ready?" she snapped at Joska.

Joska emerged from a last check of the cockpit. She gave Savina a brief smile, but Savina could see the weariness under it. "I'm ready."

Savina stepped down the loading ramp, and Joska followed.

It was late in the evening now, and there was a soft buzz and chirp of insects in the long grasses, the breeze on Savina's face cool and sweet.

She'd only made it a few steps, though, before she caught another faint scent on the breeze, something heavy and incongruous and putrid. She wrinkled her nose, glancing at Joska.

She could see the moment when the woman caught the smell, the way her posture stiffened.

She met Savina's eyes, and the sudden tight concern in her face matched the tight knot in Savina's stomach.

"I'm sorry, do you mind? I have to relieve myself. I'll take Savina with me to stand watch," said Joska to the guards. The guards must have understood enough, because they tipped their heads to the side and didn't try to follow as Savina and Joska walked off into the tall grass.

The smell grew stronger as they drew closer, and as a particularly strong gust hit them, Savina almost gagged.

Then they stepped over a small rise, and Savina had to swallow hard, bile rising in her throat.

It wasn't like she hadn't seen death before. Hell, it was all in a day's work for her.

But this …

There were about ten bodies, although it was hard to tell for sure. Animals had been at them, and now it was more a collection of limbs and gnawed bones than anything recognizably human. But they'd been human—there were enough pieces left that Savina could tell.

"How many days old, do you think?" Joska asked grimly. She'd pulled the collar of her shirt up to cover her nose and mouth and gone to kneel beside the bodies.

Swallowing back vomit, Savina did the same.

"It was hot out today—this could have happened as recently as last night or early this morning," Joska continued, glancing up. "It's hard to tell."

Savina knelt gingerly by one of the bodies and turned it over.

She sucked in a quick breath. "Joska …"

Joska stood and came over. Wordlessly, Savina gestured at the corpse in front of her.

Joska frowned, then let out a startled curse and looked up, meeting Savina's eye. "That's a pulse-pistol wound," she said.

Savina nodded, something cold and sick twisting in her stomach. "Which means, it wasn't animals that killed them. And it wasn't the yibo, either, they don't use pulse pistols."

"We have to get back." Joska's voice was tense. "We need to get back and warn the others, now."

"Wait," said Savina, grabbing Joska's sleeve. "We can't tell the yibo about this. They'll throw us out, and you've damn well given away our ship." She wiped her hands on the grass and stood carefully. "They'll find the bodies eventually, but if they aren't familiar with pulse pistols, it will look like they were killed by animals. In the meantime, we can say that there are other humans out there who may or may not be friendly, and tell them to let us know if they run into any. Whoever this was, I doubt they were hunting yibo."

Joska watched Savina for a long moment, and Savina could see the uncertainty in her face. At last, though, she gave a terse nod. "Alright," she said. "I don't like it. But you're right—Rafel and Alba won't survive us getting thrown out. But if for one moment we suspect that we're putting this village in danger for sheltering us, we tell them. I'm not going to put innocent people's lives at risk without their knowledge, not if I can help it."

Savina rolled her eyes and turned away.

When they got back to the village, Joska went to speak with the mayor. Savina walked slowly back to their quarters.

Nicolau and Ines were still outside, sitting together in the dark, and their quiet laughter floated over to Savina on the cool night breeze. But in her head, she could still see the dead, bloated bodies lying in the grass, and the scent of rotting meat clung to her nostrils.

She made her way inside and dropped down on the cot. She let her head fall into her hands, and for a long, long moment, she just sat there.

She was so tired. She was so, so tired.

"Savina?"

She jerked her head up, fighting back a curse.

Nicolau stood over her, concern on his boyish face. "Savina. Look, I'm—" he dropped down on the cot beside her. "I'm sorry. I didn't mean to—it's just, Ines wasn't—I mean, that was a hard time in her life, and she didn't want to talk about it, but—but anyway, I know you didn't mean to—look, I'm sorry, Savina."

He sounded so distressed that she found herself smiling a little, despite everything.

She took a deep breath, forcing her face back into her usual innocent, carefree expression.

Funny how that was the expression she'd worn her whole life, when there hadn't been a single moment she could remember when she'd been either carefree or innocent.

"No, you were right," she said. "Please apologize to Ines for me. I was in a bad mood, and I shouldn't have pushed her."

Nicolau stared at her for a moment, expression caught between puzzlement and the vague terror he always got when she smiled. Then shook his head. "Savina. I—I know this hasn't been easy for you. I mean, I don't know everything that happened between you and Joska and Rafel—Joska's pretty tight-lipped about it—but you were the one holding everything together when we were caught by the yibo. And you got us out, and—I guess I just wanted you to know I appreciate it." He fumbled in his pocket. "And here. Ines gave me this—it's a chip you can connect to your wavelink, and it'll download the translation program. Then you can understand what the yibo are saying. It's really useful." He dropped it into her hand. "It doesn't translate our language into yibo yet, but she's working on it. Ines is really smart."

She looked down at the chip, something odd tightening in her chest.

Then she looked back up at her brother and smiled. "Joska didn't tell you what happened?" she asked in a light tone. "I will, then—I held her at gunpoint and stole her ship, and forced her to go after the diplomatic ship because I wanted to kill Alba. I almost did, too—I would have, if the mutiny hadn't happened first. I only kept Joska and Rafel alive because I needed them to pilot the ship for me."

He was staring at her in utter shock.

She gave him another dimpled smile. "Goodnight, Nicolau."

She could feel Nicolau's eyes on her as she rolled over on her cot and pulled up the blankets.

"Savina?" he asked at last.

She ignored him.

Finally, she heard him sigh, and his footsteps moved off to the other side of the room.

She waited until everyone else had come in, and the soft, steady breathing from the cots around her told her they were asleep.

She couldn't get her mind to stop replaying the picture of the dead bodies in the grass, over and over.

There were two possibilities—whoever had killed those people was after her, or they were after Alba.

It could be either. But ultimately, it didn't matter. Because her siblings were here. Joska and Rafel were here. Her baby brother's crush was here. And once again, they were in danger.

At last, carefully, she sat up, glancing around the small cabin before standing.

Everyone seemed to be asleep.

She slipped out the door and made her silent way through the empty streets until she reached the hospital. She didn't usually worry about sneaking into places—her modus operandi was usually letting people see her, letting them convince themselves of her harmlessness, letting them helpfully guide her to where she needed to be, then cheerfully telling her that if she needed anything, anything at all, just let them know.

But her days in Yuur's employ had at least reminded her of the basics.

She waited in the shadows just outside the hospital doorway, shivering in the cool of the evening air.

She could see the stars, despite the robust force-field. There was something about the faint haziness above her, though, that made her feel just a little more comfortable.

Whoever had killed those people would have to get through the force-field before they could hurt anyone inside. And Joska had spoken to their yibo hosts to warn them not to let strangers in.

With any luck, before whoever it was had a chance to get past all those obstacles, Savina would be able to put a stop to this.

Her muscles were stiff and cramped, and judging from the faint greying in the sky, it was well past midnight by the time an opening appeared in the sheer wall next to her and a tired-looking yibo medic stepped out.

Savina stood silently and slipped through the opening before it closed behind him. She was quiet enough he didn't even look back at her.

Once inside, she kept to the shadows. She'd visited Rafel here more than once, and she could remember her way easily enough.

It was only a few minutes later that she stood outside the small room that had been set aside for the humans.

She took a deep breath and slipped inside.

It was dark inside the room, and quiet. The only sound was the soft beep and hum of the medical equipment and the slow, quiet breathing of the patients. The overhead lights were off, but the room was lit by the faint glow of emergency lighting, and the starlight from outside peeked in through the windows, casting the room in pale shadows.

Savina walked noiselessly over to the cot nearest the window.

For a few moments she stood there, looking down at the old woman lying on it.

Alba's eyes were closed, her face relaxed in sleep. She looked old and fragile, the veins on her arms and hands standing out against her loose skin, a worn maze of lines tracing across her features that reminded Savina of the wrinkled apple dolls she and Beni had made as children in the compound.

Savina drew a slim, sharp knife out of the sheath on her hip, and knelt beside the cot.

She placed it gently across the woman's throat, the sharp steel gleaming in the dim starlight through the window.

Alba didn't wake. She didn't even stir. And for half a moment, Savina had to hold back the sudden, desperate urge to slide the knife across in a quick, familiar motion, a small step back to avoid the blood-spatter, and then watch the scarlet of the woman's life-force soak through the sheets and pool on the floor.

Alba would be dead, finally. And Savina would be free.

Her hands were shaking with how badly she wanted it.

She took a deep breath and closed her eyes.

Still time for that later, if this didn't work as she'd planned.

"Alba," she whispered at last.

Alba stirred, but didn't wake.

Savina nudged her gently.

This time, Alba's eyes blinked open, confusion and irritation equally mixed in her expression.

Then she saw the knife, and her eyes went wide with a sudden, sick fear.

"Don't say a word," Savina whispered. "Not one sound, or I slit your throat. Nod if you understand me."

After a moment, Alba managed a small nod, the movement pressing the knife deeper into the loose skin around her throat.

"Good," said Savina, smiling. "Now, listen to me. When Joska and I went out to the *Dolphin* today to bring in our supplies, we found something out on the prairies. A dozen humans. They'd been picked over by animals, but there was enough left of them that we could see the pulse-gun wounds."

Alba was listening, and faint frown-lines creased her forehead at Savina's words, even through the terror clear on her face.

"As far as I can see," Savina continued, "there are only two people whoever-it-was could have been after—me, or you. So tell me, who was it?"

There was a long pause. "I … don't know," said Alba at last, in a low voice.

Savina pressed the knife against the woman's throat. "Think harder," she said through her teeth.

Alba's eyes flicked over to Savina, the fear in them tempered with a spark of irritation. "As I'm certain you've gathered over the course of the last few days, there appears to be more people than I can count who'd like to see me dead. You included, apparently." There was an impressive amount of wryness to her tone for someone with a knife to her throat.

Savina gritted her teeth in exasperation and leaned back on her heels. "Alright then," she said, her voice dripping sarcasm, "why don't we go through the list together, you and I, and we'll see if you can come up with an answer that won't lead to me slitting your throat right here." She leaned in closer. "Because believe me, I would very much like to do that."

Alba let out a long breath. "Cavaco, apparently, has wanted me dead for some time," she said. "Captain Mattin seems to share his sentiment. I suspect that weaselly scientist the captain brought with him as a replacement for Aran wouldn't be opposed to killing me either. The yibo head of government certainly wants me dead, as does the ambassador. And it would not surprise me in the slightest if there are other humans who were stranded on the planet when the diplomatic ship broke up who'd also like to kill me. Does that answer your question?"

Again, Savina was surprised by the tang of irony in the woman's tone.

She smiled at Alba. "You forgot to mention me."

"I assumed your feelings on the matter were self-evident ... Savina Moya," said Alba.

Savina narrowed her eyes. "You're walking a very thin bridge, Alba Espina, Judge of Heresies. I'd be very, very careful, if I were you, to make sure the plank doesn't break."

Alba closed her eyes for a moment. "If you're going to kill me, Savina, go ahead. I won't beg for my life, if that's what you're waiting for. Whatever your reason to hate me, I'm very sure I wouldn't be able to talk you out of it." She sounded old, and weary. "But there's something I need to do, something that might save the Joias System. Can you please let me live long enough for that? And afterwards ..." her voice broke, and she trailed off.

"You mean you want to destroy the mechanism that creates the portal and trap us all here forever, is that right?" Savina snapped. "That's what you're talking about?"

"Yes." Alba didn't offer an explanation, and Savina was glad. She wasn't sure if she'd have been able to contain her fury if the woman had tried.

"Alright, now you listen to me," Savina hissed. "You're right. I'm Savina Moya, the assassin. And I'm sure you know I'm ... I've been traveling with Beni and Nicolau and Joska and Rafel. None of this was their fault, I made them do it. I don't give a damn about the Joias System. But I don't want to see them hurt. So, here's what we're going to do. You're going to write them a pardon. You're going to write a statement, something binding, that they won't be implicated in anything I've done. You'll sign it, and you'll send it to me and to every damn person in your damn diplomatic retinue. And if you do that, and if it's good enough to satisfy me, I won't slit your throat here and now." She paused a moment. "I assume that if there are humans after you, since Cavaco's on the wrong side of the portal, they would have been sent by Captain Mattin?"

"I ... assume so, yes," said Alba. Her tone had regained some of its typical sharpness. "He's the one, as I understand, who insisted to the yibo head of government that he wouldn't go ahead with negotiations without definitive proof of my death. It could very well be that the yibo sent the group after me, but if they were human, they were almost certainly Mattin's soldiers."

Savina nodded slowly. "And presumably, then, if something happened to Captain Mattin, whoever it was would be recalled?"

"I ... would hope that would be enough. But it may not be," said Alba. "It's entirely possible that the yibo head of government would continue negotiating with his successor in authority, whoever that is."

"And what's this yibo head of government's name?" Savina asked.

Alba gave her a curious glance. "It's Kachik." She paused. "What are you—"

Savina pressed the knife harder against Alba's throat, and the woman fell silent.

"Now," Savina said pleasantly, "I assume you're well enough to dictate a statement?"

Alba nodded, and did as she was directed.

When she'd finished to Savina's satisfaction, Alba blinked to activate her wavelink.

"There," she said. Her voice was shaking, just a little, and Savina reveled in the fear in it. "I've sent it through to the others' wavelinks. I'll send it through to yours as well."

"Please," said Savina, still smiling.

A moment later, the statement popped up on her retinal screen. She scanned through it quickly, then blinked twice to banish the screen. "Good."

Alba was watching her, a mix of vulnerability and defiance in her gaze. "And now?" she asked. "Now, I suppose, you'll kill me regardless?"

Savina closed her eyes and took a deep breath. "If it was up to me, I would," she said flatly. "I'd kill you right here, and I wouldn't feel one second of guilt over it. I'd watch the life drain out of you, and I'd laugh." She opened her eyes. "But Nicolau has a crush on your poor, terrified little interpreter, and he's worried about his adoptive family back in the Joias System. Joska has a niece who just got out of prison." She leaned in closer, and she caught the way Alba flinched back. "I think they're stupid. I think they're hopelessly naïve to be more worried about people they'll never see again than they are about their own damn lives. But I can't stop them from being stupid. You want to shut down the portal. And Joska seems to think that, as awful as you are, you're actually sincere about wanting to save the Joias System. That's why I'm letting you live."

She straightened abruptly, and Alba flinched again as Savina shoved her knife back into her belt. "Don't make me regret it," Savina said in her friendliest voice. "Because if you do, I promise you you'll regret it more than I will."

"So that's it?" asked Alba at last, her voice sharp. "You're not going to kill me?"

Savina scowled at her. "You've never had to sit through Joska lecturing you about the morality of murder, have you?"

Alba stared at her for a moment, then her mouth twitched. "No. I have not had the pleasure."

"Count your damn blessings," Savina muttered. "If you call for help before I have time to get out, believe me, I'll take my chances with the damn lecture."

She turned and slipped out the door of the room, down the hospital corridors, and back outside.

The light in the sky had brightened, and the world was now the dim monochrome of early pre-dawn.

Savina walked through the narrow streets, keeping to the shadows.

Damn it to hell. Damn that bloody Alba and the whole damn Joias System to hell.

It was nothing but a stupid sentiment, sacrificing everything to keep someone else safe. To give them a chance at the life you'd never had. To spend the rest of your damn life hurting, in poverty, enslaved, in the hope that your sacrifice would save someone you cared about.

Like Savina had. Since she was seven years old. Like how she and Beni had spent their whole damn lives in the compound, pretending to buy in, pretending they agreed with everything that happened there, to keep the baby brother they hadn't seen in years safe and happy.

How sometimes Savina would wake up at night, tears dripping down her cheeks, the feeling of being trapped spreading over her like a suffocating blanket until she almost couldn't breathe from it. And how that picture of Nicolau as she'd last seen him, the happiness on his chubby little five-year-old face, would somehow make it worth it.

She swore again, viciously.

It had always been a stupid sentiment, and people who held it deserved whatever fate they got.

She deserved whatever damn fate she got.

She glanced around the uneven streets of the small yibo village and managed a small smile.

With Reka dead, Alba was right—whoever killed those humans had most likely been sent by either Captain Mattin, or some yibo politician.

Both of whom were currently in the city she'd left so recently.

And both, very likely, wouldn't be in a position to send anyone else out after them once Savina had slit their throats.

Surely someone in this village would have a ship, and a reason to go back to the yibo city. And surely even one of these bastards wouldn't be able to say no to a poor, innocent, lost human girl, who was only trying to go back and reunite with her—lover, perhaps? Father, maybe, or mother.

Not even a yibo could be heartless enough to say no to that.

She touched the familiar hilt of one of her throwing knives, running her finger over the smooth curves of it, and smiled her sweetest close-lipped smile, the one she'd perfected in the … days? Weeks? Since they'd arrived in this system.

Even a yibo couldn't say no to that. Especially not when this sweet, innocent human girl had the means to slit them open from hip to throat if they did, and no compunction whatsoever against doing it.

6

Alba

"Chief Justice Alba."

Alba jerked her head up, her eyes snapping open, panic flooding once more through her veins.

The woman striding towards her was the ship's captain, Joska. The one Savina had forced her to write out a pardon for the night before, at knifepoint.

She tried to steady her breathing. The bruises on her throat still throbbed, and she could still feel the mindless fear that had clawed at her as she'd stared up into the girl's merciless eyes.

"What do you want?" she snapped, her voice harsh.

She could call for Yosip, for Ines.

But if this woman was working with Savina, it would likely just lead to them being killed as well.

Joska let out a long breath, her posture visibly relaxing. "You're alive, Holy Mystery grant us mercy. I saw the message on my wavelink, and I came right over." She paused, pulling up a stool beside Alba's bed. "You ... saw Savina, I take it. Did she hurt you?"

Alba tried to still the tremble in her voice. "If by hurt, you mean something other than putting a knife to my throat and threatening to slit my jugular and watch me bleed out on the hospital floor, then no, she didn't." Her tone was sharp, but she wasn't sure anyone could blame her for that.

"Ah," said Joska wryly. "And that's the Savina we know and love."

"Madam!" Feliu pushed his way into the room. "Madam, what happened? What does this message—" He saw Joska, and his face darkened. "Joska. You think you can threaten Alba—"

Alba raised her hand wearily. "Feliu. Although I appreciate the sentiment, it wasn't her doing."

Feliu glared at Joska. "If she wasn't threatening you, what was she doing here?"

Joska sighed. "I had actually come for the same reason you had—to make sure Alba was still alive." She hesitated, then shook her head ruefully. "I … suppose if you don't already know, you'll know soon enough. Vina, the girl who helped us all escape, is—"

"Savina Moya. The assassin," Alba finished, her voice sharp.

Feliu gaped at her.

"Savina Moya?" Yosip's voice from the doorway was thick with concern.

"Yes," said Joska grimly. "It's … a complicated story."

"You knew this Savina was a dangerous assassin, and you didn't bother to keep tabs on her?" Alba snapped.

Joska gave her a wry glance. "As you said, she's a dangerous assassin."

"Where's Vina?" Nicolau stumbled through the doorway, a frantic look on his face, his auburn hair mussed and standing up on one side. "Joska, do you know where she is? Ines showed me the message on her wavelink, and I went looking for Vina, and I couldn't find her anywhere, and she's not answering her wavelink. Beni's still out there looking, but I thought maybe …" His gaze found Alba, and his face went dark. "Chief Justice Alba. If you've hurt my sister—"

Alba had to fight back an incongruous laugh. "Nicolau. I doubt very much I or anyone in this room could hurt your …" She peered at him more closely.

The resemblance wasn't strong, but it was there. "Your sister," she finished.

"Joska, what are we going to—" He was halfway across the floor, and Joska rose quickly to stop him.

"Nicolau, please. I'm trying to figure this out as much as you are." She paused. "And everyone here knows all the pertinent information about Savina at this point."

"Nicolau!" Ines burst into the room and skidded to a halt beside the young man, looking panicked. "Nikki, it's going to be alright. We'll find your sister, I promise. Come on, we can't—"

"Please!" snapped Alba, raising her voice high enough to cut through the chaos.

The room fell silent.

Grimacing, Alba pushed herself up into a sitting position. "All of you. Listen." She glanced around the room. "It appears we are all now aware that Vina is, in fact, the assassin Savina Moya." She turned to Joska. "I assume that's why she shot Reka Soler while we were making our escape?"

"She also saved you from the raiders," said Joska dryly. "I feel that discussions of relative virtue are better saved for another time."

Alba let out a breath. "You're right. This is hardly the time or place to discuss the morality of past actions." She fixed Joska and Nicolau with a sharp glare. "But we will not be able to escape that discussion in the future. At any rate, Savina informed me, while pressing a very sharp knife to my throat, that there were bodies on the prairies outside the village. They were humans, which presumably means they were after one of us, and I am the most likely target. And further, Yosip has informed me that Captain Mattin is still in talks with the yibo, and that they intend to go forward with opening the portal one way or another. Which, again, likely means they are seeking my death."

She paused, gathering herself.

There was no point now in wishing for the life she'd had before the portal had opened, the life in which the greatest threat was being outmaneuvered by a political rival.

She'd left that life behind, likely forever.

"This, then, brings up a number of complications. First, we don't know where Savina is, or what she's doing." She glanced at Joska. "I assume from your question of earlier that, despite your stubborn defense of someone whose actions are, as far as I can see, indefensible, you can't vouch for either her whereabouts or her intentions."

Joska's lips were pinched, but her silence confirmed Alba's statement.

"That is not our only problem, although the Holy Mystery alone knows how we got to a position where a deadly assassin on the loose is the least of our worries." She turned to Yosip, who was still standing silently in the doorway. "You've confirmed that there is more than enough reason for us to worry about pursuit. And from what Joska says, that pursuit is already here. We don't know who killed those soldiers, or why, and nor do we know where the killer is now." She turned to Joska again. "I suppose you can confirm that Savina wasn't the one who killed them?"

Joska nodded, lips still pinched tight. "I can confirm, at least, that she was surprised to find them, and that it worried her."

Alba hesitated a moment, bracing herself. "I … suppose most of you, if not all, already know the purpose of our coming to this planet," she said at last.

It was odd how uncomfortable she felt saying the words, despite the fact that it was almost a certainty that everyone here already knew what she'd say next.

"We are here because, before we fled for our lives from the yibo city, we learned that this is the planet where the mechanism to create the portal is located. And we also discovered, over the course of our negotiations with the yibo, their ultimate objective—to force the Joias System into a so-called alliance whereby the yibo would turn the system over to General Cavaco, and in turn, he would send an unknown number of humans over to the yibo to serve as a distraction in an alien war. We felt this could not be permitted to happen. And so, I made the executive decision that we would shut down the portal mechanism if at all possible."

The room was silent, but she could see from the expression on Joska's and Nicolau's faces that she'd guessed correctly—this was not the revelation it might have been.

"You're right," said Joska at last. "We'd figured that out, once we were here. I don't say I disagree with your reasoning. But—" She fixed Alba with her stern glance. "I do hope you take that into account when you judge Savina for her actions. You were prepared to lie to us, condemn us to a lifetime in a hostile alien system, use our goodwill against us, in order to get your desired outcome."

"It was the fate of the entire system at stake. I hardly think you can compare—"

"What's the value of a system, if not the lives of the people in it?" asked Joska quietly. "And who's to make the decision as to whose life trumps another's?" She shook her head. "As I said, I don't disagree with you in this instance. But if you took a little harsher judgement of your own actions, and a little softer of those you see as lesser than you, you'd see the system more clearly, if you'll forgive my saying so."

Alba glared at her.

Joska met her gaze unflinchingly.

In the end, it was Alba who turned away.

"At any rate," Alba said, "this is the situation in which we find ourselves. So. If there is anyone here who objects to closing down the portal—" She paused.

Nicolau shifted. Ines stepped closer to him, taking his hand and twining their fingers together, but no one spoke.

"Very well, then," said Alba at last. "We can't deal with Savina until we know where she is or what she's after. What we do know, however, is that we have no time to spare if we are to close down the portal permanently. And at the moment, we are virtual prisoners in this village. Even if we were to get out, we have no idea where to go. Therefore, I suggest that we concentrate our efforts on finding a solution to those two problems." She tried to keep the hopelessness from her tone.

Yosip sighed and shook his head, crossing to stand beside her cot. "As much as I hate to say it, I doubt the yibo will divulge anything to strangers who just arrived from a foreign system, a different species, with nothing to guarantee what our intentions are."

"So what do you suggest?" snapped Alba, turning on him. "That we simply give up, live out our lives in an agricultural village while everything and everyone we know is destroyed?"

Yosip pulled up a stool beside Joska's. "That's not at all what I'm suggesting. As you say, this is a matter of life or death for our entire system. But that doesn't change the calculus for the yibo who live here. If we want them to speak with us, I think our efforts are best focused on winning their trust."

Alba stared at him.

"Winning their trust?" she asked, when her faculty of speech had sufficiently recovered. "You suggest that, with the destruction of our entire system imminent and Cavaco's soldiers hunting us, we—what, sit down for tea with the yibo? Chat over a rustic agricultural ceremony?"

Yosip chuckled. "Unless you have a better idea—"

Alba shook her head sharply. "Don't play me for a fool, Yosip," she snapped. "I know perfectly well that by this time you know every single person in this damned place by name, occupation, and familial status. Don't try to tell me you can't get the information we need if you want to."

Joska looked like she was biting back her amusement.

Yosip gave Alba that mild, twinkling smile of his. "You're right, they're friendly enough. But—" he shrugged his shoulders again. "I hate to say it, Alba, but they know that you and I are friends. They're not going to tell me anything they don't want you to hear."

For a brief moment, Alba stared at him, too shocked to respond.

Friends. The diplomatic aide who'd been sent to, under her instruction, assist her in her negotiations with the aliens, or whatever they found on the other side of the portal.

Friends?

A few weeks ago, she would have scoffed at the idea and immediately asked that Yosip be replaced for forgetting his place.

But there was something about having run for one's life, dodged alien weaponry, stumbled through the jungle leaning on each other out of pure exhaustion, trusting one another with their very lives, that made for a much, much more personal relationship than she had ever asked for or wanted, before this trip.

He was watching her with a hint of a smile, as if he could guess at the thoughts running through her head.

"I—suppose that makes sense," she said stiffly.

He nodded without speaking.

"So," she said at last. "What do you suggest, then?"

Yosip's smile faded just a little. "To tell you the truth, I'm not entirely sure." He paused a moment. "Although—" he gestured to the woman sitting beside them. "Joska pledged her ship as collateral in return for our care. I believe she's been speaking with the yibo to arrange a way we can work off the debt. If we're to earn the yibo's trust, working with them isn't the worst way to do it. I've gained more friends hauling cargo or cleaning out a mess hall than I ever have through diplomacy."

"You gain friends by stepping into the damn room with them," Alba muttered, and Yosip's eyes twinkled, as if she'd given him a delightful compliment.

He turned to Joska. "If I recall correctly, you said they work textiles here?"

"Yes," said Joska, eyebrows raised.

Yosip looked back to Alba. "It's something they do together, as I understand, the older members of the village. They've assured me that it's something even someone who's recovering from an illness could do. I don't mean to be facetious, Alba, but I do honestly believe this is our best bet at finding out what we need to know."

Alba closed her eyes and took a deep breath, trying to fight back the panic. "Alright," she said at last, opening her eyes. "If I understand correctly, you are suggesting that our plan to save the entire Joias System should consist of … joining the local knitting circle."

Joska turned aside quickly, coughing loudly into her fist. Ines looked petrified, Feliu looked offended, and Nicolau looked mildly confused.

"I … suppose when you put it like that, that is indeed what I'm suggesting," said Yosip at last. He was clearly biting back a smile.

Alba sighed.

It wasn't even mid-morning, and she'd already been threatened with a knife to her throat by an assassin, called to account by a cargo-ship captain, and berated by a fresh-faced crewman who appeared to be completely infatuated by her diplomatic linguist. And now she was being encouraged to join the yibo equivalent of a knitting circle.

"I suppose it can't be any more absurd than the rest of this damnable mission has been so far," she said at last, sourly. "Well then, if that's the case," she turned to Yosip. "I suppose you may as well tell whoever's in charge that we'll be there."

7

Aran

The tiny, battered escape pod had barely made it out of atmosphere before the raider ship was after them.

Istvay swore through their teeth, glancing over their shoulder at Aran. "I sent the starmap through to your wavelink earlier," they gritted. "Give me something. We have to get somewhere out of the way, as quick as we can. There are no weapons on this thing, we're not going to last five minutes."

Aran yanked out his palmscreen and peered at it as it flickered unevenly.

Dammit, this was not the time for technology malfunctions. He glanced up at the ship screen, orienting himself, then back down at his palmscreen.

"It doesn't need to be a perfect place, just get us somewhere we can land. It's possible that once we get in-atmosphere we'll be able to —I don't know, get them off our tail somehow," Istvay snapped. Their voice was tight with strain.

Aran hesitated. "You're—not going to like this," he murmured.

A shot hummed out from the raider ship behind them, and Istvay yanked down on the controls. "Dammit, Aran, I don't actually—"

Aran crouched beside his friend and tapped a planet on the screen. "There. That's the only option, if you want something that's close, and gives us a chance of breathing oxygen instead of sulfur gas."

Istvay glanced at the map. Then they looked back up at Aran, their expression incredulous. "That's—"

Aran nodded. "I told you you wouldn't like it."

Istvay continued staring. "We're running for our lives from the raiders. And you want me to put down … on the raider's actual base planet. That's what you're suggesting."

Aran rolled his eyes. "Look. You said you wanted a place that was close and wouldn't kill us. So. That's our option."

Istvay glanced at the screen, then back at Aran, then back at the screen, their expression irresolute.

There was another shot from the ship behind them, another blue streak of energy, and Istvay yanked desperately on the controls. "Dammit, this thing was not built for maneuverability," they grunted. "And I sure as hell never studied as a damn pilot."

Another shot whispered out, and this time it must have hit, because the screen flickered crazily, the ship shaking hard enough to throw Aran against the curved wall of the cockpit, cushioned slightly by Ani's bulbous body. She grumbled a complaint and nicked the back of his hand with a tentacle spike in protest.

"Sorry, sweetheart," he gasped, wincing at the now-familiar jolt of pain shooting up his arm.

Istvay was cursing steadily. "Well, looks like the choice has been made for us. That shot cracked the shell of the pod. We have maybe forty minutes before the emergency seal gives out and she breaks up completely."

Aran stared up ahead of them at the small moon that, they'd learned only this morning, might hold the answers he'd been searching for, desperately, for years.

The place that could very well become both his and Istvay's grave.

"Well," he said, trying to keep the sheer terror from his voice. "At least we know it'll have oxygen."

"We assume it'll have oxygen," Istvay grumbled. "Those damn raiders could be adapted to breathe sulfur gas, for all we know."

"I don't think so," said Aran thoughtfully. "From what I saw of their physiology—"

"This is not the damn time for a scientific discussion," Istvay snapped. They were wrestling with the controls, trying to turn the pod towards the moon. "Because if their next damn shot breaches our fuel cell, we're going to go up exactly like the diplomatic ship did. Even if we don't get hit again, there's still a solid chance we'll go up in flames the moment we enter the atmosphere. If we can even make it through to the atmosphere, because like I said, I'm not a damn trick-pilot, and I'm piloting a bloody escape pod, and we just got shot!"

Aran glanced at his friend and bit back a retort. They were probably right, honestly.

"Can I—do anything?" he asked instead.

Istvay looked up briefly to glare at him. "I don't know, maybe you can go out there and explain to your friends the raiders that we need a little tow, maybe that would help."

Aran sighed. There was no point in even trying to talk to Istvay when they were in this mood.

He knew, deep down, that he was probably right on the edge of actually losing his crap, and that his irritation, just as much as Istvay's, was simply his brain's mechanism to avoid going into a full-scale meltdown.

"Go strap in," said Istvay tersely. "If we make it through the atmosphere—and I'm going to tell you right now, that's a hell of an 'if'—it's going to be a rough landing."

Aran closed his eyes and swallowed hard. "Yeah. Yeah, I'll—I'll do that."

Istvay glanced up at him, and underneath the frantic tension, there was that familiar concern on their face, and somehow the sight of it made Aran smile, however weakly.

"Well, there's no one I'd rather be in a crashing spaceship with than you," he managed.

Istvay blinked at him, then gave a strained grin of their own. "That's good, because it doesn't look like you're going to have much of a choice. Now go strap in."

Aran ducked back into the main body of the escape pod and strapped himself in to one of the tiny pod seats. He leaned his head back and closed his eyes, and tried, very hard, not to think about what was happening right now, not to remember where he was, and what he was bloody well doing here. Tried not to think about the fact that dying in space had quite literally been his nightmare, one that he'd woken from screaming, for as long as he had understood there was such a thing as space.

Ani seemed to have forgiven him for squashing her against the escape pod walls, because she was huddled up on his shoulder, making quiet little chirps and stroking his arm delicately with the tip of a tentacle.

He reached up, rubbing under her chin. "It's okay, Ani," he whispered. "It's okay, Istvay's got this, we'll be fine."

She purred and tried to nudge herself under his hand, and he managed a small smile as he rubbed her head. Her purring increased, her eyes closing to slits.

At least she could be stoic in the face of almost-certain death.

"We're on our way in," said Istvay shortly. "Hold on to something if you can. If the pod shell is going to fail, it'll be in the next few seconds."

And then the ship hit the atmosphere, the impact sending the small craft rocking. Aran caught one of Ani's tentacles with one hand and clung to the straps with the other, his eyes squeezed closed. His mind was going desperately over one of the hazily remembered Orthodox litanies he'd learned in childhood.

"We seek not to know, but only to be known," he muttered. "Not to question, but only to accept—"

The ship shook harder. He gulped in a quick breath, feeling Ani's tentacles tighten down on his shoulder. He didn't even have the mental energy to scold her—if she forgot and pricked him enough times to put him in a coma, maybe that would be the best outcome, all things considered.

"For what we know is foolishness, and what we perceive is illusion, and only Your everlasting presence is the true ... the true—" Dammit, he couldn't remember the rest.

The craft was shaking harder now, and when he cracked one eye open, he could see Istvay in the cockpit, their shoulders tight, their knuckles white on the controls.

He squeezed his eyes shut again.

Damn it to hell.

The craft was shaking hard enough now that he was sure he'd have bruises from being slammed against the pod walls.

Assuming he lived long enough to develop bruises.

"We're through the atmosphere," Istvay shouted back over the rush of air from outside. "But the steering on this thing is shot to hell, and I don't know if I can get the landing gear down. I've pulled all the air brakes on full, but I don't know if it's going to be enough." Their voice was sharp with strain, their words terse.

Aran didn't bother to respond. He wasn't sure he could, anyways.

There was green outside the pod windows, coming up far too quickly, then a horrific, grinding screech, loud enough to drown out Istvay's cursing. The impact jolted through every bone in Aran's body, his jaw snapping shut, his head whipping back, connecting with the shell of the pot hard enough that he saw stars, the restraints cutting into his shoulders and hips as he was flung against them. Ani clung to him, hissing her disapproval, and the screeching, tearing, ear-rending noise from outside was almost as painful as the pain itself

—

And then everything stilled.

Aran groaned in the sudden silence, taking stock for a moment of which parts of him were still attached.

They all seem to be, and he cracked an eye open. Then he remembered, and jerked his head up, the movement sending a sharp bolt of pain through his neck and back and setting his head spinning.

He ignored it.

"Pishti! Pishti, are you alright? Pishti—"

He could make out the outline of Istvay's shape slumped against the controls of the ship, and he was hit with a jolt of panic so strong that he thought he might pass out. He yanked ineffectually at the straps, then finally pulled out his bush-blade and sliced through them, hands shaking.

He tried to get to his feet, swearing at the spike of pain that shot up his hip and back at the movement.

"Pishti! Pishti, are you—can you hear me, Pishti?" He stumbled forward to where Istvay lay unresponsive, sprawled across the controls. There was blood smeared on the panel, and Aran's heart, already racing, sped up more, his muscles shaky with panic. He reached out gently, laying a careful hand on Istvay's shoulder, then let the tips of his fingers slide to the side of their throat, trying not to imagine what he would do if—if—

There was a pulse. Relief washed through him so strongly he had to catch himself on the control panel, his knees going weak.

Istvay groaned and stirred.

"Pishti!" The words choked in Aran's throat. "Pishti, you're— Pishti, you're alright!"

Istvay groaned again and pushed themself up. Blood streamed freely from their nose and split lips, and more trickled from a cut over one eyebrow, giving them a gruesome appearance. Their face was swollen and bruised, and they moved gingerly, as if trying to avoid jarring any broken bones. But they managed a brief smile through swollen lips. "'Alright' might be pushing it," they muttered. "But alive? Definitely. There's no damn way being dead could hurt this much."

Aran gave a choked half-laugh, and Istvay chuckled, then groaned again. "Ooof. Don't make me laugh, that bloody hurts."

Istvay dragged themself gingerly from the seat of the craft, Aran helping where he could, and finally they were on their feet, swaying, but upright. "Well, we're here now, anyways," they muttered sourly, glancing out the cracked window of the craft. "And I guess you were right about the oxygen, since we'd both be dead if you weren't."

Aran nodded, peering out the shattered cockpit window. "At least —" he began. Then his eyes caught movement in the sky above them, and he swore violently.

"Aran?" Istvay's voice was sharp with concern. "Aran, what—"

"They're still after us," Aran snapped. "Come on, we've got to get out of here." He was already stumbling back to the pod's storage compartments. He yanked them open, pulling out supplies and throwing them into a knapsack.

"We don't have time—" Istvay began, but Aran cut them off.

"We don't have time not to. I have no idea if the water here is even drinkable, and we won't make it far without food or something to keep warm." He shoved a first-aid kit into the pack on top of the jumble of supplies, snapped it shut, and slung it over his shoulders. Ani scrambled up his outstretched arm and took her perch atop the knapsack.

Istvay had their own supplies pouch open and was rummaging through it, their face tight with pain. They straightened, shoving something at Aran. "Here. Scent blockers. You saw the raiders back there, they were bloody well sniffing us out."

Aran grabbed the small pouches from Istvay's hand, glancing out the window again as he smeared the oily goop over his skin and clothing. He tucked the pouch in his pocket, activating it as he did so.

"They've landed," he said tersely, turning back to Istvay. "They'll be here in minutes."

Istvay gave a brusque nod and turned for the hatch, then swayed on their feet. Aran caught them, pulling them upright, and Istvay hissed in pain. Aran looked them over in concern, but they shook their head.

"Let's go," they whispered.

The pod's hull had been smashed, the hatch door jammed shut, but with some effort Aran managed to expand the broken hole in the plex window of the cockpit enough to allow the two of them to wriggle through.

Istvay followed him out, swearing in a muffled litany under their breath, then they were both on their feet again, standing amidst the cool of an evergreen forest.

The air was thick and humid, richer than the air on the previous planet, but not enough to make breathing uncomfortable.

From somewhere on the other side of the broken pod, there was the crunch of heavy footsteps approaching at a quick jog. Aran glanced around quickly, then tipped his chin in the direction of the forest, and he and Istvay ducked into the dark shadows of the trees.

Aran crept along carefully, keeping his steps light so as not to break twigs or crunch leaves. This, at least, was something both he and Istvay were intimately familiar with, and soon they fell into a steady, comfortable rhythm, Aran checking the ground before him as he placed his feet, Istvay stepping where Aran stepped and using a wide branch to brush away any sign of their passage. Ani, perched on Aran's shoulder, was silent and alert, apparently recognizing the familiarity of the routine as much as either of them.

They hadn't been walking for more than a few minutes when there was a muffled boom from behind them, followed by a shockwave that was almost enough to knock Aran off his feet. He caught himself against a tree, and Istvay, cursing under their breath, didn't.

"Pishti?" Aran hissed in alarm, but Istvay pushed themself painfully to their feet, grimacing.

"Stupid crash did something to my balance," they muttered. They blinked, shaking their head. "What the hell was that?"

Aran glanced around. "I'll be right back," he said. Before Istvay could protest, he spat on his hands and pulled himself up the branches of one of the larger of the nearby trees, just far enough up to see over the ridge of the hill they'd come over.

In the clearing where they'd left the pod, there was nothing but a massive, crackling ball of flames.

He stared at it for a long moment, then silently, he slid back down the tree.

"What?" hissed Istvay impatiently. "What did they—"

"That's—that was our escape pod," Aran said in a low voice. "It's gone."

Istvay stared at him for a moment, then dropped their head into their hands, shoulders slumping in exhaustion.

Finally, they raised their head and gave Aran a weary smile. "I guess we're staying here, then, until we find another ride," they said. "We'd better damn well hope not all the raiders are as friendly as these ones."

From somewhere behind them came the unmistakable crunch of a footstep.

Istvay swore again. "Come on. We've got to keep going."

Aran nodded, and the two of them turned, heading farther into the trackless forest.

8

Savina

Getting passage to the yibo city—Chrr it was called, apparently—had been easier than Savina had expected. She'd found an older yibo setting up for the early morning market who spoke a few words of Common Dialect, and had managed, between their few words of shared language and some pantomiming, to convey what she needed. He'd led her to a woman loading a small transport ship, and in exchange for Savina's offer of assistance, the woman had agreed to bring her along.

Savina had been at her sweetest and most helpful. How could they possibly refuse?

The trip back to the jungle planet Savina had so recently left took several standard hours. But even the small yibo transport craft had artificial gravity, and Savina was able to lean her seat back and fall into a restless sleep, and ignore the frantic wavelink messages from her damn baby brother back in the village.

She woke once to find the yibo woman asleep as well, leaned back in her chair, the controls set to autopilot. Her breath was coming slow and easy, and she was clearly deeply asleep, and it would be so incredibly easy for Savina to pull out her knife—

She sighed in frustration and leaned back again, closing her eyes.

When had her life gotten this complicated? It had never been this complicated before.

They reached the jungle planet and came down through the atmosphere as the sun was peeking over the horizon behind the city, setting it glowing in the early morning air.

The yibo woman called in on the ship radio, and when she received an answer, she brought her ship in low along the cleared outskirts of the city, terrain that Savina recognized by having run for her life through it short days previous.

There were yibo guards waiting to greet them, and they started towards the ship as it came at last to a halt.

Savina's hand went surreptitiously to her knife.

The yibo women glanced at the guards, then over at Savina, her expression indecisive. Then she tapped the radio on her dashboard.

Savina tensed.

She could make it look like a heart attack. They'd find the dead woman, and they'd never know there'd been a human here at all.

She watched the woman casually, working her needle-thin electric knife free of its sheath.

She could understand yibo now, thanks to the translation chip her stupid baby brother had handed her. And the woman had no way of knowing. That should give Savina some advantage, at least.

"Give me just a minute," said the woman over the radio. "I had some cargo shift on the way through the atmosphere, and it's blocking the exit. Let me clear it out so you can get in without tripping over it." She shut off the transmission, then turned to Savina. "Go on," she whispered, making a shooing gesture. "Best get out of here while you can."

Savina stared. Then she caught herself and shoved the knife hastily back into its sheath.

The woman shooed her again. "Go on, human," she said, as if talking to her dog. "It'll be safer for you if you get in without being seen." She sighed. "I'm talking to it like it can understand me," she mumbled under her breath.

Savina blinked at her, then recovered herself and gave the woman an innocent smile. "Thank you," she said breathlessly. "I know you can't understand me, but—thank you."

She wasn't, in fact, sure the woman couldn't understand her. It was always best not to take people—or yibo—at their word. But as long as the woman had decided not to turn her in, it hardly mattered.

She ducked out the back hatch and into the open fields, and the yibo woman closed the hatch behind her.

The rising sun warmed Savina's shoulders as she made her way across the uneven ground towards the city, birds chirping lazily from the jungle behind her, and she took a deep breath, rolling the stiffness from her shoulders.

Despite everything, she found there was a slight spring to her step, a genuine smile tugging at her lips.

It had been far, far too long since her life had been simple. Since she'd kidnapped Joska and Rafel, been hunted by Reka, found her long-lost baby brother.

The thought of Reka made something twist in her chest, something complicated and suffocating, and she shoved it back.

It was a good thing Reka was dead. It didn't matter that there was something about her that had pulled at Savina's gut with an aching longing she couldn't explain. Something about the way she looked at Savina, how her cold gaze had cut through all the affected innocence and simplicity Savina had spent her whole life perfecting, as if it wasn't there.

Savina didn't need to be seen for who she was. It was dangerous, and stupid, and it could get her killed. But in the end, her act had worked after all. Reka had underestimated her. And now Reka was dead, and Savina had killed her.

And here, just for now, everything was simple again. She had a goal, and a plan to get there. No one to worry about, no one to explain to, no complicated moral decisions, just her, and her knives, and a whole city of people to be manipulated at her will.

She closed her eyes and drew in a deep breath of humid jungle air.

This she could do. This, she was good at. For the first time in a very long time, she was playing a game she knew, with rules that made sense.

She hadn't realized how satisfying a feeling that could be.

She stayed off the main road, and when she reached the city entrance, she ducked out of sight behind some of the quick-growing vegetation that surrounded the city, and seemed to spring up here almost overnight.

She still wore yibo clothing, and although she looked nothing like the creatures, the height difference wasn't as dramatic as it would have been with Joska or Beni.

When a large group of chattering, laughing yibo workers trooped in from the field, she stood quickly and slipped in among them, keeping her head down and matching her movements to theirs. The guards at the force-field opened a gate, and the yibo passed through, Savina in their midst.

The moment she was inside, she ducked into an alley.

She was back. And this time, she was back on her own terms.

The yibo back alleys were just as dangerous as any back on Colorida, but her reputation from her time with Yuur must have proceeded her—once or twice she heard furtive footsteps behind her, but there was always a moment when they stopped abruptly, then disappeared.

She smiled to herself.

Being underestimated was her stock in trade. But still, she was hunting politicians, not criminals—although perhaps that was a distinction without a difference—and it was nice to be remembered once in a while.

At last, she saw through the streets ahead of her the massive, gorgeous architecture of the government buildings.

She made her way closer, staring about her like a Rim Mountain farm girl coming into the city for the first time.

No one paid her any notice. Which meant, probably, that whatever had happened while she was gone, the yibo no longer saw humans as an existential threat.

She had no idea whether that was a good thing or a bad one, and honestly, she didn't care. For the first time in the last damn ... however long it had been, she had no one to protect, no one to worry about, no one to lecture her on morals.

She was here to kill someone.

And she was *good* at killing people.

She waited until no one was watching, then strolled casually into the broad open courtyard surrounding the cluster of government buildings.

She could recognize the building where the humans were being kept from her conversations with Ines, and she walked casually towards it, as if returning after a night out. She had no idea if the humans here were being held captive, but if someone asked, she could always think of an excuse. That was the good thing about appearing so helpless and naïve—no one could conceive of you actually making trouble on purpose.

For a moment, she almost whispered a question for Beni into her wavelink—and then she remembered.

Still, this wasn't the first time she'd had to pull a job without Beni, and it probably wouldn't be the last. Assuming that any of them survived the next few weeks, of course.

She found a place behind one of the old trees that lined the courtyard, abutting one of the narrow alleyways, and sat, leaning back against the tree trunk as if taking shelter from the heat of the day. She studied the buildings through half-closed eyelids, taking note of the patterns of comings and goings as the aliens moved in and out.

The air was thick, humid and warm, and insects droned lazily in the muted hum of the early morning. Despite her short nap in the cargo ship, Savina found her eyes drifting closed as she watched.

She shook herself, trying to force her mind back to alertness.

Just watch. Watch, and find a way in. And when she was inside, it would be a simple matter of finding this Kachik person and killing him. Then, in the confusion, she'd go after Captain Mattin. She'd done this sort of thing so often she could probably do it in her sleep. An unsuspecting yibo government official would hardly be any different than an unsuspecting human one.

A hand clamped down on her shoulder.

Savina spun, jerking out of her assailant's grip, too shocked to react on anything but instinct. The sun, shining directly behind the newcomer's head, left their features in shadow, and Savina blinked, trying to adjust to the light.

How had she not heard them coming? She'd been tired, yes, but

—

Her attacker danced aside as Savina pulled out a knife, and a blow to Savina's wrist sent the weapon flying. A small warning pinged in the back of her brain, but she was too busy trying to stay alive to listen to it.

She yanked out another knife, fumbling with her free hand for her pulse pistol, and barely jumped out of the way as her attacker's foot swept around, almost knocking the legs out from under her. She caught a fist to her stomach and doubled over, but managed to catch herself against the tree trunk. Her attacker leapt back as Savina's knife slashed air.

For a moment, Savina and her attacker stood at the mouth of the alleyway, staring at each other.

Then the warning in the back of Savina's brain finally pushed through the noise as she stared in utter bewilderment at the familiar figure in front of her—the sharp, elegant features, the rich tone of the woman's skin, a few shades darker than Savina's own, the ice in her eyes. She wasn't wearing her armoured grey suit, but a loose-fitting soldier's uniform of a style Savina recognized from the scraps of fabric she'd seen on the dead bodies in the grasslands. Even the bulky uniform, though, couldn't hide the curves of her muscular body or the smooth, sensuous grace of her movements.

The figure Savina had last seen crumpling to the ground, eyes wide with shock and pain, blood seeping through her fingers as she clutched at the wound from Savina's pulse pistol.

The wound that should have killed her.

And despite everything, despite the muddy, ugly mix of shock and guilt and horror, just like always, the sight of her sent a jolt through Savina's entire body, a confusing spike of lust and hate that she had no idea what to do with.

"Reka?" she said at last, hearing the disbelief in her own tone. "How the actual hell—"

"Upset you couldn't kill me?" Reka's mouth curved into a cool, mocking smile that made Savina shiver, in a way that was—not necessarily unpleasant, but certainly unwanted. "You're quite something, Savina Moya."

"You're supposed to be dead, damn you," Savina hissed. Her hands were shaking, and she wasn't sure why.

She lunged at Reka again, but the woman sidestepped neatly, smirking at her. "Hush. I'd hate for anyone to hear us."

Savina cursed and lunged again, and this time Reka stepped into the blow, catching Savina's arm and redirecting the force so that Savina stumbled heavily into the alley wall. She barely caught herself, then twisted, grabbing Reka's arm and yanking her forward.

With a grunt of surprise, Reka stumbled, caught off balance.

For a moment Savina was too shocked to take advantage.

Reka was easily strong enough to have stopped her.

But she recovered quickly, grabbing Reka's hair in one hand and yanking out a knife with the other, driving it towards Reka's stomach.

Reka dodged, barely, the knife skittering across the battered body armour of her uniform, and kicked out hard, catching Savina in the shin. Savina yelped, jumping back, and Reka lunged for her, but—

But she couldn't break free of Savina's grip.

Savina shoved Reka down, slamming her head painfully into the concrete, and dropped her knee onto the woman's chest, holding her in place.

For a moment she sat there, panting, strangely reluctant to reach for the knife that would slit Reka's throat.

"Wait." Reka's voice was hoarse, and there was a raw edge of exhaustion and pain to it that Savina hadn't heard there before.

It wasn't until then that Savina noticed the greyish cast to Reka's skin, the dark stain just visible through her uniform.

For a stunned half-moment, she thought perhaps her knife had hit home after all, and the sick horror that washed over her was strong enough, and shocking enough, that it took her by surprise.

Then her brain kicked in, and she recognized the outline of bandages on Reka's torso, the way the stains on her uniform were dried and faded, not the wet red of fresh blood.

Of course. It had only been days since she'd shot Reka down on the streets of this very city, left her bleeding out on the concrete.

"How are you still alive?" Savina snapped, ignoring the hoarseness in her own voice.

Reka was still breathing heavily, and despite her obvious pain, despite the fact that Savina had her pinned to the ground, a knife at her throat, she still managed that look of cool disdain that Savina had seen so often in restless, unsatisfying dreams. "You think I'd let something like you kill me?"

Savina's heart was pounding, hard and uneven, and she could feel the ragged rise and fall of Reka's chest under her knee, the taut tendons of the woman's wrist warm between her fingers. "Well, let's see if you can survive with your jugular cut," she said at last, forcing a sweet smile. "Most people don't, but you seem to be quite extraordinary, so——"

"You idiot." Reka gasped. "You were half asleep, lying there in the shade. You didn't even hear me coming. I could have shot you in the head, put a knife in your back, slit your throat from behind. I could have killed you a dozen ways."

Savina tried to ignore the chill that crawled up her back at Reka's words. Because Reka was right. That had been the unease tingling in the back of Savina's brain this whole time.

If Reka had wanted to kill her, she'd already be dead.

"Had a change of heart, then?" Savina smiled wider, letting her dimple show. "Decided I'm too pretty to kill?"

Reka turned her head and spat into the street.

Savina pouted. "Now you've hurt my feelings."

"Believe me, Savina," said Reka, her voice hard. "I'll take great pleasure in killing you when this is all done. But in the meantime, there are more important things than your miserable life."

Savina pouted again, playing the knife across the fingers of her free hand. "Reka. That's not how you flirt with a girl." Her hands, though, were shakier than they should be.

Reka narrowed her eyes. "Captain Mattin sent a group of soldiers with me to kill you, and bring Alba back to the city. I tracked you to that agricultural planet. But I heard the soldiers talking, when they didn't think I could hear. Mattin plans to let the yibo through the portal. With the yibo's help, Cavaco will stage a coup, and in return, he'll let the yibo take whatever they want from us." She looked up at Savina with her cold, emotionless gaze. "I'd love to watch you bleed out on the pavement, Savina. But you're a nothing. An annoyance. Cavaco, though—if he has the power to do it, he'll destroy the entire Joias System."

Savina stared. "That was you who killed those soldiers?" she asked at last, stupidly.

It made sense. Whoever had killed the human soldiers who'd followed them had more than a little practice, to do it so neatly.

If she hadn't bloody shot Reka herself, watched her collapse onto the street, she'd have guessed who it was immediately.

"You found them, did you?" Reka's voice had regained its usual cool amusement.

Savina took a deep breath, recovering her composure with an

effort. "So, you came all that way to kill me, and then gave up right at the finish line so you could come back and save the Joias System. You're quite the hero, aren't you? And here I thought you were just a lapdog looking for another master."

Her heart was pounding.

Reka had been there. Reka had been on the planet, following them. And Savina had had no idea. Injured, unsuspecting—

How many of them could Reka have killed, if she'd wanted to? She'd killed a dozen soldiers, because they hadn't been watching for it.

And nor had Savina. Nor had any of them.

"Cavaco's damn well not going to take control of the Joya System, not while I'm alive to stop him." There was a sharp bitterness under Reka's flat tone.

Savina closed her eyes for a moment, her head spinning.

So Joska had been right, after all, about the portal. Alba had been right.

As much as Savina hated the Chief Justice, as much as Savina would love to see the whole Joias System implode—she'd spent enough time out in the world to know what a system with Cavaco in charge of it would look like. She could practically smell the smoke of burning bodies from the vids of the Holy Wars she'd been forced to watch, over and over, as a child. Even now, years later and light-years distant, the memories made her shaky.

"You … plan to go back with them, then, kill Cavaco?" she asked at last.

Reka shook her head impatiently. "I'm going to kill Captain Mattin and that scientist, Emeric. Once they're dead, I suspect the yibo won't be nearly as motivated to find out what's on the other side of the portal. They'll have no guarantee what's waiting for them. But if someone finds your dead body outside the government compound, it will warn Mattin that something's wrong. Your life isn't worth that."

"What a coincidence," Savina said brightly. "It just so happens I came to kill Captain Mattin as well. And the yibo head of government, because why not? Although if I'd known you were still alive, I'd have put you at the top of the list."

Reka narrowed her eyes. "You're lying." There was a flash of anger in her gaze now that sent something savage and warm into the pit of Savina's stomach.

"What?" Savina asked innocently. "Is it so unbelievable I'm here to help? I'm really actually a very selfless person, if you get to know me."

Reka sucked in a quick breath, and Savina felt a hot, vicious thrill of satisfaction.

"I don't know what you're doing, Savina Moya," said Reka in a low voice. "But I'm not going to let you ruin this, like you've ruined everything else."

Savina clenched her teeth against the hot burst of anger, her hand trembling on her knife.

She'd been the one who ruined everything?

This was stupid. She should have killed Reka the moment she had her on the ground. What the actual hell was wrong with her?

But she could still see, in her mind, Reka's crumpled body in the street, blood seeping from between her fingers, still feel the sick twist of guilt and vindication at the sight.

Besides, Reka was right. A body would be hard to explain. And Reka—who'd had Nicolau in her gun sights and let him go, because she didn't want to hurt an innocent bystander—Reka was stupid enough to be honourable about this whole thing.

"Fine," she said at last, through her teeth. "We both have people we want to kill. So, you go your way, and I'll go mine, and when this is over—" she flashed Reka her brightest smile. "I would be more than happy to renew our acquaintance."

Reka gave her a small smirk. "I might agree to that, if you were anyone else. But you're not out of my sight until we're done this. Then, if you do a good job, maybe I'll give you a day's start."

"I don't know why you think—" Savina began. Then she glanced down.

Reka opened her fingers just enough so that Savina could see the muzzle of a small, deadly pulse-pistol peeking out, pointed at Savina's stomach. "Like I said. Someone finding your dead body would make my job much more difficult, and I don't have time to go hide it somewhere safe. But I have no guarantee you won't try to kill me the moment I turn my back, since that seems to be your general method. So, we're going together. Kachik is the one who wants to join forces with Cavaco. Having him out of the way certainly won't hurt. If you really want to kill some yibo politician, I'm sure you could use the help. And I'm sure I can kill Captain Mattin, even if I'm babysitting you at the same time."

Savina blinked at her in total outrage.

Reka shoved Savina off her and pushed herself painfully to her feet, her gun still trained on Savina. "Come on," she said, as though coaxing a stubborn pack animal. "We both have the same goal for now."

"No, we don't," Savina snapped, to irritated to measure her words. "Because my goal is making sure you don't leave the planet alive."

Reka just gestured with her gun, still wearing that smirk that made Savina desperate to wipe it off. With a gun, or with a fist, of course, because there was absolutely nothing about that sensuous mouth twisted into a mocking grin, those lean, strong fingers wrapped around the butt of the pistol, that had anything to do with the sudden heat that flared in the pit of her stomach—

She turned away and shoved herself to her feet, cursing her traitorous hormones.

It wasn't actually fair that someone who she so utterly loathed should be so ridiculously attractive.

"I saw you watching the building," Reka continued, leaning casually back against the wall of the alley. Even injured as she was, her movements held a fluid grace that pulled at Savina's gaze. "Savina! Are you even listening?"

Savina blinked up at Reka.

"I said," said the woman slowly, as if Savina was very stupid, "I know how to get in. That's what you were looking for, wasn't it?"

Savina glared at her.

Reka smiled, a cold, dangerous smile that made Savina's heart jump.

She closed her eyes. This was not the state of mind she needed to be in to make a decision.

Reka wanted her dead. Savina returned the sentiment—no matter how attractive Reka might be, no matter how the memory of her lying crumpled in the street might haunt Savina, as long as Reka was alive, Savina would never be safe.

But—

Well, Reka was right. If they spent too much time out here fighting, it was inevitable they'd be discovered. And if Reka could, in fact, get them through the doors of the government building, it would make things much easier.

Anyway, at some point Reka would get sloppy. At some point,

she'd forget who she was dealing with, and she'd let down her guard, for just a moment.

And with her weakened like this, injured and slower than usual, a moment would be all it would take.

She took a deep breath, and smiled up at Reka. "Fine. I don't usually take on partners, but like you said, we would probably work really well together." Her voice was breathy and overly sincere.

Reka's mouth tightened, and Savina was mildly gratified at the flash of irritation in the woman's eyes.

It wasn't like she thought Reka would actually be fooled by the act. She was used to playing to her audience, easing them into letting down their guard. But there was something about Reka that goaded her, made her say and do things just to draw the woman's attention.

It was dangerous, and stupid, and she couldn't seem to help it.

Reka straightened, wincing, and gestured Savina ahead of her with the tip of her weapon.

"That looks like it hurt," said Savina sympathetically, glancing down at the blood staining Reka's suit. "You should probably get it looked at."

"I've had worse," said Reka dryly. "This one wasn't much—just a little girl who thought she could play with the grown-ups."

"I wonder where the little girl is now," said Savina, wide-eyed. "A big tough woman like you, I'll bet she didn't stand a chance."

"She won't, if she doesn't shut her damn mouth." Reka was speaking through her teeth.

Savina smiled to herself, and was silent.

They came around the back of the building. Savina watched Reka carefully for any sign that the woman was planning to shoot her the moment her back was turned, but it seemed the idiot was stupid enough to think that the two of them could actually work together without killing each other.

Savina didn't feel it necessary to disabuse her of that notion. At least, not while she was being useful.

Reka led them to the back of the government compound. There was more metal than glass here, but she stepped up to a small entrance—or rather, where an entrance should have been, but instead was solid glass—and pulled out a thin device from the pocket of her jacket, holding it up to the surface.

The glass dissolved.

Savina glanced at her, mildly impressed.

"One of the guards I killed had it on her," said Reka coolly, gesturing Savina inside.

Savina stepped through, and Reka followed.

"Do you know where you need to go?" asked Reka in a soft voice. The hallway was deserted, but from farther ahead Savina could hear the muted chatter of yibo voices.

She shook her head.

Reka's look turned to one of disdain. "So. You planned to just wander in here and hope you stumbled across him?"

Savina smiled. "No. I didn't need to do that. Because I can understand what they're saying." She reveled, for just a moment, in the startled look on Reka's face, then she moved ahead, Reka close behind.

9

Alba

By midday, Joska and Yosip between them had made the necessary arrangements.

"As long as you do not over-exert yourself, you should suffer no ill effects from this," the doctor said in stilted Common Dialect. "I will send a transport-drone to assist you, so you don't have to put too much weight on your leg."

Alba nodded stiffly. "Thank you."

With Joska's assistance, and the assistance of the yibo transport drone, Alba made her painful way down the potholed streets of the village.

She looked around her as she walked.

The village was small and neat, but it carried a very different flavour from that of the city they'd left.

There was a force-field around the village, just like there had been around the jungle city, and under the force-field, the streets were lined with spreading trees, the burst of green contrasting sharply with the yellow-brown of the prairie grasslands outside. The buildings here were less elegant and soaring—presumably, the wind of this place would make the tall, graceful architectural style a liability—but Alba could see hints of the same style in the oddly refractive clear walls of the buildings, and the way they stretched out in delicate branches along the ground.

The similarities, however, ended there—rather than the sleek, modern, glass-and-steel look of the yibo government buildings, these were decorated with brightly-coloured accents, the roofs of a thick red tile, the metal struts holding the glass-like material together painted or stained in cheerful oranges and yellows and greens, and decorated with closely dotted designs that spread in organic loops and whorls up the sides of the buildings and faded into the glass.

Small, large-eyed youngsters shouted and played in the streets, kicking makeshift balls in a game that was oddly reminiscent of the children's games back on the streets of Vila Nova do Sol. The more timid among them ducked back at the sight of the newcomers, but the bolder ones stared at them openly, chattering to each other in words too quick for even Ines's translator, set into Alba's wavelink, to pick up.

Again, Alba felt that strange twist of unease at the unquestioning acceptance by the yibo of humans in their midst.

She pushed it back resolutely. There would be time to worry about that once they'd neutralized the threat to the Joias System.

At last they reached a small, cozy-looking building, the walls bordered by blue, patterned struts, and Joska paused at the entrance, gesturing her inside. "I'll be helping Nicolau and Beni and Ines in the fields, it sounds like," the woman said in her comfortable, wry tone. "But Yosip and Feliu will be working with you. I expect they're already inside."

Alba nodded stiffly, letting go of Joska's arm, and limped painfully through the doorway.

With the transparent walls, there was hardly a change in the brightness from outside to inside. Still, she had to blink for a moment at the change from the glare of the sun to the softly refracted light inside the building.

She glanced around her at the group of a dozen or so yibo in the small sitting room.

They stared back with undisguised suspicion.

They all looked older, although it was hard to tell with yibo—greyish tips to the fur around their mouths and eyes, movements that bore the caution of age rather than the recklessness of youth. Their clothing was the same as she'd seen of the other villagers—tunics and trousers, the cloth worked in the same organic patterns as the designs on the buildings.

None of them looked happy to see her.

She sighed, fighting back her irritation. She was likely the only person who wanted her there less than the yibo did.

But somewhere a few million kilometres away, Kachik and Captain Mattin were discussing how her home system would be parcelled out between them. And if she failed to stop it, she would not let it be because she'd refused to put in the effort.

The chairs were gathered in small clusters, with a spreading, tree-like structure in the centre from which were hung various trays of what Alba assumed must be food and drink. Bolts of material were piled on the floor around the chairs, and delicate hand-guided drones perched on top of the piles like tiny hummingbirds.

One of the yibo gestured grudgingly toward one of the ubiquitous, uncomfortable stools that seemed to be set aside specifically for humans, and, biting back a groan, Alba made her hobbling way over and lowered herself gingerly down onto it.

"Human!"

Alba looked up, startled, into the face of an older yibo woman. "Yes?" she answered tartly.

"I asked, human, if you know what you're doing."

Alba took a deep breath. After seventy-three years of never permitting herself to show either doubt or uncertainty, admitting her own ignorance was almost a painful thing.

"I do not," she said, raising her chin slightly.

The yibo woman looked down at her condescendingly. "Well then, move over, I'll show you. We don't have time or resources to waste picking out badly made pieces."

Alba bit back a sharp retort as the woman sat beside her, muttering something in yibo that Alba's wavelink translated.

"I truly did not understand how useless humans could be," the woman was saying under her breath. "After all the stories about helpful, willing humans—I'll tell you, I don't see it. As far as I'm concerned, we should have just taken that ship rather than bargain for their help to work off the debt, for all the use they're going to be."

"You never know," said another of the yibo mildly, glancing up. "It's possible they'll learn. This one seems stubborn, but the man who works with her is friendly enough."

"That captain and those three kids are hard workers, whatever else you want to say about them. They're helping out with the harvesting, and it didn't take them long to catch on," said another. "I don't have a lot of hope for this one learning anything useful—" the speaker gestured derisively at Alba. "But the others might make up for it."

Alba had to actually bite her lip to hold back an irritated rejoinder. She was accustomed to being the most important person in the room, and she hadn't realized, until just now, how much she'd gotten used to it.

But it couldn't be helped. She set her mouth in a grim line, and set about copying her guide's stitches.

It was an intricate, painstaking process—tiny drones did the actual stitching, but you needed to manually steer them to create the patterns. The yibo hadn't trusted Alba with creating the patterns herself—with some justice, she was forced to admit—instead giving her cloth with the patterns traced onto it in light markings that she was expected to follow, but the work of keeping the drone moving correctly was far from simple. Alba's hands, still shaky and weak from her injuries, kept bumping the drone clumsily, and she had to send it back to unpick the stitches so often that by the time the other workers in the circle had finished a small pile of clothing, she was still only halfway done her first.

Yosip, sitting across from her, seemed to be having much less difficulty, his calloused hands moving the drone in sure patterns. He was deep in conversation with a yibo man, and judging from the man's wide smile, they were having a delightful time despite their lack of shared language. Feliu sat stiffly nearby, but as Alba watched, Yosip turned, drawing him skillfully into the conversation.

"You look like you could use a hand," said one of the yibo women in accented Common Dialect, coming to sit beside her, the same woman who'd spoken up for Alba at the beginning. She sat down beside her, and Alba fought back the urge to jerk her project away in irritation. "I'm Hrrr."

She took a deep breath, instead, and resisted the instinct to snatch her hands back when the yibo woman guided them along the outline of the fabric.

"—are we going to do when Kachik sends patrols next?"

Alba looked up in surprise, glancing over at the speaker.

She was one of the older women, her head down as she spun the stitching drone in intricate patterns on the cloth.

The man across from her snorted, holding up his own finished garment to inspect. "We do what we've always done. Not like we can afford to get on the bad side of Kachik, but we can't afford to get on the bad side of the government, either."

Alba frowned.

"Careful! You've got to pay attention, or the lines will be crooked."

Alba looked back to her work, biting back the flare of irritation at her companion's indulgent smile.

"What are they talking about?" she asked, trying to make her words casual.

The woman shrugged. "Taxes. With the system like it is, everyone wants to tax everyone—Kachik and Irra both. And since we're halfway between Chrr and Pria—"

Alba raised an eyebrow. "What's Pria?"

She could still see, in her mind's eye, the map that Kachik had shown her back in the yibo city, the image she'd captured on her wavelink.

She was quite certain she hadn't seen a planet or a city by that name.

The woman gave a soft, comfortable hum of amusement. "I wouldn't expect you to know much about the system yet, seeing as you're humans. Came through the portal, I hear?"

"Yes," murmured Alba.

Her mind was racing.

"As far as I'm concerned," said a man from the other side of the room as Alba's wavelink translated, "We could just declare loyalties."

The older woman who'd first spoken smiled. "Not likely. We're a bunch of farmers. You know what they think about us—stupid and unsophisticated. I'm not about to disabuse them of that, if it means we still have enough to go around. Even enough to take care of these humans."

Someone else hummed softly. "The advantage of the people who make the decisions not having any idea how much a single agricultural season should produce."

"Back to my question," said the first speaker. "You say do what we've always done?"

The older woman nodded. "We'll hide some of the designs in the warehouse again. As long as we're here sewing, I doubt they'll worry about checking there. And if they do, we can always say it was a shipment that got returned or something."

"Do—do Kachik's people come here frequently?" Alba asked in a low voice, trying to keep her hand steady on the machine.

The woman beside her shrugged. "Frequently enough. After all, after what happened the last time they opened—" she paused, glancing sideways at Alba, and trailed off.

Alba turned resolutely back to her work.

But it was mildly disorienting, looking around at the old, obviously rural yibo as they chattered and gossiped and—

Well, and, it appeared, strategized how to keep their village from both Kachik and Irra, whoever or whatever that was.

"All we need now is for the raiders to show up," said one of the women. "With how our luck's been these last few months—"

There was a communal clicking of tongues and shaking of heads.

"Stop worrying. I doubt we'll get into trouble," said Hrrr comfortably. "Last time a raider party came close, I told Captain Krevai that if he didn't call it off, I was worried that we wouldn't have enough people to finish off his last order." She chuckled. "He got his people to deal with the problem, and they dealt with it quickly." She paused, turning back to Alba and switching to Common Dialect. "Oops! Like I said, you have to watch. We'll have to pick those stitches out again."

Alba turned numbly back to her work, her mind spinning.

By the end of the day, Alba was exhausted, her hands stiff and aching, her back sore from bending over the drones. When she pushed herself to her feet and stumbled wearily to the exit, she was struck with an unexpected relief at the sight of Yosip waiting for her, his eyes twinkling, his smile wide and friendly.

"Alba," he said. "If you'll forgive me for saying it, you look tired. Shall we walk together?"

She could hear the words he wasn't saying—*You look exhausted. I'm not sure you'll make it back on your own.*

But he was right. And she had neither the energy nor the willpower to stand on her dignity at the moment. So she walked home between Yosip, with his easy smile and his light conversation, and Feliu, quiet, but smiling reluctantly at Yosip's words.

"Alba?" Yosip asked at last, turning his smile on her. "How did you enjoy your first knitting-circle-to-save-the-system?"

She blinked at him for a moment, pulled out of her spiralling thoughts.

"I suppose now they'll have to add yibo knitting as a prerequisite to Joias civil servant positions," Feliu muttered.

Alba stared. And then she let out an undignified snort of laughter.

Yosip joined in wholeheartedly, and even Feliu gave a reluctant chuckle. And for no reason she could fathom, there was a breathless relief that washed through her at the sound of their laughter. As if the fate of the system no longer rested on her shoulders alone.

As if, yibo knitting circle and all, it was possible that they could fix this.

10

Aran

By the time the sun had set, Aran was stumbling with exhaustion, and Istvay was barely on their feet. At some point during the afternoon the two of them had switched from their typical trail formation to walking side by side, Aran's arm around Istvay's back, Istvay's over Aran's shoulder. It spoke to how dire the situation had become that Istvay hardly protested. Their face was set in a stoic mask that told Aran just how much effort it was taking them merely to stay on their feet.

The forest around the two of them hadn't cleared—if anything, it had gotten thicker. The gradient of the ground had started out as a steady rise and fall of gentle hills, but it was gradually sharpening into the steeper peaks and valleys that, if Aran was any judge, meant foothills. The trees were thick enough, though, that he couldn't get a good view of the terrain ahead, so the best he could do was guess, and hope like hell he and Istvay didn't run straight into the mountains.

Ani alternated between ghosting noiselessly along beside them through the trees and huddling in a worried lump on Aran's shoulder, completely enveloping Istvay's hand and forearm and reaching out occasionally to stroke Istvay's shoulder or face with the tip of a tentacle.

As the last glowing rays of the sun cut across the gathering dimness, Aran glanced over at Istvay, stumbling along with their eyes half closed.

If there were mountains ahead, it was doubtful either of them would make it up.

The dusk turned to dark, and at last Aran stumbled to a halt, glancing around to get his bearings. Istvay slumped against him, too weary even to pretend to be alright.

He sighed, trying to hold back his concern. "Pishti," he said quietly. "Pishti, we'll rest here for a bit."

Istvay tried to raise their head. "I'll be fine," they mumbled. "I just —just let me—" their words trailed off, as if they were too weary to finish the sentence.

"No," said Aran, looking around quickly. "We haven't heard the raiders behind us in a while. Maybe they lost the trail. Anyways, if we keep going like this, we're going to get so sloppy that they find us anyways. Best to find a place to sleep for the night, I think. If they can't track us by scent, they'll need to follow our trail by sight, and even if they have night vision that'll be easier in daylight. I doubt they'll risk missing us in the dark."

He expected Istvay to protest, but they just nodded wearily.

His chest tight with worry, Aran lowered his friend carefully to the forest floor, propping them up against the trunk of one of the evergreen trees.

"Ani, watch Istvay," he whispered, and she slithered down his arm to take her place on Istvay's lap, her entire body a bright, concerned purple, her eye-pouches puffed out.

He watched the two of them for a moment, biting his lip in concern, then stepped away quickly to scout for a place to shelter.

It was almost full dark by the time he found something—a tree had fallen over, and the roots pulled up to create a small dirt cave that was almost invisible unless you were right up next to it.

By the time he returned, Istvay was slumped back against the tree, eyes closed. Ani huddled beside them, growling her soft, worried growl, and when he bent and put a hand on his friend's arm, he could feel them shivering, their skin cold to the touch.

He swore helplessly.

There was no way he could make a fire, not here, not when he and Istvay were being tracked by creatures who hunted by smell.

He crouched down and hauled Istvay to their feet, biting his lip against the panic, and Ani scrambled up his trouser leg. He wasn't sure if Istvay was even fully conscious during the short, nightmarish trek through the trees to the shelter, their feet stumbling, Aran supporting their full weight. When the three of them finally reached it, Aran pulled the survival kit from his knapsack, yanking out the compact self-inflating mat that should at least protect Istvay from the worst of the cold seeping up through the ground.

It wasn't anything approaching the cold of a Rim Mountain winter, but the night air held the familiar bite of mountain chill.

He hauled his semiconscious friend onto the mat, then carefully checked them over with the tiny emergency med scanner.

Despite the cuts and bruises that were already purpling garishly across their arms and shoulders, and the mess of swelling and dried blood on their face, they didn't seem to have broken any bones. And if they had a concussion, which they probably did, there really wasn't much Aran could do about it at the moment.

He laid Istvay out as comfortably as he could and covered them with both the thin emergency blankets. After a moment of hesitation, he crawled in beside them, adding his body heat to theirs, and Ani plopped down on top of them both like a small, lumpy, tentacled coverlet.

Istvay was completely unconscious at this point, their eyes closed and their body limp, but as the blanket slowly warmed around them, they mumbled something incoherent and snuggled in closer, burrowing into the warmth formed by Aran's body.

Aran tightened his arm around them, and just for one moment, as he closed his eyes, he allowed himself to wish, hopelessly, for what might have been.

Then even that wasn't enough, and his exhausted body gave up completely, and he was asleep.

When Aran woke the next morning, the first traces of sunlight were trickling in through the tangle of tree roots above them. He groaned softly as he blinked his eyes open.

His entire body was sore, his neck and back painfully stiff, his leg aching from the crash and then the forced march of the entire previous day. Every part of him felt bruised and battered, except for the comfortable warmth against his chest …

He turned, and saw Istvay curled into him.

Their eyes were closed, their dark lashes brushing their cheeks, their face a gruesome pattern of bruises against an unhealthy pallor, but even so, something about the sight hit Aran like a punch to the stomach.

Istvay moaned. Their eyelids fluttered open, and they blinked up at Aran.

Their eyes went wide.

Aran was suddenly very, very aware that he was lying practically on top of them, and that he could feel every centimetre of their body under his, their wiry muscles, the shape of them and the warmth of them and—and damn it to hell, his brain had figured out that this was not a relationship that was ever going to happen, but apparently his body hadn't got the memo, and everything inside him was turning into a sort of helpless, fuzzy mess …

Istvay was still staring up at him, still with that expression on their face. "Aran?" they said softly, and something in the tone of their voice made Aran's heart jump.

He swallowed hard. "I—Pishti, I'm sorry, I just—you were cold last night, and—and I was worried about you, and—"

"Aran," whispered Istvay again, their voice husky. Their hand came up, brushing Aran's cheek.

And suddenly, he couldn't do it anymore.

He pulled back abruptly.

Istvay's hand fell to their side.

"Listen," Aran began, although his voice didn't seem to want to work the way it ought to. "Listen, Pishti, you … you don't have to do this. You—I know you don't want a relationship. I—I've known that for a long time, but before, I was—I was being stupid, and selfish, and I wouldn't let it die. And that's my fault, but … but I'm not doing that anymore. You don't have to pretend just to make me feel better, okay?" He closed his eyes and ran his hands over his face "We're—we're friends, and that's all, and it's alright. I'm not looking for anything more, I promise." He opened his eyes again and managed a small smile.

Istvay was still staring at him, their face going through a rapid range of emotions that he couldn't read, and quite frankly didn't want to.

"I promise, Pishti," he mumbled, turning away. "You really don't have to pretend. It's fine. You're my best friend, and you always will be. And—and look, I'm sorry for making things awkward, before."

He could feel Istvay's eyes on the back of his head.

There was a long moment of silence.

"Aran."

There was an unfamiliar note in Istvay's voice, and Aran's stomach twisted in embarrassment. He half-turned, and managed a pained smile. "Pishti, please. I—I don't really want to talk about it right now." He turned and slid out the entrance to the cave, closing his eyes and taking a deep breath.

At last he straightened carefully and glanced around.

Ani must have taken up watch just outside the cave, because a moment later she dropped down beside him in a small shower of leaves and chirruped up at him pitifully. He leaned down with a small, rueful smile and picked her up, stroking her absently as she cuddled against his chest.

At the very least, they'd survived the night. The first rays of morning sun were peeking through the tree branches, casting bright streaks of orange light across the ground through the trees. The air smelled fresh and clean, and despite—well, despite everything that had happened back in the stupid cave, Aran found his smile growing a little more genuine.

It was better like this anyways. It was better to finally talk about it, finally get it out in the open. And maybe, finally, the awkwardness would go away, and things could go back to being comfortable again.

Istvay could finally feel comfortable again.

From behind him, he heard the rustle of someone exiting the cave. He stiffened, but didn't turn around.

Istvay's footsteps came up behind him, and their hand landed on his shoulder. He stiffened more.

"Aran," said Istvay, still with that strange note in their voice. "I—I packed our things into the knapsack. Normally I'd say maybe we should just lay low and hope they miss us, but they proved pretty thoroughly yesterday that they can follow a trail as long as they have the light to do it. So we'll need to keep moving. We'll have to have the energy bars for breakfast, and probably dinner too, but at least they should have enough calories to—" they trailed off.

For a moment the two of them stood in silence. At last, Istvay cleared their throat and shoved an energy bar into Aran's hand. "You should eat something, you'll feel better after you've eaten. I wasn't the only one who got beat up in that crash, and you've been doing most of the work, hauling me after you, so … " They trailed off again. "Um. About … About what you said back there—"

Aran gritted his teeth. "Look, Pishti, I—can we please not talk about this right now? I'm just—I'm not sure I'm—I can—"

The sharp crack of a twig made both of their heads jerk around, as if they were two puppets pulled by the same string, and Ani gave a low growl, her eye-pouches puffing out. Aran's eyes met Istvay's, every trace of lingering awkwardness replaced with grim realization.

"I'll grab the pack," said Aran. "We've got to get out of here, now."

By the time the sun was fully up, they were on the run again.

The day passed in a haze of exhaustion and strain. Istvay's strength began to give out by midday, and between Aran's own injuries and the fact that he was all but carrying Istvay as well, by the time the sun began to set he could barely put one foot in front of the other.

The pursuit hadn't flagged throughout the day, and more than once they'd only escaped by the sheerest of luck.

And now …

Aran stared at the steep slope ahead of them in blank despair.

"Aran. What is it?" Istvay mumbled, opening their eyes with an effort.

"I was right," said Aran grimly. "Those were foothills." he gestured at the foot of the mountain ahead of them, the evergreens clinging to the side of the steep slope.

Istvay groaned. "I—don't suppose there's a way around it?"

Aran shook his head. "No such luck. Even if there was, there's no way we get around this, not being chased like we are. And from the sounds of it, they've spread out. It feels like they're trying to cut us off. We can't turn off, or they'll catch us."

Istvay swore, and something about the hopelessness in their tone caught in Aran's chest.

"Aran," they began softly.

"Shut up," said Aran in a flat voice. "Don't even damn well think about it."

Istvay sighed. "Aran. Listen. I—" they broke off, their voice catching. "I can't make it up this. Do you think I don't realize you're practically carrying me as it is? There's no way both of us get up the mountain, so at least one of us should—"

"I said, shut up."

Istvay sighed and fell silent.

In the distance, Aran could hear the sound of the raiders pushing through the trees behind them. Ani shifted on his shoulder, growling uneasily.

The raiders hadn't caught up yet, but it wouldn't take long.

He turned back to the steep slope ahead of them.

"Well," said Istvay at last, and Aran could hear the utter exhaustion in their tone. "I guess we'd better get going."

Aran took a deep breath. "I'm going to carry you, okay?"

Istvay scowled at him. "I'm not going to let you."

The footsteps were getting closer.

"We don't bloody have time to argue," Aran snapped, and Istvay sighed.

"Fine," they said wearily. "Fine, we'll do it your way."

Ani reached out a tentacle to pull herself off Aran's shoulders and onto an adjoining tree branch as Aran crouched, hoisting Istvay onto his back, and straightened with an effort. He tried to hide his stagger, glancing over his shoulder quickly. From the look on Istvay's face, he wasn't sure he'd been successful. But they didn't say anything, and Aran stumbled forward up the grade.

He hadn't gone more than a hundred metres before he was panting, his legs almost ready to give out. He was holding Istvay in place with one hand, and with the other halfway-dragging himself up the slope, supporting himself on the branches of the ubiquitous evergreens.

Behind him, he heard a shout, and he swore breathlessly as more voices joined in.

Dammit, they'd been spotted.

Ani hissed a threat from the trees above him, but even she wouldn't be able to take on that many raiders.

He tried to pull himself along faster, but his muscles were shaking with the effort, his breath rasping in his throat.

Maybe if he could get far enough up the mountain, he and Ani could turn and make a stand at least long enough to distract them from Istvay—

Behind him, someone shouted again, and the footsteps came to an abrupt halt.

Aran didn't have time to worry about it, or to do anything but mutter a brief, semi-coherent gasp of gratitude to whoever or whatever was helping them out.

At last the steep slope flattened into a shallow ledge, and he came to a halt, gasping for air.

"Aran," said Istvay quietly.

"What is it?" he panted.

"They've … turned around. They're not following us anymore."

Aran leaned against a tree, closing his eyes for a moment as he caught his breath.

"Are you sure?" he asked, when his breathing had steadied a bit.

"Look," said Istvay. There was a grim note to their voice.

Aran looked.

From this height, he could see for some distance. Far out, he could make out the smoking ruins of what had once been their escape pod —their only way off this planet. But below them, in the trees, he could see—nothing. No footsteps, no movement. Down a slope like this, as steep as it was, he should be able to see or hear something, if the raiders were still after them.

Even Ani had stopped hissing, and she dangled from the tree beside him, her posture watchful, but relaxed.

"Maybe—maybe they decided to come around and cut us off from the other side," said Aran, trying to push back the unease in his stomach. "I'm sure they know the terrain better than we do."

Istvay shook their head. "Maybe. But I have a feeling it's something else. You're carrying me, and I'm completely useless. There's no way they didn't realize they could make it up this mountain faster than we could."

Aran glanced ahead of them up the slope. In the darkening evening, the mountain seemed to stretch to the sky. For one brief, ridiculous moment, he felt a touch of what could only be called homesickness, memories of the Rim Mountains pushing themselves into his brain.

Memories of a time when Istvay wasn't dying.

But he'd only been fooling himself. Istvay had been dying that whole time, he just hadn't realized.

"Put me down," said Istvay, their voice cracked with weariness. "You're about to fall over. If they're not coming up after us, we may as well rest. Goodness knows we both need it," they added in an undertone.

"Let's get a little farther first." Aran could hardly make himself say the words, his entire body rebelling against the thought of climbing even one more step. But he and Istvay were still much too close to where the raiders had left off chasing them. If they were going to hide, he'd rather it be somewhere that wasn't quite so obvious.

For a moment, he thought Istvay would argue, but they just nodded wearily.

Aran struggled up the mountain until it was almost too dark to see, his muscles shaking, his stomach roiling with nausea from the effort. The next time the slope flattened off, it was almost full dark. Wearily, he lowered Istvay to the ground, and then dropped to his knees and tried not to vomit.

He and Istvay slept back-to-back in a small hollow beneath the spreading lower branches of a tree, Ani pressing herself into the narrow space between them. Aran was unreasonably grateful when Istvay simply crawled onto the mat and closed their eyes, without trying to revisit the conversation of that morning.

It might be a while before Aran felt ready to go down that particular track again.

His sleep was broken and uneasy—he kept waking to imagined sounds from outside, his heart pounding, and each time it took him far too long to fall back asleep.

In the end, Istvay woke before he did in the morning. He rolled over, blinking awake to the beam of sunlight across his face, and felt a momentary jolt of panic at glancing over to find them gone. He took a long breath, trying to slow his heart rate, and finally, his muscles aching at the movement, crawled out from under the spreading branches of the shelter.

Istvay was standing silhouetted against the rising sun, and they turned as Aran straightened.

"They're—gone," they said quietly. "Either that, or they found a way to be a hell of a lot sneakier than they were yesterday."

Aran nodded silently, looking up towards the formidable bulk of the mountain.

Istvay voiced his thoughts for him. "If there's something up there the raiders are afraid of—"

"You never know," said Aran, trying desperately not to think about the implications of Istvay's words. "It could be just—I don't know, superstition or something. A religious thing."

"You know as well as I do that most superstitions have some basis in fact," Istvay muttered.

Aran sighed. "Well, it's not like we have much choice. We can't exactly go back the way we came, not unless we want to be eaten."

Istvay turned, and managed a weak grin. "I guess you're right. At least you won't be literally carrying me up the damn mountain this time."

"There is that," Aran murmured.

Istvay sighed and turned back to the slope ahead of them, a grim look on their face. "Well, like you say—it's not like we have much of a choice."

11

Savina

Savina and Reka crept down the halls of the government building, keeping to the shadows, inasmuch as there were shadows in a place made mostly of windows.

Savina glanced at Reka occasionally, but to her surprise, it seemed the woman actually intended to leave her alive until they both finished killing their marks. Which was—gratifying, if ridiculously naïve.

"At this time of day, Kachik will most likely be in the afternoon ministerial meetings," Reka whispered. "You're lucky one of us knows where those are."

Savina shot her a glare, and Reka raised an eyebrow in that infuriating calm amusement.

The two of them made their way silently through the hallways, and with Reka's device, up a set of odd lifts that brought them to one of the higher floors. Savina glanced out the window, and wished abruptly that she hadn't.

It wasn't that she was afraid of heights. But standing six stories above the ground on a translucent surface wasn't the best way to deal with them, in her opinion.

Reka was watching her, still with that hint of amusement under her emotionless expression. Savina scowled and stepped back.

"Come on," Reka whispered. "You can sightsee later." She gestured Savina ahead of her down a hallway.

At last they turned down a long corridor that ended in a blank, semi-translucent wall that blocked their way into what appeared to be a large room filled with yibo. Reka ducked into a small side corridor, and Savina followed suit, trying to appear nonchalant.

"Alright," whispered Reka. "When we go in, Kachik will probably be sitting in the centre of the room." She paused a moment. "Do you know what he looks like?"

Savina's scowl must have been answer enough, because she sighed heavily. "It's a good thing for you that I found you," she said. "You would have just marched in there and started shooting, was that your plan?"

"No!" snapped Savina. "My plan was to sit outside and observe, listen in, figure out who he was and where he'd be. Then I was going to wander in here, looking lost, get myself into the right room, and shoot him dead. But that was before someone forced me into helping her do the job she couldn't do alone!"

Reka paused a moment, biting her lip. Savina looked away quickly, cursing herself.

"I would have done it differently, but your plan isn't as bad as I would have expected," Reka said at last. "Alright. I know what Kachik looks like, and you don't. So you go over there. Look stupid and confused, that seems to be your specialty. And while the guards are watching you, I'll kill them, slip inside, and kill Kachik. It won't take the yibo long to call in the army once Kachik's dead, so we'll have to move quickly after that. You follow me to where Cavaco's people are stationed, since you have no idea where that is. You can hold off the guards again—distract them, shoot them, I don't care— and I'll take out the captain and Emeric and as many of the soldiers as I can manage. But we'll have to get there before the yibo have time to lock it down, or it'll be impossible."

"And once you've killed everyone you want to kill?" asked Savina, turning back to her. "I assume you have a plan for afterwards?"

Reka shot her an amused glance. "You're quite the optimist if you think we'll be alive to have plans after that."

Savina smiled, narrowing her eyes. "You should know something about me, Reka—I don't do suicide missions. I don't do anything that doesn't leave me better off than when I started."

Reka gave a small, dry chuckle. "Of course. You wouldn't, would you? Do your best, then, I suppose." She gave an indifferent shrug. "If we both survive, I'll try to kill you. But it's always possible, since I'm the only one of us who actually gives a damn about what happens to the Joias System, that you might get off free and clear. And then you can go right on murdering your way across the system."

Savina looked up to make some cutting rebuttal, and found herself caught in Reka's gaze. There was an intensity in the woman's eyes, something sharp and intelligent and relentless, and it cut through Savina like a knife.

She swallowed hard and tore her gaze away, pulling out her pulse pistol and checking to make sure her knives were loose in their sheaths. "Fine," she snapped. "Are you ready?"

Reka give a brusque nod and straightened, the movement as fluid and graceful as a jewel-backed adder uncoiling in the sun. "I'll follow you," she whispered.

Savina took a deep breath, straightening her tunic and mussing her hair artfully. She widened her eyes and stepped out into the corridor, looking around dazedly, her steps hesitant. The guards at the door saw her a moment later and turned, annoyance in their postures.

"I'm … I'm sorry, I was just—" Savina began in a nervous, breathless tone.

One of the guards' eyes widened, and then they collapsed to the ground with a strangled noise. Savina fought the urge to whip around—she hadn't even heard Reka behind her, how was that possible?—as a second guard gave a shout of alarm. Two more guards fell, screaming, and the others were bringing their weapons to bear in panicked confusion.

"Good," Reka's voice hissed in her ear, and Savina had to fight not to jump. "Scream or something, I doubt they'll try to hurt you."

Savina opened her mouth to comply. And then a sound from behind her made her stomach lurch.

There were footsteps from the corridors, and barked commands in the yibo language. Dozens of footsteps. Many, many more than the number of guards there should have been.

She spun on Reka, opening her mouth to shout something at the woman's betrayal—but Reka looked as shocked as she felt.

For an instant, the two women stared at each other.

"I'll take the ones coming in, you finish off the guards," Savina hissed through her teeth.

Alarms wailed, footsteps pounding out from every corridor. Savina fired, and fired, and fired again, but the yibo kept coming, more than a dozen, more than two dozen, more than five dozen—

She ducked a shot and yanked her knives out, sending them through the throat or shoulder or stomach of the approaching yibo. The yibo soldiers screamed as the knives found their marks, but even as they stumbled and fell, more came behind them.

There were so many, so many more than there should have been.

From behind her, she could hear Reka's steady fire, picture the set look on the woman's face.

But the guards kept coming. They kept coming, and no matter how many of them Savina shot, there were more—

Something hit her full in the chest, and she staggered back at the impact, waiting for her mind to register the pain.

Then it did, and she gasped, weaving on her feet.

Another impact. She felt her legs give out under her, her knees slamming into the hard floor. She heard, faintly, behind her, Reka's alarmed shout, but everything was blurred and unsteady. She tried to lift her hand, tried to pull the trigger on her gun, but her muscles wouldn't respond, and her movements felt thick and slow.

And then the wavering shapes, the noise and the shouting around her, faded, and the last thing she remembered was the floor coming up to meet her.

When Savina woke, it was to a bright burst of pain.

She groaned, trying to make sense of what had happened.

Her entire body ached, and her face throbbed, her nose swollen and dried blood crusted down her face. Which meant, probably, that she was alive, at least.

She'd been with Reka. And then she'd … fainted? Been knocked out somehow, more likely.

And now … she shifted experimentally.

She appeared to be sitting upright, which meant she must be propped up against something. Her hands were bound behind her, and there was a cramp in her neck where her head had been slumped to one side.

She sifted through her muddy memories.

She must have been moved recently, which would explain the jolt of pain. Her ribs felt as though she'd been kicked, hard, and the bruises had stiffened. But there was nothing to indicate serious injury, which was something of a surprise. She couldn't remember much of what had happened, but she had the vague recollection that it had involved people shooting.

Well, not people, per se, but yibo. And more of them than she'd expected, and—

The memories came crashing back, and she had to bite back a whimper.

She was going to be killed. There was no way out this time. She'd used up all her luck, and now she was going to die, and Beni and the others would never even know what had happened to her.

This was supposed to have been a simple job.

She took a deep breath.

The yibo had had a chance to kill her, and they hadn't done it. Which meant they'd underestimated her. Which meant maybe she still had a chance.

Carefully, she blinked her eyes open.

She was in a brightly lit cell of sorts, propped against a wall, and there were yibo guards at the door. They had weapons trained on her, but their postures were casual, and they obviously didn't think she'd pose a threat.

Reka was tied next to her, still unconscious, her head slumped on her chest.

For a quick, ridiculous moment, worry clenched in Savina's stomach.

Then Reka groaned and stirred, and Savina let out a breath of relief.

Reka's eyes fluttered open, and she glanced around quickly. Savina could see the sharp calculation in her expression as she took in the room, their surroundings—and then Reka stiffened.

"Reka Soler." The voice spoke Common Dialect in a singsong yibo accent, tone amused, and Savina jerked her head around to find the speaker.

He stood in one corner, his outfit fine enough that she could guess he was someone important.

"Captain Mattin warned me you'd gone rogue. He told me to watch out for you. I suspect," the yibo man added, a hint of humour in his voice, "that he was more concerned that I find you before you killed him than he was for my wellbeing." He straightened, watching Reka as if she was a fascinating new specimen. "I am a politician, which means I'm adapt at reading the truth through the lies. And I suspect that you hate General Cavaco, and by extension our good captain, very, very much."

Reka didn't respond. But Savina could see the faint stiffening of her posture, and she knew the yibo could see it as well.

"I don't blame you," he said, crossing the room towards them. "I'm sure there's a very good reason for your dislike. But I need the captain, so I can't let you kill him. Still—" The yibo man paused. "I don't see why you hating Cavaco is worthy of a death sentence."

"Don't bother, Kachik." Reka's voice held that cold, calm matter-of-factness that Savina was so familiar with. "I won't work with Captain Mattin, and I won't work with General Cavaco. So," she shrugged, her mouth twisted into a small, bleak smile. "You may as well kill me now."

The yibo made a soft hum of amusement. "You're just as fierce as those humans told me you'd be. But I think you're missing an option." He stopped in front of Reka and leaned in closer.

"The other option is, Mattin never knows you were here. Mattin never finds out I caught you trying to sneak into our meeting. You hate Cavaco. I need him, for the moment. But I know nothing about him, other than what Mattin has told me. I have no guarantee that he will keep his end of the bargain once we have allowed him into power. From what I've heard of him, he's not one to share power easily. You, though—you could change that dynamic." He paused a moment, a small, close-lipped smile on his face.

"You're exactly as deadly as Captain Mattin said you were. You killed almost a full company of my guards, even taken by surprise as you were. You can give me information on Cavaco that Mattin is hesitant to share. And if Cavaco should try to walk away from the terms of his agreement—I have no doubt of your capabilities, or your lethality. So that's the other option, Reka. You remain here as my guest. You and I work out a plan to keep Cavaco honest. You have the satisfaction of knowing that Captain Mattin will be looking over his shoulder for the rest of his time here, waiting for you to slip in through his window and cut his throat. If things go well, at worst, you're back to your own system, free and clear. And if things don't go well, and Cavaco tries to betray me—then you take your revenge, kill Cavaco, and we replace him with someone more cooperative. I sincerely hope it doesn't come to that, but from what I know of humans, you are exceptionally arrogant and ambitious. And you have a tendency to think more of yourselves than you really deserve."

Reka said nothing, her lips pinched tightly shut, but Savina could see the tension in her posture.

The yibo man turned his attention on Savina.

Now that he was focused on her, Savina could study him more closely. He was average-sized for a yibo, his fur a sort of honey brown, with grey on the tips that she'd learned meant he was older. His tail was draped neatly over his arm, and the tunic he wore was clearly finely made. The circles around his eyes were dark brown, contrasting with the golden colour of his fur, and Savina assumed that by yibo standards he was probably attractive—although in honesty, she had no idea and didn't want to.

He was watching her, his head cocked to one side, as if she was a puzzle he was trying to figure out.

She found she was shaking, a sharp, bitter taste of fear in the back of her throat, but she widened her eyes, letting the hint of tears start in their corners. She had years of practice of bringing tears on demand.

"You, though," the yibo man mused. "I have no idea who you are. And that could pose a problem."

Savina drew in a shuddering little breath, dropping her head as if trying to compose herself. "Reka is my—my lover." It was the first thing that had popped into her head, and she was going to die anyways, so it hardly seemed to matter. "She told me she was doing this, and I couldn't let her do it alone. I—I knew it was dangerous, and I couldn't bear for her to die without me ..." She broke off, her voice choking, and squeezed her eyes shut as if fighting back tears. "I just—I couldn't wait back with the others and not know whether she was—whether she was alive, or—" she sniffled loudly, and watched through her lowered lashes as the yibo's posture relaxed just a little, and tried not to think about how much of the shakiness in her voice was affected, and how much was genuine.

From the corner of her eye she could see Reka's glare, the fury in it hot enough to scald, and she felt a trace of sick satisfaction, even through the fear.

She was going to die anyways. May as well get in one last jab.

Kachik hummed in amusement, still watching her. "Somehow, I doubt that. Mattin told me that Reka was working alone. So. I'll ask you again: who are you?" There was an unspoken threat in his mild tone, a soft viciousness that made Savina's stomach clench.

"I told you," Savina tried again. Her mouth was dry. "I'm—"

Kachik gestured to a guard. The yibo woman stepped forward, raising her pistol, and Savina shrank back.

"This is your last chance," said Kachik pleasantly. "And then she'll shoot you."

Savina strained her fingers, reaching for one of her hidden knife blades, but they were all out of reach.

"I—" Her words choked in her throat.

The soldier stepped forward.

"She's telling the truth."

Savina's head jerked up in concert with Kachik's and the soldier's.

"I'm sorry. What did you say?" asked Kachik, turning back to Reka.

"She's telling the truth. She's my lover." Reka was speaking through clenched teeth, not looking at Savina.

Savina stared.

"And you let her come with you?" asked Kachik, that hint of amusement back in his tone.

Reka took a deep breath, her posture relaxing once more, her usual unflappable calm reasserting itself. "It was no use trying to stop her. There's no talking sense into her when she's come up with an idea. But then, she always needs protecting, so I'm used to it." Reka gave a low, soft chuckle that did something to Savina's insides. "She's a pretty little airhead who'd trip on her own feet going up the stairs. But I'm used to getting her out of scrapes, so I didn't think this would be any different."

Savina was too speechless with shock even to be offended.

What the hell was Reka playing at? Was she waiting until they were alone because she wanted to kill Savina herself? Was she trying to get Savina to let down her guard so she could betray her?

Reka ignored her, smiling calmly at Kachik.

Kachik frowned and turned back to Savina. Savina pasted a look of innocent confusion on her face, as if she hadn't quite figured out whether what Reka had said was an insult or a complement.

Inside, though, she felt as knocked-off-balance as if Reka had hit her over the head.

"Well," said Kachik, shrugging. "I can't let her go, of course, but maybe she'll make your temporary captivity more bearable."

Behind his back, a muscle in Reka's jaw jerked. But the woman's voice, when she spoke, was as calm as ever. "Yes, I suppose it would give me someone to talk to, at least. Although as I said, conversation isn't her strong point."

Kachik chuckled. "Well, I'll leave you two lovers to work out the details. In the meantime, I'll have my guards take you somewhere safe." He paused. "Reka. If you cooperate, there is no downside to this for you—either you get your revenge on Cavaco, or failing that, you get back to your home in safety. But I'm very busy trying to arrange things with Mattin, and I don't have time or energy to spare on you right now. So I'll do everything in my power to keep you happy, and you, in turn, will do everything in your power to keep me happy. Are we clear?"

Reka leaned back against the wall and fixed him with that cool, indifferent gaze that she'd used on Savina so many times.

He watched her, smiling slightly. "Well. I have plenty of work to do. I'll have my guards take you to your quarters." He turned to the yibo woman who appeared to be captain of the guards, and Savina's wavelink translated his speech as he switched back to the yibo language. "Keep Reka alive. She's dangerous, but she's an asset I don't want to waste, so her life is worth more than any guard's right now. Provoke her at your peril. You won't kill her unless I determine it's necessary."

Then he turned on his heel and strode out of the room.

12

Alba

"And how's your leg feeling this morning?" asked the yibo woman who seemed to have adopted Alba.

"It's much better, thank you," Alba said, trying to keep the irritation from her voice. She took a deep breath. "And you?" she asked. It was … more awkward than she'd expected, asking someone about their private life. "I … understand your granddaughter was ill?"

The yibo woman hummed comfortably. "She's much better this morning. But thank you for asking." She waved a hand over her wrist device, and a small, holographic image of a skinny, large-eyed creature that must be a yibo infant appeared over her wrist. "That's my Prii," she said, smiling a fond, close-lipped yibo smile.

Alba inspected the small creature critically, and the yibo woman laughed. "Not much for babies, are you?" She said it as though it was the most natural thing in the world. "When they're your grandbabies, you can't help but love them. But I'll admit, they are funny-looking."

Alba stared at her for a moment, then gave an undignified snort of laughter, and the yibo woman joined in.

When she'd recovered herself, Alba glanced back at the tiny, odd creature in the image.

It truly was funny-looking. But there was something about the way the yibo woman had spoken of the child … "I'd … like to meet her sometime," said Alba quietly.

She wasn't sure who she surprised more by the words, the yibo woman or herself.

"I didn't take you as one who cared for such things," said the woman, her expression softening. "But I'm sure she'd love to see a human. If you don't mind being stared at a little, that is."

There was a commotion at the doorway, and Alba glanced up to see one of the younger yibo burst into the room, chattering so rapidly that Alba's wavelink struggled to translate. Whatever it was, though, it sounded serious.

The mayor, who was in attendance that day, said something sharp, and the younger yibo nodded, tipping their head to one side, then disappeared out the door.

"Kachik's people are on their way," the mayor said in yibo, turning back to the rest of them. "I'll speak with them." She paused, as if not wanting to say the next words. "And—I suppose we'd best keep the humans hidden." She said it with a faint air of distaste. "If they see we have something like that, they'll ask for more in taxes."

Hrrr stood, offering her hand to Alba. "Come," she said.

"What's happening?" asked Yosip.

"Our planet happens to be smack in the middle of the two factions," said Hrrr, gesturing the humans to follow her. She pulled back a transparent curtain for them to slip behind. As Alba opened her mouth to protest, she realized the curtain wasn't, in fact, transparent—it was painted in such a way that it looked to show an empty room behind, but in fact, it was opaque, enough so that it would be difficult to see anything through it.

"It's the problem of living here," the woman continued as she settled them in seats. "Don't make a sound, you don't want their attention. Kachik's people don't think much of humans. They've gotten high and mighty since they opened the portal. We'll never hear the end of it now."

She turned back to Yosip. "Difficult to live where we do. Growing season is good, but ever since Kachik made Chrr his headquarters, we've been caught between him and the government, and both want their due in taxes."

"The—" Alba began, not certain she'd heard right.

"Hush. They'll be here in a second."

The yibo woman slipped out, and Alba glanced over at Yosip and Feliu.

By their expressions, they were just as confused as she was.

From the other room they could hear the chattering voices of the yibo, then heavier footsteps as, apparently, whoever it was that the mayor had been worried about stepped through the doors.

"We're here for the taxes," came a bored yibo voice.

"Well, thankfully we're just finishing up," said Hrrr, her tone homey and comfortable.

The newcomer snorted. "Let me see." There were a few moments' silence, then the sound of rustling cloth. "Twenty-two units?" he asked at last. "It's unfortunate that you work so slowly."

Hrrr hummed. "It is. But artisan workmanship takes time."

The man snorted in irritation. "Very well. I'll take these, and we'll be back in a month."

"Of course," said Hrrr, and Alba could hear the smile in her voice. "You're welcome anytime."

"Well, come show me the units you've set aside," said the man impatiently, and Alba heard footsteps moving off.

It was long enough later that Alba's muscles had stiffened when Hrrr came back to fetch them.

"You can come out, they're gone," she said. Her face was uncharacteristically grave. "But … from the sound of it, they weren't just here for the taxes. They're looking for someone else, as well." She fixed Alba with a sharp glance.

Alba took a deep breath.

Every instinct inside her told her to prevaricate, try to find some half-truth to hide behind. But … she pictured Yosip's easy smile, Hrrr's soft expression as she spoke of her grandchild.

"I believe I know what they were looking for," Alba said at last, in a low voice. "I believe they were after us. After me."

The yibo woman was silent, watching her. Under her placid expression, her gaze was surprisingly, uncomfortably perceptive.

Alba sighed. "Perhaps we should have told you. Joska, at least, advocated for that. But we were desperate. We were not sure those of us who were injured would survive if you chose not to shelter us, and after some conversation, we concluded anyone after us would likely not pose a threat to you."

"And you were the ones who could make that decision for us?" the woman asked. Alba couldn't read her tone.

Yosip and Feliu were watching, Yosip looking concerned, Feliu offended, but neither seemed inclined to interrupt.

Alba almost wished, irrationally, that Yosip would. This was his forte, not hers.

"Perhaps I was wrong," she said at last. "I don't know. But these people were depending on me to keep them safe, and I couldn't bear to—" To her horror, she found her voice choking.

There was a long moment of silence. At last the woman sighed and pulled up a seat of her own. "Well. Maybe we should all have a talk, then."

Alba closed her eyes for a moment, steadying herself. "There— were more than just us that made it through the portal," she said finally. "And you are not the first yibo we encountered."

Hrrr nodded, watching her with an unreadable expression. "You ran into Kachik's people, then?"

"Yes. And some of the other humans who arrived with us were … more willing to negotiate with him than we were. Or rather," she added wryly, "were more willing to give him what he wanted, consequences to our own system be hanged."

The yibo woman was still watching her. "And for us, here, stuck between the government and Kachik—you truly didn't think taking you in would affect us?"

Alba paused, frowning. "Stuck between the government and Kachik? I thought Kachik was the head of government."

An amused smile appeared on Hrrr's face for a moment. "Oh, he'd like you to think that. They've been a thorn in the government side for over a decade now. A bunch of nativists. The government never took too much notice, until they used the old mechanism here to open the portal." She shook her head. "There's some of us think humans deserve more than what they got last time we found one of their colonies." She glanced at Alba sideways. "I'm sorry. I don't mean to open up bad memories."

"I—" Alba began. Her mind was blank with shock.

Kachik wasn't part of the government, but a splinter group. A nativist group.

So many nagging questions falling into place.

And then this. The last time the yibo found a human colony.

Alba cleared her throat. "I apologize. I didn't … I wasn't fully aware of the politics here. And I … was never told what happened to the Labirinto colony. We'd been trying to contact them without success for some time now."

Hrrr turned to her, her eyes surprisingly compassionate. "I'm sorry." She sighed. "I should tell the mayor all of this, by rights. But if I do, you're probably right, you'll be thrown out. We can't afford to get on Kachik's bad side, not living so close."

"If they don't know we're here—" Feliu began.

Hrrr shook her head. "That won't last forever. But, I don't see how we can just throw you out. I'll talk to her about keeping you somewhere safe at all times, so you're not seen. That means while you're here, I'll be keeping an eye on you, and when you're not, you're back in the hospital. In fact, I think I'll try to get the rest of your group moved to beds in there as well."

"And then what?" asked Yosip softly.

Hrrr shook her head again. "I don't know. As far as I'm concerned, what happened with the last human colony was wrong. After the massacre, there were those in the government who believed our contact with humans should be made along other lines. But—" she shrugged. "Kachik's party has always believed differently. Said the raiders have the right of it, seeing humans as livestock. Said we should go in and take what we want, and not let them contaminate our society any further. They're trying to remove every hint of human culture from the yibo, though with how far back it goes, I doubt that's even possible. These precautions are for your benefit as much as for ours. If Kachik's people find you, they'll almost certainly kill you. Better for everyone if you stay out of sight, and leave as soon as you're able."

"We were not planning on staying forever," said Alba softly. "But there is information we need before we can leave. Information about the portal, and about what happened to the Labirinto colony."

Hrrr studied her. "Well," she said finally, "it's getting late. But you asked to see my grandchild earlier, didn't you? Perhaps you and your friends can come by my house after work tomorrow, and we can talk."

Alba nodded.

She wasn't sure she could have spoken if she'd wanted to.

13

Aran

After a quick breakfast, Aran sighed, glancing up at the slope stretching ahead of them.

"Well," said Istvay. "Shall we?"

Aran nodded grimly. He tried not to think about how weak and pale Istvay looked in the early morning sunlight as they started off.

"I don't like this," said Istvay as the two of them scrambled up the steep slope. "But let's at least get somewhere high enough that we can catch our bearings, and maybe we can figure a way out of this."

Aran nodded. "How long do you think they'll follow us?"

Istvay gave a wry chuckle. "That's the question, isn't it?" They sighed. "I have no idea. But considering they've followed us half-way across the system so far, I'm not really very hopeful of them giving up." They paused. "Do you have any idea what the hell they were talking about, somebody killing one of their people?"

Aran shook his head. "I wish I did," he muttered. "I'd like to see the person who could kill one of those things and walk away from it."

The forest around them was silent, and Aran tried not to think too hard about why that might be.

Maybe it was just a superstition, maybe that was the reason the raiders hadn't followed him and Istvay up the mountain. Or maybe —maybe there was some religious significance attached to the place, or maybe they had indeed come around the back, and were waiting for Aran and Istvay, watching as they struggled their way up the mountain, unwitting, into a trap—

The snap of a twig under his foot jerked his attention back, and that was the only thing, probably, that saved his life. He managed a choked curse, then Istvay had grabbed him, dragging him back from the edge of the pit as it opened up under his feet. He didn't move quite fast enough, and for a moment he was dangling in midair, then Istvay yanked him up, and his feet caught the ground under him, and he was standing, gasping, on the edge of a pit, covered with twigs and leaves to look like the surrounding forest floor.

Aran and Istvay stared at each other for a moment, then down at the pit. The bottom of it was lined with thick metal stakes, sharpened and pointing straight up, ready to catch and disembowel the unwary creature who stumbled on it, and there was a thin blue laser tripwire across the path in front of them.

"What the hell—" Aran began, but Istvay give a sharp shake of their head.

"Please, Aran, I'm trying really damn hard not to think about what might have happened. Let's just thank the damn Mystery that you're alive, and watch our step."

Aran nodded, swallowing hard. He wasn't about to argue with Istvay's logic.

He and Istvay hadn't gone more than another half-kilometre when they sprang another trap. This time it was Ani's hissing that warned them, and they both leapt back as a massive boulder crashed through the trees centimetres away from where they stood. It tumbled past, leaving mangled, flattened undergrowth in its wake, and Aran stared after it, shaken.

When the third trap sprang, and Ani, with an insulted yowl, was yanked into a net, which she promptly melted with her acid, Aran and Istvay eyed each other.

"Maybe—maybe that's why the raiders didn't want to follow," said Istvay, as Ani, hissing, proceeded to destroy the last remnants of the net that had so thoroughly insulted her. "Maybe it's a hunting ground, and they didn't want to risk being caught."

"Maybe," Aran said, looking around uneasily. "But traps like these would require someone to be checking them. Otherwise we'd see dead animals lying around. So either they're very inefficient, or—"

"Please," said Istvay, their voice grim. "Like I said. Unless there's something we can damn well do about it, I really, really don't want to think about this."

Aran shrugged, and they moved forward.

"I think—I think we're getting close to the top," Aran panted as the sun reached its midday zenith. They were moving slowly— between the steepness of the grade and Istvay's obvious weakness, they hadn't made it nearly as far as they should have.

But then again, if it was true the raiders were waiting for them on the other side of the mountain, they might be merely delaying their own demise.

He glance surreptitiously at Istvay, worry twisting in his stomach.

"I'm fine," Istvay snapped. "I'm not about to keel over, if that's your question."

Aran sighed. Istvay had never been the most even-tempered when they weren't feeling well. "It's fine, Pishti. Don't worry about it. We'll just—look, as long as the raiders aren't actively chasing us, we're not in any hurry. This planet is supposed to be populated, we'll just keep going until we find a friendly settlement."

They were in a hurry. They had maybe enough food to last two more days. They'd already begun rationing, but he couldn't ration much more, not with Istvay as weak as they were, and neither of them could afford Istvay simply collapsing on the trail. As much as he wanted to—as much as he would if he had to—if Aran tried to carry Istvay the entire way, there was no way he'd be able to outrun anything following them. And he wasn't nearly naïve enough to assume that the raiders, who had followed them across half the galaxy, would have a change of heart and decide that after all, it wasn't worth waiting for them to come back down the mountain.

"Let's go a bit farther, then we'll take a break," he said instead.

He'd have preferred to suggest a rest right away, but judging from the stubborn expression on Istvay's face, they would see through his ploy and utterly refuse.

"It looks like it might flatten out a little up ahead," said Istvay, peering up the mountains, and Aran nodded. The two of them started forward again, Aran staying close to Istvay's side, both to increase the chance that one of them would see any traps at their feet, and also to be in place to grab Istvay should they collapse.

At last, the two of them broke through a stretch of trees and into a patch of open ground. Aran turned, offering his hand to help Istvay up the last scramble, and then, at Ani's startled growl from his shoulder, turned around again, taking an unconscious step forward to catch his balance—and ran full-on into something warm and solid.

"What—" he began. Whatever it was he'd run into made a similar exclamation of surprise—then he heard Istvay startled yelp, and Ani's furious hiss, and his mind caught up with the rest of his body.

He leapt back, grabbing for Ani instinctively as she jumped forward to either melt, liquify, or poison the newcomer, and yanked out his pulse pistol with the hand that wasn't holding Ani, levelling it at the raider woman in front of him.

She stood where she was, blinking at them in shock.

She looked similar to the raiders who were chasing them—her skin deathly pale, her eyes red, fangs changing her disturbingly human face into something from a horror tale—but her black hair was cut into a short bob, and her outfit a practical blue shirt and trousers rather than the grey-and-black armoured suits of their pursuers.

She said something in a guttural, rich tone, words that didn't sound at all familiar, but made something click in the back of Aran's brain.

She sighed at his look of utter incomprehension, and tried again, in Common Dialect this time. "You are—you are humans?"

Aran was still holding his pulse pistol with one hand and clutching onto an irate Ani with the other. "Um," he said. "Yes. Yes, we're—we're humans."

The smile she turned on them was utterly delighted, despite the large fangs visible through the expression. "Wonderful! I'd been so hoping to meet one of you."

Ani was still hissing angrily, struggling to get free of Aran's grasp.

Aran and Istvay simply stared.

"Oh, don't worry," the raider said breezily, waving a casual hand. "I'm not going to eat you. I've been wanting live specimens to study for quite some time now. Come, come!"

They were still staring as she turned, beckoning them to follow.

She seemed to realize, after she'd got a few steps, that they hadn't, in fact, followed.

"What's the matter?" She was looking at them as if they were an interesting scientific problem. "You're still afraid that I am going to eat you?" She laughed. "You're so funny. If I wanted to eat you, I'd just kill you now. It would be much easier than waiting for you to climb the rest of the way up to my research station."

"Your—your research station?" Aran managed, his brain grasping desperate hold onto any words that seemed to make sense.

"Yes," she said impatiently. "I assume that you have scientists on your planet? It's a place we go to study things in their natural habitat."

"I—I know what a research station is," said Aran stupidly. His brain seemed to be having trouble firing on all synapses.

"Well, good, then. Let's go," she said. "Your friend there looks like he's not going to last much longer on his feet anyway."

Aran glanced reflexively at Istvay, who was swaying a little. They shot him their signature glare. "I'm fine," they muttered.

They were very clearly not fine.

They turned to the raider, who was watching them curiously. "'Aran's friend here' is entirely capable of speaking for themself," they said. "But yes, you're right. We could both use a rest. So—" they glanced at Aran, and gave a helpless shrug. "I suppose, lead the way."

It wasn't far to the research station, or wherever the hell the raider was taking them, but it seemed to take an absurdly long time to get there. Istvay was stumbling, and after his recent panicked flight and the three days of travel previous, combined with the leftover panic of running into the raider woman, Aran's legs had turned to something akin to jelly. But at last, the group of them stepped through the tree line and out into a small mountain clearing, neat and clean, with an oddly shaped shelter erected in the centre. It was circular, with a peaked roof and walls made of a thick material that at first glance Aran took to be synthetic, but on closer look made him wonder if it was some sort of animal hide.

He almost asked out of curiosity, then caught sight of the grim look on Istvay's face and sighed.

Istvay was right—there were more pressing concerns than the construction material of their captor's shelter.

"Come in, come in," the raider said cheerfully, sliding the door open along a sort of track. Ani was growling uneasily on Aran's shoulder, but she seemed to have decided that, at least at present, their host was not posing an active threat to their lives, and had decided to extend to her the same courtesy.

Istvay hesitated a moment in the doorway, then stepped inside. Aran followed.

Then he almost forgot the imminent mortal peril they were in in his surprise.

The room was set up like a field science lab, similar to what he and Istvay would put together at their basecamp. There were measuring devices hung neatly on the walls, and beakers of sample material, neatly labelled, set on the table.

And at the sight of the labels, the niggling familiarity of the raiders' speech clicked into place in Aran's mind, and he almost gasped.

It was the same language as the samples they'd been sent through the portal, however many lifetimes ago that seemed. He hadn't recognized it the first time he'd heard it, in the strain of the raiders screaming at each other for his and Istvay's death—to be honest, he'd been a bit distracted at the time—but now, with no immediate threat to his life—

He took a deep breath, trying to push back the sudden giddiness.

They'd been right. Ree, back in the yibo city, had been right. Somehow, these raiders had sent that box through the portal. Which meant that somewhere out here, on this planet or another, was the answer—the path to a cure for Istvay's death sentence.

"Sit," the raider was saying, and he blinked out of his daze to find Istvay watching him in concern.

"Aran," they began quietly.

He shook his head. "It's—it's nothing, I'm fine," he muttered.

"Go on, sit down," the raider said again, pushing two cushions across the floor towards them. Aran sat automatically, and Istvay fell more than sat, unable to stifle a groan of relief.

The raider woman had her back to them, going through her supplies, and a moment later she came over with the platter of— well, Aran wasn't entirely sure what they were, but they were apparently supposed to be for him and Istvay to eat.

"I've been studying humans for some time, but I've never had any here in person," she said, thrusting the tray out towards them. "I'd love to see how you react to this food. I have a theory that—"

"Um," said Aran quickly. "We, um, we just ate."

The raider looked faintly disappointed. "Maybe next time, then," she said philosophically. "You humans get hungry fairly frequently, if I understand correctly."

Aran took a deep breath. "Listen," he said. "I've—we've been—"

Now that he was here, he found it was almost impossible to get the words to come out. "You—listen. There was a portal that opened up. And—and one of you sent something through it. A raider did, I mean."

He didn't dare to look at her. He couldn't bear another disappointment. The chance of finding someone who had any idea about what he was looking for—

"Oh!" Her tone was so delighted that Aran blinked and looked up at her in surprise. "You got my box? I wasn't sure when I sent it through that it ended at the right planet. But I was pretty confident. Like I said, I've been studying you for some time now. And I had so hoped that you would respond. But I had no idea you'd actually send someone through yourselves, especially before Captain Sharda shut down the portal." She was smiling, an expression that, even with her red eyes and sharp incisors, was intimately familiar to Aran—the smile of someone whose scientific theory has just been validated.

He, however, felt a little like he'd been hit in the head by a brick.

"You—" his voice was choking, and he almost couldn't get out the words. "You were the one who sent the box?"

"Of course!" She glanced over at him. "You don't think anyone else would have, do you? Most raiders see you as a food source which … in fairness, you are delicious, but that's no excuse not to further our knowledge in this area." She shook her head. "I've been researching this for years now. There's undeniably human DNA in most of our bloodlines, if you go far enough back. Which means our two species are clearly sexually compatible, and if we're genetically close enough for sexual reproduction that can produce fertile offspring, it seems not only logical, but vital that we make a thorough and careful study of your culture, as it almost certainly ties in to ours." She spoke with the tone of someone who was intimately familiar with her area of study, and who seldom was able to find a captive audience to hear her theories out.

"Um," Istvay volunteered, sounding almost as shellshocked as Aran was. "You—excuse me for interrupting, but—you shut down the portal?"

She glanced at Istvay and laughed. "I didn't. I told you, that was Captain Sharda. She wanted to make sure that we had time to communicate with the other raider ships. I understand your species is quite gregarious, but we raiders tend to exist in semi-isolated societies, which makes communication difficult at times. Last time the yibo opened a portal to a human system, they went through and took what they wanted, and we had to make do with the leftovers. But this time, Sharda thought if she could shut down the portal and give herself time to send word to the others, by the time the yibo opened the portal again, we'd be prepared to go through and harvest what we needed first. The yibo are frightened enough of us that they're not going to stand in our way, so—"

"When—when you say harvest—" Istvay sounded faintly sick.

The scientist glanced over at them. "I'm sorry, that was probably insensitive. I wasn't thinking. I … don't like it myself, I'll be honest with you. But I've tried to talk to Captain Krevai, and he's impossible to convince. I say that you're a sapient species, and that you deserve to live as much as any of us, but he insists that it's part of the natural order of things, and everyone needs to eat, and so it hardly seems that morality needs to come into it."

Aran glanced over at his friend. They were staring at the raider woman, an expression of mingled surprise and horror on their face.

Which, in fairness, Aran understood—he was certain that once his brain had the opportunity to process the fact that, had the portal remained open any longer, these raiders would have come streaming through, intent on slaughtering their way across the Joias System, he would be just as horrified as Istvay was.

But right now, he had something much more important to worry about.

"You—you sent the box," he said again. He could hardly recognize his own voice.

"Yes," she said.

"And you say that your people interbred with humans somewhere back along the lines."

She nodded. "It's not a popular theory, but I've done enough studies to be very confident in my findings."

Aran nodded again. "Can—can you tell me who gave the blood sample that you sent?"

She stared at him for a moment, a rapid flurry of emotions tracing over her face. "I—I can tell you who gave the sample," she said, a note of hesitation in her voice. "As a matter of fact—" she glanced out the window to the research station uneasily. "Listen, it might be best if you—"

Ani, on Aran's shoulder, perked up, her eye-pouches puffing out as she growled.

It was only then that Aran realized that the sound he'd been hearing in the back of his mind, and paying no attention to because he was much too concerned about what this raider woman was telling him, had been footsteps.

And then the door to the small shelter burst open, and someone ducked inside.

The newcomer was another raider, taller by a full head than the scientist. He was wearing full body armour, although it was a dark, glossy bluish-purple rather than the grey and black of their former pursuers, and carrying a weapon that made the yibo's atom-guns look like child's toys. A flowing scarlet cape draped off his shoulders, and his hair fell almost to the floor. He smiled, light glinting off his sharp incisors and his blood-red eyes as he surveyed the tiny group.

The scientist jumped to her feet. "Captain—Captain Krevai!" she said, a trace of nervousness in her voice. "I—see you've come earlier than you planned."

The raider captain laughed, a low, chilling sound.

Aran could see through the open door behind the captain an entire crew of raiders, all in the same bluish-purple uniforms, filling the small clearing where the research station had been built.

"You don't look happy to see me, Dessi," said the captain, in a rich voice that vibrated through the cabin. "You should be, I'm very pleased with you. I'm hungry after this last week's work, and it looks like you've provided a feast."

14

Alba

Alba slept poorly that night.

By the end of the workday the next day, her muscles were so tight her entire body ached. But at last the endless day ended, and Alba and the others were gathered at Hrrr's home.

Like most yibo buildings, the small space was bright and airy, the warm evening sun streaming in through the translucent walls and plants and greenery spilling from every available surface. The seats in the house were set up similar to the ones Alba had seen in the yibo city—rising in tiers up the wall. Hrrr looked around quickly. "Oh, I apologize—I'd forgotten. I don't have the kind of stools you humans like—"

Alba could scarcely refrain from a small sigh of relief. Her posterior ached at even the thought of those damnable hard stools. "I think we'll manage," she said dryly.

Yosip gave her an amused glance.

"Well, if you're sure—" said Hrrr, her voice uncertain.

"Your thoughtfulness is appreciated," said Yosip, the sincerity in his voice unmistakable. "But really, please don't distress yourself. It's your company we came for, not your furniture."

The yibo woman hummed in amusement and nodded, gesturing to the tiers of seats.

They weren't uncomfortable, despite their odd appearance, and as Alba sank down into one of the lower seats, she breathed a small sigh of relief at getting the weight off her broken knee.

Hrrr brought out a plate of food. Nicolau and the others of the crew who'd been working at harvesting all day dug in with a will, and Alba ate to be polite.

She could hardly taste it.

At last, Hrrr put down the platter and took a seat. "I … suppose you have questions," she said.

"The—the Labirinto colony." Alba took a deep breath. "Is it really destroyed?"

The yibo woman sighed. "I'm sorry to be the one to tell you. It happened about—" she frowned, as if making some calculation in her head. "Perhaps three decades ago, in our years. I'm not sure what that would be in your time. But at any rate, it was around the time my daughter was born." She shook her head. "They told us, back then, that we were looking for humans because we were worried. Some time ago—twenty generations back or more, probably—our ancestors encountered humans. We don't have many records from that time, but at some stage humans and our ancestors intermingled, to the point that you'd be hard-pressed to find a yibo today without human blood, however small the amount." She paused, her gaze distant.

Alba glanced at Yosip. "It must have been one of the missing generation ships that ran across this system," she said quietly, and he nodded.

They were in touch with a few of their sister colonies, back in the

Joias System, but there were ships they'd never heard from in living memory.

Alba turned back to the yibo woman. "Do you have any idea who the humans were? Where they came from?"

The woman shook her head. "I'm sorry. It was so long ago, and whatever happened, there was an event that destroyed most of the records. We don't know, really, much of what our society was like back then, or what happened. Maybe there was a disease that decimated the population, maybe it was a war. As I said, we have very few records. But over the last hundred years, more and more people have been getting curious about our history. Because despite the societal crash that happened around the time when the yibo met the humans, there was a technological jump of a magnitude we haven't seen since. Most of our technologies can trace their roots back to that era. And we thought, for some time, that humans had been wiped out—that that was the only group of humans in existence. But as more and more people became interested in our history, and began going back through what records we had, they found indications the perhaps it was not. That perhaps there were still humans out there. And that, of course, led to a debate—was it worth trying to find humans? And if so, what should our relationship with them be? We had the technology to open portals by that point, and we were using it regularly for exploration and travel to more distant systems. So if we were to find another human colony, it was well within the realm of possibility that we could initiate contact."

She shook her head. "I don't think anyone really intended for there to be a massacre. But—" she shrugged. "We had word of them. We opened a portal, and those in power in the government at the time were either aggressive, or afraid, or both. They demanded the humans prove their peaceful intent by surrendering, and humans didn't. And—" she trailed off.

"You've seen the difference between our weaponry and yours. As I said, we had a technological leap when our two cultures met. But it didn't mean that what the people in the Labirinto System, as you call it, had created wasn't valuable. And our system was split—there were those who were horrified at what had happened to the humans, and wished to protect any other colony of humans, to enter into a friendly, two-sided relationship, rather than a one-sided massacre, and those who believed that our society was advanced to the point that humans were the equivalent of animals, and that they should be utilized for their technology, and then destroyed. I'm certain you have guessed, by now, which side Kachik's party was on," she added dryly.

Alba's mind was spinning, and her brain balked at the implications of what she was hearing.

An entire human civilization. The equivalent of the entire Joias system—not just the planet of Colorida, but the entire system—gone. The sheer destruction that would entail, the number of lives lost—she wasn't sure she could comprehend it.

She wasn't sure she wanted to.

"And that's why these rebels opened the portal?" asked Yosip at last. There was a sick tone to his voice that told her the news had affected him as much as it had her.

Hrrr nodded. "It—wasn't quite that simple, I don't think, but it's part of the reason. There's been unrest in the government for a while. Kachik's party was formed supposedly to protect the purity of the yibo culture. They don't want anything to do with anything human. They were a legitimate political party for a while, but as they became more radical they slowly lost their moderate followers, until now they're mostly a party of fanatics. When your system was discovered, there was a fight over whether to leave it alone, or whether to open a portal in the hope of another leap in technology. In the end, Kachik didn't have enough political support to convince the government of his views, so he and his supporters relocated to Chrr and declared themselves an independent government. Everyone was shocked when they managed to open a portal, except for those of us on this planet, because we've been watching them work on their mechanism for the last decade. But we're just a little rural planet, so no one in the government pays us much attention. I think Kachik wanted to get to your technology first, and then use it to open a rebellion against the government proper. But who knows?"

There were a few long moments of silence.

"Did any of the humans in the Labirinto System survive?" Alba asked at last, quietly.

"There are still some survivors," said Hrrr. "That's why we weren't all that surprised to see humans here. It's difficult to wipe out an entire civilization, even if the raiders did their best. There are humans throughout the system, and probably some back in their own system as well. But—" she shrugged. "If what I hear is correct, if there are any back in their system, they're living on bombed-out planets. Not somewhere easy to survive."

For a while they sipped their drinks, not speaking.

Alba didn't dare look at the faces of the others—she already knew what she'd see. But she caught a glimpse of Nicolau's stunned expression, the pallor in his face, and the way Ines was squeezing his hand like she couldn't let go if she wanted to.

There was a small, high-pitched squeal, and Alba turned quickly to see a tiny yibo child, with wide eyes and dark fur, come running in, followed a moment later by another yibo woman, slightly younger than their host.

Hrrr got to her feet and crossed the floor, picking up the child in one arm as it squealed and chattered. She tugged its ears affectionately, then put it down and turned to talk to the adult.

The child approached the group of humans cautiously, glancing at them out of the corners of its eyes, taking small, sidling steps as if ready to run at the first hint of a threat.

Yosip smiled and held out a hand. "Hello there," he said, his tone warm and friendly. "What's your name?"

The child watched him with large, wary eyes, but at last came closer.

The yibo women had turned and were watching with indulgent expressions as the child reached out tentatively and touched Yosip's hand, then skittered backwards.

"That's my granddaughter," said Hrrr. There was no mistaking the pride in her voice. "Her name is Prii."

Yosip smiled and held out his hand again. "Hello there, Prii," he said.

This time, the child came close enough to take Yosip's outstretched hand, examining it curiously. Then she turned to Feliu, and he gave an undignified squeak of surprise as the child took his hand as well, yanking it over to compare it with Yosip's.

Yosip smiled, and Feliu sputtered, and Hrrr called something to the child, who pouted, but let go of the two men's hands.

Alba almost smiled herself at the look on her old clerk's face.

And then the child turned to Alba, reaching up to touch the wrinkles on her face.

She jerked back, startled. The child scampered a few steps off, eyes wide with fright.

Alba took a deep breath. "Hello, Prii," she said, somewhat stiffly. "I apologize for startling you."

Prii took a cautious step forward, then another, until she was at Alba's knees, her wide, dark eyes staring up into Alba's.

Alba forced herself not to react as the child reached up again, running her small hands over Alba's face.

She'd never particularly liked children. But ... there was something about the soft, hesitant fingers brushing her skin that sparked something warm in her chest, like when she herself was a child and a butterfly had settled on her hand, resting there for a moment before fluttering off.

Something small and wild, that for whatever unknowable reason trusted her enough to let down its guard, just for a moment.

When she looked up, Hrrr was watching her, a soft expression on her face.

When the yibo woman came to sit down again, the child scampered over and climbed up on her lap. The woman seemed not to mind being poked and prodded by childish fingers as she spoke.

"Your granddaughter is lovely," said Alba, and she was surprised at the sincerity in her tone.

Hrrr's eyes glinted with pride. "She's very intelligent for her age." She glanced down indulgently as the child slid off her lap to scamper across the room after some distraction or another. "And you? Do you have grandchildren?"

Alba cleared her throat. "I ... do not. But I think Yosip—"

She caught the way Yosip's face changed, the brief flash of pain in his eyes, and she felt a quick pang of guilt.

She should have paid more attention.

"I had a grandson," he said after a moment. "But he died a few years ago. He—" he paused a moment, clearing his throat. "He would have been thirteen years old this year."

"I'm sorry," said the yibo woman, and for a moment, they sat in silence. At last, though, Hrrr shook her head. "She is a little troublemaker sometimes. Still, it's been harder and harder to keep anyone out of trouble, since Kachik's people opened that portal machinery on our planet." There was a wry note to her voice, and Alba exchanged glances with Yosip.

"The portal mechanism is here on your planet?" said Alba, her heart rate speeding up. She tried to keep her voice neutral. "I'm sure that must make things difficult."

The woman made a small gesture with her hand, but there was something sharp in her expression that told Alba the topic hadn't come up by chance. "The government doesn't have the political will to start a full-on war with Kachik's people yet, which, thank the gods, means we're not in a war zone. But powers above protect us all when that happens."

"I'd be interested in seeing this portal mechanism," said Alba at last, carefully.

"I imagine you would be," said Hrrr. She paused. "I will tell you, though, as a friend—stay away from it. Kachik's people are guarding it. It would be next to impossible to get close. Believe me, there are those of us who'd love nothing more than to see the thing destroyed, but they watch it closely."

"And where is it, exactly?" Alba asked.

The woman studied Alba for a moment. At last, she stood and walked over to her table. She picked a small metal sphere and tapped the base of it, and a holographic map appeared, spreading around her hand like a halo.

Alba's pulse was racing, a sick feeling of something between anticipation and dread tightening her throat.

Carefully, she blinked twice, activating the scan-and-record on her wavelink.

"This is our village," Hrrr said, tapping a point on the map. She rotated it a half-turn. "And the mechanism is here." She tapped the map off and returned to her seat. "But please be careful. There are far too many guards, and even if—you'll excuse my impoliteness— even if you were all young and strong like these ones," she gestured to Beni, Nicolau, and Ines, "you'd be shot down for certain. It's a bunker, for all intents and purposes. And after the raiders attacked last time and took down the defences, they've doubled or tripled the guard. You may as well give up the thought."

The rest of the evening's conversation was stilted. Alba's mind was far too caught up in the enormity of what she'd learned for her to pay much heed to the small talk, but Hrrr seemed to understand, and didn't press her.

It was dark by the time they left Hrrr's house. The yibo woman escorted them down the narrow streets to the hospital in the light of the hovering artificial lamps. But Alba noticed, as Hrrr left them at the hospital door, a handful of guards who hadn't been there the evening before standing at the entrance.

On the one hand, it made it less likely Alba or any of the others would be murdered in their sleep. On the other—they wouldn't be leaving here without the yibos' consent, unless they made some mad escape. And for what? To try to sneak into a heavily guarded bunker and take it down, like in an audio-romance?

She glanced at her companions, and almost laughed at the absurdity of it all—a handful of geriatric bureaucrats, a world-weary cargo-ship captain and her ex-military crew who was clearly past his prime, a timid interpreter from the Rim Mountains, and the two younger siblings of the Joias System's most notorious assassin, trying to take on armed yibo soldiers who could take down the raiders.

For just a moment, she pictured the creatures who'd intercepted them on their way out of the yibo city, with their blood-red eyes and sharp fangs.

No. It was impossible. Even with Joska and Nicolau and Ines, it was impossible.

When they reached their rooms, Alba sank down on her cot. "Well," she said at last, glancing around at the others. "At the very least, we've discovered what happened to the Labirinto System."

Joska studied her for a long moment, her expression grave. "I'm sorry, Chief Justice," she said at last. "I know this wasn't what any of us hoped for."

Unwanted tears were welling in Alba's eyes, and she forced them back. This was not the time for self-pity.

"At least we know where the portal mechanism is," she said finally. "And it appears we still have time to make plans. Although what those plans may be—" she trailed off.

Then she frowned. "Where's Yosip?"

"He's in the hallway still," said Feliu. "Someone was calling him on the wavelink from back in the yibo city."

Something uneasy stirred in Alba's stomach.

Yosip's friends back in the yibo city shouldn't have any reason to contact him.

"I'll go speak with him," she said sharply. "The rest of you, please stay here."

She forced herself to her feet, despite the jolt of pain through her broken knee, and limped out into the hallway.

Yosip stood there, leaned up against the wall. He didn't seem to notice her come out, just stared straight ahead, his face blank.

She realized, with an uncomfortable jolt, that the news of the Labirinto System's destruction must have hit him as hard as it had hit her. And she hadn't thought to offer him even a portion of the comfort in return that he'd offered her.

"Yosip?" she said quietly.

He turned.

"What's wrong?" Her voice was sharper than she meant it to be. But she was so accustomed to his smile that his exhausted expression was jarring.

His smile in response was wan. "I'm … afraid I have bad news. Captain Mattin has apparently withdrawn his requirement for proof of your death prior to opening the portal. Now it's just a matter of them finalizing their agreements. They'll be opening it any day now."

For a few moments, she simply stared at him.

He shook his head, still with that wan smile. "I'm … sorry. I suppose we should go tell the others."

Alba nodded. And then, slowly, she looked up, meeting his gaze. "You're right. We need to tell the others. But I think perhaps we have more going for us than you're considering. If you recall, we're not the only ones who escaped Kachik. And, you remember, one of our fellow escapees has a weapon of mass destruction for a pet, and, if the news packets are to be believed, a lifetime of experience of sneaking into places while things are trying to kill him."

Yosip met her eyes, his wan smile growing a little more genuine. "You know, I'd forgotten that."

Alba smiled back, surprised at the relief seeing the familiar twinkle in Yosip's eye brought. "I think, Yosip, there's just a chance this may not be the end yet."

15

Savina

When Kachik was gone, the guards pulled Savina and Reka roughly to their feet and marched them down the corridors of whatever building they'd been taken to. They ended in a small room lit by an artificial light, with a cot in one corner and something that could have been the yibo equivalent of a table in the centre, along with two of the ubiquitous stools.

"We'll be bringing you your meals regularly," said the captain of the guards who brought them there. She spoke in accented Common Dialect, biting off her words, and there was a look on her face that told Savina that, while Kachik may have been impressed by Reka's ability to kill guards, this particular captain had a very different view of the matter. "If you make trouble, I can't guarantee your safety."

Reka looked at her with that indifferent gaze and gave a small nod.

"Good," said the captain. "If you need something, there's an alert button on the door that you can use. You'll be taken out for air and exercise once in the morning and once at night. You will be guarded at all times. I would advise you not to try anything." There was a tone in her voice that told Savina she very much hoped Reka would try something.

Reka just gave her another cool, emotionless nod, and turned away.

When the guard had left, there was a long, long moment of silence.

At last, Savina turned to Reka. "What the hell," she began, her voice shaking a little.

Reka deliberately turned her back.

And abruptly, the sick combination of fear and guilt and suspicion and the fact that she was stuck here in a cell with Reka, of all the damn people in the universe, condensed into a white-hot anger.

She'd be damned if Reka would get away with pulling a stunt like that, then ignoring her.

She yanked out one of her hidden knives, her hand trembling. "Reka," she purred. "Is that how you treat your girlfriend?"

Reka's posture tensed.

Savina took a step closer. "Reka. Darling."

Reka spun.

She was clearly furious. But there was something under the anger, a desperate helplessness that Savina had never imagined in Reka.

"How dare you?" Reka hissed. "How dare you? Isn't it enough that you've ruined every last damn thing in my life? Isn't it enough that I fell for your damn, stupid act again, your 'poor helpless pitiful me,' even though you tried to kill me? Isn't it enough that I saved your damn life? I'm locked up in here because of you, and I'm sure under that shocked expression on your pretty little face you're laughing at me. Believe me, I don't care. I have nothing left to lose. But how dare you imply that I owe you anything?"

Savina gaped, her hand loosening on her knife hilt, her mouth hanging half-open.

"What the hell are you talking about?" she snapped at last, but her voice came out more shaky than angry. "If you'd gone after Mattin you'd have been shot. He's expecting you, didn't you hear that? There's no way you would have gotten out of that alive, even if you did manage to kill him."

Reka's face twisted, her voice going cold. "And that would be worse than this how? I don't want to be here. All I wanted was to stop this, kill Mattin. I never expected to get out of it alive. But I have no intention of wasting any more breath on you. If you touch me, I'll kill you. But quite frankly, you're hardly worth the effort." She dropped onto the cot, deliberately turning her back again. But there was a tension to her posture that told Savina that if she tried anything, one of them wouldn't live through it.

For a few moments, Savina simply stared.

At last, she dropped down into the corner and tipped her head back against the hard wall of the cell.

Had Reka been telling the truth? She'd saved Savina because … she'd felt sorry for her?

She had to be lying. Reka was a killer. She had a reputation as a government agent—no mercy, no quarter. No failures. She had to have had another motive.

But an uncomfortable recollection surfaced in Savina's brain—the confused look on Reka's face when Savina had her pinned up against the wall, a knife at her throat, and accused her of trying to kill Nicolau.

"If I'd wanted to kill your brother, you little idiot, he'd be dead."

And Savina had heard the truth in the words. Nicolau had been in Reka's gun sights, and all it would have taken was a twitch of her finger on the trigger. Anyone would have agreed he'd be an acceptable casualty.

Savina cursed under her breath.

Morals like that were what got people killed, and they deserved what they got, as far as she was concerned. Reka deserved what she was going to get, whenever they got out of this.

The cell was uncomfortably cool, and Savina wrapped her arms around herself, trying not to shiver. Reka still had her back turned, steadfastly ignoring her, and outside she could hear the footsteps of the yibo guards, steady and measured.

And suddenly she was hit with a memory, strong enough she almost gasped—Joska's voice, warm and amused, telling Savina that she was being absurd, and she was a bad one through and through, but Joska knew what it was like to be young and stupid and as much as she wanted to, she couldn't entirely blame Savina. The feeling of that calloused hand on her shoulder, surprisingly gentle, the concern in the woman's eyes. Her dry, faintly indulgent smile when Savina did something ridiculous, the quiet, calm reassurance of her presence.

Savina squeezed her eyes closed, trying not to let tears spill out from between her eyelids.

With the memory of Joska had come the memory of Rafel, his scowling face and irritated grumbling, Nicolau's eager, boyish grin, the way he'd looked at Savina, half like he was terrified of her, half like he was desperate for her approval. Beni's quiet, unassuming, comfortable presence.

It wasn't fair. It wasn't bloody fair. She didn't need them, she didn't need any of them.

The tears, though, wouldn't be pushed back, and one trickled down her cheek.

She blinked it away angrily.

She didn't need a stupid ship's captain and her idiot crew, and Beni and Nicolau were babies. They needed her, not the other way around. She was the one who did the protecting, not the one that needed protection, and… and…

She choked back a small sob.

From the corner of her eye she saw a Reka stir, but the woman didn't deign to look in her direction.

Savina took a deep breath and scrubbed savagely at her eyes.

This was stupid. Joska and Rafel were probably thrilled she was finally gone. As Joska was so fond of reminding her, the only thing she was to the woman was a kidnapper and a ship hijacker.

She leaned her head against the wall, huddled into a ball for warmth, the after-effects of the stun weapon still jittering through her body.

"Savina!"

She jerked her head up, looking around quickly, half-convinced she'd drifted off and the voice she'd heard had been a dream.

"Savina? Savina, if you can hear me, I need you to find a way to answer." Joska's voice through the wavelink was thick with concern.

Savina stared blankly for another moment, then blinked twice to activate her wavelink speaker. "Joska?" she asked.

She was rewarded with a dry chuckle. "So you are alive, after all. We were wondering." There was a pause. "You didn't—kill whoever it was that took you out there?"

"It's not your damn business," she snapped reflexively. "But no, I didn't," she added in a grudging tone.

She could picture the smile of approval on Joska's face, and she gritted her teeth against it.

"I'm proud of you, Savina." Under the touch of irony in her voice, Savina could hear a real warmth. "I assume you're in the yibo city? Chrr, I think they call it?"

"Yes," Savina whispered through her link. "I'm here. But … I got caught. I'm locked up."

"Caught? By who? Are you alright?" Joska's voice was sharp with sudden concern.

"Kachik. And yes, for the moment," said Savina bitterly.

"Good." There was unmistakable relief in Joska's voice. "When we found you were gone, we'd decided to come after you in case you needed help. But … it seems we're needed here at the moment. I promised Nicolau and Beni that the moment we can safely get away, we'll come find you. So—just hold on, okay? We'll come for you, as soon as we can."

Savina's throat tightened so she wasn't sure she could get the words out. "I—" she managed. "I don't need—" She was trying to make her voice harsh, but she wasn't fooling anyone, not even herself.

Joska chuckled. "I have tried to tell you this before, Savina, but it's never a bad thing to have friends. Or, if you're not ready for that, at least allies."

Savina nodded mutely, even though she knew Joska couldn't see. She took a deep breath. "What's happening there? Is everyone alright?"

There was a long pause from the other side of the line.

Savina narrowed her eyes. "You said you were needed there," she said flatly. "You're helping Alba, aren't you?"

Joska sighed. "Savina. I know you don't agree with this, but … I can't sit by and let the system burn. And Nicolau—"

"You're letting Nicolau help?" Savina's heart was pounding. "I thought you were going to keep him safe! If anything happens to him—"

"If you'd like to try to talk him out of this, you're welcome to," said Joska dryly. "I hate to say this, Savina, but he's old enough to make his own decisions. And he's determined the yibo won't kill his parents. His adoptive parents, I suppose." She paused, her voice growing serious. "But I promise I'll do my best to keep him safe. Although I can't say I like our odds at the moment if Kachik decides to come after us."

Savina closed her eyes and drew in a long breath. It hardly seemed to matter where she went or what she did, Nicolau would find a way to get himself into danger.

"Savina," said Joska at last. "We're working blind right now. I know you're locked up, and I don't want you to put yourself in any more danger. But if you can find any way to delay the negotiations … it could mean the difference between whether we succeed, or whether we die trying."

"Yeah," said Savina. "I'll … I'll do what I can."

"Thank you," said Joska quietly. "And—we'll come for you, as soon as we can. I promise. But please take care of yourself until then."

There was a click, and the connection died.

Savina sat where she was for a long, long moment, staring at the wall.

It could mean the difference between whether they succeeded or whether they died trying, Joska had said.

She was locked up in a damn cell with her worst enemy, probably about to be killed.

But, idiot that she was, she'd find a way. Somehow.

She leaned against the wall again, shivering at the cool seeping into her skin. It was late in the day, judging from the light trickling in from outside, and she wasn't sure how long she'd been sitting.

"Hey. Reka," she said finally.

Reka didn't answer.

Savina turned to look at her. She was still lying on the cot, her body stiff, her shoulders set in anger. She must have overheard at least Savina's portion of the conversation, but she didn't give any sign whatsoever.

Savina narrowed her eyes. The worry and the ache in her chest had twisted together into a tight, uncomfortable knot, exacerbating her restlessness.

This wasn't going to end well. She knew it wouldn't, but she couldn't help herself. Like back in the Rim Mountains, poking at one of the slow yellow-crested lizards with a blade of grass until it turned to bite you, and you had to jerk your hand out of the way.

"Reka." She made her voice plaintive and innocent.

"Shut up," Reka snapped, not turning.

"Reka," she whined, "come on, talk to me. I'm bored. You say I'm not worth anything. What about you, then? Now that you're all locked up, what's your life worth?"

Finally, Reka rolled over and sat up, leaning back against the wall behind the cot. The sharp, harsh anger was gone from her expression, replaced once again with that infuriating cool indifference.

"If I tell you, will you shut up?" There was a weariness under her aloof tone that Savina didn't remember hearing there before.

"I suppose my life is worth however many guards and politicians I can take down with me before I die." Reka smiled, a small, humourless smile. "I'm sure they'll bring me in front of Kachik again at some point. I probably won't kill him, but I may be able to kill some others before they kill me." She wasn't looking at Savina, just staring at the wall, and Savina watched her in silence for a few moments, an odd, uncomfortable emotion stirring inside her.

Reka hadn't sounded afraid to die. Which, honestly, wasn't that much of a surprise—Savina couldn't remember ever seeing Reka look afraid.

But … she'd expect at least some emotion. Elation, or sadness, or … something.

"What the hell is wrong with you?" Savina asked at last, irritably. "You won't kill who you need to if you do that, and you'll just die yourself."

Reka glanced over, as if she'd forgotten Savina was there. "Why does it matter?"

"It doesn't!" Savina snapped.

But something about the dull resignation in the woman's eyes was … unsettling. Uncomfortable.

She hadn't known Reka for long, and since knowing her, this was the longest she'd been in Reka's presence without one of them trying to kill the other.

And, she realized—she knew nothing at all about Reka Soler.

There was a tap on the door to their cell, then the *click* of a lock. The door swung open, and a yibo woman in a fine tunic stepped through, flanked by two guards. One of them held a tray of food.

The woman in front ignored Savina, smiling a close-lipped yibo smile at Reka. "Kachik asked me to come make sure that you were comfortable."

Reka studied her. "You're Kachik's defence chief, aren't you?" she asked at last.

The woman nodded, smiling wider, and Savina caught the glint in Reka's eyes, the grim, almost imperceptible smile, the way she shifted, as if readying herself to move.

"I suppose my life is worth however many guards and politicians I can take

down with me before I die."

Reka didn't care that she'd be killed, only that she could take someone with her. And this was Kachik's defence chief—probably important enough, from Reka's point of view.

Reka shifted again, her muscles gathering like a cat prepared to pounce. And almost without thinking, Savina jumped to her feet. Her heart was pounding a fast, unsteady rhythm as she stepped quickly forward, placing herself between Reka and the yibo politician. "Oh!" she gushed, turning to the guards with a wide, genuine-looking smile. "You brought dinner! Thank you, I was so hungry!"

She wasn't sure why she'd done it, to be honest. Reka was old enough to deal with the consequences of her own stupidity, and maybe Savina would have found a way to escape in the confusion.

But something about the look on Reka's face when she'd talked about dying …

The guard looked at her askance, and she could feel Reka's glare burning a hole in the back of her tunic.

Damn it, she needed something more distracting.

Savina took a step closer to the guard, her eyes wide and guileless. "I'm sorry, I'm not used to being locked up like this. I'm—" she gave a faint little laugh. "I've been crying and crying. I'm sorry, it's just so embarrassing." She sniffled. "I … I hate to ask, but is there—is there still blood on my face? I haven't been able to look in a mirror since we got caught, and it's just so awkward—"

The guard frowned, but put the food down and leaned closer. "You're fine," he said. "There's just a smudge on your jaw."

She widened her eyes again. "Oh, here?" She rubbed a hand helplessly on her cheek.

He gave an indulgent smile, and reached in. "No, here—"

His fingers brushed along her jawline.

Savina widened her eyes, glanced over her shoulder at Reka. "Sweetheart?" she whispered. "Reka, are you going to let someone do this to your girlfriend?"

A quick sequence of emotions played over Reka's face—disgust, irritation … and then, what Savina had been waiting for. A sudden flash of realization.

Reka smiled a little, got to her feet, and crossed over to the guard.

"No," she said thoughtfully. "No, I don't think I will."

She grabbed Savina with one hand, pulling her around behind her. With the other, she hit the guard, hard enough to send him staggering back into the wall.

The yibo politician jumped back with a curse, and the guards who'd been waiting outside shouted in alarm, pushing the door open, but Savina had regained her feet, and she caught one of them by the arm, redirecting his momentum and sending him slamming into the cement wall beside her.

Reka had already taken out two other guards, and Savina snatched the pistol from the guard she'd disabled, turned, and slammed it into the skull of a fourth.

The nearest guards had rushed the politician out of the cell to safety as the fighting started, and Savina breathed a quick sigh of relief. As she and Reka finished off the guards in the cell, another company came pounding down the stairs, a dozen at least, their weapons at the ready.

"Back! Step back and drop your weapons, this instant!" their leader shouted.

Savina and Reka glanced at one another. Slowly, they complied.

"Don't move," the yibo guard panted, glaring at them.

The yibo politician straightened, brushing herself off. "Reka

Soler," she growled. "I thought you and Kachik had a bargain. You attacked these guards without provocation. We want to work with you, but if you refuse to work with us—"

Reka took a deep breath, her eyes brushing over Savina quickly. Then, as if she'd made a decision, she closed her hand possessively around Savina's arm.

"He was trying to flirt with my girlfriend," she said in a flat voice, turning back to the politician.

Savina fought back the small shiver of—well, something. Certainly not pleasure, because she would have to be literally out of her mind to enjoy being touched by Reka Soler.

The woman stared at them. "I'm ... certain that was not the intention ..." she said at last, her tone hovering between belligerent and tentatively appeasing.

"I said I'd work with you," said Reka, her tone icy, her hand still possessively around Savina's upper arm. "But if you think this is not flirting—" she reached out, sliding her fingers gently along Savina's jaw.

Her touch was warm, fingers strong and calloused, and Savina's stomach did a strange flip-flop.

"Savina was willing to come with me, risk her life because she didn't want me to get hurt. And I'm supposed to repay her by standing by to watch any time a yibo guard gets the urge to feel her up? Savina is not an object. And she won't be treated like one."

She slid her arm around Savina's waist, her body angled so she stood between Savina and the angry guards, and again, Savina had to fight back the strange flutter in her stomach.

The politician's expression turned wary. "I'm ... sorry," she said at last. "I'm sure it was a misunderstanding, but I'll make it very clear that this sort of thing is not to happen again."

Reka's expression was cold. "I hope it doesn't."

At last, the woman nodded again and turned. "I shall … inform Kachik of what happened. And I will personally vet the guards that are permitted to come down here from now on."

"See that you do," said Reka.

Once the yibo were out of sight, Reka dropped her arm from around Savina like the touch burned her. Savina stepped back quickly, trying to slow her pounding heart.

For a few moments, the women stared at each other.

"What?" snapped Savina.

Reka's forehead was creased in a frown. "Why?" she asked finally, something like genuine bewilderment in her tone.

"Maybe I was fooled by your 'poor helpless pitiful me' act too," Savina muttered sourly, turning away.

She still had no idea why she'd stepped in, saved Reka's damn life. Something about the look on Reka's face when she'd talked about what her life was worth, maybe, or the helpless desperation in her expression earlier.

Maybe her answer was truer than she'd thought.

There was a soft sound behind her, and she spun, hand going to her knife.

And then she stopped in complete shock.

Reka was hunched over, shoulders shaking. She leaned back against the wall and slid down to the cot, bending over, elbows on her knees, face in her hands, laughing helplessly.

Savina stood, utterly stupefied.

At last Reka recovered herself and straightened slowly, wiping at her eyes. She took a deep breath, and finally, she looked up at Savina.

"So," she said. "Savina Moya has a heart after all. That, I didn't expect."

Savina narrowed her eyes, heart still beating too quickly. "You're wrong, Reka. I'm a selfish, heartless person with no redeeming qualities, and I don't give a damn if the entire Joias System burns. As far as I'm concerned, every last person on Colorida could be killed by the yibo, or hunted down by the raiders for food, and I wouldn't lose a moment's sleep over it."

Reka's mouth twitched, just a bit, and Savina scowled.

Damn Reka.

Then she paused. "But … Reka," she said slowly. "You do care. You want to stop Cavaco. And I might not care about the damn Joias System, but my baby brother does, and I owe him." She was talking faster now, her mind catching up to her words. "He and my friends are trying to stop Kachik from getting through the portal, but they need time. Kachik needs you, and he underestimates me. And as much as I hate you … that, just now, worked better than I thought it would. Maybe …"

Reka's eyebrows were raised, her gaze turned serious. "Your friends are trying to stop Kachik," she said at last. "I assume that's who you were talking to earlier? How are they going to do it?"

"They're going to shut down the mechanism that makes the portal." Savina's heart was pounding.

There was no way. This was absurd, ridiculous. It would mean working beside Reka …

For a moment, her mind jumped back to Reka's hand tightened possessively on her arm, the warmth of Reka's body against hers as Reka pulled her out of reach of the guard.

She shoved the thought away.

Reka's head was cocked to one side, and she studied Savina thoughtfully.

"If we do this, and we somehow survive, this doesn't pay your debt," she said at last. "I still have a warrant out for your arrest."

Savina smiled her most innocent smile, with a trace of viciousness behind it. "Believe me. The only reason I saved you just now is so that I could have the pleasure of killing you myself when this is over."

Reka's mouth twitched again, just a bit. "Well then. It seems we understand each other. And as you say … what you did with that guard worked better than I expected." She paused, closing her eyes briefly as if bracing herself before she looked back up at Savina. "So, I suppose, you may as well tell your friends we'll see what we can do to give them time."

16

Aran

For a long moment, Aran, Istvay, the raider scientist, and the captain stood staring at each other. Then the captain stepped towards them, pulling a long knife out of his belt, a dangerous grin on his face.

The scientist threw herself forward, landing just in time to plant herself between the captain and Aran as he and Istvay scrambled to their feet. "No!" she shouted. "You can't kill them! Do you know how long it took me to get to live specimens?" Aran recognized the panic in her voice.

She grabbed the captain's wrist as the knife came down, and Aran leapt back out of the way, holding tightly onto Ani, who was hissing on his shoulder.

"Listen, Dessi, I'm sure we can find you some more—" the captain was saying, struggling to extricate himself from the frantic scientist.

From behind him, one of the other raiders, dressed in the same uniform as the captain minus the cape, stepped forward and grabbed Istvay by the arm. Istvay swore helplessly as the raider dragged them towards the door, already pulling out a knife. Aran leapt after them and grabbed the raider by the shoulder, even though she was a solid twenty centimetres taller than he was, and jerked her around.

"You can damn well take your hands off Istvay," he snapped, and snatched up a beaker from the table beside him, smashing it across the raider's face.

Istvay stared at him.

The raider staggered back, looking more surprised than hurt, but her hand loosened from Istvay's arm. Aran grabbed his friend, pulling them around behind him, and yanked out his pulse pistol. His heart was pounding, his hands shaking with adrenaline, but no one was bloody well going to touch Istvay, not while he was alive to prevent it.

And then Ani, who he'd let go of in the struggle, launched herself off his shoulder, landing on another raider who'd come around behind him, their long knife raised.

The raider behind him gave a grunt of surprise, and Aran half-turned, his attention split between the raider he'd hit, now apparently recovered and after his blood, and Ani.

"Ani—" he started, then the raider in front of him grabbed for Istvay again.

Aran snatched up a long pole that was probably a delicate piece of scientific equipment and swung it with all his strength, connecting hard with the raider's rib cage. The raider staggered back, eyes wide with astonishment.

"Stay the hell away from Istvay," Aran snapped, bringing the pole back for another swing.

In the background, he could hear the scientist and the captain shouting at each other, and the raider Ani had landed on was spitting muffled curses. The raider growled something and yanked out a knife to slash at the furious land-devil.

"No!" Aran shouted. "Don't do that, she'll—"

It was too late.

The raider brought down the knife.

Ani spat.

There was a moment of silence.

Then the raider dropped to the ground, screaming and writhing as steam hissed up from his protective suit.

"Ani! Get over here!" Aran snapped, his heart in his mouth.

Ani spat at her victim again, then sulkily wriggled across the floor to latch herself onto Aran's trouser leg.

The entire crew of raiders had gone silent as their companion's screams faded to a muffled gurgling.

"Ani," Aran said sternly into the silence, his heart pounding sickeningly in his chest. "Ani, you know better. He wouldn't have been able to hurt you with that knife, and you know it. There was no reason for you to—"

He trailed off.

Everyone in the room was staring at him.

"Um," Aran said uncomfortably, glancing around. "I'm. I'm … sorry about that. I was trying to warn your friend not to—" the words sank into the silence like stones into a still lake.

At last, carefully, the raider captain broke the silence. "What in God's name," he said, "is that thing?"

Aran glanced guiltily over at Ani, who had made her grumbling way up his leg to perch on her usual place on his shoulder. "She's. Um. She's a land-devil."

It didn't seem quite like enough of an explanation, but then, he wasn't sure what he could say to salvage a situation like this.

"She's my pet. She—she's normally very well behaved, it's just she doesn't like it when people threaten me or my friend, so—"

The raider captain was still staring at him. "That thing … that thing is your pet?"

Aran nodded, not quite meeting his eye.

There were another few moments of silence.

And then the raider captain burst into hearty peals of laughter.

Aran stared as the captain bent over, howling and wiping at his eyes.

No one else in the small shelter moved or spoke.

Aran exchanged glances with Istvay, but they seemed just as confused as he was. He edged closer to them. "Listen," he whispered. "They all have body armour on, but if they're afraid of Ani, we might be able to—"

The raider captain held up a hand, still doubled over with laughter. At last he straightened, wiping his eyes and hiccupping with the remnants of mirth. "I'm sorry," he said, the words wheezing from repressed laughter. "I'm very sorry. If I'd known you were such ferocious warriors, there's no way I would have tried to eat you." He turned to the scientist. "Dessi?" His tone was still thick with mirth. "You said these are specimens you wanted to study?"

The scientist's eyes were wide, and she was staring between Aran, Ani, the body on the floor, and the captain.

She swallowed, and nodded. "The whole point of sending that box through the portal was to initiate contact. I need humans that the yibo haven't domesticated if I want to do a proper study to round out my observations, and this may be my only chance. Like I've told you a hundred times, they're a sapient species. By learning more about their natural habitat and their behaviours—"

The captain waved a dismissive hand. "Yes, yes." He glanced at Aran and Istvay, and Aran could see, under his laughter, the dangerous glint in his red eyes as he studied them. "It appears you picked some impressive specimens," he said at last. "I can admire that. And here I thought humans were just a sort of especially stupid version of the yibo. You say you need these particular humans?"

Dessi nodded. There was a stubborn look to her face that told Aran she was willing to leap in front of them again if necessary.

The captain grinned and turned to Aran and Istvay. "I suppose, then, we may as well get acquainted."

"Um," began Aran, his eyes flicking to the dead raider on the floor.

The acid was now foaming a weak greenish colour.

The raider captain snorted dismissively. "He knew better than to try to go after prey I'd marked." He gestured, and two of the raiders stepped forward, grabbing the body by the shoulders and the ankles, and dragged it out the door.

The captain turned his attention back to them, smiling in a way that showed his sharp incisors to full advantage. "Alright, then. I am Captain Krevai. These people here are my crew. I won't bother introducing them all, I'm sure you'll get to know them as time goes by. And this, here—" he grabbed the scientist, pulling her in for an affectionate one-armed hug that she squirmed out of indignantly, "is our resident scientist. She's very peaceful, as I'm sure you noticed. And she's fascinated by humans. She hasn't killed a single person yet, not even a yibo." He cupped a hand to his mouth, as if whispering a secret. "That's why she's got short hair—never killed anyone and earned the right to grow it out. She's practically a vegetarian."

The scientist glared at him and brushed herself off haughtily.

"We adopted her when we took the ship she was raised on, but they treated her like a servant anyways. No love lost. And now she's our good luck charm. We let her do her experiments here in her lab to keep busy, and the rest of the raiders know the mountain is out of bounds to anyone but us. Had to kill a few crews and burn out a few ships to get the message across, but everyone stays away now. And our little scientist can work away as peacefully as she pleases." He reached out to give the scientist another affectionate squeeze, but she stepped out of reach huffily.

Again, Aran and Istvay exchanged glances.

No wonder the raiders who'd been chasing them had turned around when he and Istvay stepped onto the mountain. From the captain's nonchalant attitude towards death, it seemed getting on his bad side would be a very permanent bad decision.

"And now, who are you?" the captain asked, turning to Aran. There was a dangerous glint in his red eyes.

Aran cleared his throat. "Um. I'm—I'm Aran Romeu. I'm also a scientist."

The captain stared at him, then burst into a fresh wave of laughter. "A human scientist! Look, Dessi, the humans have scientists too! Maybe you were right all along."

Dessi shot Aran an apologetic look, like a teenager embarrassed by their parent.

"Anyways," Aran continued awkwardly, as the captain was obviously waiting for him to go on. "This is Ani. She's—she's very friendly once you get to know her. And, um, this is Istvay. They're—they're my friend. And my research assistant."

The captain frowned. "I see. And Ani—she's a larval stage? Or is that how the mature females look, and you and your Istvay are males? I haven't seen one that looks like her before, but then—"

Dessi, in the corner, looked like she was choking.

Aran stared, then had to fight to keep his face straight. "No, no. No, I mean, yes, I'm a male, but Istvay's not, they're non-binary. And Ani is—she's a different species. The human genders all look roughly similar."

The captain raised his eyebrows and nodded. "Ah. I see. So we have a scientist, and a research assistant, and a … whatever that is. And a male, a non-binary, and a female." He turned to Dessi with a grin. "You were very thorough in your samples."

"The creature is not a human female," snapped Dessi, annoyance in her tone. "It's—" she glanced at Aran.

"A great tree-dwelling venomous tentacled land-devil," Aran muttered. He had completely lost the thread of the conversation at this point.

"Of course, of course," said the captain breezily. "Just like I was saying. We have Aran, and his Ani, and his Istvay."

"They're not my Istvay," said Aran, in some irritation.

The captain raised his eyebrows in mild surprise. "You're not mates?"

Aran stared at him blankly.

"You know. Mates," said the captain patiently. "You know? Like …" He made an unmistakable gesture with his fingers.

Aran coughed abruptly, not daring to glance over at Istvay. "No! No, um, no. No, we're—we're not mates."

"Ah," said the captain, sounding mildly disappointed.

For a few moments, they stood there staring at each other. At last the captain grinned again.

"So. Aran. What brought you and your Istvay and your Ani here?

"I told you, they're not my—" Aran began, then gave up. "Um. You—I mean, Dessi, sent something through the portal that had a blood sample in it. I was … we were looking for the person the sample was taken from."

The captain looked confused.

Dessi cleared her throat and looked away, appearing slightly embarrassed.

"You told me you needed a sample to check my blood sugar levels," Krevai said, turning on her with lowered eyebrows.

She didn't appear intimidated. "Well, I needed a sample to send through, and I couldn't have all the samples be from me. If I wanted someone to respond to me, they couldn't think I was the only inhabitant of the entire system."

He was still glaring.

She cast a resigned glance at Aran. "And besides," she continued grudgingly, "I wanted blood samples from someone who was a strong physical specimen."

The captain watched her suspiciously for a moment, then he beamed and turned back to Aran. "Well, it looks like you found him, then."

"Why were you interested in the blood sample?" asked Dessi, frowning. "I assume you weren't studying us independent of what I sent through. If you're interested in doing some analyses, you and I could—"

"Actually," Aran broke in, "it's—" he paused, glancing around, then sighed. "It's just, there's—there's a genetic mutation endemic in our population. I don't know where it came from, but it's been there for a long time. It's a combination of several genes, as best we've figured out, which means it's difficult to test for, and also that most of the population is a potential carrier. But when someone has the defect, they—they die. Usually within twenty or thirty years. We've never been able to find a cure." Even now, he could hardly speak the words without his throat tightening.

He cleared his throat. "Anyway, we—the blood sample you sent, we did DNA analysis on it when it got to our planet. The captain has the same combination of genes that causes the genetic defect. And he's at least two decades older in our planet's time than the longest any survivor of the defect has lived back in the Joias System. I—I'd hoped that maybe, if I could do some analysis, perform some studies …"

"Do you have this defect?" the captain asked, frowning.

Aran shook his head mutely, unable to speak.

The captain's frown deepened. "But one of you do, don't they? It's your Ani or your Istvay, isn't it?"

"Yes," said Istvay at last. They hadn't spoken during this entire exchange, but now they stepped forward, placing themself between the captain and Aran. "Yes, it's me. So if there's a problem, I'm the one you should talk to. Aran was doing all this for me."

The captain was still frowning, glancing between Aran and Istvay. "No, no, of course," he said at last. "I wondered why the three of you were willing to seek us out."

He glanced over at the scientist, and a wordless communication passed between them. She nodded, and he turned back to Aran and Istvay, grinning.

"Well," he said. "You want to know about this genetic defect. And Dessi wants to know about you. And I heard rumours that Captain Sharda is prowling around the base of my scientist's mountain hunting for some rogue humans, and she's been testing my strength for a while now. So I think I've found a solution that will make all of us happy—you will stay here with us. You can do your research or tests or whatever, and Dessi can study you to her heart's content, and no one will bother you unless they want my crew to hunt them down. My crew has a reputation among the other raiders." His smile widened, and there was an unmistakable menace under it. "And next time I talk to Sharda, I'll be able to rub it in her face a bit. She's begun to think a little too highly of herself lately."

Aran stared.

Istvay recovered themself first. "That sounds very nice," they said, and Aran could hear the challenge in their tone.

In fairness, Istvay had never been particularly tactful when they were injured, and in this case, he could hardly blame them.

"We stay here, and your scientist does studies—I assume her studies will be on us?"

The captain smiled benevolently. "Well, of course, but she doesn't want to hurt you. I'm sure they'll all be harmless."

Istvay gave the captain their signature glare. "Oh yes, I'm sure they will. And what exactly do you get in exchange for all this? Food storage for when hunting is bad?"

The captain burst into uproarious laughter again. "Aran," he said, when he'd recovered somewhat. "Your Istvay is very fierce."

Aran turned his own glare on the captain. He probably should be more polite right now, but after everything that had happened, he quite frankly couldn't bring himself to care. "Listen," he said through his teeth. "They're not *my Istvay*. They're their own person. And you can damn well—"

The captain held up a hand, still chuckling. "I apologize, Aran," he said. "I didn't mean to offend you. I am deeply happy to have you as part of our crew."

Aran and Istvay exchanged glances again.

"Part of your—" began Aran uncertainly.

"Part of my crew," said the captain. "It's been a long time since I've met anyone who's made me laugh this much. We'll make sure you have food and clean water, a comfortable place to sleep—you can be … you can be our mascots. I'm sure the crew will love you." He grinned, showing his teeth. "And Sharda will be spitting blood."

"Your—your mascots." Aran could hear the incredulity in his own voice.

"We're their food storage," said Istvay flatly. "This is ridiculous, we don't have to—"

"Not food storage, I swear it," the captain said jovially. "Dessi is always asking me for something we can adopt, but it's so hard to find a creature that would fit into the crew."

Aran turned to Istvay. "Pishti. He's right, this isn't about food storage. He's damn well keeping us as pets."

Istvay glanced between Aran and the captain, their eyebrows raised almost to their hairline. "He's—" They sounded like they couldn't decide whether to laugh or start shouting.

"That's what this is, isn't it? You want to keep us as pets," said Aran, half in disbelief, turning back to the captain.

The captain chuckled. "Don't be silly, of course you won't be our pets. You'll be members of our crew."

"I'm not a pet," said Aran through his teeth. His heart was still pounding far too quickly from the too many near-death-experiences to count that he'd suffered over the last hour. "And nor is Istvay."

"Of course you're not a pet," said the captain soothingly. "You're a member of our crew. Just like any other member of the crew."

One of the raider crew stepped through the door, eyeing them suspiciously. "Captain? You sent for me?"

"Yes," said the captain over his shoulder. "I need you to prepare that spare cabin on the ship. Make sure it's got food and clean water and some bedding so they can make their little nests or whatever they need. Talk to Dessi when we're done here—I want to make their habitat as accurate as possible, so they can adjust."

"Our—habitat?" said Aran flatly.

"They're not doing sex with each other," the captain continued. "At least, that's what Aran said. I don't really know human mating habits. But I think it's alright to put them in the same habitat anyways, they seem to get along." He turned back to Aran and Istvay, peering at them. "You do get along, don't you? If we put you in the same room, you won't—fight, or eat each other, or something?"

"Humans live in complex social groupings," said Dessi importantly, stepping forward. "These two look like they've formed their own social grouping with each other and their land-devil, so they should be fine. And humans have complex methods of communication, so there are usually some warning signals before they resort to dangerous levels of violence within their chosen social grouping. At least, generally speaking," she added, glancing suspiciously at Aran and Istvay, as if worried they might start a fistfight in the middle of her laboratory.

"Good, good," said the captain, turning back to the newcomer. "Then that's how we'll arrange it."

"Listen," began Aran again, helplessly. "We're not pets. We're—"

"Of course you're not pets," said the captain soothingly. "You're … scientists. Human scientists."

He seemed to be trying to hold back laughter at the words.

Aran glared at him, his entire body still buzzing with adrenaline. "Listen," he began.

"As soon as you get settled in, come back here to my lab, and we can start looking at some information on the DNA," Dessi broke in. "I suggest we start by taking some of Istvay's blood, and we'll compare it to the captain's. You can show me the DNA markers for the defect, and we'll see if we can figure anything out."

Aran turned to the scientist quickly, his annoyance forgotten in an instant. "Do you have a DNA analysis machine here?" he asked. His heart beat with a mixture of excitement and a sort of frantic disbelief.

"I keep the more delicate machines in the back, but yes, I certainly have the equipment for basic DNA analysis. If we can pinpoint the genetic differences, perhaps we can figure out what exactly this defect is, and why it doesn't affect us like it affects humans." She cleared her throat importantly. "Since we almost certainly have genetics in common, there's a high possibility that we'll be able to figure something out."

Aran's legs went weak with relief. Istvay grabbed his shoulder in support, but when Aran looked at them, they didn't look any better than he felt—face pale, eyes wide with shock.

"You can do that tomorrow," the captain broke in firmly. "Look at them. They look like they're about to fall over. Orud should have finished fixing up some bedding for them. They need sleep, and it looks like they've been injured. You don't want damaged specimens, do you?"

Dessi's eyes widened, and she glanced quickly at Aran and Istvay. "I didn't even notice. Yes, yes, of course. Let's get them food and rest, and I'll see what I can find as far as medicine that should work with their biology—" She turned, rummaging through her shelves and muttering to herself.

"I'm—I'm fine, actually," Aran began. "I'm not tired at all, we can start setting things up right now—"

"No," said the captain firmly, stepping over to them. Ani hissed, but it was half-hearted, as if she'd decided the captain no longer posed a threat. "It won't be nearly as satisfying to gloat to Sharda about you if you're dead. Besides, you won't find a cure for your Istvay if you're falling asleep standing up. Go on, you can do your ... your little science in the morning."

Istvay glanced at Aran with a rueful smile. Their face was pale, and their expression still held a dazed, sickly look of exhaustion. "I hate to say it, Aran," they said quietly, "but I agree with the raiders on this one."

Aran and Istvay were led to a small, comfortable cabin on the large raider ship now parked in the centre of the clearing. Aran tried not to think about how much time the raiders must spend in space, if their home was the ship itself. He could worry about that when it came to it.

Right now there was only one thought on his mind, turning over and over in his brain, pounding through his chest like a heartbeat.

They'd found the person who'd sent the box. He could finally start on finding a cure.

Istvay might live.

He hadn't realized, until just now, how much the constant worry for Istvay had weighed down his every damn thought for the last … well, too many years to count.

Even before they'd started showing signs, he'd worried. Because Istvay was his whole world. How could he not worry?

The raiders left them, and Istvay dropped wearily down onto a thick pile of blankets. They looked exhausted, but they glanced up at Aran with concern. "Are you alright?" they asked softly.

Aran dropped down beside them. "I'm fine," he said, although he could hear the tension in his own voice. "I'm fine, just—" he trailed off.

Istvay smiled faintly. "I'll admit, this wasn't on my list of things that I was expecting to happen today."

"I can't believe they made us their pets," Aran grumbled, and this time, Istvay did laugh.

Something about the cheerful, carefree sound of it caught Aran off guard, and he had to close his eyes for a moment to regain his composure.

Finally, there was a chance that Istvay would to live. They'd have a chance to be happy, and he'd have a chance to hear them laugh years in the future, not just a few short, precious, tragic more months.

The relief that washed over him at the thought was almost enough to leave him shaky.

The buzz of his wavelink up the nerves of his arm jolted him out of his thoughts, and for a moment he stared around stupidly, trying to figure out where it had come from.

"Aran? Istvay?" The voice through his earpiece was Yosip's.

"You're … you're alive?" he asked, hearing the incredulity in his own tone. "What the hell—where are you calling from? Are you still with the yibo?"

Yosip chuckled. "It's good to hear your voice. We weren't sure you'd made it out, to be honest. You're too far away to show on our sensors." He sighed. "And no, we're not with the yibo. At least, we are, but not with Kachik and his friends. Are you two alright?"

Aran stared blankly at Istvay. At last he said into the wavelink, "Yes. Yes, we're fine."

"Good." There was clear relief in Yosip's voice. "I tried to call Istvay as well, but I couldn't get through to them. But they're alright? Where are you? What are you doing?"

Aran glanced at Istvay and squeezed his palmscreen, so Yosip's voice would carry through the amplifiers loud enough that Istvay could hear.

"Pishti? Your wavelink …"

Istvay clenched their fist around their own palmscreen experimentally, then shook their head in disgust. "Must have been damaged in the crash. The damn thing was already glitching, and that must've finally killed it."

"Um," said Aran helplessly, turning back to his own wavelink. "Istvay's here, we're both here. We. Um. We found the raiders. And they—may have made us into their pets. I think. But—it's fine. They're going to help us find the cure. So."

There was a long silence from the other end of the line. "I probably shouldn't ask, should I?" Yosip said at last. He sighed. "Aran. I hate to interrupt you when you're so close to your goal. But we have a problem."

By the time Yosip finished his explanation, Aran and Istvay were staring at each other in horror, their exhaustion forgotten.

"The yibo plan to destroy the Joias System?" Aran repeated at last.

"I'm afraid so," said Yosip quietly.

"Well, I don't think our news is much better on that front," said Istvay, their voice grim. "The raiders are waiting for the portal to open for the same reason. The captain we ran into took a liking to us for some reason and decided to keep us alive, but he doesn't have any qualms about killing humans. They're gathering the various raider crews to go through the portal and kill everyone. But I'm not sure what we can do to stop it, if they're as close to reopening the portal as you say."

"We've discovered where the mechanism that creates the portal is," said Yosip in a soft tone. "If we can destroy it, the portal can't reopen. That's how we stop this."

Aran stared at the wavelink implant on his wrist.

He was finally here. He finally had the cure for Istvay right in front of him …

"We may not need your help. This may not even be a possibility. And if it is, I'll do everything I can to keep you out of it." Yosip paused a moment, and Aran could hear the reluctance in the man's voice. "I am sorry," he said at last. "I know how much saving Istvay means to you. But this could be the entire Joias System at stake." He sighed. "But we should know within twenty-four Colorida hours, give or take, whether we'll be able to do this at all, and whether we'll need your help. So. I just wanted to give you a chance to think about it."

"Thank you," said Aran numbly.

He tapped his wavelink off, and turned to glance at Istvay. They were watching him, and there was an expression on their face that he couldn't read.

They noticed him watching them and managed a shaky smile.

Aran scooted closer to them on the pile of blankets and laid a hand on their arm. "Pishti," he said quietly. "We'll figure this out. I promise. Get some sleep, okay? I'll keep watch for a bit, just in case."

"Aran," Istvay began, and Aran could hear how their voice caught.

He shook his head. "Pishti, listen. I don't care what we have to do. We're going to figure this out. You're not dying, not while there's something I can do to stop it, Joias System be damned. Do you understand me?"

"Aran—"

Aran sighed. "They might not even need us. Let's … let's talk about this tomorrow, okay?"

Istvay swallowed, their eyes still fixed on his, and then, with an effort, they nodded. "Alright," they said quietly. "We'll talk about it tomorrow."

"Pishti," Aran said, turning them to face him. "You're my best friend. And we're going to figure this out."

They watched him for a moment, something unreadable in their expression. At last they managed a faint smile. "Yeah."

They lay back, curling up on the pile of blankets, and Aran watched them until their breathing evened out in sleep.

Then he stood restlessly, pacing back and forth from the door to the far wall.

Despite the exhaustion that tugged at every muscle in his body, he couldn't bring himself to sit down.

He was going to bloody well save Istvay.

He had to.

17

Savina

"Savina." Reka looked up from their shared breakfast.

The guards who'd brought it had been very respectful, keeping their eyes conspicuously averted from Savina and leaving the food tray at the door of the cell before backing away quickly.

Savina had had to work to fight back a grin at that.

She glanced up at Reka. "Yes, sweetheart?" she cooed.

Reka's gaze darkened, but she didn't take the bait. "If we want to delay Kachik, it will take more than just a fist-fight in our cell."

"I know," said Savina at last, letting her smile drop. "Besides, last time was mostly luck. We'll need something a lot bigger."

Reka was watching her. "You've thought of something, haven't you?"

Savina smiled. "Come on, now, I'm the stupid one. You're supposed to be the one with the plans. I can't bother my pretty little head about details."

Reka narrowed her eyes, and reached out as if to snatch the bowl of breakfast from Savina.

Savina yanked it out of reach. "Hey, it won't look convincing if your girlfriend is starving to death." She paused a moment. "Fine. I do have an idea."

Reka leaned back against the wall, watching her warily. "Well?"

"Kachik said he wanted to meet with you today, didn't he? Talk through the plan to deal with Cavaco? Do you think you could convince him you need your girlfriend along for emotional support?"

Reka's eyes narrowed further. "And if I did that?"

Savina fluttered her eyelashes. "Well, then I'd be soooo proud of you, sweetheart." She ducked out of the way of the spoon Reka tossed with deadly accuracy. "Hey!"

Reka smirked as Savina rubbed at her shoulder. "Is that all you need from me?"

"That's not the only thing." Savina tried to keep her voice light to hide the sullen murder in her tone. She lowered her voice to a husky whisper. "I need you to hold me, Reka." She yelped and covered her head with her arms as Reka's empty bowl followed the spoon "Not like that, you idiot!"

"Do you see the cameras?" whispered Reka from where she was supporting the stack of rickety stools Savina perched on, right in the cameras' blind spot. "Can you get to them?"

"Can you shut the hell up?" Savina hissed back. "If you think this is so easy, you could do it yourself."

Reka made an amused sound, and Savina glanced down in surprise, almost losing her balance.

Reka caught her easily, propping her back up. "Easy there. Mind on the job, Savina."

Savina glared at her. "I have my mind on the job! Just because—"

Then she noticed the twitch at the corner of Reka's mouth, the humour in her eyes.

She scowled, and turned back to her work.

Damn Reka to hell.

It didn't take her long to figure out the mechanism, but she stayed there for a few moments longer just to make Reka wait. At last, she let herself carefully down.

"There," she said, dimpling. "I know what I'd have to take out to disable them. I doubt the yibo will see much on their screens when I'm through."

Savina saw a small glint of approval on Reka's face before the woman caught herself.

Savina smiled wider. "You'll just need to distract them while I do it. Too bad you're not as pretty as me. But I'll bet if you took your clothes off, they would—"

Reka's expression turned dangerous, and Savina stepped back quickly. "You can't hurt me, Reka. Sweetheart. You need me." She fluttered her eyelashes.

Reka narrowed her eyes. "Call me sweetheart again without the guards here to listen and I'll pin you to the wall by your throat, *sweetheart.*"

That tone of voice shouldn't make Savina's stomach twist, it *shouldn't*, and it didn't, and Savina glared at Reka's back for a few moments, and she absolutely did not have to wait for a moment for her heart to stop pounding before she could sit back down in her corner.

Damn Reka.

"Reka. We've been asked to bring you to speak with Kachik."

The guards were still very obviously not making eye contact with Savina, and Savina bit back a smirk.

"Alright," said Reka. She stood, then turned to help Savina gently to her feet as well, and put an arm around her, pulling her close.

Savina almost swore at the sudden giddy flutter in her stomach.

What the actual hell was wrong with her?

"Um. Kachik asked for you, specifically. Perhaps your girlfriend —"

Reka shot them an icy glare. "You think I'm going to leave Savina here alone? After what happened last time? She's coming, or I'm not."

The guards conferred for a moment, and at last, the leader said reluctantly, "Alright. She can come this time, but she'll need to be quiet and not make trouble."

Savina looked up at them with big eyes, then back at Reka, her lip trembling.

Reka gave her a tiny grin, then swore, turning back to the guards. "You're making her cry. If you think you can come over here and insult my girlfriend until she cries—"

"I'm sorry!" the guard said in a panicked voice, backing up quickly enough to trip over his own feet. "I didn't mean—I just meant—" He trailed off, swallowing hard. "Let's—we should go, if you're—if the two of you, that is, are ready."

"Savina?" Reka's voice was warm and solicitous.

She hadn't actually realized Reka's voice could sound warm. But it did, deep and soft, like the smell of cedarwood and dark chocolate, the low sweetness of a note pulled from a cello string with a newly rosined bow.

"Savina?"

She shook herself from her reverie and smiled up at Reka in mock-adoration. "Of course, my love. I'll go wherever you go." She made sure Reka could see the mockery in her glance, and she was rewarded with the tiniest tightening around Reka's eyes.

And she wasn't sure why the words left a sour taste in her mouth.

Somewhat to Savina's disappointment, the guards kept a respectful distance, so neither she nor Reka had an excuse to kill anyone.

When they reached the room where Kachik was waiting, the guards gestured them politely through. Reka, her arm still around Savina's waist, went, drawing Savina after her.

Savina glanced quickly around the room as Reka fussed over her, offering her a seat and making sure she was comfortable, and tried to pick out the technology she was looking for.

It was better than watching Reka, anyway, and her feigned solicitude.

"Reka," said Kachik at last, when they were finally both settled. "Thank you for coming. I have the assurances of Captain Mattin that Cavaco is backing him, but I'd like to go over those assurances with someone who's worked with Cavaco before, in order to attempt to parse out any potential issues."

"Of course," said Reka, her face cold and emotionless once it was turned to Kachik.

Savina shuddered, just a little.

Reka was bloody terrifying, and she should probably not forget it.

As Kachik and Reka talked in low voices, bent over a holodisc, Savina studied the room more closely.

For the look of things, she cast a few flirtatious glances at Reka, and was rewarded with a small tightening around the corners of Reka's mouth.

She smiled to herself.

There were cameras installed in the corners, as they'd expected.

And … there. What she'd been looking for. An alarm.

She blinked innocently and stood, stretching.

Reka glanced over at her. "Savina?"

"It's alright, darling, I just need to stretch my legs." Savina laughed guilelessly. "I'm sorry, I'm not really able to follow everything you and that yibo person are talking about."

Reka nodded, smiling at her fondly, and Savina looked quickly away.

She wandered along the edge of the room, keeping her eyes surreptitiously on the guards. At first they stiffened, watching her warily, but as she meandered aimlessly, they slowly turned their attention back to the conversation between Reka and Kachik.

Reka certainly looked like a greater threat, her lean body set with that whip-crack readiness, her expression cold and indifferent, the air of danger she wore like a second skin.

And Savina … well, she'd spent her entire life working on looking harmless, and innocent, and earnest, and just a little silly.

When she was certain she'd lost their attention, she moved over to one of the cameras. After her practice earlier, it only took her a moment to pull out the wire that would disconnect it, then yank a tiny component free.

She moved on to the next.

She'd only have a few minutes at most between when she disabled the first camera, and when someone realized what she'd done. But she was very good at moving quickly while looking lost and aimless.

She had four of the cameras disabled before she caught sight of a guard listening intently to his communicator, a slight frown on his face.

She looked up, as if suddenly noticing something, and walked quickly over to the alarm.

Before any of the guards had time to do more than glance in her direction, she raised up on her tiptoes, studying the device, then yanked hard on the dangling chain.

A harsh wail filled the room, the noise grating against her eardrums. But painful as it was, it seemed to affect the yibo even more.

Kachik jumped to his feet, glancing around quickly. When he caught sight of Savina, his face darkened, and he said something to Reka.

Reka's face went even colder than usual, but she strode quickly over to Savina. "Savina. Are you alright?"

"I'm—" Savina looked up at her, face frightened, and Reka led her gently out of the room after Kachik, who looked on the verge of spontaneously combusting.

Outside, the groups of panicked yibo were running down hallways, opening lifts.

"This way," one of the guards grunted in the yibo language, and hurried them down a corridor, down a lift, through another corridor, and finally outside into a rapidly filling courtyard.

"What happened back there?" Kachik hissed, rounding on Savina. "What did you do?"

"I … I didn't—" Savina stammered, tears welling in her eyes. "I was just … I was trying to help!"

"Trying to help by disabling the cameras and pulling the emergency alarm?" Kachik's voice was rising in a mix of outrage and disbelief. "What exactly are you trying to do, Savina?" He turned to Reka. "I thought we had an agreement. What—"

"I wasn't disabling the cameras!" Savina wailed. "I was trying to help! There were these bits sticking out, and they looked messy, and I thought I'd clean them up. And then when I was going over to look at the alarm to see if there was anything I could clean up there, the guards startled me, and I pulled it on accident!" She burst into sobs and buried her face in Reka's shoulder.

"I thought we had an agreement as well, and it did not involve terrorizing my girlfriend!" Reka hissed.

"They evacuated the entire building, because they couldn't see through the cameras what had happened in the room!" Kachik shouted.

The alarms blared in the background, and the courtyard was filled with the over-excited chatter of far, far too many yibo, and Savina smiled into Reka's shoulder.

One extra day for Joska, at any rate.

It was a long time before they were returned to their cells. Kachik had been fuming, but from what Savina could see, there was going to be no further negotiations with Captain Mattin happening that day.

Reka had stood stoically between Savina and the fury of both Kachik and a diplomat named, if she recalled correctly, Harroch, and any number of guards, as Savina alternately cried and babbled nonsense in her own defence.

Now, back in their cell with the door closed and locked behind them, Savina let the stupid, innocent look drop from her face and leaned against the wall of the cell, rubbing a hand wearily across her face.

When she looked up, Reka was watching her with a small smile that, for once, looked almost genuine. "That was ... not bad, Savina," she said quietly.

The words sparked a small, unexpected ache in Savina's chest, and she gritted her teeth.

She didn't need this. She didn't need any of this.

After a few moments, Reka dropped down to sit on the cot, and gestured to a stool.

Savina sat warily, watching Reka for any sign of a trick.

"Oh, for the Mystery's sake," said Reka with a sigh. "If we're going to work together, you're going to have to stop acting like you're terrified of me."

"Maybe I am," said Savina, widening her eyes again. "You're so big and strong and scary, and I'm just a little Rim Mountain country girl."

Reka snorted. "That's enough. There's no one watching, stop wasting both our time."

Savina smiled and batted her eyelashes. "It's not a waste of my time. You're so cute when you're angry."

Reka's mouth twitched, just a little. Savina pulled her gaze away quickly.

"After what happened today, there's no way I'll get permission to bring you with me tomorrow," Reka said. "But ..." she paused. "Based on how well you play stupid, Savina, I may have another idea."

Savina gradually scooted her stool closer to the cot as they mapped out the plan. When she looked up, she realized suddenly that they were shoulder to shoulder, hunched over a diagram Reka had sketched out in wrinkles on the blanket. Reka hadn't noticed, her focus on the small map she'd moulded skillfully from the fabric, her lean hands moving over the surface as she spoke.

Savina pushed her chair back, feeling suddenly awkward.

Reka wanted to kill her. Reka was the reason she was trapped here in the first place. She had to remember that.

But somehow, she was finding it more difficult than she'd expected.

18

Alba

It was late that night when Joska stood from her position at the window and turned to the others.

"I think they're asleep," she whispered. "If we're planning on getting out, this is going to be our best chance."

It only took a few minutes for the small group of them to gather their things.

"Nicolau," Alba whispered. "You were going to find a way to get us out of the hospital without being seen, correct?"

Nicolau cleared his throat. "Um," he said. "Beni got them to leave a window open in our room when they came to check on us earlier this evening. It opens up on the back of the building, and I've been watching—it's a back alley, and no one goes that way. We shouldn't be seen if we climb down. And I couldn't get my hands on any rope, but I thought if we took the bedsheets and tied them together—"

Beni's face took on an expression of sudden interest. "Like in the Steamy Alien Nights audios?"

Joska turned her head aside, coughing into her hand.

Alba glared at him. "You—you want us to tie bedsheets together and climb down the wall?"

Nicolau flushed. "I mean, they do it all the time in the audios—"

Ines stepped forward, her eyes flashing. "It's a good idea," she said. "Unless any of you have a better one."

Alba looked at the young interpreter in astonishment.

"No, no, it's not a bad idea," Joska said. Her voice was carefully neutral, but she was obviously biting back a smile. "It'll certainly be better than trying to climb down hand over hand."

It didn't take long to get the bedsheets gathered and torn into strips. Nicolau was surprisingly adept at the knots, and between him, Joska, and Rafel, they soon had a small, serviceable length of rope.

Joska examined it critically, then nodded. "I think it'll hold. Now —"

"I'll go first," said Ines. There was determination behind her frightened expression. "I'm the lightest, I can test it to make sure it'll hold."

Nicolau looked at her in concern. "Ines, you don't have to—"

She lifted her chin and looked him directly in the eye. "I trust you," she said quietly.

Even in the dark, Alba could see Nicolau flush.

"Well anyway, I'll secure the rope, but I'll be holding it too, just in case," he said, his voice rough.

Joska was no longer even attempting to hide her amusement, but thankfully, the two young people were entirely focused on each other, and seemed not to have a thought to spare for their elders.

With Nicolau bracing himself to secure it against one of the cot frames, Ines grabbed the makeshift rope. Her eyes were wide in the moonlight through the open window, her expression that same sick determination Alba had seen there so many times.

"Ines," Alba said quietly.

Ines jerked her head up, startled.

"Good luck."

Ines gave a nervous little bob of her head. Then she took a tighter grip on the rope and let herself carefully down off the side of the wall.

The rest of them watched as she lowered herself slowly to the ground, but she reached it without incident. She untangled herself from the rope, shook it loose, then stood back, nodding up at them.

Nicolau let out an audible sigh of relief and turned back to the others. "Alright, it looks like it's safe. Who's next?"

Joska went down next, then Beni, and then between the three on the ground and Nicolau on the wall, they lowered Yosip, Feliu, and the still-injured Rafel, despite his grumbling protestations that he was perfectly fine and didn't need help.

When it was Alba's turn, she had to swallow hard against the vertigo as she looked down at the drop below her.

But both Feliu and Yosip had gone, and she couldn't bring herself to show hesitation where they hadn't. So she closed her eyes and seated herself in the uncomfortable makeshift harness Nicolau had improvised, holding back a gasp as she was lowered gently over the window ledge.

The wind jostled the thin rope, bumping her against the wall of the building painfully more than once before she reached the bottom, and by the time her feet touched something solid, she felt like a pig that had been twisting on a spit.

She closed her eyes in relief as the harness settled her back on solid ground, then Yosip and Joska were there, unstrapping her from the harness and helping her out.

Her legs were shaky enough from the trip that she was grateful for Joska's firm grip on her arm, steadying her.

"Easy there, Chief Justice," Joska murmured, but she stayed until Alba's legs steadied under her and she could move stiffly over to stand with the others.

Nicolau followed last, untying the rope and looping it around the legs of the cot he'd dragged up against the window, then wrapping both ends of the rope around himself and abseiling down with practiced ease. When he reached the ground, he loosened the rope from around himself and pulled one end up and over, until the whole thing lay in a pile at his feet. He coiled it quickly and stowed it in his knapsack, then looked up with a grin.

"I knew it was a good idea," said Ines, coming over to stand beside him. He looked down at her, his face flushing again in the moonlight, but his smile was wide and genuine.

"Alright. Now all that's left is getting out of here before the yibo notice we're missing," said Joska.

The group of them stepped cautiously out into the dark, silent streets. The village was quiet, and it didn't appear that their escape had been noted. As long as they kept to the shadows, no one seemed concerned with finding them out.

Although, Alba was more than certain, the guards would be very interested indeed in finding them out should they realize what she and the rest of her motley group were planning to do.

The breeze off the dry grasslands carried a sharp, fresh, musky smell. Beside Alba, Feliu was muttering under his breath.

"Are you alright?" she whispered.

He glared at her. "Madam. With all due respect, considering what we've been through in the last few weeks, I hardly think that's a question that deserves an honest answer."

Alba bit back a small smile despite herself.

By the time they reached the edge of the village, Alba's knee was already stiff. Feliu was still grumbling, and from behind them, Alba could hear Rafel muttering swear words under his breath.

Feliu cast the occasional irritated glanced back at the crewman, but honestly, the tone of Rafel's swearing was so similar to the tone of Feliu's grumbling that Alba had to hold back a chuckle.

At the last street before the force-field, they came to a halt.

"Well done," said Joska quietly. "Now we just have to get past the guards."

"Let me take care of the guards," Yosip whispered. "They know me, and I was meaning to ask one of them for their porridge-soup recipe anyway, so I don't think anyone will think it's too strange."

Alba refrained, with an effort, from commenting, but she could see the twitch of amusement in Joska's face.

"No," the woman said, with an obvious effort to keep her voice solemn, "I—don't expect they would."

"Alright," said Yosip, stepping out of the alley. "The rest of you go while I'm talking, I'll join you in a minute."

They watched as he strolled up to the two guards on duty. She couldn't hear the conversation from this distance, but Alba saw the tension in the guards' movements as they spun at the sound, and its sudden release when they caught sight of Yosip.

It wasn't long before he and the guards were leaned back against the wall of one of the buildings, postures relaxed, clearly shooting the breeze. One of the guards laughed at something Yosip said, and Alba could picture the twinkle in Yosip's eyes.

"Come on," Joska whispered, and the small group of them crept silently out of the alley. When they reached the forcefield, they ducked behind a building, out of sight of the guards.

"Yosip," Joska whispered into her wavelink. "We're here. We just need an opening to get through."

It was several endless minutes before they heard soft footsteps. Yosip rounded the corner, and as he did so, an opening appeared in the forcefield. As Alba had predicted, his eyes were bright with good humour, and his smile was wide and infectious. He glanced behind him, then beckoned the rest of them through.

"Apparently, Eeda's son should be glad that she hasn't told his new boyfriend exactly what she thinks of him," he whispered as they joined him.

Joska caught Alba's eye, and they shared an amused glance.

"I told them I wanted to look at the stars, and they said that should be fine, as long as I'm careful and stay close."

"Well, best take advantage of it," said Joska.

Alba sighed inwardly. Her body ached, and her knee ached, and if she stopped to think of it, there didn't seem to be a single part of her that didn't ache.

But Joska was right—best go while they had the chance.

"Lead the way," she said.

At least, Alba thought as she forced her exhausted body to keep moving, this escape attempt they weren't being pursued by raiders. At least there was that.

It was hard to hold on to any sort of positive thought, though, with every muscle in her body aching, and her knee burning with pain.

"Are you alright?"

She turned to see that Yosip had come up beside her.

He looked as tired as she felt, but somehow, his face was still creased in a wan smile.

"I suspect you know the answer to that as well as I do," she said wryly.

He chuckled, and they walked for a while in companionable

silence.

"Yosip?" she asked at last. "Do you ... do you think we have a chance at this?"

She wasn't sure what had prompted the question—maybe just something to keep her mind off the never-ending torment of walking.

Yosip smiled, the expression unaccountably reassuring. "If you'd asked me a few months ago if we'd have a chance of surviving a mutiny, a ship break-up, being stranded on an alien planet, captured in an alien city, and almost eaten alive by raiders, I'm not sure how I would have answered you. But here we are."

She returned his smile. "I suppose you're right. Here we are."

By the time they reached the *Dolphin,* neither she nor Yosip had energy to spare for conversation. They staggered into the ship, and Alba almost fell onto one of the cots.

"Well," said Joska quietly. "We made it." She glanced around. "I didn't see any signs of pursuit, so I think we have time. I suggest we contact Aran again. I don't know what we're going to find out there, but I doubt we'll have even a chance without his and Istvay's help."

Alba nodded, almost too weary to answer.

"I'll talk to him," said Yosip quietly. "I ... don't think he's going to be happy about this. But perhaps I can convince him."

Alba glanced up. "It's the entire Joias System," she snapped. "I should certainly hope he can be convinced."

"It's his friend's life," said Yosip softly, meeting her gaze. "But I'll do what I can."

Alba frowned, watching him as he tapped in the code on his wavelink.

And it struck her, once again, how very little it appeared that she understood the people in the system she was supposed to have been governing all these years.

212

19

Aran

Aran woke late the next morning, his entire body stiff and aching and a dull pang of hunger gnawing at his stomach. He rolled over to find Istvay sprawled out across the blankets next to him, still fast asleep.

He smiled a little, watching them, then rolled carefully up to a sitting position.

Ani chirruped questioningly from a nest of blankets beside him, and he reached over to rub her head. "Hey sweetheart," he whispered. "Sleep well?"

She sidled closer, purring, her bulbous eyes watching him pleadingly, and he grinned, shaking his head at her. "Come on then, let's see if we can find something for you to eat."

He tucked the blankets up around Istvay gently, and they stirred but didn't wake as Aran pushed himself carefully to his feet.

Someone had left a plate of food outside the door to his and Istvay's cabin, an assortment of foods that Aran couldn't readily identify—three cuts of meat, one raw, one medium-rare, and one cooked to approximately the consistency of charcoal, along with a variety of other fruits and vegetables, most of them split neatly into cooked, raw, and charcoaled lumps.

He bit back a small grin. He was willing to bet the scientist had provided this particular tray.

He pulled out his scanner and did a basic scan of the fruits and vegetables. At least three of them seemed edible, and they could almost certainly eat the meat—the scientist had said he and Istvay were the first humans she'd seen, so he wouldn't be committing cannibalism, at the very least. He tasted a couple of the items, and if they tasted halfway palatable he set them aside for Istvay. Ani helped herself to anything he didn't eat, although she didn't touch the burnt food—that was apparently too much even for her.

When he glanced back, Istvay had opened their eyes and was watching him. Aran managed a small smile and came over to sit next to them.

"Here, none of these should kill you," he said, pushing the tray over to them.

Istvay sat up, then groaned. "Hell. I feel like someone ran into me with a damn transport."

Aran grinned. "Well, I mean, you crashed an escape pod into a forest then spent the next three days running for your life, so …"

Istvay groaned again and picked up one of the pieces of fruit. "Don't remind me. Please. I'm doing my best to wipe the last three days from my memory."

Aran laughed, trying not to think of his conversation with Yosip the previous evening.

It would be fine. The others probably wouldn't need him and Istvay after all.

Istvay shook their head, chuckling reluctantly, and took another piece of fruit.

A loud pounding at the door made Aran jump. The door swung open before either he or Istvay had time to react, and the raider captain stepped in, grinning broadly.

"Aran! Istvay! Ani! Slept well, I hope?"

"Um, yes, we——" Aran began.

"Good, good!" The raider captain was grinning even broader now, his sharp canines glittering in the artificial light. "Come, let me show you around before I take you over to our scientist friend. I'd hate for you to go somewhere you shouldn't, and be killed—Dessi would never forgive me."

Aran and Istvay exchanged glances. Istvay gave a small shrug, and the two of them stood and followed the captain, Ani scrambling onto her accustomed place on Aran's shoulder.

"… and this, here, is our cockpit. I understand you humans travel in space as well?"

"Um, yes," said Aran warily.

"Good, good, we'll make sure we take you out with us on trips. And over here is where the crew bunks. Their places are sorted out by how many kills they have. A raider kill counts twice as much as a yibo kill and three times as much as a human." He glanced over at them quickly, and added in a placating tone, "But don't feel bad. I may have to revise humans to the same level as a yibo after meeting the three of you."

Aran had to bite back a laugh at the look on Istvay's face.

"What are those?" asked Istvay, gesturing.

The captain glanced over. "Ah. These are the key chips to the attack pods. The pods are in a clearing closer to the foot of the mountain—I leave my ship there, usually, but I wanted to come say hello to Dessi. But don't touch them. I don't want you leaving the clearing without my permission. As I said, Dessi would be so angry if

I killed you."

"You've—known Dessi for a long time, then," said Aran warily.

The captain roared with laughter and slapped him on the shoulder. Aran flinched back at the unexpected touch, and Ani growled.

The captain laughed. "Now, now. I thought you were brave. Best get used to—"

He reached out to slap Aran on the shoulder again, and Aran grabbed for Ani and hunched his shoulders, bracing himself …

Istvay stepped forward quickly, catching the captain's wrist. "Don't touch him unless you ask him first," they said, something steely in their voice.

The captain blinked at Istvay in utter bewilderment. Then his face darkened. "How dare you grab my arm? I'm the captain here. I—"

Aran glanced quickly between the captain and Istvay and took a firm grip on Ani, ready to jump between his friend and the captain. From the look on Istvay's face, Aran wasn't completely sure which of them he'd be protecting from the other.

Istvay took a deep breath. "*Please* don't touch him unless you ask first, then," they said, sounding like they were forcing out the words. "It … causes him a great deal of stress. I didn't want you to inadvertently harm him, and upset Dessi."

The captain stared at Istvay for a moment. Then he chuckled, and Aran's shoulders dropped in relief.

"You're right, best not to upset Dessi. I'm very sorry, then, Istvay," he said, good humour seemingly restored. "I had no intention of harming your Aran."

Aran's heart jumped a little at, "your Aran," but he forced his expression neutral.

"I'll tell the crew, then, if that's the case," Krevai continued. "We want to make sure we treat our humans with nothing but respect." He turned back to Istvay. "Anything else I should know?"

"It's, um, it's really not that important—" Aran began, but Istvay shot him a glare.

"He doesn't like loud noises, and he doesn't like crowds, and he doesn't like being touched without permission," said Istvay. "And he doesn't like space travel."

"Ah. That is very good information," said the captain, eyebrows creasing into a small frown. "I'll make a note of it." He reached into a pocket and pulled out a tablet, tapped it, and began writing something with the tip of his finger.

Aran stared at Istvay, and then at the captain, in frank astonishment. Istvay looked just as nonplussed as he felt.

The captain finished his note, tucked the tablet back into his pocket, then beamed at the two of them. "I'll ensure the crew knows this. And if they don't respect you, you have my permission to set your Ani on them."

"Um," began Aran in alarm. "It's really not that big of a—"

The captain had already started off again.

"Captain," said Istvay at last, as the captain led them through the ship with what seemed like utter delight. "This portal. Dessi said something about you going through it and killing humans on the other side."

The captain turned in surprise, pausing mid-sentence. "Yes," he said at last. "That's the plan. Captain Sharda took the portal down because she wanted to give us a chance to get through before the yibo, or at least not too long after. The last time they opened a portal through to a human settlement, it was only those of us who were in range and happened to see it who were able to go through." He shrugged. "It wasn't fruitless—I'd say we took a few hundred thousand humans—but it certainly wasn't what it could have been. So this time when we saw the portal opening, Sharda took it down to give herself time to spread the word to the rest of the raider ships. This way, we can all go in when they're ready to reopen it." He gestured around. "We raiders generally live on our ships as crews, as Dessi told you. But this moon here is where we come when we need to be planetside for a while, to pick up supplies or find mates or whatever. There are cities here, and we all make it back here eventually. She knew that, given enough time, we could ensure that most of the raider ships knew and were waiting."

Aran blinked, the horror of what Krevai had just said sinking in. "You—" he began at last, his voice shaky. "You—killed that many humans?"

He felt sick to his stomach.

The captain shrugged. "It's not like we didn't treat them well. The yibo destroyed their planet and kept the survivors caged up. We let them run free, and just took the ones we were going to use. If we lay first claim to the planet, the yibo won't dare, so really, it's better for everyone."

"But—but you killed—"

Krevai frowned. "I didn't realize you'd find it so disturbing. Surely humans kill each other too? And besides, sometimes there are humans we take a liking to, and they sign on with our crew, just like you're doing. Dessi even claims we have some human DNA, so we're a little related."

Aran took a deep breath, trying to push back the horror. "Captain," he said quietly. "What would it take to convince you not to do that?"

There was a long moment of silence. The raider captain studied him, still frowning. "Not—" he began, as if not entirely sure what

Aran was asking.

"Not go through the portal. Close down the mechanism again. Not wipe out the humans. Surely there's something you want, something we could offer you—"

The captain was still frowning. "Do you—do you have family back there?"

"Not family, no," said Istvay grimly. "But friends. People we care about. And we'd just as soon not see them hunted for food."

The captain's face cleared. "Ah. Is that all?" He paused, then took a breath, as if preparing himself to offer something priceless. "Istvay. Aran. I like you two. And you're part of my crew. So, if you have specific humans you'd like us not to kill, tell me their names, and I'll do my best to arrange for something. And you don't need to worry about yourselves—you have friends here now." He gestured expansively around the ship. "Every one of my crew would put themselves in the way of a shot for you—or if they wouldn't, they know they'll be facing a shot from me." He laughed. "Besides, it's not like there aren't other colonies of humans, so you're not an endangered species or anything, whatever Dessi and her little theories say. So no need to worry—you give me a list of your friends, and we'll figure out a way to identify them."

He strode off, and Aran and Istvay had no choice but to follow. They glanced at each other, and Aran could see the horror in Istvay's face, but the captain was clearly not open to further conversation on the subject.

"… and here we are at last," said Krevai, ducking out the hatch of the ship. "You've eaten this morning, yes? Good. I promised Dessi I'd hand you over to her the moment I finished our tour."

Aran's protest died on his lips, a quick jolt of hope starting in his chest.

From the corner of his eye, he could see the sudden tension in Istvay's expression.

He swallowed hard.

He couldn't even tally how long his fear for Istvay had been tickling at the back of his brain, never quite letting him relax.

Almost as long as he could remember. Probably since he'd seen Istvay's mother die. The genetics of the defect weren't that straightforward, and he'd known that the fact Istvay's mother had it didn't necessarily mean Istvay would as well. But the fear had started back then. The terror of 'what if.'

And then, around three years ago, that niggling fear had bloomed into full-on panic as the first signs of the illness took hold.

Istvay had never spoken about it much. Istvay had always been stoic and matter-of-fact about their condition, about the fact they were going to die and there was nothing either they or Aran could do about it.

But looking at his friend now, Aran knew suddenly that it had all been nothing but an act.

Neither of them spoke as the captain escorted them to the small research station. He pounded on the door, then shoved it open. "Dessi!" he bellowed, then, noticing Aran's unconscious wince at the noise, clapped a hand over his mouth with an expression of alarm that was almost comical.

"Dessi!" he tried again, this time in a hissed, exaggerated whisper.

Aran gave Istvay a rueful glance.

Dessi appeared through a small door in the back of the research station and hurried over. She reached out to grab Istvay by the arm, but the captain stepped quickly in front of them.

"No," he said firmly. "Humans don't like being touched without permission. You have to ask first."

"I don't—it's not—" Istvay began.

Dessi raised her eyebrows in interest. "My studies didn't mention this. Interesting. Is there anything else I should know?"

"I have a list of some of their human preferences," the captain said, a trace of smugness in his voice. "I'll send it to your data pad."

Dessi looked mildly annoyed, but she nodded. "I'd be grateful," she said stiffly. "And I, of course, will send you the results of my studies on their eating and sleeping preferences."

The captain didn't look annoyed in the slightest, just grinned broadly. "Good, good," he said, ducking back out the door with a cheery wave. "I'll leave the three of you to it, then. Four of you, sorry Ani."

Once he was gone, the three of them stared at each other.

"We're—we're his pets, aren't we," said Istvay.

Dessi sighed heavily. "Yes," she said. There was a hint of exasperation in her tone. "I spent hours last night trying to explain that you were sapient species, and that you deserved to be treated with autonomy, and he just grinned and promised of course you would, he wouldn't dream of doing otherwise. But yes. You're his pets. He tried to bring back a charak once, and we only convinced him to get rid of it when it had mind-melded with half the crew and forced a mutiny." She shuddered.

"A charak?" asked Istvay, resigned dread in their tone. "What are —" They shot a quick glance at Aran, and shook their head grimly. "Actually, forget I asked. The less we know about any deadly species that live in this place, the better, probably."

Dessi blew out a breath. "They live in very deep space, so I doubt you'll run into them." She shuddered again. "Which is lucky for you. Anyone who doesn't manage to run into them is lucky. Now then." She stepped back, her gaze running over Aran and Istvay. "Which one of you is the sick one? I'm not sure, because I've never been able to study live human physiology—but I'm assuming the pale skinny one?"

Aran bit down hard on his grin, and Istvay scowled.

"Good," she said brightly. "Then I think the first thing we want to do is draw some blood. I spent last night thinking up a few different tests we could do to figure out the cause of this, but I think this is our first step. First, though, I'll need each of you to step into the isolation chamber for measurements. Ani too, if she'd like, but I'm mostly interested in you two. I'd like to do some base metabolic measurements on a healthy human specimen and an unhealthy one. Oxygen intake, CO_2 output, basic caloric output, so forth."

Istvay narrowed their eyes. "The captain sees us as pets," they said flatly. "But you? You just see us as sapient data-mines."

"No! Of course not! Whatever gives you that idea?" Dessi sounded slightly uncomfortable, and she turned away quickly without meeting their eye.

Istvay muttered a curse under their breath.

Aran, though, couldn't possibly have cared less. If they could find a cure for Istvay, he'd be a sapient data-mine for as long as Dessi wanted.

In the end, Aran persuaded Ani to wait in their cabin after procuring her some food, but once he got back, the baseline observations Dessi insisted on took the rest of the morning. Aran was practically dancing with impatience by the time she beckoned them both through the small door in the back of the research station, and into her lab.

She gestured Istvay to a stool, then she pulled out a small vial with the sharp needle on one end.

She studied Istvay for a moment, her face registering uncertainty, and Aran sighed and stepped forward, kneeling beside his friend.

"This is the easiest way to take blood, generally," he said, taking Istvay's wrist and turning their hand palm up. He glanced at them for permission, then pulled back their shirtsleeve, running his fingers up their forearm to rest on the blue vein at the inside of their elbow.

Istvay shivered, and he glanced up at them in concern.

"It's … chilly in here," said Istvay, scowling.

Aran stood quickly, shrugging out of his jacket, and draped it over his friend's shoulders. "Better?" he whispered, and Istvay gave a grumpy nod.

Aran knelt beside them again, repositioning his hand, and turned back to Dessi, his fingers resting lightly on the inside of Istvay's elbow.

He wasn't sure whether or not the room was actually cold—the adrenaline pumping through his veins was enough to make a thin sheen of sweat form under his hair.

"May I?" he asked. Dessi hesitated, then handed him the vial, coming closer to hover over his shoulder, eyes wide with curiosity.

"Vacuum sealed?" he asked.

She nodded. "It's made for raiders. I don't know how much blood you humans can spare before it affects you, so you'll have to pull it out once we have enough for an analysis."

Aran nodded. "Okay, Pishti, it'll be just a poke …" he mumbled, and with a quick, precise motion, he tapped the small needle into Istvay's vein.

"Clench your fist," he said out of habit, but it was hardly necessary—bright red blood sprayed out in a thin stream, coating the inside of the cylinder and dripping down the sides. Aran waited a couple seconds, then pulled it out with a quick jerk, pressing his finger over the puncture wound to stop the bleeding. He handed the vial to Dessi with his free hand, and she took it, turning to her equipment.

"Let me run a quick DNA analysis," she muttered as she worked. "I had the captain give me a fresh blood sample yesterday as well. I thought having a more recent sample to analyse might be helpful." She turned back to Aran as the machine behind her hummed quietly. "Can you pull up the analysis you did back on your planet, and show me where this defect is located on a human genome map?"

Aran nodded. Carefully, he lifted his pressed fingers from Istvay's arm, checking to make sure the bleeding had stopped.

They were watching him, their eyes dark, jaw clenched as if they were in pain, but they shook their head shortly when he gave them a questioning look.

Aran closed his eyes for a moment, trying to steady his breathing. Then he tapped his palm screen open, paging through to the readout from back on Colorida. "I assume your DNA analysis machines are similar to the ones the yibo use?" he asked, his voice shaking. His heart was pounding far too quickly.

What if he'd been wrong? What if there was no defect to be found in the captain's new blood sample, and it had only been the effects of the faster-than-light travel that had sent the box through to their planet?

"Broadly similar, yes," said Dessi, not seeming to notice his nerves. "The readouts will be more or less the same, if that's what you're worried about."

Aran nodded. "Our readouts are completely different. But I put together a key between the yibo readouts and ours, so I should be able to—" he trailed off in concentration, squinting down at the readout Dessi placed in front of him, comparing it to the painstaking map he'd made from the yibo readout back in the city.

At last he grinned, letting out a long breath. "There. That's it, right there." He expanded the screen and tapped the place.

Dessi frowned down at the section Aran had indicated on the readout, then nodded slowly. "I see it," she said. "That's—not really uncommon in our population—it's a mild genetic abnormality. We've never really tracked it, because it doesn't seem to have any measurable effect on health, but I'd say at a guess it's present in ten to fifteen percent of the population."

Behind her, the machine beeped, and she turned. She crossed over to it, tapped her data pad to the screen, and brought it over, placing it on the small lab table.

"Alright," she said, leaning over it beside Aran. "This is your friend's readout." She glanced at him. "You don't have this—genetic abnormality, do you?"

Aran shook his head.

"Good. I'll take a sample from you as well, then, so we've got a control. We'll see if we can determine why this is deadly to humans, and not to raiders. That should at least give us a starting point."

Istvay had stood up from the stool and was leaning against the doorframe, hands in their pockets. Their head was tipped back, and they were staring blankly at a point where the wall of the lab met the ceiling.

Aran could read the tension in every line of their posture.

Normally, they'd be peering over his shoulder—or more likely, they'd be the one talking excitedly about the results with Dessi. They'd always been more interested in the laboratory analysis aspect of things than Aran had.

"Pishti?" Aran asked quietly, once he'd handed the raider scientist the vial half-full of his own blood and she'd turned back to the machine. "Why don't you go outside for a bit, look around? It wouldn't hurt for us to have a sense of where we are."

Istvay turned to glare at him. "I know what you're doing, Aran. I don't need to be babied."

Aran grinned a little. "Okay, fine. But it wouldn't hurt to get our bearings, either way." He paused. "Besides, you're making me so nervous that I had to try three times to get the vein when I was giving my blood sample, and now I'm going to have a bruise."

Istvay narrowed their eyes at him, then sighed. "I suppose you're right," they said at last, ruefully. "Fine. I'll go."

Aran put a hand on their shoulder and gave them a reassuring squeeze. "Pishti," he said in a low voice. "I promise. I'll do everything I can do. Everything."

Istvay studied him for a few moments, their eyes unreadable. At last they reached up, putting their hand over Aran's. "I know you will," they said quietly.

Then they turned and stepped out the door.

Aran looked after them for a long moment. Finally he turned back to the lab table, bending over the data sheets again.

His stomach was tight, every muscle in his body tense.

This might be his only chance.

He wasn't naïve enough to think they'd simply stumble across a cure the first time they took the time to look. But if Yosip called again tonight, he had to at least have gotten far enough to know what data he'd need to take with him when they left.

"Alright," said Dessi, coming over with the new readout. "Do you have a genome map accessible? Let's get started comparing the human map with the raiders'."

Aran had no idea how long it had been when he went to pull up and merge the next batch in the endless sequence prepared by the program, and realized he'd reached the end of the list.

He stared blankly down at the long line of notes on his palmscreen, until Dessi crossed over to him in concern.

"Aran?" she asked. "Is there something wrong?"

He shook his head, still in a daze.

A comparative map of the raider and human genome.

If there was a key to saving Istvay, he was holding it right now in his battered palmscreen.

"Are you sure you're alright? Aran?" Dessi's voice seemed to come from a long way away.

He blinked, reaching out to steady himself on the table. "Yes," he said, his voice breaking slightly. "Yes, I'm fine."

A faint nausea churned in his stomach, and he felt lightheaded, his legs almost too unsteady to hold him.

"Well. I think that's enough for today anyway," said Dessi briskly. "We can't really do anything further until I feed your data into the machine and we can do a clean analysis on the samples." She paused. "Are you in pain? What's the matter?"

Aran chuckled weakly, wiping his eyes with the back of his hand. "No, I'm fine. It's just—I just didn't think—I never thought I'd be able to—" he found he couldn't continue.

Dessi pulled out her data pad and jotted something down, probably a note about human habits around crying.

He honestly couldn't care less.

"I'm—I'm going to tell Istvay how far we got," he said, and turned quickly to the door.

"Wait! Wait, are you hungry? I've put together some samples based off your selections this morning—" her voice faded behind him as he half-jogged out of the lab and into the open clearing.

The clearing was large, but he knew Istvay well enough that it didn't take him long to track them down.

They were seated at the base of an old tree just outside the clearing, leaned up against the trunk where the tangled roots made a small hollow. Their head jerked up at his approach, but they didn't turn, just sat where they were, staring straight ahead. They were twisting a small twig absently between their fingers, their jaw clenched tight.

Aran came over without speaking and dropped down beside them. He leaned back against the tree, and for a while the two of them sat in silence.

At last, Aran reached out and caught the twig Istvay was twisting.

Their hand stilled, but they didn't turn.

"Pishti," he said.

And then he found he couldn't speak at all, his throat too tight, tears stinging at his eyes, his chest constricting so he could hardly breathe.

Istvay turned quickly, the tension in their face overlaid with sudden concern. "Aran," they said. "Listen, it's fine. I didn't expect —I never expected that we'd be able to—look, it's fine if we can't—" They shifted to face him, putting their hands on his shoulders like they always did when they were trying to reassure him.

Aran shook his head, managing a trembling smile. "Pishti, no," he choked. "That's not it. I … Dessi had the information we needed, and we were able to compile a comparative genome map. We can feed her blood and mine in for controls, and we should be able to … I think we'll be able to … Pishti. I never thought we'd be this close. I never thought—" He broke off, unable to say anymore.

Istvay had stilled, their face gone bloodless. They turned away quickly, dropping their face into their hands. "Aran—"

"Pishti," he whispered. "Pishti, I think we're going to be able to figure this out."

By the time Dessi tracked the two of them down, carrying a tray of food, Istvay had brought themself under control again. Their face was still ghastly pale, but they managed a smile of thanks as they took the food.

Dessi, it appeared, had decided to further her research by sitting and watching them eat while she took notes, and after the hours she'd spent in the lab with him, Aran could hardly bring himself to complain. So, with a rueful glance at each other, Aran and Istvay ate in silence.

"Alright," she said when they'd finished. "I'm going to let some more analyses run overnight, and tomorrow morning we can get to work again. In the meantime, you can wander around if you'd like, or you can get some rest. I told the captain to leave you alone."

Istvay still wasn't speaking by the time they and Aran got back to their room on the ship. They looked like they were in shock.

"Pishti?" asked Aran cautiously. "Pishti, listen—"

Istvay took a deep breath and attempted a smile, although their face was still very, very pale. "Sorry," they said. "I'm—I'm fine, I promise, just—" they squeezed their eyes closed, blinking back tears.

Aran came over to sit beside them, putting an arm around their shoulders. "Pishti," he said quietly. And Istvay leaned against him, and dropped their head into their hands again, and cried.

The lights had gone out on the ship, and the restless exhilaration from the day's efforts was starting to fade from Aran's tight muscles enough for him to think about lying down, when there was a buzz through his wavelink.

He glanced down at it, his stomach tightening suddenly in worry, rather than excitement.

"Yosip?" he whispered, tapping his wrist to activate it.

"Aran." Yosip paused a moment. "I'm … I'm very sorry. But it looks like there's no way we can do this without the two of you."

20

Savina

When they heard the footsteps of the guards approaching the next afternoon, Reka turned to glance at Savina, who was stretched out on the cot.

"Be careful," she said in a low voice. "Kachik is more dangerous than he looks."

Savina smiled lazily up at her. "Reka! Worried about me? So you do like me, after all!"

Reka smirked, reaching into the pocket of her suit and pulling out a small electronic device. "In your dreams. Here, I stole this off one of the soldiers I killed." She tossed it at Savina. "It should let you pick the lock and open a doorway, but I can't promise anything."

Savina almost didn't see the device, too distracted by the mesmerizing grace of Reka's movements, and barely snatched it out of the air before it hit the ground.

She scowled.

It wasn't fair of Reka to be this attractive. If she'd been bad at what she did, it would have been one thing, but it simply wasn't fair that she was this good at everything, and this stupidly hot at the same time.

"Savina?"

She blinked out of her reverie. Reka was watching her, a dry smile on her lips—dammit, why was she looking at Reka's lips?

Savina looked up at her, pouting prettily. "I don't know why you're so mean to me all the time."

"Because you're a thief and a murderer without a single redeeming quality?" said Reka dryly. "Focus on the job, Savina."

Savina narrowed her eyes and gave Reka a sweet smile. "I'm always focused, sweetheart."

The glance Reka shot her was … more amused than furious.

Savina closed her eyes, and refused to think about the way that small, barely-there grin made something tighten pleasantly in the pit of her stomach.

The guards arrived a few moments later, and Savina let her breathing go slow and soft.

"Shhh. She's asleep," Reka whispered as the guards pushed the door open, gesturing towards Savina. "She was upset after what happened yesterday, so I told her to take some time to recover."

Her tone was so concerned that Savina almost frowned.

There was clearly someone, somewhere, that Reka cared about deeply, for this concern to come so naturally to her. And Savina realized, yet again, that she knew next to nothing about Reka Soler.

Reka slipped out the door after the guards, and Savina waited until she couldn't hear footsteps in the corridor any longer.

Then she sat up and made her way over to the door.

She listened at it for a few moments, then carefully picked the lock. It was more complicated than Reka had made it look, and she was swearing steadily under her breath by the time the cell door swung gently open.

She pulled up the map of the building that Reka had sent through on her wavelink and studied it for a moment, then stepped out into the hallway. She crept down the corridors, always keeping near the wall so she could slip into a cross-hallway if necessary.

The hallways were all but empty, which probably meant the yibo bureaucrats were busy doing—whatever they did in their meeting rooms. Savina had never had much time for politics, besides learning the names and likely locations of whoever she'd been hired to kill.

It took her almost half an hour to get to the room she and Reka had identified the night before. When she reached it, she ducked behind a decorative plant, breathing heavily. Six flights of stairs were more than anyone should be expected to climb, for any reason.

Her muscles were tense with a mix of anticipation and terror.

Why had she agreed to this again? She was having a hard time remembering.

Because her kidnapping victim had asked nicely? Because she was trying to prove something to a woman who wanted to kill her?

For half a second, she heard Joska's measured voice through her earpiece, the concern in it. The confidence, probably unmerited, that Savina could handle whatever she got herself into.

Damn it to hell.

Savina closed her eyes, steeling herself. Then she straightened, stepped briskly out of her hiding place, and strode towards the conference room door.

The guards turned in surprise at her approach, raising their weapons, and Savina batted her eyelashes at them. "I'm so sorry, I'm lost, and I don't know where I'm going. Can you—"

One of the guards heaved a sigh of exasperation and started towards her, lowering his weapon and beckoning to his companion.

She stood still, waiting as they approached, a look of confusion on her face.

And then, as the first guard grabbed her arm, she reached down, snatched the gun from his other hand, and shot him in the face.

He disintegrated at the weapon fire. His companion let out a shout of alarm, and Savina whirled and shot her as well.

She could hear footsteps in the hallway, a reaction to the guard's shout. She smiled grimly to herself and stepped up to the conference room door, pulled out the electronic device Reka had loaned her, and slid it across the glass.

The glass melted.

She stepped through the opening, holding the gun with both hands. She kept a look of frightened bewilderment on her face, and as one of the yibo politicians stood, she turned the weapon, firing at the column beside them.

The column melted. The politician screamed, and Savina let out a startled shriek, dropping the weapon. She raised her hands, babbling something meaningless.

Her heart was pounding.

She hated being helpless. She was used to looking the part, an act to lure her marks into complacency—but actually being trapped, wholly dependent on her captors' mercy, was a sick, ugly feeling.

She forced herself to stay still, not to dive for the gun she'd dropped.

Two yibo guards grabbed her roughly, shoving her to the floor, and she whimpered, tears welling in her eyes. "I'm—I'm sorry, I'm so sorry, I was just trying to find my girlfriend—"

Had she come to the right place? Reka had told her she'd be in a room on this same hallway, but how the hell would Reka know that? It would have been a guess at best, and damn it, Savina knew better than to trust someone who wanted to kill her ...

The guards pulled her hands behind her back and secured them tightly, then yanked her to her feet.

Tears were rolling down her cheeks, her eyes wide and frightened. "Please, I'm so sorry, I really didn't mean—"

There was a shout from outside—apparently someone had found the two in the hallway.

"She killed two guards," Savina's wavelink translated. "She's not some helpless human."

"I thought she was supposed to be harmless!" one of the politicians was shouting angrily. "I thought it was that Soler woman we had to worry about. Who is this girlfriend?"

The yibo ambassador, Harroch, stood from his seat at the head of the room, where he'd been talking to a human man who must be Captain Mattin. The yibo's face was tight with anger, and Savina couldn't help a small prickle of satisfaction in her chest at the sight.

"I have no idea," Harroch said in yibo, his voice low and dangerous. "But she's going back to her cell, and Reka is going to have some explaining to do." He gestured with the tip of his tail. "Get these other humans out of here. I'll deal with this."

Savina was still whimpering, trembling with fear when Harroch strode over to her.

It was an act, mostly. But her stomach twisted at the expression on his face.

"Who the hell do you think you are?" he snapped in Common Dialect, once the remainder of the humans were out of the room. "Why did you kill my guards? Where's Reka?"

From the doorway, there was a shout, abruptly cut off. Harroch's head jerked up, and Savina let out a short, quick breath of relief.

"It's—" Savina's wavelink translated another guard's shout, then that guard, too, went silent.

The glass melted open, and Reka stepped through. She looked as sleek and deadly as a jungle cat, not a hair out of place, her eyes cold and her expression deadly.

She took in the room quickly, then spun the gun in her hand, using it like a billy-club to knock aside a swath of yibo guards.

One of them made the mistake of bringing their weapon up, and was dead before he'd managed to bring it level.

"Take your hands off my girlfriend," hissed Reka, her voice cold and sharp as a knife edge.

The guards holding Savina stared, uncertainty on their faces.

Reka didn't waste her breath asking a second time, just brought up her weapon.

"What in the system—" Savina's wavelink translated, then Kachik, who'd stumbled in behind Reka, snapped, "Let her go!"

The guards jumped back with impressive alacrity, and Savina stumbled, falling to her knees on the floor.

She dropped her head to her chest, sobbing quietly. Reka was over to her in two strides and dropped down beside her, her arms going tenderly around Savina's shoulders.

Savina refused to think about the way her body responded to Reka's touch.

"Are you hurt?" Reka's voice was quiet enough Savina was the only one who could hear it, and thick with real concern.

Savina managed a faint shake of her head. Reka gave her shoulders a gentle squeeze, then looked up, glaring at Kachik.

"What the hell is this?" she snapped. "You promised she'd be safe if I left her in the cell. And now I find this? What exactly are you trying to do?"

Harroch drew in a deep breath, as if trying very hard to control his temper. "Your girlfriend," he said, ice in his tone, "shot two of our guards, came bursting in here, fired a gun that took out one of the pillars, and sent this entire section of the building into lockdown. We had to cut off negotiations for the second day in a row. I, too, would like to know what the hell is going on."

"Savina?" Reka's voice, now that it was loud enough to be overheard, was gentle.

Savina swallowed the stupid lump in her throat. "I—I was just—" she sniffled. "I woke up and you were gone, and I was afraid to be left all by myself because I know the guards don't like me, and—" she broke off, her voice trembling. "Anyway, I know they don't like me, but they respect you, Reka. So I thought—I didn't want to bother anyone, so I thought I'd just go find you myself."

There was a long moment of silence. At last, Kachik turned to stare at her. "You thought shooting two guards and bursting into our main conference room was a good way to find Reka." His voice was flat and disbelieving.

"No," Savina sobbed. "I'm not stupid! I just—I got lost, and then —and then your guards pulled their gun on me, and I went to grab it away because I didn't want to get shot, and—and the gun went off, and it was awful, and—"

Everyone was staring at her now, their expressions registering total disbelief.

"You killed two of our guards on accident." Kachik's voice was even flatter than before. "You want me to believe this?"

"I don't know what you believe. I don't care what you believe, just don't hurt me. They tried to shoot me, Reka, they were going to shoot me—" She buried her face in Reka's shoulder.

Reka put a comforting arm around her, pulling her close, and Savina nestled into her shoulder. Her body was still shaking, and something about Reka's grip was more soothing than she'd like to admit.

"You're making her cry." There was a hard menace in Reka's tone. "I would appreciate it if you would stop."

Kachik took another long breath. "Savina," he said at last, through his teeth. "If there is something that you need, you are more than welcome to ask the guards. You don't have to let them in if you're afraid of them, you can just call through the door. You are not, however, welcome to go wandering about the government buildings by yourself. You could have been hurt very badly if things had gone differently."

Savina gave a terrified little whimper.

Reka glowered at Kachik.

"And you, Reka," he hissed, turning to her. "You'd better figure out how to either control your girlfriend, or give her a milligram of common sense."

"I'm not stupid!" Savina sobbed. "I was only trying to—" she broke off.

Reka's arm around her tightened. "You do not call my girlfriend stupid."

Kachik stared in disbelief. "You." He said after a moment. "You just said yourself, just the other day—"

"I am telling you, for the last time—do not make Savina cry." Reka's voice was icy.

There was a long, long moment where no one spoke.

All of the yibo politicians were staring at them.

Savina sobbed harder.

Finally, Kachik turned to Savina, his teeth gritted. "I—am sorry," he said, as if forcing the words out.

Savina blinked at him, then up at Reka.

Reka gave her a soft smile, reaching down to wipe the tears from her cheeks. Her fingers were rough and warm, and even though it was just an act, the touch felt almost frighteningly intimate. "There now, Savina," she said. "He apologized. No need to cry."

Savina sniffled, trying very hard to fight back the ridiculous heat in her chest.

"Now," Reka said coldly, turning back to Kachik. "Now that you've finished terrorizing my poor girlfriend, may we please go back to our cell? We'll have to finish our conversation tomorrow. I can't possibly leave Savina alone after all that. I thought this was supposed to be a straightforward arrangement when I agreed to it."

Kachik mumbled something under his breath, which Savina's wavelink translated as, "So did I." But he just gave Reka a small, forced smile that was wearier than it had been the day before.

It looked, Savina thought with some satisfaction, like he hadn't slept well recently.

"Yes," he said. "Let's get you back to your cells."

Reka gave a dignified nod. "That would be appreciated."

Kachik turned to Harroch. "I'm sorry," Savina's AI translated. "Reka is still too useful to kill, which means we can't kill Savina. You can have the cell guards killed, though. They know better than to let either of these two out of their sight."

"I'll do that," said Harroch. He still sounded furious. "And now I'm going to spend hours trying to reassure that stupid human captain and his friends again."

Kachik's tail twitched in a dismissive gesture. "Once we get him and his pet soldiers on a ship and back through the portal, things should be easier. We'll kill the rest of the humans as soon as they're gone—we can kill them as a group in their sleep if we're in a hurry, or if you think the people could use a morale boost, you can bring them out and shoot them one by one in front of the government buildings. It's just a matter of getting the captain and the others through the portal, and if what you're telling me is correct, we're close. But in the meantime, I still need Reka, and she's made it clear she's only going to cooperate if we treat the other one gently. So we're stuck with her for the time being."

"She's not as innocent as she looks," Harroch hissed. "There's no way she killed two guards on accident."

"I know." Kachik's look was wry. "But I'll kill her later. When it's more convenient. I'm just asking you to hold things together until then. How close are we?"

Harroch sighed. "Before this happened, I'd be able to tell you for certain. This—" he gestured at Savina and Reka, "may have thrown things off, but before it happened, he was willing to start through the portal as early as tonight. I suspect it will be longer now, since I'll have to placate him, but still … I'd estimate no more than a day or two."

"That's good news," said Kachik. "I have every confidence in your ability."

Savina's entire body felt very, very cold.

A guard stepped forward, reaching for Savina's hands, and Savina gave a little gasp.

Reka turned, and the guard jumped backwards.

"Don't—" Reka began.

"Touch your girlfriend, I know," Kachik finished in resignation, switching back to Common Dialect. "Perhaps it would be best if you took the restraints off Savina yourself."

He gestured to the guard, who handed the unlocking mechanism to Reka. Reka worked deftly, her strong fingers finding and unlocking the restraints, and Savina sighed in shaky relief as they dropped free.

Her heart was pounding, her mind racing almost too quickly for her to keep up.

With Reka shooting threatening glances at the guards, who stayed well behind them, she and Reka made their way to the cell without incident.

Savina stumbled once, and Reka caught her automatically, depositing her back on her feet before she could fall. She frowned at Savina in concern, but Savina shook her head, and Reka turned her gaze forward once more.

When they were back in the cell, the doors closed behind them, Savina dropped to the ground, sagging back against the cell wall.

"Savina."

She glanced up, startled. Reka was crouched beside her.

"What the hell do you want?" Savina snapped. Her arm throbbed where the yibo guard had jerked it around, and there were tears that were desperate to well in her eyes.

Reka was looking at her, her strange hazel-grey eyes catching Savina's and holding them. Her face was lined with weariness, and there was tension written across her expression, but her gaze was dark with concern. "Savina. Are you hurt?"

"I'm not ... I'm not hurt." Savina tried to make her voice sharp, but it came out more of a squeak.

Reka frowned and ran a hand down Savina's arm, and Savina shivered at the touch, then winced as Reka's fingers reached the place where the guard had twisted her arm. Reka's frown deepened, and she tugged Savina's sleeve up gently.

"That looks like it hurts." She ran the tips of her fingers over the reddened skin, and again Savina shivered at the touch. "I'll put a bandage on it."

Savina snatched her arm out of the woman's grip, scowling. "Don't bother. We're not actually lovers, remember?"

Reka sighed. "I haven't forgotten. But we still need to make the guards think I can stand being around you. So sit still and shut up." She turned away brusquely, reaching down for something to wrap Savina's arm with.

Savina blinked savagely. "Anyway, that's not our biggest problem, sweetheart." She put as much spite as she could into the word. "We're damn well out of time. They're going to open the portal any moment—it would have been tonight, if it wasn't for what we just did."

Reka stared at her. "Are you sure? What did they——"

Savina shot her a humourless smile. "They're also going to kill me and every other human here once they get Captain Mattin and his friends on the ships. Murder them in their sleep or shoot them in front of the government building is the plan. They might let me live until we reach Colorida again, Kachik didn't specify."

Reka's face had gone stony, her lips pinched into a tight line. "You're sure of this?" she said at last, the words sharp as knives.

Savina nodded silently.

Reka closed her eyes for a moment. When she opened them again, her expression was set and hard, like it always had been before. When they'd been trying to kill each other.

"Alright, then," she said, in her dispassionate voice. "Your friends won't get to the portal mechanism in time, so our first goal has to be getting the rest of the humans to safety. Then we can think of a different plan to shut down the portal."

Savina narrowed her eyes. "What are you talking about? My baby brother is on his way to help shut down the portal mechanism right now. If we don't help him, he dies."

"And if you don't listen to me, hundreds of people die," Reka snapped. "Savina, I'm honestly sorry about your brother. But you said it yourself—it's too late. There are hundreds of people out there. We can't let them get slaughtered. We have to change the plan."

Savina took a deep breath. Her heart was pounding so quickly she was almost dizzy with it, and she felt vaguely sick to her stomach, but those seemed like distant problems, something happening to someone else. "If you decide not to help me," she said lightly, "I'll make sure Kachik kills both of us, right here, tonight."

Reka turned to look at her, her face blank with shock.

"I'll do it," said Savina. "He's going to kill me anyways, he said so. And I'll make him kill you, too, right here, locked up in this cell. You won't save the rest of the humans either way. I won't let you."

"Savina." Reka's voice was sharp with a mixture of fury and disbelief. "You'd sacrifice hundreds of people on the off-chance you might help your brother? At the very least, we have to warn them."

Savina pushed herself to her feet, and tried to ignore the hurt and betrayal in Reka's expression.

It didn't matter. They were enemies. It didn't matter what Reka thought.

"You said it yourself, Reka—I'm a thief and a murderer, without a single redeeming quality. I burned five people alive, when I was twelve years old. I tricked them into a house, and then I locked the door and set the whole place on fire and listened to them scream as they burned, because they would have killed my baby brother. One of them was my aunt, another was my uncle."

Reka was still staring at her with that mix of loathing and shock.

Savina gave her a tight, mocking smile. "So if you think I would hesitate, for one second, to let every damn human on this planet burn, you don't know me at all. Your choice, Reka Soler. We stick with the plan we agreed on, or we both die tonight, for nothing."

Something shuttered over Reka's eyes, her face going once more blank and expressionless. "Do you have any idea how long it would take your friends to get the mechanism taken down, assuming they could do it?" she asked at last.

"I have no idea," Savina spat. "It's my two baby siblings, a stupid cargo captain and her crew, and a bunch of geriatrics. Longer than tomorrow, anyway."

Reka nodded, her gaze distant. "Alright. If that's our only option, we'll do it." She glanced over at Savina. "So after everything, you're exactly the heartless murderer I thought you were when I first got your warrant."

Savina's heart was pounding, her hands shaking with a mix of helplessness and anger.

"Oh, Reka," she said, her voice mockingly sweet. "I thought you'd have learned that a long time ago. I leave the people who think they see some good in me bleeding out on the street, remember?"

Reka's expression was frigid. "You're right," she said in a distant tone, turning away. "I was forgetting."

21

Aran

Aran stared blankly at the walls of the cabin. "I—Yosip, I can't leave right now. We've—were just starting to figure out a cure. I spent all day with a raider scientist, and she thinks there's a possibility—"

"I understand," said Yosip quietly. He hesitated. "Aran. I can't tell you to give this up. I know you've been searching for it your whole life. And goodness knows we'll all be more than grateful for the cure if we ever get it back home. But—this is the entire Joias System at stake. And I don't know anyone else we can turn to." He paused. "I can't make you do this. And I can understand why you wouldn't want to. But ... we don't have anyone else."

Aran glanced over. Istvay had sat up and was watching him.

"Aran," they began in a low voice. "If it's the fate of the Joias System—"

"Just a minute," said Aran tersely into his wavelink.

He tapped it off, and turned to face Istvay.

"Aran—" they began again.

Aran shook his head. He crossed over and sat down in front of them cross-legged on the pile of blankets. "I promised you that I'd do whatever it took to get you that cure. But … but I also promised you—promised myself—that I wouldn't make decisions that affect both of us all on my own, and just expect you to come along. So." He looked up, catching Istvay's gaze. "Yosip said he and Alba and whatever's left of the diplomatic corps are trying to destroy the mechanism that opens the portal. They think that would save the Joias System. It means the rest of us are stranded here, but quite frankly, I don't care about that. If you're here—if you're here and we find a cure—I don't care where we end up. But he says they can't do it without us. Which means—" He hesitated, drawing in a deep breath. "Which means, we would have to find the cure just from the information we have, or what we can gather in the next day or so. So. What do you think?"

Istvay was staring at him, mouth half-open in shock.

Aran grinned weakly. "Pishti. Was I really that bad when we were back with the yibo?"

At last, Istvay managed a small, wry chuckle. "Aran. You'll have to stop shocking me like this, or I'm going to die from a heart attack before we have time to find a cure." For a few moments, they were silent. "I made a promise, too," they said finally. "I promised you that I would take this seriously. That I'd stop being a self-sacrificing idiot, I think you called me. But—" They shook their head, and even in the dim light Aran could see the strain on their face. "But this is the entire system at stake. More lives than either of us can count. And I'd never be able to live with myself knowing I survived only because they died." Istvay took a deep breath. "I want this cure. I want it more than I can possibly explain to you. But—but we can't leave this." Their voice choked.

Aran nodded quietly.

Istvay took another deep breath. "I suggest we sneak out tonight, see if it's even possible. The captain isn't going to let us go without a fight, and neither will Dessi, if I read her correctly. But just maybe, if we can find the attack pods and they're not too heavily guarded, it's just possible we can make an escape. And tomorrow, we can—" they swallowed hard. "We'll get all the information we can from Dessi, and maybe it'll be enough we can keep working on a cure without her help." They tried to grin. "We've done more with less information before now."

Aran watched them for a minute. He had to bite down hard on his teeth to keep his jaw from trembling.

But Istvay was right. He knew them well enough for that. If he told Yosip no, even if he found the cure, Istvay would blame themself for what had happened until their dying day.

And he'd promised himself. He'd sworn it. He was going to do whatever he needed to do to see Istvay happy.

At last, he managed a nod. "Are you—are you sure you're alright with us leaving?"

Istvay grinned a little, although their face was pale. "In the twenty-something years we've known each other, I think you know that I'm not usually very coy when I disagree with something."

Aran gave a snort of laughter despite himself, and Istvay's grin widened.

"I guess … I guess I'll call Yosip back, then," Aran said.

Istvay nodded without speaking.

The two of them waited a little longer, until any noise from the ship had died away. Then Aran lifted Ani onto his shoulder, crept to the door of their cabin, and tried the handle.

It opened easily, and he turned to Istvay, raising an eyebrow, and pulled the door gently ajar.

The hallway outside was deserted, and it was easy enough work to creep through the empty corridors and down the open hatch until the two of them were standing on the soft ground of the clearing, Ani still perched on Aran's shoulder.

The night air was cool and smelled of moonlight and evergreens, and Aran closed his eyes and breathed it in.

"It's been a while, hasn't it?" whispered Istvay. "I mean, since we've been outside at night and not been running for our lives."

The two of them crept quietly out of the clearing, back to Dessi's makeshift trail that led down the side of the mountain.

Aran shivered involuntarily at the memory of the last time he and Istvay had stood on the trail—injured, exhausted, at the end of their strength, with the party of raiders after their heads.

Istvay gave him a wry glance that told him they were having similar thoughts.

They beckoned with their head, and Aran nodded, and the two of them started forward through the trees.

"I did actually scout around a little yesterday," Istvay whispered as the two of them walked single-file down the narrow trail. "I couldn't see much, since we're not above the tree line, but it looked like there was a bit of a saddle in the mountain in that direction, and it was more a scree slope than anything. If we can get there, we should be able to get a clear view, at least." They pointed. Aran nodded, and the two of them stepped off the faint trail and into the trees.

Istvay was stumbling more than usual, and Aran consciously slowed his footsteps—Istvay's stubborn expression told him his friend wouldn't accept 'being babied,' but at least Aran could give them both a level of plausible deniability.

With as slow as they were going, and with the forced caution of having to look out for any more of Krevai's traps as they went, the moon was high in the sky by the time they reached the scree slope

Istvay had seen earlier from the clearing.

Aran glanced up at one of the trees on the edge of the slope. "I'll climb up. I should be able to see the landing pad from there, if it's where the captain said it was."

"I'll come too," said Istvay. "It'll be better with two pairs of eyes." There was a familiar stubbornness to their expression that told Aran it would be no use to argue.

He sighed. "If—if you're sure you can make it—"

Istvay glared at him. "I told you I was going to stop faking being alright when I wasn't. So if I say I can make it—"

Aran chuckled. "You mean, you gave yourself an excuse to be even grumpier than usual when I ask you about it?" he whispered.

Istvay glared, and didn't dignify his question with an answer.

Aran started up the tree with Istvay close behind, and soon both of them were high enough up that they could see over the lip of the slope and across the stretch of the mountain below them.

"There," said Istvay at last. Aran looked over to where they were pointing.

Sure enough, there was a distant glimmer in the moonlight, the sleek black outlines of what must be the raider attack pods nestled into a clearing on the far side of the saddle.

Istvay fumbled one-handed in their supplies pouch and brought out a pair of battered binoculars. "It's not guarded too heavily," they said after a few minutes, passing the binoculars to Aran. "From the sounds of it, Krevai has a reputation. So maybe he's not too worried."

Aran raised the binoculars to his own eyes, dialling them into focus. Istvay had been right—there were only two guards, and both had the casual stance and relaxed posture of people who weren't expecting trouble.

"Look on the far side of the clearing," Istvay whispered. "From the look of it, there are a couple of pods that are out of the sight-range of where the guards are positioned. It's just possible, if we could get through there and the pods are as quiet as the raider ships are, that they wouldn't notice the pod was missing until the next morning, depending on how alert the guards are."

Aran nodded, lowering the binoculars. "I'm sure they have trackers on them, though."

Istvay grinned at him. "They do, as a matter of fact. I talked to one of the crew this afternoon. But I looked at the mechanism, and assuming the tracker is similar to the one on their main ship, a standard blocker would shut it down, at least temporarily."

Aran turned, grinning back at his friend, and for a moment they were staring into each other's eyes.

It would have been incredibly awkward, honestly, even a few weeks ago. But now, Aran was able to feel nothing but happiness.

Istvay's eyes widened, darker than usual in the moonlight. There was an odd expression on their face, and they didn't pull their gaze away, even when he expected them to—

He turned away, breaking off the gaze, feeling a little shaky, and pulled his mind back to the present.

Behind him, he heard Istvay let out a long breath.

"Well," they said at last, their voice not quite steady. "We'd best get back. From the look of that moon, we'll barely make it back in time as it is."

"Yeah," said Aran, clearing his throat. "Yeah, you're right."

The two of them made their rapid way down the tree in a shower of bark and needles, and Ani protested irritably from her perch on Aran's shoulder.

"You could have climbed up yourself, Ani," he grumbled. "It

would have saved me carrying both of us."

She latched herself tighter onto his shoulders.

"I think we're going to have to go down and around," said Istvay. They were standing at the lip of the scree slope. "It'll take too long to go all the way up and around that outcropping like we did on the way here, and we don't have a lot of time left."

Aran nodded silently, and the two of them started down the mountain.

It wasn't until they reached the foot of the mountain and made their way around the thin outcropping of cliff that Aran realized that something was wrong.

He wasn't sure he would have noticed it even then if it hadn't been for the way Ani tensed on his shoulders, her posture perking up, suddenly alert.

Then he did notice. The quiet sounds of the nighttime forest—the soft hum of insects, and the faint rustle of small animals through the undergrowth—had stilled.

"Oh, hell," Istvay whispered.

And then from the trees behind them came a soft, all-too-familiar voice.

"Hello, little humans. There are lots of people looking for you these days, aren't there? Humans, yibo, raiders … But it looks like we got here first."

Aran and Istvay looked at each other for a split second, then dived into the undergrowth, Aran holding Ani firmly to his shoulder despite her spitting protests, and shoved frantically through the brush towards the slope of the mountain.

"That must be Captain Sharda's crew. Good hell, how long were those damn raiders planning to wait for us?" Istvay said through gritted teeth as they climbed. "They clearly have way too much damn time on their hands. And what the hell were they talking about with their yibos and humans? Here." They threw back a small pouch of scent blocker, and Aran caught it neatly. He smeared it over himself as the two of them stumbled along, the sound of pursuit clear in the background, then activated the pouch, shoving it in his pocket.

"You alright?" he whispered.

Istvay give a terse nod. "But we're not going to make it far enough up the mountain. They're too close, and they're faster than we are."

"Then let's find somewhere to hide until we can damn well figure out how to get rid of them," Aran whispered through his teeth.

Istvay slowed, already breathing heavily. A moment later, they gestured to a small depression that looked like it had been cut out by seasonal runoff.

Aran nodded, too breathless to speak, and the two of them tumbled down the short, steep slope and into the ditch.

Their pursuers were only metres behind, from the sounds of it.

"In there!" Aran hissed, shoving Istvay towards an undercut in the bank. Istvay wriggled inside, and Aran clambered in after them.

The space was barely big enough for one, let alone two, and they were crammed in so tightly there was hardly room to breathe, but as long as they were perfectly still, they should be out of sight. He pulled Ani against his chest, whispering something soothing in her ear, and for a wonder, she didn't protest.

Then they were quiet, waiting.

Above them, he could hear the approaching raiders, their footsteps quiet on the forest floor. They walked slowly, as if trying to catch a trail, but without Aran and Istvay's scent to guide them the trail would be difficult to follow in the moonlight.

The footsteps paused on the bank above them. More footsteps

approached, and there was whispered conversation, then the rustle of someone making their quiet way into the ditch.

Aran held his breath, willing his heart to slow, one hand loosely around Ani.

If they were perfectly still, he was pretty sure their hiding place was virtually undetectable.

But then, he'd never been hunted by something like these raiders before.

He was pressed so tightly against Istvay that he could feel every rise and fall of their chest, the rapid pounding of their heart, the warmth of their breath against the back of his neck.

The raider was close enough he could hear the creature's quiet breathing.

Aran shifted, and he felt Istvay's breath hitch.

He was very aware, suddenly, of the warmth of Istvay's body pressed against his, the way their arm had come up around him, pulling him close to make more room.

He closed his eyes. This was not something he needed to be thinking about right now.

In the ditch below, the raider's footsteps were slow and methodical, a steady back-and-forth.

Aran gritted his teeth, trying to steady his breath. Istvay must have felt him stiffen, because they tightened their hand on his arm in a reassuring gesture, and he put his hand over theirs with a quick squeeze of gratitude.

At last there was another whispered conversation, then a quick, light scramble of footsteps as the raider pulled themself up the side of the ditch. There was more quiet conversation, and the footsteps above them faded away.

Aran squeezed Istvay's hand again in warning, listening closely.

It was possible this was a trap. The raiders could have left someone behind, waiting to see if they emerged.

Istvay must have come to the same conclusion, because they didn't try to move, and for a few minutes the three of them stayed pressed into the hollow, Aran's back pushed up against the warmth of Istvay's chest, his legs tangled with theirs, Istvay's arm slung low over his hips.

At last Aran lifted his head, trying to peer out. He gave Ani a soothing pat, then pushed back against Istvay, trying to see through the narrow opening. Istvay's breath hitched again.

But there was a small gap in the tree roots above him, and he was pretty sure if he could just maneuver himself a little farther up—He wriggled, trying to find a position that would afford him a view of the bank.

Istvay gave a muffled groan.

"You okay?" Aran whispered, shifting again in an attempt to give them more room. "I can just—maybe if I—"

"Aran." Istvay's voice was strained. "For the love of the Holy Mystery, would you please stop moving!"

Aran froze, and he felt Istvay take a long, shuddering breath.

"Sorry," he whispered.

"It's—it's fine." Istvay's voice was still strained. "Just—just give me a sec."

Finally, when Istvay's breathing had evened out a little, their heartbeat steadying from the spike of earlier, they said carefully, "Are they gone?"

"I—I think so," whispered Aran, being careful to stay entirely still. "I was trying to check when—anyway, there's a gap in the roots up here, but I can't quite see out of it from where I am."

He felt Istvay take another deep breath. "Alright. I'm—I'm going to push you up so you can see better. Okay?"

Aran nodded.

Istvay's arm slid off his hip, and he felt an odd pang of disappointment, then their hands were on his shoulder blades, lifting him.

He peered out through narrow opening. "I can't see anyone," he whispered. "I can't see the whole bank, but at least there's no one right over top of us." He glanced quickly to one side. "And Ani doesn't seem upset."

"Well, if we don't get back soon, there will be two groups of raiders hunting us. And I'm not sure either of us wants to deal with that. So we'll have to take our chances."

Aran nodded carefully. He scooted back, trying to get his feet under him, which despite his best efforts shoved him against Istvay once more.

Istvay sucked in a sharp breath.

"Pishti?" he asked anxiously, turning back.

"Just—just get up, okay?" Istvay was speaking through their teeth.

Aran sighed, but did as Istvay asked, and a moment later he was out.

It was another moment before Istvay emerged, and when they did, their face looked slightly flushed in the moonlight.

They didn't meet his eyes, just glared up at the sky. "We should get going. We'll be pushing it to make it back to the ship before morning as it is. We'll worry about getting our hands on a key for the pods when we're back there."

Istvay was right—by the time the three of them reached the raider ship again, the sky was beginning to grey, and they could already hear the soft hum and bustle of the ship waking up.

On the bright side, the night guards were tired and not paying much attention, and it was easy enough to sneak past them.

It was harder to make their way through the ship's corridors, now that raiders were coming and going with their morning tasks, but they reached their room undetected, slid through the door, and managed to drop down onto the nest of blankets moments before someone tapped on the door with their breakfast.

22

Alba

By the time Alba woke, the ship had come to a halt.

She blinked and rolled up into a sitting position. The sky through the small portholes was dark—she must have slept the day through.

Her entire body ached, but it had become such a familiar feeling that she was no longer certain how it felt not to hurt when she woke.

She made her way stiffly out of the small cabin and into the messroom, where Joska, Rafel, Beni, Nicolau, Ines, and Feliu were already gathered. Yosip joined them a few minutes later.

"I've been looking at that map of yours, Chief Justice," said Joska quietly. "We should be close to where the mechanism is. But from what I can tell, they have quite the security apparatus around it. I suggest we walk from here, since I'm pretty sure an unidentified craft is going to cause more concern than we want to deal with, and we don't know how well it's guarded."

"We don't know how well it's guarded, but I think 'pretty heavily' is a safe bet," Rafel muttered.

Joska sighed. "As much as I hate to admit it, you're probably right."

Rafel gave a snort of laughter. "You never like to admit I'm right, Captain. You may as well save your breath on that point."

Joska chuckled, and glancing between them, Alba saw the genuine affection in their faces.

"Well," said Joska. "I suppose no point in wasting any more time. I should have some nightvision goggles on board somewhere, although if you've got the retinal implants in your wavelinks, you probably don't need them."

Joska had parked the ship near the base of a large hill. The walk, and then the climb to the top, couldn't have been more than a kilometre or so in total, but it felt like fifty. If it hadn't been for Nicolau's assistance, Alba wasn't sure she'd have made it at all.

Then, at last, they crested the hill, and their destination came into sudden, unmistakable view. It was a massive complex surrounded by a heavy spiked fence, and covered over with a force-field. From the top of the fence, brilliant floodlights shone out across the small valley.

"Well," said Joska, after a long moment of silence.

Alba didn't have anything more articulate to add.

The valley below them was flooded with lights and swarming with guards, and watching the scene, Alba felt her stomach sink.

"Well," said Joska again.

"There's no way we're going to get in there," whispered Nicolau.

Alba was tempted to snap at him, but—he was right.

This was simply impossible.

She felt the weariness to the very core of her being. She turned, at last, to Yosip. "You spoke with Aran and Istvay. Are they going to come?"

Yosip hesitated. "They're in a bit of a difficult position at present, and they weren't sure they'd be able to get out. But they said they'd do their best."

"Perhaps if we made it clear that the fate of the entire Joias System depends on them being able to get out?" Alba snapped. She knew her irritation stemmed more from the sick panic she felt of the sight in front of them than it did from either Yosip or the errant scientist and his friend, but she was too exhausted to temper her words.

Yosip sighed and shook his head. "I'm sure they'll do the best they can. And we will simply have to hope."

Alba could still hear Aran's words from back on the escape pod: *"I am damn well finding that cure, if I have to die to do it."* And she could still see the way he'd looked at his friend when he said it.

All at once she was hit with a sudden, unexpected pang, an odd sort of ache at the realization that this ragged young man who'd spent his life in the most remote reaches of the system had the one thing she, who's life had been dedicated to the public trust, had never allowed herself even to dream of.

Yosip shot her a weary smile. "He was worried that if he and Istvay come, they might put the raiders on our trail, but I took the liberty of informing them that at this point, that's the least of our concerns."

There was no sentimentality in his words, just a simple matter-of-factness. But Alba knew he understood the implications of what he was saying. If the raiders found them after they'd destroyed the portal, they'd be killed. But then, once she'd made the decision to destroy the portal mechanism, Alba had never expected to come out of this alive.

She lifted her head. "Thank you," she said quietly. He smiled at her, a soft, weary smile, and Alba realized that something would leave the system when Yosip died—something fragile, and fleeting, and precious.

By the time they made their weary way back to the ship, Alba was thoroughly exhausted. Joska sent Nicolau, Beni, and Ines off to bed with the admonition to get as much rest as they could, as they'd likely be needed soon. Then she and Rafel settled themselves with Alba, Yosip, and Feliu on the cramped main deck of the ship.

"Chief Justice?" Joska asked quietly. "This is your plan. What do you think?"

Alba drew in a long breath. "It's no more than we should have expected, I suppose," she said, trying to keep the exhaustion from her tone. "I suggest that—"

"Joska!"

Alba looked up, irritated at the interruption, to see Nicolau stumble into the cabin. His face was pale, his eyes wide in panic. "Joska! Joska, we need—"

Joska stood quickly, putting out a hand to steady the frantic young man. "What is it, Nicolau? What's wrong?"

"Sa—Savina." His voice choked. "They're going to kill her. She called to warn us that the yibo will be opening the portal soon, and when I told her we'd come for her as soon as we were done here, she said … she told me that once the portal was down, there was no need to come back. And …" He took a deep breath. "I'm going after Vina. I have to. She's—she's my sister, Joska." There was a pleading look in his eyes, and desperation in his tone. "Beni's coming too, we already talked about it. You can stay, captain, but this—"

Joska put up a hand to stop him and turned back to Alba and the others, a wry look on her face. "Give me a minute," she said, then put her hand on the young man's arm and steered him out of the cabin.

Alba, Yosip, Feliu, and Rafel were left looking at each other.

At last, Rafel shook his head. "That little idiot is going to lose his mind if we don't come up with a way to save his sister," he said gruffly. "Heaven help us if we were ever that young and stupid." But there was a reluctant fondness in his tone.

Joska came back a few minutes later. Her face was grim, but Nicolau, who was trailing behind her, looked a little calmer.

"Well," said Joska, resuming her seat. "It looks like our favourite murderer is in trouble. And Beni and Nicolau aren't going to leave it unless we do something." She sighed. "I figured of the three of us, Nicolau would be the most use here. And Rafel, as fond as I am of you, your days of storming a building are over. Between you, Alba, with your map, and Yosip's apparent ability to make friends with the rain clouds themselves, I figure that once Aran and Istvay get here, Rafel and I will be a bit redundant anyway. And there's no power in the Mystery's vastness that will persuade Beni to stay behind when Savina's in danger. So. When our scientists get here, I'll leave Nicolau and Ines with you, and the rest of us will go see if we can keep Savina alive a little longer."

For a long time, there was silence in the cabin. At last, Alba nodded. "I suppose that will have to do," she said, trying to keep the irritation from her tone.

23

Aran

"Aran!"

He blinked his eyes open, his head snapping up.

Dessi was watching him in mild exasperation. "I thought this was something you were interested in."

"Oh—it is, I'm very interested," he mumbled, blinking hard and scrubbing at his eyes with his knuckles. "I'm sorry, I just—I guess I didn't sleep well last night."

He'd gone out to check on Istvay when Dessi had insisted they pause for a noonday meal, only to find them sprawled out on the forest floor, fast asleep. He'd pulled off his jacket and draped it over them, smiling, then gone back into the lab. But even the fresh air hadn't really been enough to wake him up.

"I'd love to see the genotype analysis that ran overnight," he said, trying to bring himself back to full alertness.

Dessi chuckled. "Here I thought we were working on developing this cure together, and all you keep doing is asking for my baseline information. If I didn't know better, I'd think you were trying to get all my data so you could develop the cure on your own and one-up me."

Aran managed a smile that he hoped didn't look too guilty.

The raider scientist had already bent over her data pad, paging through the information. "Here it is," she said at last. "Actually, perhaps that's a good idea after all—I'll give you everything I have, and we can look at it separately as well as together—perhaps one of us will find something that the other hasn't seen yet." She paused a moment, then turned, handing him a data pad. "There. I transferred it all onto here. I don't know how your devices work, that's not my specialty, but you know how to work a datapad, right?"

He gave the datapad a wary look, and she sighed. "Here. Let me show you."

By the end of the day, Aran had not only all the underlying data, but a working knowledge of how to use the datapad.

His heart was pounding strangely.

Yosip had said he'd call them again when they got to the mechanism. And then …

And then he'd have to leave. Because it was what Istvay wanted.

Sure enough, he and Istvay barely had time to finish dinner when Yosip's call came through Aran's wavelink.

"Aran." Yosip's voice was weary and strained. "We're here. The portal mechanism's heavily guarded, and none of us has the experience we need to get inside."

Aran glanced at Istvay. Their face was tense, and they were watching him steadily.

"We'll come," said Aran softly. "Tonight after the raiders are asleep, we'll come."

Ani had snuggled her bulbous body up next to him, seeming to sense his distress, and he stroked her absently. His hands were shaking.

Yosip let out a long breath that told Aran clearer than words how relieved he was. "Thank you. I'll send the map and directions to your wavelink." He paused. "How long will it take you to get here, do you think?"

Aran glanced at Istvay. "Pishti, do you know—" he began, then yawned so widely that for a moment he couldn't talk.

Istvay gave him a tight grin.

Aran's wavelink buzzed, and he tapped his palmscreen. A holographic map sprang up around his hand, and Istvay came over to peer at it.

They frowned at the map for a few minutes, then shrugged. "In the escape pod, I would have said something like thirty-six Colorida hours. But from what I've seen of these raider ships, I think we can cut that down to something like twelve."

Aran relayed the information to Yosip.

"And you'll be able to get away?" Yosip asked.

Aran glanced at Istvay and managed a small smile. "I hope so. We have some experience with this sort of thing. Istvay was able to to steal a key to one of the pods, and with any luck, it will be a few hours before the raiders notice we're missing. But I can't promise they won't come after us the moment they do."

"I know," said Yosip quietly. "If we had more time, perhaps we could take better precautions. But as things stand—as long as we have a few hours to take down the mechanism, we'll have to worry about the rest afterwards." He paused. "We'll wait for you here. Get here as soon as you can. I don't know how much longer we have before the portal opens."

"Yeah," said Aran quietly. "We'll get there as fast as we can."

He tapped off his wavelink and turned to Istvay. "I spent today getting all the baseline information from Dessi, so we could keep working on the cure. We'll go help them, but I'm not going to leave this. I'm not giving up."

"I know," said Istvay, their voice almost inaudible.

For a while, the two of them tried to pass the time until the raiders went to bed with a game of dice, but soon Aran was yawning so hugely that Istvay chuckled and shoved him over towards the pile of blankets.

"Lie down, I'll wake you up when it's time. I had a nap, I'll be fine."

Aran nodded and stumbled over to the nest of blankets. He didn't even remember closing his eyes.

He awoke to a soft touch on his shoulder, and a voice whispering, "Aran?"

He sat up with a jerk, and Istvay caught him before he overbalanced, and he blinked his eyes open centimetres away from Istvay's face.

Their arms were around him, holding him steady, their mouth close to his, and he could see where their lips were chapped, and he must have been still half-asleep, because he reached out to touch where the dry skin was cracking. And then he came fully awake, and realized, suddenly, where he was and what he was doing—his thumb brushing Istvay's lips, his face so close to theirs that all he would have to do was lean in, just a little—

Istvay didn't pull back, though, just stayed there, watching him. Their eyes were wide and dark, and Aran found he wasn't actually breathing—

"Aran," they said at last, their voice rough. "It's—it's time to go."

Aran swallowed hard and nodded, but still Istvay didn't pull away.

"And, um," they said. "If—look, Aran, you and I … we—we need to talk. Okay?"

Aran's mouth was suddenly very, very dry, but he managed to nod anyways.

"Alright," said Istvay, their voice not quite steady. "Alright. We—we'll talk as soon as we get this stupid portal shut down. Okay?"

"Okay," said Aran, his mind gone completely blank.

His heart was still beating quick and strange in his chest as the two of them, with Ani perched on Aran's shoulder, made their way out of their room and off the ship.

Istvay didn't seem to be doing much better—twice, Aran had to grab their jacket to hold them back from stepping out in front of one of the guards.

They shot him an apologetic grin both times, but neither incident seemed enough to re-focus their attention.

Finally, though, they made it out of the clearing and reached the attack pods.

Istvay took a deep breath and closed their eyes for a moment, visibly trying to regain their focus. At last they opened their eyes and grinned shakily. "Well," they said. "Shall we?"

There were raider guards posted, but they didn't seem overly worried about a challenge, and in the dim moonlight, it was easy enough to creep past them. The key Istvay had stolen opened the pod hatch, and once inside, it only took Istvay a few minutes before they looked up, a gleam of satisfaction in their eyes.

"Got it," they whispered. "Better strap in. I set the blocker on the tracking device, and we'll fly low for a bit to get some distance, so our trip through atmosphere won't be quite as noticeable. But if they see us leaving, we're going to be in a hell of a hurry."

Aran nodded, swallowing hard.

He hated this part. He'd never not hate this part.

"It'll be over soon," said Istvay, their voice softening. "You can go into the back as soon as we're clear, okay?"

Aran nodded, closing his eyes to fight back the helpless panic.

Istvay laid their hand on his arm for just a moment. Then they turned to the controls, and the pod rose silently, then shot forwards.

Aran choked out a curse as his stomach dropped. The ground blurred under them, and he clenched his teeth, trying not to be sick.

"Going up," Istvay whispered a few minutes later, and the ship's trajectory turned vertical. The entire craft shook as they pushed through the atmosphere, and Aran squeezed his eyes more tightly, Ani's tentacles gripping his shoulder the only thing keeping him from hyperventilating.

At last the craft steadied, and Aran let out a short, shaky breath.

"Aran." Istvay's voice was gentle. "Aran, go on. Into the back, okay? I didn't see anyone after us, so I think we're clear."

Aran nodded, swallowing hard against the sick panic. He managed to unclench his hands from the arms of the copilot seat, and stumbled toward the back of a ship, where at least he wouldn't be able to see the blackness of space around them.

Istvay came to find him a few minutes later. They put a hand on his shoulder and sat with him, and Ani stroked his cheek gently with her tentacles, chirping softly, until at last he was able to open his eyes.

"Are you alright?" Istvay's eyes were dark with their typical concern.

Aran managed a weak nod.

Istvay smiled, but their hand stayed on his shoulder. Aran couldn't help but remember a few hours ago, sitting so close to Istvay he could feel the warmth of their breath on his face, his thumb running gently across their chapped lips, their arms around him …

"Pishti," he began, his voice hoarse. "Pishti, you said you wanted to—that we should—"

Istvay cleared their throat. "Yeah," they said, looking away. "Yeah, I—I wanted to—" They shifted, dropping their hand from his arm. "It's—look, it's late, and you haven't had any sleep. We should—"

"No, it's fine, I'm fine, I—" Aran stammered. His heart was pounding, and he couldn't seem to catch his breath.

"We'll—we can talk when we finish with the portal," Istvay muttered. Aran could practically feel the tension from his friend. They stood abruptly, and Aran stood as well, quickly enough that Ani gave a startled grumble and grabbed his arm for balance.

"Pishti. Wait."

Istvay froze.

"I—can't we—" He wasn't sure how to finish the sentence.

Istvay took a deep breath and turned back to him. "I promise," they said with a wan half-smile. "I just—look, I'm … sorry. I just … I need a little time, okay?" They squeezed his shoulder, and just for a moment he was caught in their gaze again, and it was as if all the work he'd done over the last however many weeks to actually damn well deal with this hadn't happened at all.

Then they turned and were gone, leaving Aran staring after them.

He was certain he'd never be able to sleep ever again for the rest of his life after that. But the strain of the last few days, combined with the previous night's adventures, was enough to overcome even his Istvay-induced insomnia, and the next thing he remembered, Istvay was shaking him awake.

"Aran," they whispered. They looked like they'd just woken up themselves. "We're almost there. Are you ready?"

Aran nodded groggily and sat up, and Istvay shot him a strained smile before turning back to the cockpit. "I'm going to take it off autopilot," they called back. "If you can manage it, come up here. I've never piloted a ship like this before, and I wouldn't mind a hand."

Between the two of them, they put the ship down not far from the coordinates Yosip had sent, and started off on foot.

When he and Istvay reach the others, they found them in a small camp in a dip between two hills.

Aran frowned, glancing around. "How did you get here? I thought you had a ship?"

Yosip smiled, although the expression was weary. "We did. But it turns out a friend of our captain was in trouble. Once we knew you were coming, she said she was going to fetch her."

"What happened to you?" asked Istvay.

"The question should be, what didn't happen to us?" said Feliu sourly.

"Aran, Istvay." Alba stood, crossing over to them. She looked exhausted, puffy circles under her eyes, the bones in her face standing out as if she'd hardly been eating or sleeping. "I appreciate you coming," she said quietly.

Aran stared.

Of all the greetings he'd expected from Alba, this was not one of them.

Istvay looked as taken aback as he felt, but they didn't comment, just nodded.

"Aran!"

He looked over to see a young man who looked vaguely familiar from his time on the ship.

Aran had to fight back a groan at the hero-worship in the kid's face.

"Aran!" He was grinning widely. "I honestly never thought I'd—" he paused, trailing off. "I'm—I'm sorry, it's probably not the time."

"No, no, it's fine," said Aran weakly.

As much as he hated the attention, there was a boyish eagerness in the young man's face that he couldn't bear to crush.

"So," he said instead. "What are we working with?"

In the end, they eschewed long explanations in favour of Nicolau leading them the the top of the hill overlooking the compound.

Istvay gave a low whistle. "Well, they're not exactly being subtle about this, are they?"

Aran pulled the binoculars out of his pouch, scanning the compound quickly. "It's—not going to be easy getting in there," he said after a moment.

"No," said Istvay dryly. "No, I don't think it will be." They paused, holding their hand out for the binoculars.

Aran handed them over, and they peered through them for a few moments before lowering them and looking over at Aran. "Are you seeing what I'm seeing, though?"

Aran grinned. "That bit over in the far corner?"

Istvay nodded, grinning as well, and dropped their knapsack to the ground. "I'll stay here. I need to figure out the guards' patterns. You go back with the others, try to get some sleep. One of us has to be awake if we want to get in there."

Aran dropped his own knapsack. "Pretty sure I've slept on the ground before. It'll be easier if I stay, that way I can spell you off if you need it."

Istvay gave him a reluctant smile. "Fine. But I don't need you falling asleep on the job like you were back on the raider ship."

Aran rolled his eyes, and Istvay chuckled.

"Alright," Aran whispered to Nicolau. "You go back, Istvay and I will stay here. Tell the others we'll be back in a couple hours, hopefully with a plan of some sort, and in the meantime they should get as much sleep as they can."

The wide-eyed Nicolau nodded, and turned back the way he'd come.

The silence when he was gone was somehow much more awkward than Aran remembered it being.

Istvay was on their stomach, the binoculars propped up to their eyes, looking fixedly down at the compound below.

Aran sighed and unstrapped his equipment pouch, pillowing his head on it, and stared up at the unfamiliar stars. Ani pushed her way up under his arm like she did most nights, with diffident little movements like she thought maybe if she was careful, he wouldn't notice. He shook his head and hid a fond smile, rubbing her under the chin as she purred.

"Put on a blanket, idiot."

He looked up in time to get hit in the face by Istvay's emergency blanket.

"Idiot yourself," Aran grumbled, grinning. "Anyways, you need a blanket too—not like it'll be warmer just because you're awake for it." He rummaged in his knapsack and pulled out another blanket, which he tossed at Istvay.

It hit them, covering them and the binoculars. They sputtered, fumbling their way out, then turned to glare at Aran. He gave a snort of laughter, and Istvay rolled their eyes, chuckling reluctantly.

Aran lay back again, pulling the blanket around him and Ani.

He'd barely closed his eyes, though, when a bright light seared across the sky, visible even behind his closed eyelids.

He opened his eyes, blinking.

Istvay had turned as well, and they were frowning, pointing their binoculars towards the sky. Then they cursed. "Aran. I know exactly who that is." Their voice was strained.

Aran frowned, then, abruptly, he swore as well. "It's Captain

Krevai, isn't it?"

Istvay nodded.

Aran tipped his head back. "Dammit. I thought we'd have a least a few hours." He blew out a quick breath. "We've got to get back to warn the others. This is not good."

"No," said Istvay grimly. "No, it's really not."

24

"Reka, darling," Savina purred, sitting on the cot and curling up against Reka's back.

Reka turned, her face dark with anger. "What is it?" she snapped. "This had better not be another one of your jokes, Savina."

Savina widened her eyes, then thought better of it. "No," she said quietly. "It's no joke."

She sent the scan of the building with her markup to Reka's wavelink, and waited as the woman pulled it up.

"I have it," said Reka shortly. "What are you planning?"

Savina took a deep breath. "Do you see how the water lines are laid out?" she asked. Her voice was quiet, because she was afraid it would tremble, and she didn't want Reka to hear that. "If I got out, and I set off an explosion in the pipes where I've marked—if you look at where the switches are, this wouldn't show up on the sensors for a while. I bet we could flood the entire records room. That might keep them busy enough trying to fix it that they delay for a little longer—they're not going to want to lose the records of all their discussions with Mattin."

Reka was quiet for a moment, studying the diagram. At last she looked up, her eyes hooded. "If they catch you, they'll kill you."

Savina swallowed hard. "I know." She'd meant it to come out carelessly, but her voice shook too much for that. "I told you. I'm good at getting myself out of bad situations."

She was a bit more successful with the carefree tone this time.

Reka studied her for a long moment, then shrugged. "Like you say —we're just trying to buy time for people who actually matter." She turned away, and Savina couldn't fight the sharp, stinging ache at the careless dismissal.

"Well, Reka, we'll see if the yibo can succeed where you failed," she said lightly. "It takes talent to be as bad at this as you are—follow me all the way through the portal like an over-eager puppy, team up with the raiders, and still not be able to kill me." She slid off the cot, and she could hear the bitterness in her own voice. "But as long as you follow orders like a good little soldier, right? I hardly know why you're doing this, to be honest—if you just need orders to follow, it seems to me you could follow Kachik's orders just as easily as you could follow—"

Reka grabbed her by the front of the tunic, and Savina sucked in a quick breath, a mix of fear and sick vindication. Something inside her craved the sight of Reka losing her stupid, stupid calm, that disdain, that detached amusement she looked at Savina with. Savina wanted to see it gone. Savina wanted to make Reka so angry she couldn't see straight. She wanted—

Reka yanked Savina upright, and Savina glared into those eyes, dark with fury, and she wanted—

She *wanted*—

Then Reka took a deep breath and stepped away, letting go of Savina with a gesture of disgust. "Better get ready, then. I'll unlock the door for you when it's dark." Her voice had regained its old indifference, and she turned her back on Savina.

The day seemed endless. Savina wrapped herself in the blanket Reka had thrown her and tried to nap in the corner, but she couldn't seem to fall asleep. When she finally did, it was to restless, unsettling dreams that she couldn't remember when she woke.

At last, the guards appeared with their dinner. They looked around the cell warily, but on seeing both Savina and Reka where they belonged, they left the food and stood at a respectful distance outside the cell while Savina and Reka ate. Then they carried the dishes away.

When they were gone, Savina and Reka sat in silence for a few minutes. Savina didn't deign to look at Reka, glaring instead at the corner of their cell.

She still wasn't sure whether she was more angry with Reka, or with herself.

At last Reka stood and made her way over to crouch next to her. "Are you ready?" she whispered.

Damn her to the Void.

Savina pasted on a smile as she turned. "I'm always ready, sweetheart. You forget that at your peril."

"Good," said Reka indifferently, rising. "Then I'll get the door open for you."

It only took her a moment to pick the lock. But she hesitated as Savina came over. "What are you going to tell them as an excuse this time?" she asked. "There's a limit to how much I'll be able to do to help you, and this may cross that line."

Savina frowned. Reka looked actually ... worried.

That same ache from earlier jabbed into Savina's chest, cold and sharp.

This was pretend. It was all pretend, and Reka would be laughing about it the moment Savina was gone.

She gave Reka a dazzling smile. "Don't bother your pretty head about it, sweetheart. I can take care of myself." She pushed past Reka and slipped out the door without looking back.

By the time she reached the hallway that led down to the pipes, the furious, seething anger in her chest had dulled to a cold emptiness. But her hands were trembling as she broke through the lock into the room that held the main water line.

Reka was right. There really wasn't a whole lot she could say to cover this one up. Hard to argue that she'd gotten lost in the middle of the night, stumbled into the waterworks, and accidentally set off an explosion.

Maybe she'd get back to her cell before they caught her. That was her only hope, really.

If Reka would even let her back in.

It didn't matter. She was trying to save her brother, and what some damn government agent thought of her didn't matter at all.

She took a deep breath, trying to still her hands. It would be difficult to set off an explosive if her hands were shaking so hard she blew it up before she'd managed to plant it.

The thought of the smirk on Reka's face at the news gave her the jolt of fury she needed to steady herself.

She reached into her pocket, retrieving the explosive Reka had given her. The woman had said once it was set, Savina would have about sixty seconds to get out. It was possible Reka was lying—the memory of the glittering hatred in the woman's gaze after their argument the night before still shook Savina, just a little.

But she probably hadn't been lying. As long as Reka had a use for her, she'd keep her alive.

She glanced one final time at the diagrams she'd sketched out, wishing irrationally that Beni was here—Beni had always been better at planning things than Savina was—and pinpointed the place she'd need to plant the explosive to cause the maximum amount of damage. Then she crept across the empty room, her breath catching in her throat at every sound.

By the time she reached her destination, all her original bravado had disappeared.

She sucked in a breath, staring at the tangle of pipes.

The yibo would kill her for this.

Not that it bloody well mattered to anyone but her.

She pulled out the explosive, taking another deep breath to calm her shaking nerves. She activated it, tapped the timer, and nestled it in the centre of the tangle of pipes, then jumped to her feet and took off running.

She made the door, and was outside and three quarters of the way down the first hallway when the explosion went off. It was soft, nothing to attract too much attention—but a few seconds later, a trickle of water bloomed along the hallway by her feet. In moments, the trickle had turned into a stream, and the stream into a flood. Soon Savina was splashing through water high enough to soak her shoes, then high enough to wet her ankles.

She walked as quickly as she could, trying to balance the need for speed with the need for silence.

The closer she could get back to the cell before they found her, the higher her chance of living through this.

And then she heard the sound she'd been dreading—the splash of running footsteps, and a guard's voice shouting. Her wavelink translated their words: "There she is! It's that stupid human girl again."

Savina turned, her eyes wide, raised her hands to show she was weaponless. "I didn't do anything! I saw the water, and I came to find someone—"

There was a soft *pop*, and Savina gasped at a sharp, shocking pain, her right leg buckling under her.

The guards had reached her by now, and one of them grabbed Savina, slamming her head against the wall. She bit her tongue, tasting blood.

He smashed her head into the wall again, and she gave a choked scream, blood pooling in her mouth and streaming down her throat as she gagged. He backhanded her, and there was another explosion of pain, sharp and sudden and hot as her nose burst with blood. The guard shoved her away from him in disgust, and she collapsed into the water, sobbing.

She wasn't sure, anymore, if she was sobbing for real or in a last, desperate attempt to save her life.

Another guard splashed over and hauled her to her feet, fastening restraints around her wrists.

"Where do we take her?"

"Take her with the other. Onto the ship."

Savina heard the words through the fog of pain. Blood streamed down her face and chin and dripped onto her tunic, splashing into the water below her. The water around her was a bright, shocking red, and tendrils of darker red blood twisted in streams from her injured leg.

When the guard let go of her again, she dropped to the ground, choking and whimpering, heedless of the water soaking through her thin tunic. The pain in her leg was almost enough to make her woozy, and blood soaked through her clothing, clinging hot and sticky to her skin.

The guards jerked her to her feet again, and this time there was nothing faked in her whimper.

"Should we just kill her?" asked the guard holding her. "Even Reka can't possibly believe this idiot is doing this on accident." He yanked out his gun, shoving it up against Savina's ribcage. "How many guards has she killed? I can't even remember anymore."

The muzzle of the gun was hard and cold, and through the odd, sick dizziness, Savina could feel the outline of it, a small, bruising shape.

She wasn't going to live through this. She was going to die here, and no one would ever know or care what had happened to her.

The guard's captain shook his head reluctantly. "Best not. It would be a shame to lose Reka after all this work."

The words were still coming through the translator in Savina's wavelink, but everything had gone a bit hazy, and she couldn't spare the energy to interpret them.

When her brain finally wandered back into focus, she was being dragged along the corridor, stumbling and whimpering at every step.

It took her a few moments, in her pain fogged state, to realize that they weren't going back towards the cells. The icy wash of panic at the thought was almost enough to jolt her from her stupor. Were they taking her somewhere to kill her?

Then she remembered what the guard had said.

Not killing her, then. But not taking her back to the cell.

She stumbled to a halt at one of the glass walls of the building, and the guard in the front of the procession opened an entryway and gestured them through.

Savina blinked at the sudden shock of night air on her wet skin and clothing. Then she was dragged along a crowded, busy launchpad, packed with ships, until at last she was prodded up an open hatch. She stumbled up it, her stomach roiling in sick despair.

The yibo were getting ready to launch their ships.

The portal was going to open.

They'd been too late.

25

Alba

Alba glanced up with a start at a sharp buzzing, and she looked around, disoriented.

"You've got to get out! You've got to get out, right now!"

It took her a moment to realize the voice was Aran's, and it was coming through her wavelink.

"The raiders are here." His tone was grim. "I didn't think they'd be this fast. Alba, you've got to get everyone out."

She blinked herself awake, and staggered to her feet. "Yosip!" she snapped. "Feliu, wake up. Everyone out, now!"

Now that she was awake, she could see the bright light of the descending ship.

"What the hell—" Nicolau's voice was groggy as he staggered out of his tent.

"Out!" snapped Alba. "It's the raiders."

"Find somewhere to hide." It was Istvay this time, voice coming faintly through Aran's line. "Best stay away from the ship Aran and I came in, I don't want them after you, too."

"And what are you two going to do?" Yosip had emerged from his tent, looking tired, and older than his years.

"We'll figure something out." Aran's words were strained.

"And it'll be a hell of a lot easier to figure something out if we're not worried about the rest of you," Istvay added.

"We can't just—we can't just leave Aran and Istvay—" Ines began, her eyes wide.

"You heard what Istvay said," snapped Feliu. He sounded more like his old self than he had in a long time.

"Um." Ines' voice was very quiet. "I—I'm not sure that's an option anymore."

Alba swung around to follow the girl's gaze, and froze.

A raider stood at the entrance to the camp, a few metres away. They were smiling, but it didn't look like a cheerful smile.

"What have you done with the captain's humans?" The question came out sharp-edged and menacing.

"I am not sure who you're talking about," said Alba, stepping forward. Her tone held its usual tartness, but her legs were strangely reluctant to take that step towards the raider.

But if it could buy Aran and Istvay time to get away, somehow …

"If you're looking for someone, I would suggest—"

"They're here," said the raider, their smile growing. "We saw the ship. Where are they? The captain wants them alive, I think, but I doubt the same holds for you."

The others were watching Alba.

She took a deep breath. "I'm sorry to say I really can't help you."

"Well then." The raider stepped forward, grabbing Alba by the upper arm. Claws dug into her flesh, and she had to bite back a gasp of shock and pain.

"Madam!" came Feliu's horrified voice.

And then there was a commotion from the other direction, the sound of running footsteps.

Aran and Istvay burst into the camp. They were both breathing heavily, and Istvay was staggering, their face drawn with effort.

"Wait!" gasped Aran. "Wait."

The raider turned, loosening their grip on Alba, and she staggered back. Nicolau caught her, but she shook him off, forcing herself to straighten.

"Wait." Aran paused a moment, sucking in a breath. "It's—you're looking for us, aren't you?"

The raider's expression had turned to one of dangerous delight. "There you are! The captain was—not happy to find you gone."

Aran and Istvay exchanged glances. "I imagine he wasn't," Aran murmured dryly.

"Excellent," said the raider, with a sharp smile. "I'll take you back, then, and you can explain things to him. And best hope you catch him in a good mood. The rest of these, we can—"

"Aran." The new voice was deep and menacing, and there was a threat in the words that needed no interpretation.

Aran took a deep breath and turned, and Alba caught the way Istvay's hand tightened protectively around his arm.

"Captain Krevai," said Aran.

"Aran. You hurt my feelings, you and your Istvay."

Ani squirmed on Aran's shoulder, growling a warning.

"I told you," said Aran. His voice was quiet and hopeless. "We need to save our friends. If that portal opens, everyone we know back on Colorida will die."

The captain frowned, starting across the clearing towards them. "Aran. Maybe you should be a little less concerned about your friends on Colorida, and a little more concerned about your own survival." He reached out a hand as if to grab Aran by the shoulder, then seemed to remember something, and dropped his hand hurriedly. "I'm sorry, I forgot."

"I gave up my chance to find a cure for my best friend." Aran's voice was low. "Maybe you don't understand. But if you want to stop me from doing this, you'll have to kill me."

Alba stared at the young scientist, a little taken aback.

The raider captain seemed taken aback as well. "Aran. You're a scientist. You know how prey species and predator species work. You can't fault us for—"

"This has nothing to do with fault." Aran broke in. "If you tried to hurt me, Ani would kill you. She doesn't give a damn about morality. She loves me, and she doesn't want me to get hurt. If any one of you tried to touch Istvay, you'd have to slit me open first. Because I—" he glanced at his friend, who was standing beside him, their eyes wide.

He cleared his throat, turning back to the raider captain. "I—I care about them very much. I'm not going to argue with you about whether it's moral for you to kill the people on Colorida. But I won't stand by while you do it. So." He shrugged. "Go ahead and kill me, if you need to. That's the only way you're going to stop this."

The raider captain glared at Aran. At last, he sighed, turning to one of the raiders standing next to him. "We'll deal with these three later. Restrain them and put them on the ship. His Ani will try to kill you, so be careful."

Something bright and sharp blazed across the sky. The raider captain glanced up, then swore.

Aran and Istvay exchanged grim looks.

"What is it?" Alba snapped.

"Um," said Aran. "The, um—other raiders. They want to kill us. I mean, even more than these ones do."

Alba stared, her mind spinning.

"If you'll excuse me for asking," began Yosip, "exactly how many groups of raiders want to kill you?"

"At least two more than we'd like!" said Istvay. "Get out of here while you damn well can!"

"If Sharda thinks she can lay claim to my humans," the raider captain growled, turning to the raider beside him, "then she'd better think a little harder. Get Dessi to watch the humans, the rest of us will take care of her. She's been getting a bit too confident lately."

He snapped out orders, and raiders scattered, heading towards the small attack pods.

In the distance, Alba could see the lights on the portal mechanism flaring up.

Feliu must have noticed it as well. "Madam," he said quietly. "Perhaps with the raiders here, they'll be distracted enough that—"

For a moment, Alba allowed herself to hope it was true.

And then there was a flash of light, like a lightning strike, but a million times more brilliant.

Feliu gave a choked curse. "Madam—" he started.

Then, like fabric aged and weakened by use, the sky ripped apart, revealing a familiar black jag of nothingness.

"No." The word was soft and choked, and it took Alba a moment to realize that she was the one who'd said it.

After everything they'd done—the exhaustion and the pain and the sacrifice—it couldn't be too late. It couldn't be.

She could vaguely hear the shouts of the raiders around her, the hiss of weapons fire, the screams of the injured. But none of it seemed to register properly in her brain.

All she could do was stare at the gaping black rent that moments before had glowed bright with pinprick-lights of unfamiliar constellations.

She'd always known, academically, that they were going to die here. If she managed to pull this off, if she managed to shut the portal down, she'd die in this alien, unfamiliar landscape, among unfamiliar people in an unfamiliar place. But she'd managed to push it all to the back of her mind, because it was for something greater than herself. Because this time, no matter how many mistakes she'd made in the past, this decision was the right one. The only one she could make in good conscience.

She'd still die here, now that she'd failed. But everyone in the Joias System would die too.

The portal was open.

They'd lost.

26

Aran

Aran stared at the gaping rift in the sky. He was still clutching Istvay's arm, and he realized it, but—well, but dammit, it hardly seemed to matter anymore.

One of the raiders had grabbed the two of them and dragged them to the side of the clearing, but gently. Ani was still on his shoulder, her eye pouches bulged out threateningly.

He'd been ready to tell her to go after the raiders. But it hardly seemed worthwhile now. It would just end up getting more people killed.

"Maybe we can talk them into keeping Alba and the others alive, anyway," Aran whispered.

Istvay's face was pale, but they gave him a wry smile. "Aran. This isn't your fault. We did our best."

Aran took a deep breath. "I know," he mumbled. "We both did. It just wasn't enough." He sighed. "That's the thing, Pishti. It's not that I don't care about all of this. I just—I'm a good scientist. That's all. I never had to worry about trying to change things I couldn't change."

Istvay looked at him for a long moment. "If that's the case," they said at last, "why did you spend so long looking for a cure for me? You knew that was something you couldn't change. Why didn't you just give up?"

"Because," Aran said quietly, "I didn't want to live in a world where you didn't exist. Because that was the one thing I wasn't willing to do."

Istvay closed their eyes for a moment. "Aran," they began.

"Aran, Istvay, listen."

Aran blinked at the unexpected voice, turning quickly.

Dessi stood beside them, looking nervous. "You want to close the portal and keep the humans from being wiped out, right?"

Aran nodded cautiously.

"Well, go on!" she hissed. "The captain left me to guard you. You can leave now, if you're quick."

Aran stared at her. "What—what about the others?"

"They're back there in the woods," she whispered. "I sent them out already, since I knew you'd insist on it."

Aran was still blinking in astonishment. "Won't you—won't you get in trouble for this?"

Dessi shook her head in exasperation. "Let me deal with that. I've known the captain for a long time, I'll be able to talk him down. I'll just tell him your land-devil creature tried to eat me or something. He knows I'm not a fighter."

"Why are you—" Aran began.

"Because," she snapped, "I've tried to work with laboratory animals who are pining their hearts out, and they always just die. I can never get the data I need. And I'm confident that, no matter how much data you think you stole from me when you left, you're going to need more if you want to find your cure, so you're not going to run for good. So. If you swear that you'll come back when this is done, I'll promise to keep the captain from killing you for it. I get my data, you get your portal closed, we all win."

Aran stared at her, then turned to Istvay, who was also staring.

"Um," he said at last. "Um. Yes. Thank you."

Dessi looked relieved. "Back there," she hissed. "They're waiting for you in the trees. But don't forget, you promised to come back."

"I promise," said Aran fervently.

He could still feel the ache of his decision to leave the small, neat research station to go after the portal.

"Well, go on then!"

Aran nodded, in a stunned fashion, and Istvay dragged him out of the clearing and into the trees.

Alba and the others were waiting a few metres in, as Dessi had promised.

"What in the Mystery's name—" Alba began in a shaky voice, but Istvay shook their head briskly.

"No time for that. If we want to get this portal taken down, we've got to go now." They turned to Aran. "Aran," they began in a softer voice.

"Pishti. Listen." He took a deep breath. "You know as well as I do that of the two of us, I'm the best one to do this. You get Alba and the others to safety. When you've done that, and they're somewhere safe, head back to the camp, and when I'm done with the portal mechanism, I'll meet you there."

Istvay studied him for a long moment. Then, at last, they nodded. "You're right," they said quietly. "But if I'm not coming, you'll need to take someone with you."

Aran stared at them in panic, and they gave a small smile. "Aran. I promise, I'd do this for you if I could. But—I can't. I—"

Aran swallowed hard.

He could work on his own. And he could work with Istvay, because he knew Istvay almost as well as he knew himself. But … but he wasn't a leader. He wasn't about to take a group of people he didn't know, who looked up to him as some damn hero, into a situation he had no idea if he'd be able to get them out of again.

Istvay was still watching him, and he could see the pain on their face.

He tried to smile. "It's fine, Pishti. It'll be fine. You stay with the others, I'll be fine on my own. I have Ani with me, anyways, and—"

"I'll go with you." Ines stepped forward. She looked just as nervous as he remembered, but there was a new determination in her face. "I can help. I grew up in the Rim Mountains, and I used to go hunting with my mom. And—" She shot a frightened, defiant look in Alba's direction. "And I'm not going to let my family get hurt, not again."

Aran closed his eyes for a moment.

"Aran," whispered Istvay.

He took a deep breath, and nodded. "Thank you, Ines."

"I'll come too," said Nicolau quickly, stepping forward. His face, too, was set and determined, if a little paler than usual. "I—I let Joska and the others go off to rescue my sister without me. This is the least I can do."

Aran nodded again, trying to fight back the panic.

He wasn't sure how well he was succeeding.

"Aran." Istvay stepped close, and Aran glanced up at them, surprised, for a moment, out of the spiralling terror in his brain. "They'll be able to help. I'll get the others somewhere safe, and we'll get a distraction ready. Set off a flare when you need it. I don't know how long we'll be able to keep things interesting over here, but we'll do our best."

Aran nodded. He couldn't seem to form words.

Istvay stepped closer, putting a hand on his arm. Aran was suddenly acutely aware of how close they were to him.

"Aran—" their eyes were wide and dark, and he could feel their hand tighten on his skin.

He swallowed, unable to look away.

Dammit. It didn't matter how often he did this. It didn't matter how many times he told himself this, he couldn't seem to—

"We still haven't had our talk," Istvay whispered. "So—so you need to come back to me, okay?"

Aran wasn't sure whether he was still breathing. "Okay." It came out as a hoarse croak.

"And Aran?" Istvay's voice was rough. They reached up, and Aran watched, almost as if he were in a trance, felt their hand brush across his cheek, slide into his hair, their fingers cup around the back of his head.

His heart was beating so that he thought it might actually break its way completely out of his chest.

"Can I?" Istvay whispered, their other hand coming up to cup his jaw, their thumb brushing across his lips. "For—for luck?"

"For ... luck," Aran managed, his voice almost inaudible.

Very, very gently, Istvay tightened their hand into his hair, drawing his face close to theirs. They leaned in, their breath warm against Aran's cheek. And then their lips brushed his, and he suddenly couldn't think or breathe or feel anything at all except for the warmth and softness of their lips, that familiar, remembered pressure from years ago. Something warm and soft and intoxicating flowed through his entire body at their touch, his brain sparking and fizzing, his entire existence narrowed to Istvay's mouth on his.

His hands had come up, resting on Istvay's hips, and he pulled

Istvay towards him. The brush of their body against his set off another wave of sparks that threatened to overwhelm him completely, and he pulled them closer, leaning into the kiss. Istvay's breath was coming quick and unsteady, their fingers tightening in his hair, their lips parting …

At last, Istvay drew back. Their eyes were wide, pupils large and dark, the rise and fall of their chest fast and uneven. Even in his addled state, Aran could feel how their hand trembled against his skin.

For a few moments, the two of them stared at each other.

"For luck," Aran repeated stupidly.

Istvay managed a small smile. "Just—come back to me, okay?"

They turned away, and Aran swayed as their hand left his arm.

"Aran!" someone hissed. He blinked, and realized it was Nicolau. "Come on! We need to go."

It took a moment for Nicolau's words to penetrate the fog that was his brain, and when they did, it took a moment more to persuade himself that this was more urgent than the memory of Istvay's lips on his.

"I—" he began, and then realized there was no way he would be able to force his brain into forming words at this point.

Nicolau and Ines were shooting amused glances at each other. At last, Ines took him by the arm and tugged. "Aran. Let's get moving, we'll talk about our plan on the way."

He stumbled after her, his brain slowly coming back to the problems at hand.

But there was a dreamy smile that had painted itself across his face that he wasn't sure he be able to get rid of, even if he wanted to.

27

Savina

Savina could hardly think over the roaring in her ears, her mind not quite able to process what had happened.

How had they been too late?

It had been a desperate hope anyway, she'd always known it, but it was all they had. How had it been too late?

She was dragged down the ship corridors to a small hatch in the back. There were a handful of guards at the entrance, but they stepped aside as Savina's guards approached, pulling the door open.

Savina landed on the floor in a heap as the door slammed behind her.

She lay there, dazed and dizzy, in a sticky pool of her own blood.

Hazily, she felt warm hands on her shoulder, a concerned voice whispering in her ear. But she couldn't really make out the words, and she figured she must be dreaming, anyway. The hands slid around her gently, and she gave a little gasp of pain as she was lifted, like a small child.

"Easy, Savina," the voice soothed, and she relaxed into the warmth. She remembered being carried like this by her mother, when she was very small, back in the compound. When she was still young and innocent and trusting. Before her life had been set on a road she'd never be able to turn back from.

She felt herself laid on something soft, and someone was wiping the blood from her face, their touch surprisingly gentle.

"Savina?"

This time, she recognized the voice, and her eyes blinked open in dull astonishment.

Reka was leaning over her, the expression on her face one of unmistakable concern.

"Reka?" she managed.

Reka looked up, sucking in a quick breath. "You're conscious. I wasn't sure."

Again, Savina caught what sounded like actual worry.

She struggled into a sitting position, shoving Reka's hands away, although her own hands were almost too shaky.

She wasn't about to do this again, let Reka's stupid fake concern cut through all of her defences, send her sniffling in the corner about how hard her life had been.

"I'm fine," she snapped. "Leave me alone. It's just a bloody nose." She had to stop for a moment, clenching her teeth against the nausea roiling in her stomach at the movement.

"It looks like a bit more than a bloody nose." Reka's tone had regained its usual dryness.

Savina scowled at her, and pushed herself to her feet.

The room spun, and she swayed—then a pair of strong arms caught her, lowering her gently onto the cot again.

"Sit down, you little idiot. Where are you hurt?"

"None of your damn business," Savina choked, biting back tears.

Reka ignored her, looking her over carefully, then slid her hands gently down Savina's calf. Savina gasped as Reka's probing fingers touched the centre of the throbbing pain.

Reka sucked in a quick breath. "When did this happen?"

"When the hell do you think?" Savina hissed. "They caught me in the corridor, and they——" she cut off her words, biting down hard against the sick tears trying to well up in her eyes.

Reka studied her for a moment, her eyes uncomfortably perceptive. At last she looked down at Savina's leg and sighed. "I'm sorry. This is going to hurt," she said. "Are you ready?"

Before Savina could respond, there was a lightning jolt of pain in her leg, and she gave a little, muffled scream, her vision going momentarily blurry.

Reka held up a jagged shard of sharp steel. "I'm surprise you were still conscious, with this stuck into you."

Savina stared at the bloody shard of metal, then turned away and vomited onto the floor at the foot of the bed.

When she'd finished, she stayed where she was for a moment, the acid burn of vomit sharp in her throat, her eyes stinging with tears.

She waited for Reka to say something cutting. But instead, the woman laid a gentle hand on her shoulder. "Are you done? Then lie back, let me tie this up so you don't bleed out."

Savina swore weakly, but Reka ignored her, ripping a strip from the bottom of Savina's tunic and using it to bandage the wound.

"You'll need to get that cleaned out sooner or later, but this is the best I can do at present. At least it'll slow the bleeding," she said in her cool voice.

"Me bleeding to death isn't really our biggest worry right now! They're going to open the portal."

"I noticed." Reka's tone was, if possible, even drier than before. "In fact, I hate to break it to you, but judging from the chatter over the lines, the portal is already open."

"Then why aren't you doing anything?" Savina's voice was harsh with a mixture of panic and tears. "We need to stop this. I thought we were bloody well going to stop this."

Reka leaned back on her heels where she sat crouched at Savina's feet, and looked up at her with those piercing slate-hazel eyes.

"Why does this mean so much to you?" she asked at last. "I thought you said you hated the whole Joias System."

"I do! I hate the whole damn thing. But—" she closed her eyes for a moment, waiting until she was sure her voice would be steady. "But my little brother might still be alive, and he's almost as much of an idiot as you are, Reka. He said he'd rather die on this side of the portal than see his stupid adoptive parents die. He's a stupid, naïve little idiot. But I'm not going to let him get hurt again."

Her words choked a little at the end, and she clamped her mouth shut.

Reka studied her with an unreadable gaze. At last, she asked quietly, "Hurt again? What happened to him?"

"None of your damn business," she growled.

"I suppose it isn't," said Reka.

For a while, they sat in silence.

"You?" asked Savina at last, when she couldn't bear the quiet anymore. "Why do you want this so badly? You don't have a baby brother with an adoptive family in the Joias System, do you?"

"No," said Reka, in an emotionless voice. "I don't. But it's the right thing to do."

Savina scoffed. "The right thing to do."

Reka ignored her, turning so her back was leaned against the cot.

From outside, they could hear the sound of the yibo fleet preparing for departure—the muffled shouts, the sound of heavy objects being moved, punctuated by occasional curses.

"As I said, from the sounds of it, the portal's already open," said Reka at last, not looking over at Savina. "We can't stop that. And we can't save the humans on this side of the portal, we're too late for that, too. But … we may have one last option to do something."

Savina frowned. "Well?" she asked at last. "What is it?"

Reka turned to look at her at last, a small, humourless smile on her face. She reached into the pocket of her suit and pulled out another explosive, twin to the one Savina had used in the water pipes in the government building. "The yibo military formations are pretty closely packed, here on the loading pad. The ship we're on isn't particularly important, but we're close to a formation of heavy gunships. I analyzed the composition of the fuel they use with my wavelink. If we plant this in the ship's fuel supply and set it off, the resulting explosion should at least take a few of them with us. It doesn't solve our problem, but—" She shrugged. "Maybe it will give the Joias System at least a bit more of a chance."

Savina stared at Reka for a long time. She felt very cold.

"Why do you want to do this so badly? Really?" she asked softly, at last.

Reka turned away. "It doesn't really matter why, does it? What matters is, whether it's worth it for you. Because I can't do it by myself."

For a while, Savina just watched her.

This would be her and Reka's death. And for what? If Nicolau had survived the portal opening, it wasn't like this would affect him personally. If the yibo went through with their bargain, maybe his stupid adoptive mother and father might get sucked into whatever hell Cavaco had planned, but if Nicolau would be fine.

She remembered the look on Joska's face, back on the outskirts of the small yibo village. *"I have a niece, down on Colorida. And if I'm trapped here in exchange for keeping her alive? Giving her a chance at a life that I never quite got, as much as I tried for it?"*

It was a stupid sentiment.

The farmer back in the Rim Mountains hadn't needed to take in the small, dirty bundle Savina had left on her doorstep twenty years ago. And even if she had taken him in, she hadn't had to raise him like her own, abandon her farm to keep him safe when he was in danger. Her life would have been far easier if she hadn't.

But she'd given Nicolau something that Savina couldn't, and would never be able to.

And Joska, too—what family did she have back in Colorida? The only one Savina knew about was the niece who'd gotten into trouble.

A niece who Joska loved enough that she was willing to give a second chance to a murderer, a thief and a ship hijacker, just because Savina reminded her of the girl.

It was a stupid, stupid sentiment.

But she had a quick flash of memory, the evenings in Yuur's safehouse—her, Nicolau, Beni, Joska, and Rafel chatting, or playing dice, or simply relaxing in comfortable silence after a long day's labour.

Maybe, after all, she was just as stupid as all those people she looked down on for their sentiment. Because she'd do anything at all —including what Reka was suggesting—to stop the look on Joska's face, if the woman lived through all this, when she found out her niece had been killed. To give Nicolau back that gleam of hope as he realized his adoptive parents were safe, no matter what was going to happen to him.

"Alright," she said quietly. "This is probably the stupidest thing I've ever done, but alright. I'll help you."

Reka turned to look at her, her expression unreadable.

"What about you?" asked Savina, as she pushed herself carefully to her feet. Pain jolted up her body as she put weight on her injured leg, but it was dampened by the tight bandage Reka had tied. "Do you have anyone back there you're going to miss?"

"No."

Savina glanced at Reka in surprise, but her expression forbade further questions.

And she was hit with a sudden, small jolt of pity.

No one in Colorida that Reka would miss.

Savina wished that was true for her.

It wasn't.

It didn't make sense, of course—all her worst fears, her deepest hatreds, were caught up in her memories of the compound. Her memories of her family, of her mother, who'd been willing to bury her son alive. And mixed in with the hate and the anger and the frustration, a sick, bittersweet nostalgia. Homesickness. Love and hate, resentment and bitterness and longing, all wrapped together in the same tangled mass.

And Reka didn't have even that, if what she was telling Savina was true.

"Alright," said Savina. "No point in putting it off, I guess."

She took a tentative step, and her leg almost buckled. Reka put out an arm to steady her, and Savina grabbed it without thinking.

Reka's skin was warm, her touch surprisingly gentle.

Savina scowled, and dropped her hand deliberately.

"The fuel storage is on the second floor down," said Reka, as if nothing had happened. "We'll have to get past the guards by the door without them sounding the alarm, but it should be fairly straightforward from there. Like I said, this isn't carrying anything too important, and it shouldn't be guarded heavily. We'll need to be quick. Once they get into the air I'm not sure they'll stay in close enough formation for us to do any damage."

Savina nodded, trying not to think too hard on the implication of Reka's words.

It wasn't like she hadn't been close to dying plenty of times on this damn trip. Mostly thanks to the woman next to her.

But it didn't make the terror go away.

"Do you have a knife?" asked Reka.

Savina nodded.

"And I have my pistol. Between the two of us, the guards shouldn't be a problem. It'll just be a matter of getting from there down to the fuel storage before they call in enough backup to kill us. I'll send a copy of the map through to your wavelink, in case one of us doesn't make it."

Savina nodded again, a tight mixture of anticipation and fear bubbling in her stomach. "I should call Joska," she whispered. "See if they're still alright. Let her know what we're doing so they can take advantage of it."

Reka glanced at her, then nodded.

Savina tried to ignore the way her stomach twisted.

She wasn't actually calling to warn Joska, much as she might tell herself so. She was calling because she wanted to hear the voice of one person who actually cared about her before she died.

Maybe Joska would let her talk to Beni and Nicolau for a minute. Although she wasn't sure if that would make things better or worse.

There was silence as the wavelink buzzed. And then, at last, she heard Joska's voice, and a flood of relief washed over her.

"Savina!" Joska's words were tense. "I've been trying to get a hold of you for the past standard hour, but you weren't answering."

Savina frowned, then remembered the hazy delirium of pain after she'd been captured. "Sorry," she muttered. "I was—I was busy." She paused. "Listen, Joska," she said at last. "The portal's either open, or about to, and the yibo have taken us onto the ship. But—" she swallowed hard. "But there's one last thing we can do. We're going to blow the ship up. The loading pad is packed tightly enough that we may be able to take out a few of the yibo gunships. If they stop to figure out what's going on, it might give you a chance to get the portal shut down still." She cleared her throat. "And. Um. I'm not sure if it's good news or bad news, but I'm—not going to make it out. So tell Beni and Nicolau—" she stopped, her voice choking off.

There was a long moment of silence from the other end of the wavelink, then Joska's wry voice. "Savina." There was an unfamiliar emotion in her tone.

Savina blinked.

"That … can't have been an easy decision for you to make. I'll be sure and tell Nicolau and Beni what you were willing to do for them. But—" she paused, a hint of humour creeping into her voice. "But I'm going to ask you to refrain from blowing up the ship just yet, since Rafel and Beni and I are on it. While I don't relish the thought of being blown sky-high, perhaps the more relevant fact is, we've hijacked the ship. So we may be able to find a way to keep the yibo busy that doesn't involve all of us being killed."

Savina stared at her wavelink, almost unable to process what she was hearing.

"Now. If you can, take out the guards—although I'd prefer you not kill anyone unless strictly necessary—and come up to the cockpit. We'll see if we can discuss plans that don't involve any of us dying."

28

Aran

It took until they were halfway to the compound before Aran's brain started functioning again.

Ines and Nicolau were clearly trying to be respectful, and also were clearly trying very hard to bite back smiles.

He honestly couldn't have cared less.

Istvay had kissed him. Istvay had said—

His brain shorted out any further thought.

It didn't matter. They were going to talk about things, finally, when he got back from this.

If he got back from this.

Which meant he was damn well determined that he would get back from this.

At last they reached the place overlooking the security compound, where he and Istvay had sat a few hours before. Behind them, he could still hear the sounds of the raiders fighting, the shrieks and screams and the hiss of weapons.

He took a deep breath and shook his head to clear it, then pulled out his binoculars, dialling them in.

Then he swore.

"What is it?" Ines' voice was as timid and worried as ever, but he knew damn well that didn't have any effect on her ability to do what needed to be done.

"Looks like they've noticed the raiders," he whispered.

Nicolau glanced back as a large explosion blossomed above the treetops. "It's … probably hard not to, at this point."

Aran nodded grimly. "You're right. But it's not going to make this any easier." He paused. "Give me a minute." He brought the binoculars back up to his eyes.

It was—well, honestly, even worse than he'd been expecting. The guards were scuttling around like insects, weapons ready, everyone on full alert.

"Alright," he said at last, lowering the binoculars.

Ines and Nicolau were watching him, their gaze eager and trusting, and he had to refrain himself from cursing.

He wasn't a leader. He didn't want to be. He was a damn scientist.

He closed his eyes for a moment, trying to tamp down the creeping panic. Ani gave a little chirrup, moving restlessly on his shoulders, and he rubbed her head to calm her. "If we keep to the trees, we can get around to the back of the compound. It looks like they've cleared the area around it, but in the back right corner it looks like there's a dark spot between the spotlights. We'll have to get through the forcefield and then through the fence, but I think it's our best bet at this point."

Nicolau and Ines nodded, that trace of hero worship in both their gazes.

Aran swore under his breath.

The three of them crept through the cover of the trees towards the brightly lit compound. The spotlights lit the night, their brightness dampened only slightly by the force-field surrounding the outer walls.

They reached the edge of the trees, and paused.

Aran gritted his teeth and sighed. Damn it to hell, he was rubbish at telling people what to do.

"Okay," he whispered. "I'll go first, you follow. Ani's acid does a lot of things, but it's not going to get us through a force-field. I have an emergency disrupter, but it doesn't work very well on yibo force-fields either, so we'll have to think of something else—"

"Wait!" said Nicolau, his face brightening. "Listen, when Savina and Beni and I were back with the yibo criminals, they used to have to get through force-fields all the time to get into places. They used something that was similar to a disrupter, and I ... I think I remember how to do it." He glanced at Aran. "If—if you don't mind me trying," he added awkwardly. "I mean, I'm sure you already know all—"

"No, no, please, go ahead," Aran broke in quickly.

Nicolau flushed, looking simultaneously wildly excited and hideously embarrassed. "We're going to have to get right up to the force-field, and it'll take me a minute or two after that."

Aran nodded. "Alright," he said. "It looks like the guards come by on a five-minute rotation. So from the looks of it, taking the sightlines into account, we'll have about two minutes. Is that enough time?"

Nicolau frowned dubiously. "It ... should be."

"If you have a pair of cutters, I can probably get us through the fence," said Ines.

Aran fumbled in his pouch, pulling out a small pair of cutters. "Will this do?"

Ines nodded, swallowing hard.

"Alright," said Aran, fighting back his sick terror. "We'll … we'll go in as soon as the next guard turns the corner."

Nausea churned in his stomach. He might get them killed. They might get into trouble he couldn't get them out of, and it would be his fault if they died.

He took a deep breath.

No point thinking about that right now. Focus on the task ahead. Focus on the guard on top of the wall.

"Now!" he hissed, and the three of them darted forwards.

They reached the wall moments later, and Nicolau took the device Aran handed to him and pulled a utility knife from his belt. He shoved the knife into the mechanics of the disrupter, prying it open. He was working steadily, his hands sure, but Aran could feel the sweat beading the back of his neck.

They must have used at least thirty seconds already.

The device popped open, and Nicolau shoved it against the outside of the force field, pressing it to the translucent surface.

A small crack appeared in the glowing field, and he pushed the tip of his utility blade through it. "I need something to pry it open," he hissed, and Ines snatched up a stick from the ground, handing it to him. Nicolau jammed it into the space, then dragged the device down the surface of the force-field, running the sharp blade of the knife after it, until there was a long, thin crack, held open by the branch.

Then he shoved the knife back into his pocket, braced his feet, and put his weight against the branch, the force-field straining back against the edges of the wood.

"In!" he whispered, his voice strained, and Ines glanced at him, then slipped through the crack.

Aran took the branch from Nicolau. "You next."

Nicolau looked conflicted, but when Aran gestured again, he did as he was told.

Aran braced the edge of the stick against the ground, then slipped through, tapping the stick with the toe of his boot as he went.

The stick sprang free, and the force-field snapped shut again with the three of them inside.

Aran bit back a curse. They were crammed into the narrow few centimetres between the force field and the razor-wire fence. He could already hear the sound of the guards' footsteps—

"Got it," hissed Ines, and he turned in surprise to see that she'd already managed to cut a long, neat slice down the wire of the fence.

Nicolau ducked through the opening, and Aran did the same, Ines close on their heels.

Aran glanced quickly around, then shoved the other two behind the shelter of a small outbuilding and threw himself down after them just as a guard rounded the corner. For a few moments they lay there panting, their breathing sounding harsh and loud in Aran's ears. Ani growled softly from her perch on his shoulders, and he gave her a reassuring pat. "Easy, sweetheart. You're such a brave girl, but we … probably shouldn't pick a fight right now."

The guard didn't seem to notice anything amiss, just kept on her way, and Aran let out a long sigh of relief. "Alright," he whispered when she'd turned the corner out of sight. "I've got a couple detonators, but we'll have to figure out where to plant them, because if we don't take down the mechanism completely, we're not getting another chance at it."

Nicolau and Ines nodded gravely as Aran took a quick scan of the building layout.

The problem was, he had no idea what the mechanism looked like or how it worked. His best guess was that the majority of the compound was dedicated to providing a power source, but where the hell would he need to plant an explosive to take out the mechanism itself?

He took a deep breath. "I guess we start at the main building and try some reconnaissance."

The three of them waited until the coast was clear, then scampered quickly to the shelter of the next building.

Their progress was agonizingly slow. Aran could still see dim flashes of light through the force-field that must be the raiders fighting, and he wondered for a hysterical half-second what would happen when they figured out the humans they'd been fighting over were gone.

At least it was distracting the yibo guards' attention—they should have been caught at least twice, but both times the guards were so busy trying to see what was happening outside that they paid no mind.

At last they stood in front of a side-door, Nicolau and Ines looking around nervously as Ani spat, and the lock mechanism steamed and hissed.

Aran pushed the door carefully, and it swung open. He glanced inside, then beckoned the others in, blinking in the dim light.

Then he groaned.

The building was a maze. It would take them hours to search this place.

Ines made a soft, startled sound, pointing to the wall. "The diagram, on the wall. The program I wrote won't read it, because it looks like it's a lot of numbers and symbols, but—but I might be able to decipher it myself, if you can give me a minute." She crossed quickly over to the diagram.

"Nicolau," Aran whispered. "Get your weapon out. If anyone sees us, we'll need to keep them occupied until Ines is done."

Nicolau nodded, pulling out a small pulse pistol. Aran did the same, moving to stand on one side of the hallway while Nicolau took the other.

Ines frowned over the diagram, her lips moving silently. Aran could feel the tension building in his muscles, but he fought it down.

At last, her face brightened. "It looks like the mechanism is underground, and I know where the entrance is," she whispered. "Two buildings down from here."

By the time they reached the small building Ines had indicated, and Ani had melted the lock on the door, Aran could sense a change in the atmosphere of the place—guards calling to each other, running footsteps, barked orders.

"Istvay?" he began through his wavelink. Then he remembered, abruptly, that Istvay's wavelink wasn't working.

It was odd how the thought made his stomach sink.

He took a deep breath.

Get this done and get out. That was all. Don't think about the fact he was on his own, without even Istvay's comforting voice through his wavelink, or the fact that the Chief Justice and the entire Joias system were depending on him. He couldn't think about any of that right now. Just get in, get this done, get out.

Whatever was happening outside, it must be something big—there was the sudden blare of an alarm, then another, more pounding footsteps from outside the building.

"We don't have much time!" he hissed as they slipped inside. "Ines, do you have any idea what the mechanism looks like?"

She shook her head. "The diagram didn't say anything about that."

He forced himself not to swear. "Well, I'm sure there'll be some sort of signage on the machine itself, maybe we can work it out from there."

There was nothing but empty rooms on the main floor of the building, and they located the stairwell easily enough. When they reached the bottom and stepped through the doorway, Aran stopped in astonishment.

The machine was huge, stretching out in a massive snarl of technology through an impressive underground bunker.

He groaned.

Ines had already moved to one corner of the machine, and was reading through the signs. Nicolau had gone over to help, although from the looks of it, he was being less helpful than he thought he was.

Aran scanned the room quickly.

This was going to take forever. And it would probably not take forever for them to be found out. He grabbed a large metal stool, wedging it firmly behind the door.

It might give them a few extra moments, at least.

He closed his eyes for a moment. The tension was a hard knot in the pit of his stomach, and he felt a bit like he was going to throw up.

The noise from outside was growing louder, and he could hear guards shouting.

And then there were footsteps on the stairway outside.

He cursed. "Ines—"

She looked up at him, her eyes frantic. "I'm—I'm sorry Aran, I haven't—"

"It's fine," he hissed, "just get away from there, get down—"

A fist slammed against the door, and Aran's AI translated, "Why's the door shut? Who's in there? Answer me!" There was a moment's pause, then the voice shouted, "Sound the alarm! Someone's in the machine room. Send in backup!"

Aran looked around frantically, then beckoned Ines and Nicolau over, pushing them down behind a large crate. It wouldn't do much, but it might protect them from the first wave of shots.

The yibo were pounding on the door.

Aran took a deep breath.

He could still feel Istvay's kiss on his lips, see the look in their eyes as they pulled away, heavy with longing.

"Come back to me, okay?"

He yanked out the two detonators and shoved one into Ines' hand and one into Nicolau's. "You stay hidden, I'm going to try to get out and signal Istvay for a distraction. When it's safe, keep trying to figure out where to plant the detonators. Understand?"

"But—" Nicolau began.

"Just do it, okay?" Aran whispered. "And—and if you get back and I don't, tell Istvay—" he paused, swallowing hard. "Tell them I'm sorry."

He stood, making his way at a crouching half-run towards the door.

He reached it, and positioned himself against the wall where it would open.

The yibo guards were still pounding on it, and someone shouted, "Stand back!"

There was a crackling, electric buzz, and the door dissolved.

The yibo burst in, stumbling over each other. Ani hissed, and the yibo closest to Aran stumbled backwards in alarm. Aran yanked the guard out of the way, dove past her, and pounded up the stairs. There were shouts behind him, but the yibo wouldn't risk shooting their atomizer weapons in here, not this close to the machine they'd been working so hard to protect.

He stumbled out into the courtyard, slapping the base of the flare against his thigh, and held it up. A brilliant red flame blossomed into the night, flattening against the force field.

A shot whizzed over his head, and he dropped the spent flare and dived to the ground as another shot impacted against the building behind him.

Then he scrambled to his feet and ran, blindly, not caring in which direction.

29

Savina

Savina paused for a moment outside the cockpit of the ship, wiping blood from her knife blade. Reka stood close behind her.

"Vina? Is that you?" Beni's voice came from inside as the door slid open.

Savina barely had time to answer before Beni launched themself at Savina and grabbed her into a tight hug, burying their face in Savina's shoulder. "Vina! I was so worried about you …"

For a moment, Savina was too stunned to react. And then she wrapped her arms around her sibling, and Beni clung to her, and for a moment she was just a kid again, before the whole world had become cold and complicated.

"What the hell happened to you, Savina?"

Savina jerked her head up at the dangerous tone in Joska's voice. Then she remembered, and glanced down, wiping blood from her face with her sleeve and swallowing back the nausea at the bloody mess that was her leg.

"Reka." Joska's voice had gone, if possible, even more dangerous. "Did you do this to her?"

Savina blinked at Joska. The woman's expression was hard, and so stern that even though her gaze was focused on Reka, Savina found her brain automatically searching through her own actions of the past few weeks to figure out what she should be apologizing for.

Reka looked, for once, completely nonplussed.

Beni pulled back. "Vina? Are you hurt?" They spun on Reka as well. "Reka Soler, I swear to you, if you touched my sister—"

"No," Savina stammered. "It wasn't her, it was the yibo. And— and anyway, it's not as bad as—"

Joska shot her a look that told her as clear as words what she thought of the excuse, then turned back to Reka. "I expect an explanation."

Savina stared at Joska, unsure she'd heard correctly.

Reka was still staring as well.

Rafel had limped out from the cockpit, and was glaring at Reka over Joska's shoulder.

"Well?" said Joska in that infuriating tone she had, that managed to convey both stern disapproval, and a sincere belief that you could do better.

It was … gratifying to hear that tone turned on someone other than Savina, for once.

And for the first time in her life, she caught Reka looking faintly sheepish.

"I'm sorry," the woman said at last.

Savina almost sputtered in astonishment.

"You're right. She presented me with the plan, and I was angry, and I didn't sufficiently consider the risks when I agreed to it. I was negligent, and I apologize." Reka must have seen the look in Joska's eyes, because she turned to Savina. "I … apologize, Savina," she said quietly. "I didn't mean for that to happen to you. I didn't take the precautions I should have. That is my own fault, and I'm truly sorry you suffered the consequences of it."

There was a sincerity in her tone that Savina hadn't expected.

Savina couldn't do anything but blink at her.

Reka gave Savina a small, wry smile, and turned back to Joska. "So, Joska. I assume you have a plan?"

"I believe I do," said Joska. "I know Savina can work ship's guns —I assume you can as well? While you're right, an explosion on the loading dock would take out a few ships, I think we'll be better served if we can keep them from getting off the ground in the first place, perhaps damage the infrastructure as well. We won't have to keep them occupied permanently, just long enough for our famous adventurer Aran to get the portal mechanism taken down."

"Aran Romeu? Aran Romeu is working with you?"

Savina glanced over, and caught a glimpse of admiration on Reka's face that was entirely unexpected.

Joska smiled a little. "He is, he and Istvay. Or, working with Alba, at least. When I left, the two of them had just made their escape from some raiders they'd tracked down and convinced to … help them with genetic analysis, from what I understand? As far as I've seen, Aran is … more or less exactly what the rumours paint him to be. I have no doubt between him and Istvay, they'll figure it out."

Savina had never expected to see a tinge of something like hero worship on Reka's face. But then, she'd seen a hell of a lot of unexpected things in the past few hours.

It took them only a few minutes to get situated: Reka and Savina in the gun tower, Joska in the pilot seat, Rafel as copilot, and Beni navigating.

Savina was absurdly grateful that Joska had managed to talk Nicolau into staying behind. Not that it was that much less dangerous there than here, from what Joska had said, but—well, but she couldn't imagine it being much more dangerous.

"I'm no trick pilot," said Joska quietly into the amplifier. "I can fly us a straight course, and I can keep us pointed at the target, but that's about my skill level. Beni? What have you found for the shields on this thing?"

"I found how to set them up," said Beni, their voice tight with worry. "I have the specs on their relative strength, but I'm not familiar with yibo measurements, so I don't have any idea what it means realistically."

"Well, we'll do what we can," said Joska. "I'll do my best to keep us from being hit, but Savina and Reka, this will fall mostly on you. You'll have to disable ships, and take out all the infrastructure targets you can. And you'll have to keep them busy enough that they're focused on defending themselves instead of attacking."

"From what we saw on our way in, this is mostly an air-based offensive," Rafel grunted through the wavelink. "They don't seem keen to land troops on Colorida, which makes sense for what we know of their motives. They'll want a show of force, not an actual war. So as far as I'm concerned, take out the biggest guns you can find. The moment they no longer look intimidating, they'll start having second thoughts about going ahead with this."

"Rafel's right, I think," said Joska. "I don't know how long we'll last. I don't know whether or not this will be effective, and to be honest, I'm not even sure what's happening back with the others. But we'll do our best to buy them some time." She paused a moment. "And Savina," she added. "You know how I feel about unnecessary casualties."

Savina rolled her eyes from habit. "Only kill if you have to, blah blah blah," she grumbled, but she found she was smiling.

She could hear the smile in Joska's voice in response. "Very good. I knew you were a quick learner." She paused again. "Are you ready, then?"

"I'm ready," Reka's voice was as calm as always.

"I'm ready, too," said Savina shortly.

Her hands were still shaky, and she wasn't sure whether it was the shock of the injury, or the shock of the rescue, or something else entirely.

Reka glanced over at her. "Are you alright?" she asked.

Savina scowled. "I can do what I need to. I know damn well that's all you care about."

Reka frowned. "Savina," she said at last. "Your captain friend was right. We were working together. And as much as I might have … personal disagreements with you, that carries with it a degree of responsibility. I'm sorry I—"

"Shut up," Savina said through gritted teeth. "I'm not your responsibility. I don't need your damn pity. We pretended we cared about each other because we both needed to stay alive. You don't have to pretend anymore. Joska's not stupid enough that you can fool her like you fooled Kachik, and nor am I."

Reka raised her eyebrows, but said nothing.

Savina turned back to the gun controls. "Joska?" she snapped.

"Beni's sending me the information," said Joska. "And… we're moving. Hold on, this might get interesting in a hurry."

Savina settled herself into her seat as the ship lifted off the ground. She could hear the shouts through the cockpit radio, her wavelink translating the yibo's consternation.

"Paging ship 879. You do not have permission to embark. Repeat, you do not have permission to embark. Please return at once to your station …"

"Remember, disable them." Joska's voice was strained. The ship turned, so they were pointing towards the loading pad.

"And—when you're ready."

Reka got off the first shot, taking off the wing of one of the larger gunships. The yibo shouted through the radio, and Savina could see them fumbling about like ants whose hill had been stepped on.

Savina aimed her sights towards another gunship, lining up with the body. Then she cast a sideways glance at Reka and scowled.

It was clearly a shot to maximize casualties, so she'd have to play it off as a mistake to Joska. And she wasn't damn well about to admit making a mistake in front of Reka.

She shifted her aim to one side, and the entire tail section of the ship exploded.

Reka fired on a communications tower, and Savina recalibrated her aim to another gunship.

"You're going to have to be faster," said Joska through the radio. "They're getting the ground guns out, it looks like. I'm going to have to go up in a minute."

Reka fired again, then once more, and the communications tower went up in a ball of flame.

Then there was a roar of sound, and the entire ship shook. Savina was thrown against the straps, and gasped out a breathless curse as pain blossomed across her side from her bruises.

"Go!" shouted Beni. "If we get hit with another of those, the shields are gone."

Joska spun the ship, and there was the unsettling gut-punch of acceleration as it shot upwards.

Behind them, crews were scrambling for the gunships.

"Once we're out of atmosphere, this is going to be a dogfight," said Joska through the radio. "Hold on."

Then they were through, and out into the clean black of space.

The yibo ship must be equipped with artificial gravity, because despite a slight disorientation, Savina didn't feel the now-familiar weightlessness of the *Dolphin*.

Other ships were bursting through the atmosphere behind them, and she spun in her seat, lining up her gun sights on the fleeing ships.

She shot, and one of them spiralled off, its tail section split open.

Savina wasn't certain if that was technically not killing them, but really, there was only so much that could be expected of her once they were in space.

Reka was firing steadily, and between the two of them, the ships leaving atmosphere were being shot down almost as they came through.

But they couldn't hit everyone. There was no way. There were too many of them, and they were coming through far too quickly, and it was taking more than just one shot to take them out now that their shields were up.

And to make matters worse, the survivors were forming up, their combined shields heavy enough that Savina's and Reka's shots could hardly make a dent.

"Joska," Savina said through her teeth.

"I know," said Joska quietly. "I know."

The ship rocked, and from the cockpit, Beni gave a startled yelp.

Joska swore. "We're not going to be able to afford many more direct hits."

"We're doing the best we can back here," snapped Savina. She was firing as fast as she could aim, and so was Reka, but—it wasn't going to be enough.

The ship rocked again.

"Savina," said Joska quietly through the link. "Before you knew we'd taken the ship, you were telling me there was one last thing you could do."

Savina turned to glance at Reka.

"Yes," said Savina. "Yes, we did."

"It looks like we're not going to make it out of this alive," said Joska. "I don't suppose you still have that explosive?"

Savina glanced at Reka again. The woman nodded grimly.

"Yes," said Savina. "We do."

"Good," said Joska. She paused. "Their formation is still tightly packed. If we were to fly in there, and if we timed the explosion right ..." she didn't finish the sentence.

"That would mean a hell of a lot of casualties," said Savina. She was trying to make her voice mocking, but it wasn't really working.

"I know," said Joska. "But ... I can't sit by and watch the Joias system be destroyed." She paused a moment, then added wryly, "At the very least, I suppose I won't be alive to feel bad about it afterwards."

30

Alba

A few minutes after Aran and the others disappeared, Istvay returned to where Alba waited with Yosip and Feliu. Istvay seemed more distracted than usual, but when she glanced at them questioningly, they just glared at her.

"Let's get out of here," Istvay whispered. "As far away as we can. If any of the raiders find us, all bets are off. And we need to be somewhere we can make a distraction for Aran when he needs it."

They glanced around quickly, and she could see in their face the sudden realization of what exactly they were working with—an old woman and two old men, Feliu the youngest of them.

Istvay didn't say anything, though, just gestured with their chin for the others to follow and started off through the trees. But they matched their pace to Alba's, and didn't try to rush her.

It wasn't until the group of them reached a dip between two of the rolling hills, the crest of the hill above them high enough that they could barely see the top of the yibo facility over the edge of it, that she realized that Istvay wasn't only going slowly to let her and the others keep up. They were breathing heavily even with the minor exertion, and their face was pale and drawn.

"Listen," they said. "The three of you stay down here. I'll go up and watch for Aran's flare." They paused. "I'll need your help once the flare goes off. I can't create the distraction by myself."

"I suggest we make a distraction immediately." Alba's muscles were trembling with strain, and the remembered despair at the thought they'd lost everything still buzzed uncomfortably through her body. "If we can get the guards watching over here—"

"No." Istvay's voice was flat. "We're going to do this Aran's way."

"But—" Alba began.

Istvay cut her off with the brusque gesture. "We're doing this the way Aran asked."

Alba turned to glare at them. "Aran is down there," she said, her voice icy. Her whole body was still shaky from the panic. "We can see what's going on better than he can. I suggest that we find out—"

Istvay spun on her, and she almost stepped back at the fury in their expression. "I am not going to discuss this any further," Istvay said through their teeth. "Do you ever, even once, stop to think about the fact that other people might know better than you how to deal with their own circumstances?"

"And do you ever stop to think that sometimes people misjudge their own situations? That sometimes, it's better for someone with a higher vantage point to make the decisions?" she snapped back.

Istvay looked at her for a long moment, and the expression on their face was odd—anger mixed with something that was almost pity.

"No," they said quietly. "I don't. Because I trust Aran. Aran knows what he's doing. If he needs help, he'll tell me. That's the only reason we can work together the way we do—I trust Aran with my life, and he trusts me with his. And so, no. I won't try to make a decision for him."

They paused. "I've—done that before," they said at last. "Made decisions that I thought were in Aran's best interest, instead of letting him make them himself. And—and I'm learning just how much I regret that. There was—I—" they broke off, and drew in a deep breath. "I almost ruined maybe the most important thing in my life because I did that. And I'm still not sure I can save it, but I'm damn well going to try." They studied her. "And you, Alba. Chief Justice of the Joias System. You've never once trusted someone that much, have you?"

Alba was silent.

She felt suddenly very, very tired.

She couldn't dispute what Istvay had said. She'd always carried the burden of the decisions, even when that burden was far too heavy, because she'd never been able to trust someone else to make them.

She'd never trusted someone else enough to take her own hands off of the controls.

She glanced back at Istvay. They looked exhausted, sick and weak, and she could see the bones of their face in sharp relief.

Istvay didn't have long.

But they trusted Aran. Trusted him enough to let him make decisions that could shape both their own fate, and the fate of the Joias System.

"I suppose you're right," she said at last, quietly.

Istvay's head jerked up in shock.

"We'll do it your way," she said. "We'll wait for Aran's signal."

Istvay was still staring at her. At last, they gave a brusque nod and turned away.

But the look in their eyes as they turned had been less enmity than it had been surprise.

They'd been expecting a fight, she realized.

She realized, too, how close she'd been to giving them one. Weeks ago, she would have simply ignored what Istvay had to say completely.

She took a deep breath and let it out again slowly.

Maybe this alien landscape was teaching her more than just her own capacity for discomfort. Although whether the lessons were valuable or dangerous, she wasn't entirely sure yet.

"Alright," said Istvay. They fumbled in their supplies pouch and withdrew a handful of small metal devices, then handed one each to her, Yosip, and Feliu. "When the flare goes off, I have an idea how to make a distraction. But in order for it to work, we're going to need to spread out. These are transmitters, and they're going to—"

From the direction of the compound, a bright red glow lit the sky.

Istvay's head jerked up, and they cursed. "We're out of time," they said tersely. "The transmitters will mess with the raider ships' signals. I don't have time to explain, we've got to do this now. Feliu, I need you twenty metres that way. Yosip, over the hill and twenty metres in the other direction. Alba, stay where you are. You'll all need to hold the transmitters over your head. Don't worry about the rest, I'll take care of it, just stay where I put you."

They pulled another small device out of their supplies pouch, activated it, and clipped it to their belt.

"I'll come back when I can," they said, then they started off towards the top of the hill.

Alba watched them go, her teeth clenched.

This wasn't going to work. Istvay was clearly at the end of their strength. They'd never make it far enough to do—whatever it was they were planning on doing.

Istvay reached the top of the hill, staggering a little, shouting and waving their arms.

Alba's chest tightened in sudden, unreasoning terror.

Istvay was bringing the raiders here. Right down in the centre of them.

She closed her eyes for a moment. It didn't matter. It hardly mattered if they were killed, as long as the portal was taken down—

But the portal was still open, and the distraction was their only hope, and Istvay was bringing the raiders here.

She took a deep breath and forced herself to steady.

In the back of her mind, she heard Istvay's words. *"You've never once trusted someone that much, have you?"*

It was true. She didn't trust anyone that much.

But she'd seen the way Istvay looked at Aran.

Whatever else she believed about them, she could trust that—that Istvay would never, ever do something that would hurt Aran, not if they could help it. That Istvay wouldn't lie to Aran. And if Aran needed a distraction to take down the portal …

The raiders must have seen them—the ships had turned in their direction.

"You have to hold up the transmitters," Istvay shouted back, and started off down the hill toward the raider ships at a stumbling run.

Feliu glanced at Alba. She gave a small, brusque nod.

Her heart was pounding. She had no idea what the transmitters were supposed to do, but—

Well, she was out of her depth now. Trusting Istvay was the only option.

Yosip had already activated his device, and the three of them stood where Istvay had showed them, holding the devices up as the raider ships swooped closer.

There was a stuttering burst of weapons fire from the other side of the hill, and Alba closed her eyes, trying not to imagine how Istvay's body would look if they'd been caught in that. The expression on Aran's face, if he came back and found them.

There was another burst of weapons fire. Alba's heart was in her throat.

The ships appeared over the edge of the hill, almost on top of her and Yosip and Feliu.

Istvay must have miscalculated. Istvay must be lying dead, and now she and Yosip and Feliu were all going to die as well.

She'd trusted them. She'd let Istvay and Aran make the decisions they thought would be best, the ones she should have made herself. And the two of them had miscalculated somewhere. There'd be no distraction for Aran, no way to stop the yibo and the raiders from streaming through the open portal, destroying everything on the other side. Everything she knew, everything she loved. Everything she'd given her entire life for.

Still, she held up the transmitter the way Istvay had demonstrated.

And then, as suddenly as they'd appeared, the raider ships pulled up short. They spun, all of them, and shot back the way they'd come, towards the yibo compound at the bottom of the hill.

31

Istvay would give him a distraction. They'd promised. But until then, Aran was the only distraction any of them had.

He made it behind the shelter of one of the smaller outbuildings and dropped to the ground, yanking out his pistol.

Ani was hissing on his shoulder, bridling, barely restraining herself.

"Easy, girl," he said soothingly. "I'll tell you when, okay?"

The yibo soldiers skidded around the side of the building, saw Ani, and stumbled to a halt, jumping back out of sight. Ani spit on Aran's whispered command, leaving a smoking hole in the floor of the courtyard where the guard had just been.

"What the hell?" Aran's AI translated.

"Stay back," said Aran, trying to keep his voice steady. "Just … stay back."

"Human." The voice was deep, with a strong accent and arrogant tone. "Human, whatever it is you're doing, you may as well stop. We found the two down by the machine, and we have them trapped. They're going to die, and if you don't want to die as well, you'd best give yourself up."

Aran's stomach tightened at the yibo's words.

Ines and Nicolau. They'd damn well trusted him. Dammit, he hadn't asked for this, he'd never asked for any of this.

He took a deep breath, and let it out slowly. "Listen," he said, trying to keep his voice from shaking. "If I give myself up, will you keep the other two alive?"

From outside, the man spat out a sudden, panicked curse in yibo.

There was the sound of running footsteps. And then … nothing.

Aran stared around him in bewilderment.

Then something crashed into the force field above him with an impact loud enough to set Aran's ears ringing.

There was an explosion. The force field flickered.

It died.

Aran blinked, not quite believing his eyes, as a raider attack pod tumbled through, followed by four others.

In the compound, yibo were running, screaming, diving for cover. A raider ship shot through after the pods, and this one Aran dimly recognized as the ship that had hunted them from the yibo city.

He shook his head to clear it and sprinted back towards the entrance to the underground bunker.

One of the ships must have seen him—he leapt out of the way of a blast that scorched a smoking hole in the concrete, then dived into the small building. The door of it exploded behind him, then he was pounding down the stairs. He ducked through the doorway at the bottom to find the underground room devolved into pure chaos, yibo shoving and screaming and trying to get out of the way.

"Ines! Nicolau!" he shouted. "Are you in here?"

"Aran? What the hell is going—" Nicolau began in a strained voice from where they'd sheltered in a corner, but Aran cut him off.

"Ines, did you figure out where we can plant the detonators?"

Ines nodded.

Behind them, the stairwell exploded.

"Then let's get the hell over there," Aran shouted above the noise.

Nicolau and Ines jumped to their feet. Ines beckoned, and Aran and Nicolau followed her through the twisting maze that was the heart of the mechanism.

Another explosion rocked the entryway to the bunker.

It appeared the raider ship had decided to simply blow its way down the stairs after Aran.

"What the hell is going on out there?" panted Nicolau. "Why is there someone—"

"Long story," muttered Aran. "Let's just get this damn detonator planted and get the hell out."

There was another explosion behind them.

"Here!" Ines whispered. "If we can take this section down, it should shut down the portal. This connects the mechanism to the energy generator, and it should set off a chain explosion."

Aran grabbed a handful of detonators from his pouch and tossed them in a loose pile at the centre of the place Ines had indicated.

"I'm going to shoot a pulse blast to trigger the detonators and start the reaction," he whispered. "We'll have to run like hell if we want to make it out alive. You two get started, I'll follow."

The two of them hesitated, their faces tight with strain.

There was another explosion from the raider ship, and the ceiling above their heads creaked with the strain.

Aran aimed his pistol at the detonators. "Go!" he gasped, and fired.

Then he turned, and the three of them ran, the sharp *pop* of the detonators sounding behind them.

"This way!" Ines panted. "There's an emergency exit—"

They reached it, and Nicolau fired a shot from his pulse pistol into the door. The lock exploded, and he shoved it open with bare force, then the three of them were pounding up the stairway.

The shock from the bunker's explosion caught them just as they emerged, picking them up and flinging them across the courtyard. Aran landed hard, gasping, the breath knocked from him, Ani clinging desperately to his shoulders. His leg ached, and there was a sharp, stinging pain in his arm.

He looked around frantically for Ines and Nicolau, and saw them laying on the concrete a few metres away. Ines was already pushing herself into a sitting position, but Nicolau's eyes were closed, his face pale, blood trickling from a cut on his forehead.

The raider ship swung around, hovering over them.

Then it rocked back with the force of another explosion as a second raider ship appeared.

Aran could make out Krevai in the cockpit. He was grinning maniacally, sharp incisors gleaming, as the two ships turned their attention to each other.

"Let's go!" Aran hissed.

Ines pushed to her feet, hurling herself towards Nicolau. "Nikki! Nikki, are you—"

Nicolau groaned, his eyes fluttering open.

Ines gave a small sob of relief.

Aran grabbed Nicolau on one side, pulling the young man's arm over his shoulders, and Ines steadied him on the other side.

"Nikki, you're—you're alright, you're—" She went up on her tiptoes and kissed him.

Nicolau flushed a deep red, a dazed smile on his face.

Aran looked away, fighting back the ache in his chest.

"Come back to me, okay?"

Soon.

"Come on. We've got to get out of here," he muttered, and, supporting a stumbling Nicolau between them, he and Ines ran for the opening the raiders had blasted through the force field.

As they slid through the opening, there was a sharp crack of light bright enough to momentarily turn the night to midday. Aran glanced up on instinct, then shielded his eyes as the light brightened

—

And then it disappeared.

And the portal disappeared with it.

32

Alba

Alba watched in shock as the raider ships crashed through the force-field, fighting like two dogs in the street. The entire compound lit up with explosions as she watched in disbelieving silence.

Yosip and Feliu had come to join her, and the three of them stared down at the destruction below.

"Well," said Feliu at last. "I suppose that should provide a distraction."

Alba just nodded, too stunned to speak.

There was another explosion, more massive than any of the ones that had come before, and an entire section of the courtyard caved in as yibo scattered in every direction.

The rumbling boom had scarcely died away when the sky above them, where the portal cut a gash through the emptiness of space, lit up, brighter and brighter, until they all had to shield their eyes against the brilliance.

It brightened even more, momentarily so brilliant that it burned even through her closed eyelids.

And then the light vanished. She opened her eyes, blinking.

When her sight had readjusted to the darkness, she looked up in the sky where the portal had been.

It was gone.

They'd done it. Somehow, they'd done it.

Yosip was grinning so wide that his smile hardly fit on his face. Even Feliu was smiling, an expression of mixed wonder and happiness, and just a touch of regret.

And suddenly, the implications of what they had done finally hit.

Alba took a deep breath, closing her eyes.

She wasn't sure, exactly, what she was feeling—happiness or horror.

She'd done it. She'd done what she set out to do, saved the Joias System.

And now the portal was closed, and hundreds of humans trapped here, forever.

From everything she'd seen, they were doomed to an existence of slavery or outright death. And she'd been the one responsible.

"You've never once trusted someone that much, have you?" Istvay had asked.

In the end, though, she had trusted them, them and Aran. She'd trusted them to take down the portal. But as for the decision to take the portal down in the first place—she'd made that decision herself. And she'd have to live with that, for however long the remainder of her life would be.

There was a noise behind her, and she spun in time to see Istvay. Their face was pale and damp with sweat, their expression one of grim determination, and they moved slowly, as if every step was an effort, but they were grinning.

"I told you Aran knew what he was doing," they said, coming up to stand with the three of them. Their voice was ragged with exhaustion.

Alba turned to them, frowning. "Istvay," she said. "Are you—"

She wasn't sure how to finish the sentence.

She'd known plenty of people who'd died from the defect—you could hardly avoid that, growing up in the Joias System. But most of the people she'd known had died years ago—no one with the defect survived much past thirty, and she was well into her seventies.

Even when she'd been in her thirties, she hadn't known what to say to someone dying of it. What did you say to someone whose body was slowly killing them?

Istvay managed a small smile. "I'll be alright," they said. "Anyways, until Aran and I find something, there's nothing I can do about it."

Alba nodded stiffly, and turned back to watch the chaos below them.

There was a sound from above, and she looked up, startled, to see three large yibo ships approaching.

She tensed. "If they're here to—" she began.

Istvay had tensed as well, but they shook their head. "If they're here to fix the portal, they won't be able to, at least not easily. Aran knows what he's doing."

Alba nodded. "I suppose if that's the case, we can hardly complain if we lose our lives to Kachik's people rather than the raiders. At least the yibo shouldn't eat us."

Istvay looked at her in surprise, then gave a small snort of laughter. Yosip chuckled as well.

Feliu looked scandalized. "Madam," he began.

Then the first of the yibo appeared over the top of the hill.

Alba could tell at once that these yibo were military. Something about their posture and their uniform was somehow universal.

The yibo stopped on seeing them, appearing taken aback. More came over the hill, and the yibo who appeared to be the commanding officer snapped at them, "What are you—"

She trailed off, staring down at the humans. Then she shook her head. "Humans." There was a note in her voice Alba couldn't interpret. "Well, it looks like we found the cause of this." The captain paused a moment. "Go get Jair," she called over her shoulder.

One of the yibo soldiers jogged off in the direction she indicated, and the captain gestured her people to stay back.

At last the yibo soldier returned, with a tall figure in tow.

Alba frowned.

And then her heartbeat sped up.

The figure wasn't yibo. It wasn't a raider either.

It was a human. One who was completely unfamiliar.

"Hello," said the man, stepping forward. His face was weathered and weary looking, and his accent one she hadn't heard before. "What are you doing here?"

The explanations took some time.

Jair, as he introduced himself, was, it appeared, originally from the Labirinto System. He refused to elaborate, though, when Alba asked, just said in a quiet tone, "If you're caught by Kachik and his people, you'll be killed. Irra is offering you asylum. It's the same offer she's made to any humans who have come through the portal."

Alba stared at him in confusion. "Asylum?"

Jair nodded grimly. "We saw the portal open, but Irra wasn't ready to start an outright war with Kachik over it. A human system wasn't exactly worth a civil war." He shrugged dryly. "She planned to come down here and see if she could talk Kachik into peace, and then the portal opened again. We came as fast as we could, but—"

he shrugged again. "It seems you've taken care of the problem yourselves." He paused a moment, then leaned in closer. She saw the tension in his face. "Thank the Holy Mystery you did," he said quietly. "If you have anyone you love back in that system, thank the Holy Mystery that you managed to shut the portal down."

Alba watched him for a long moment, her heart pounding. "They're offering us asylum?" she asked at last. "As a fellow human, would you advise us to take it?"

The man nodded without hesitation. "If Kachik gets his hands on you, you're as good as dead. This is your only safe option." He paused. "And if you come, you may be in a position to do some good. The government is debating how to handle the human issue, including any refugees who may have arrived through the portal. Having someone here from your system would be—helpful."

Alba watched him. At last she said quietly, "I'll need to talk with the others before I can make a decision."

Jair nodded and stepped back.

Alba walked slowly back to where the others were waiting, and gave them a brief summary of the conversation. She could sense Istvay's tension as she spoke, see the frown of concern growing on Feliu's face.

"I don't know that we have much of a choice," said Yosip quietly when she'd finished. "And—" he paused. "And Alba. This may be our chance to do something, at least, for the others we've stranded here. I think we have a responsibility to do that."

Slowly, Alba nodded. "Istvay?" She asked at last.

Istvay shook their head. "You go on. I'm going back to camp to wait for Aran. I told him I'd meet him there, and I don't want him to come and not find me. He'll worry. Besides, we promised to go back with the raiders, and Aran's not going to change his mind about that

—he's far too stubborn." They paused a moment. "If you see him, tell him I'm waiting." Their voice was quiet, and there was something soft and fond and sharp with longing in their tone.

Alba nodded, and Istvay turned back to the camp, walking slowly.

Jair watched them go, concern on his face.

Alba turned to him. "We accept your offer of asylum," she said briskly. "Istvay, however, and their friend, had some unfinished business with the raiders they needed to take care of. And we're waiting for a few others. I can't speak for them, but I assume they'll want to come with us as well."

Jair nodded and sighed. "Alright. I'll let the captain know and we'll prepare quarters for you in the ships. In the meantime, we were planning on taking over the facility to stop Kachik from rebuilding, but—" he glanced down at the smoking destruction below them. "It appears that will not be necessary."

"I very much doubt it would be," Alba murmured.

She watched Jair leave, saying something to the yibo captain as he passed. The woman nodded brusquely and barked a command, and a handful of soldiers started back to the ship at a smart march.

"Well, what do you think?" asked Yosip. "Do we have a chance?"

"Of course we do."

Alba turned to look at Feliu in surprise.

He was looking at Yosip. "I'm not sure what you think of Alba," he continued, in his usual curt tones. "But I think you've been around long enough to know that she won't give up, not as long as there's a chance to save lives." He paused. "People have asked me, before, why I've served as her clerk for so long. I could have gone on to do other things, I suppose. But—" he turned, catching Alba's eyes for just a moment. "But of all the politicians I've worked with, the Chief Justice is one who actually tries to do the right thing. She doesn't prevaricate, and she doesn't compromise her morals, whatever the personal or political cost. And I have always been proud to work with her."

Alba stared, her mind gone completely blank.

Yosip smiled, that warm, friendly smile he had. "Yes," he said quietly. "I've noticed the same thing." He turned to Alba. "Very well, Alba," he said. "I suppose we'd best go see if it's still possible to save our friends back in Kachik's city."

Alba blinked rapidly for a moment, and she had to clear her throat before she could speak. "I suppose we'd better," she said.

The three of them started after Jair towards the yibo ship.

33

Savina

Savina watched the packed ship formation, the open portal black and threatening behind them.

There was a sick feeling in her stomach.

They'd failed.

Nicolau had failed, and she couldn't stop and think, right now, what that probably meant.

Because she was going to die, too, in just a few minutes.

The defensive formation had turned, focused now on sheltering the ships headed for the portal, rather than attacking Joska's ship. And, as they'd all learned after the breakup of the diplomatic ship, the portal was much closer to the yibo planet than it had been from Colorida. Even the injured escape pods from the diplomatic ship had been able to make the planet in less than twenty-four hours.

And these yibo ships were much, much faster than the escape pods.

"I'll hold them with the guns," said Savina, glancing at Reka. "You plant the explosive."

Reka nodded without speaking, and slipped down from the

gunner's seat. She pulled out the explosive from the pocket of her suit and activated her wavelink. "I can give us up to five minutes once I set the explosive. How long will you need to get us into the middle of them, Joska?"

Savina felt something tighten in her throat.

Before, it had only been her who was going to die. Well, her and Reka—but then, it had seemed fitting, somehow, that the two of them would die together.

But now it was Beni. Rafel. Joska.

Savina would have never imagined worrying about someone like Joska—someone whose ship she'd hijacked, someone who insisted on treating her like a rebellious teenager, someone who constantly got in the way of her plans.

Someone who, against all odds and against all common sense, actually cared about Savina. Someone who, when Savina was lying on the floor in the basement of the yibo government building, wondering if she was about to be beaten to death, was the person she'd thought of. The person she'd wished, sharply and irrationally, could be there. Not to save her, just—just so that there'd be someone who'd care when she died.

She took a deep breath, turning back to the guns. "I guess you don't care about me killing them now, since we're about to send all of them to the damn Void," she said through her wavelink, trying to make her tone snarky.

"'Not care' might be a stretch," came Joska's familiar dry voice. "But realize the necessity? Reluctantly, yes."

"Realize I'm right about killing, you mean," said Savina, in an attempt at humour.

Joska snorted. "May the Mystery strike me down if that ever happens."

"I don't think you'll have to wait for the Mystery to strike you down, from the looks of things," said Savina. She lined up a shot and sent it off, and a yibo ship disintegrated.

"I'm in the fuel storage room," came Reka's brisk, emotionless voice. "Let me know when you want me to set it."

"Give me a minute," Joska muttered.

The ship shook as another shot hit them, and Beni made a small sound of distress.

Savina closed her eyes.

She was supposed to keep Beni safe. And Beni was going to die here, without even Savina there holding their hand …

"Alright," said Joska. "As soon as I get—"

She broke off with a choked curse.

Savina whirled, staring out the gunner's viewport.

The portal overhead was spitting and crackling like a grease-fire with water tossed onto it.

"What in the hell—" Rafel began in a strained voice.

The portal cracked and snapped again, glowing whipcracks of energy flying off it and hurtling into space.

"Someone gets hit with one of those, they won't be around long enough to complain about it," said Joska, her tone awed.

"Vina? Vina, what's happening?" Beni's voice through Savina's wavelink was frantic.

"It's alright, Beni," said Savina, her voice oddly soft. "I think … I think—"

"The portal's closing," Rafel broke in gruffly. "The Chief Justice or that scientist or someone must have figured something out. The portal's closing."

The yibo ships had obviously realized the same thing they had. The ones closest to the portal had turned tail and were fleeing at top speed.

As Savina watched, another bolt of energy cracked out, hitting one of the ships. It disintegrated, and Savina was hit with an awful, horrifying flashback to the sight of the diplomatic ship exploding as the *Dolphin* fled for its life.

And then, in a shuddering burst of light so bright that the afterimages were seared across Savina's eyelids—the portal was gone.

For a long time, there was stunned silence across the ship.

At last, Joska said in an awed voice, "Well." She fell silent, as if unsure how to continue.

"Is—is it closed?" Beni's voice was quiet.

"It's closed, for good or for ill," said Joska, her tone still quiet. "And we're trapped here. But Joias is safe."

Slowly, Savina became aware of the background noise, the frantic chatter through the radio as yibo ships raced to try to pull survivors from the broken hulls of the ships that had been too close.

Once, Savina might have suggested shooting down as many as they could while the yibo were distracted. But the horror of the diplomatic ship's breakup weeks ago, the thousands of lives lost to the void of space, was still playing in her memory, and she couldn't seem to make herself bring it up.

Joska would never have agreed, anyway.

"We won't be any help with survivors," said Joska at last. "They'll think we're going in to attack. So I think the best we can do is leave them to salvage what they can." Her voice was quiet and grave.

They came back down through the atmosphere, and Joska piloted them to the tiny clearing where they'd landed the *Dolphin* weeks earlier.

The ship was there now, battered and worn, but familiar. Waiting for them.

They left the damaged yibo ship where it was, and gathered in the cockpit of the *Dolphin.*

"So," said Joska, when they were all together. She looked beyond tired, worn and exhausted, strain lines written across her weathered face.

Savina waited for her to continue, but she seemed not to know what to say next.

"What do we do now?" asked Beni.

Joska turned to them and tried to smile. "I suppose that's the question we should all be asking. The portal's gone, and if things turned out as planned, the mechanism is completely destroyed. So we're here for the foreseeable future. Likely the rest of our lives, however long that ends up being. Because as far as I can tell," she added wryly, "we are not on the yibo's best-friend list."

Savina gave a half-hearted snort, and Joska smiled.

"While we were back on the agricultural planet, we found out some more about the politics of this place," Joska continued at last. "Apparently, the yibo in this city aren't the actual legal government. They're some sort of rebel offshoot. I—don't know what that means for us, but I suppose it's possible there's at least a chance at diplomacy left, for those of us trapped here. I expect that's Alba's intention. However, Savina, she knows who you are. And I know how you feel about that. So. What are your thoughts?"

There were a long few moments of silence.

At last, Reka spoke up. "Joska. You seem like a good person, and an honest one. And I'm well aware that you saved my life just now. And so I'm going to be honest with you, as well. You know who this is." She gestured at Savina. "I … have also worked with Savina. I know how easy it is for her to subvert your expectations. But—" she paused, an odd reluctance in her tone. "Regardless of your or my personal feelings on the matter, I was charged with a warrant to bring her to Alba. Perhaps Savina is … not exactly what I'd been led to expect. But she's dangerous. And it's my duty as well as yours to ensure that she's somewhere she can't cause harm."

Savina's heart had begun to pound, a sick feeling welling in her stomach.

"Don't you touch my sister." Beni's voice was quiet and frightened, but there was a determination to it. "You're not hurting Savina."

Reka ignored them, her gaze fixed on Joska. "Let me take her in. At the very least, let me lock her up. I have some business to take care of, but the moment it's done, I promise you I'll take her back to Alba. Alba can decide what's to be done with her. Savina and I worked together, and I appreciate what she's done. But I have a duty, and that duty is no less now that we're trapped behind the portal. Allowing her to go free here, where our very survival as a species is in question, is far too dangerous, both for us and for all the humans trapped here."

Joska was simply watching, her face impassive.

Savina's heart beat painfully in her chest.

If Joska tried to grab her, Savina could shoot her and slip out of the ship in the confusion, or slit the woman's throat with one of her knives. Joska wouldn't be expecting it, and she wasn't wearing armour. She probably couldn't afford it if she wanted it, honestly.

But even as Savina thought it, she knew she was fooling herself.

She couldn't kill Joska.

And she knew perfectly well how Joska felt about what she'd done in the past.

"I won't kill her," Reka was saying in a level tone. "Not unless she gives me no other choice. If nothing else, for your sake, Captain, and in repayment for your cooperation, I'll keep her alive."

It wasn't true, though. Because Savina knew very well what it would mean, being taken captive and brought before Alba.

She'd die anyway. So just as well to die in an attempt to escape. There wasn't anything to lose. And if she tried to get away, Reka wouldn't hesitate. She'd seen enough of the woman to know that.

Joska was still watching Reka, in that evaluating way she had.

Finally, she stepped forward, toward Savina.

Savina flinched back, her hand on the hilt of her knife. But Joska stepped past her, standing between her and Reka.

"I can understand why you feel the way you do, Reka," she said. "But I'm going to say this once, and I hope it sinks in—if you want to take Savina, you'll do it across my dead body."

Rafel sighed reluctantly and shoved himself up out of his chair. "I suppose you have to do it over mine, too," he grumbled, limping over. "Because you're not touching the captain, not while I'm alive to stop it." He shot a glance at Savina, and under his irritable expression, she caught the faintest hint of something that might have been a smile. "Besides, this little murdering thief has saved my life twice now. I can't let her die with the ledger that unbalanced."

Savina blinked. Her heart was still pounding an uneven rhythm, and her head felt strange and dizzy.

Beni stepped up beside her, slipping their hand into hers like they used to do when the two of them were children. Savina glanced over at them, and found her eyes were blurred with tears.

Reka raised her eyebrows in mild surprise, watching them. Her gaze caught Savina's just for a moment, and Savina looked quickly away.

At last, Reka sighed and shook her head. "Well, it looks like I can't persuade you otherwise. And after you saved my life, I can't exactly shoot my way through you to get her." She paused a moment. "I'll ask that you let me off here, then. As I said, I have business to take care of back in Chrr that's rather urgent." She turned. Her grey-green eyes found Savina's, and for a moment, it could have been only the two of them in the room. "I'll give you a day's start, Savina. I owe you that, I think," she said quietly. "And then, I'll come for you."

Joska nodded slowly. "Since I doubt I could keep you here if I wanted to, Reka," she said, "you're free to go."

Reka gave her a small nod. "Thank you for what you did back there," she said. "We would have died without you, as would most of the Joias system, I suspect." She glanced at Savina. "Savina," she said quietly. "Until we meet."

Then she turned, and without so much as a backward glance, strode down the loading ramp and out into the jungle.

Savina watched after her for a long, long time.

Finally, Joska shook her head. "Well, I suppose at this point, none of us would know what to do if we weren't being chased by Reka Soler." She turned to Rafel. "Do you have that map the Chief Justice gave us? We'll need to find a place to refuel and resupply, and we can make our plans after that. I'm not sure the yibo even use the same fuel we do, but perhaps we can find something we can make work anyway. Beni, can you give him a hand, please?"

Rafel nodded, and turned back to the copilot seat.

Beni paused a moment, then squeezed Savina's hand. "I won't let Reka take you, Vina," they whispered. "She'll have to kill all of us if she wants to get to you. I promise." Then they slipped their hand from hers and followed Rafel into the cockpit.

Joska paused, her eyes lingering on Savina. There was a quiet sympathy in her expression that Savina realized she'd come to expect, a kindness beneath her stern gaze. "Savina?" Joska asked. "Are you alright?"

Savina swallowed hard. "I'm—" she started.

Then, to her horror, she felt the tears that had been welling in her eyes spill down her cheeks, and she couldn't speak for the thickness in her throat. She turned away, tears burning tracks down her face, choking back thick sobs.

She felt a rough hand on her shoulder, and she fought back the urge to shake it off.

"Savina." Joska's voice was gentle. "Savina, you're safe. It's alright. We weren't ever going to leave you."

And then, despite her best efforts, Savina was sobbing, her shoulders shaking, her eyes blurry with tears.

Joska rubbed her hand back and forth along Savina's shoulder blades, as if she was calming a skittish horse. "Come on, Savina," she murmured. "You've been through a lot in the last few days, I imagine. Let's get you to the med bay, we'll take a look at your injuries as soon as we're away from here and somewhere a little safer."

Savina let Joska take her arm and lead her down the *Dolphin's* familiar corridors to the med bay. She swallowed the painkiller Joska gave her, then lay back on one of the cots at Joska's prompting and stared numbly up at the ceiling as Joska left to talk to Rafel.

The *Dolphin* lifted gently, and once it had started off, Joska reappeared. Wordlessly, she handed Savina a tissue to wipe her face, then checked her over with quick, competent hands.

She sucked in a sharp breath once or twice as her fingers brushed over the worst of the injuries. When she'd finished her examination, she gave Savina a wry look. "It's a good thing we came when we did. For all that Reka's a government agent, she certainly didn't take much care treating that wound on your leg."

Savina sniffled. "Well," she said, her voice still thick. "We both thought we were going to die in five minutes' time. So there probably wouldn't have been time for it to get infected."

Joska chuckled, a soft, comfortable sound. "One day, when you're rested up, you'll have to tell me exactly what happened back there," she said. "From the sounds of it, there was plenty of excitement to go around. Although after knowing you this long, I'm not sure I'd expect anything different."

Savina managed a wan smile. "This from the woman who hijacked a yibo ship."

Joska's smile in return was genuine. "It wasn't nearly as exciting as all that—by the time we got to the loading pad, Mattin and his soldiers were in the process of embarking, so no one was too concerned at the sight of a few humans. We found a place to lay low, and when we saw the yibo bring Reka on board one of the ships, we assumed you'd follow shortly. We managed to get aboard without drawing attention, and since the pilot wasn't expecting us, it was hardly a fight. Now." She looked Savina over quickly. "You lie down. We should be at the yibo settlement in a couple of hours to pick up supplies, then we'll head off-planet. How are you feeling?"

"I—I think I just need some sleep," Savina said, swallowing. "I'll go into the room off the sick bay and lock the door—don't wake me up when we get there. I think I'll feel better once I get some rest."

Joska studied her for a moment, then, at last, she nodded. "Alright, Savina," she said quietly. Then she turned and left.

Savina stayed on the med bay cot for a few minutes longer.

Her injuries still hurt, but the pain had faded a little.

She couldn't remember the last time someone had taken care of her like this. Not since she was a child in the compound. It had been her mother back then. Her mother's hands smoothing her forehead, soothing a cut, rubbing a bruise.

The same hands that had lowered her baby brother, his tiny face screwed up in pain and fear as he wailed his weak newborn cries, into a shallow grave, and turned away, tears running down her face, as dirt was thrown over his small, fragile body.

She'd cried. She'd stood there crying, and done nothing to stop it.

And from that day on, those gentle hands had never felt quite the same. Savina had felt the death in them.

She took a deep breath, watching the door where Joska had disappeared.

She hadn't expected Joska to stand up for her. She wasn't sure what she'd expected, exactly—but not that.

Joska had somehow managed to talk Nicolau into staying back with the others. She'd kept Beni safe. She'd come back for Savina, even though Savina would never have asked.

If Savina could trust anyone with her siblings' lives, it was Joska.

And after what she'd seen over the past few weeks … If there was one person who was even more dangerous than the yibo, it was Reka Soler.

She remembered, far too well, the sight of the blood from Reka's weapon staining Joska's collar.

Reka wouldn't hurt Joska or the others on purpose. But accidents were far, far too easy.

At last Savina slid off the med bay cot and made her way into the small cabin off the med bay, closing the door behind her. She waited until the *Dolphin* came to a gentle halt and the engine shut down. She could hear voices outside, then the *hiss* of the loading ramp.

When at last it was silent, Savina sat up. She pulled out the sheet of writing paper she'd been creasing between her fingers and straightened it out, pinning it to the bedsheets.

She glanced at it one last time, her eyes scanning the words.

Joska. I've spent enough time around Reka to know we'll never be safe with her after me. She'll be a danger to you, and to Beni and Nicolau and Rafel, no matter what we do.

I know Beni and Nicolau will want you to come after me. Don't. This is the only way I know to keep them safe. And Rafel, too, since he's probably too stupid to do it himself. My wavelink will be turned off, and you won't be able to contact me, so you'd never find me anyway.

Get them somewhere safe. Get them to Alba. And if you ever get the chance— get them home. They'd like that, despite what my stupid baby brother says. He's just as stupid and self-sacrificing as you are.

And … thank you.

It wasn't enough, really. But then, there probably wasn't anything she could write that would tell Joska what it meant to her, that there was someone watching over Beni and Nicolau. That there was someone who'd put themself between Savina and someone who wanted to kill her, not as a joke or a decoy, but simply because she wasn't willing to stand by while Savina was hurt.

But … maybe Joska would understand anyway. Joska had always been far too good at understanding what Savina wasn't willing to say.

She smiled to herself just a little, then stood, gathering her things. She was still limping, and the sight of the blood on the bandage around her leg made her feel mildly woozy, but it was nothing she couldn't handle.

She opened the door carefully and glanced around. The ship was empty. She limped back to the supplies room and took enough to last her for a week or so, shoving it into a knapsack. Then, quietly, she slipped out the door.

The *Dolphin* had put down close to the outskirts of the small town, and Savina walked down the well-trodden path from the jungle. She saw no sign of the others, and so she made her way towards the market section of town.

As she slipped through the stalls, she heard a familiar voice.

She peeked through between two buildings.

Joska, Rafel, and Beni stood around a stall. Joska was pointing to something and saying, in her wry tone, "Listen, I might not be from around here, but that's three times the price it was in the city. Don't try to take us for a ride."

Savina smiled to herself, and ducked back.

She looked around her at the yibo hurrying about their business, her smile widening.

It shouldn't be hard to find a ride back to the city. This close, the yibo must travel back and forth frequently. And who could resist a helpless, sweet, innocent human like her?

Especially one with the knife, and no compunction about using it.

She widened her eyes, pasted on her most innocent close-lipped smile, and started towards the transportation hub in the centre of town.

She'd always known it would come to this, eventually, as much as she'd tried to avoid the thought. As long as Reka was alive, no one Savina loved would be safe.

The people Savina loved were stupid, and naïve, and ridiculous, and they'd proved it over and over. Stupid enough to risk their own lives for Savina's, even when they shouldn't. Even when she didn't deserve it and didn't ask for it and didn't want it. And she couldn't stop them, but neither could she let them do it.

And so Reka would have to die.

Resolutely, she shoved back the sick feeling the thought carried with it. Then she switched off her wavelink, and started towards a likely looking ship.

34

Aran

For a long time, Aran, Nicolau, and Ines simply stared at the space where the portal had been.

The relief washing over Aran was so thick it was dizzying, and he almost had to reach out to support himself against a tree.

"Did we—did we actually—" Ines's voice was soft with wonder.

"Yes," he said, his voice choking. "I think we did. And from the looks of it—" he glanced over his shoulder at the steaming ruins of the compound, where the raider ships were still dogfighting under the half-formed force-field. "It might take a while for them to put that back together."

Nicolau was grinning like a small boy opening presents on his saint's day. He turned to Ines, pulling his arm off Aran's shoulder. "Ines, you were brilliant." He swayed, but Ines caught him. He pulled her into his arms, and then the two of them were kissing, a long, passionate kiss.

Aran looked away awkwardly. After a few moments, he cleared his throat. "Um. Listen, I don't mean to … but maybe we should get farther away before we—"

Reluctantly, Nicolau pulled back. His expression was dazed, and softer than Aran had ever seen it.

Ines' eyes were sparkling, her entire face lit up. "Yeah," she gasped, a little breathlessly. "Yes, that's—that's probably a good idea."

Aran grinned despite himself, and the three of them started back the way they'd come.

By the time they reached the top of the hill, Aran could see what had caused the disruption back in the facility.

At least a dozen yibo military ships had landed in a semicircle around the hill beyond their encampment. They were at a respectful distance from the raider ships, but they were heavily armed enough that they probably didn't have much to be afraid of.

From the look of the yibo soldiers, though, and the way that the military captains were gesturing and barking orders, it didn't look like the raiders were their main target.

Aran frowned. "Who the hell—" he began.

Nicolau glanced over at him. His eyes were still a bit stary, and he was grinning like a kid. "Oh. You didn't hear, did you? I guess the yibo we met in the city when we first got to this system are actually not the government. They're—" he shrugged. "Some rebel group. Anyway. I'm guessing these are the actual military."

Aran stared at him, but it was clear he wasn't going to get any better explanation from the young man at the moment.

"Humans?"

Aran jerked his head up in time to see—

He frowned.

It was a human he didn't recognize. His accent was strange, nothing like anything Aran had heard back in Colorida. But the words themselves were understandable enough, the Common

Dialect they still used for scientific research.

"Excuse me, are you travelling with Alba?"

Aran gave a wary nod.

The human smiled, his drawn face relaxing a bit. "Good. You're safe, then." He strode forward and clapped a hand on Nicolau's shoulder.

When he tried to do the same with Aran, Ani hissed, and Aran stepped back quickly.

"I'm sorry," he began. "She's just—she's a little—"

The man gave Ani a wary glance, then shrugged. "The group of you have done an immense service. We didn't have the precise location of the portal mechanism, or the ability to take it out without starting a full-on war. But you've taken it out yourself, it appears, and Kachik's people have been thrown into enough disarray that I think we'll be able to take this place without bloodshed. Now, if you head back to the ship, the others are waiting for you."

He turned, and cautiously, Aran, Ines, and Nicolau followed him back towards the military ships.

Alba stood beside the loading ramp of one of the ships, in conversation with a yibo soldier. She turned when she saw them, and her face went slack with relief. "I'm glad to see you made it," she said in her sharp tone. "After that explosion, I wasn't sure." She paused. "These yibo have offered us asylum, and I think it's best we take it. The choice, however, is up to each of you."

"Where's Istvay?" Aran interrupted, his pulse pounding in his ears as he scanned the small group. "Where the hell is Istvay? Did something ... Are they—"

"It's alright," said Yosip, stepping forward. "Istvay's in the camp. They said they'd wait for you there. They weren't sure where you'd come first, and they didn't want you to worry."

"They're alright?" asked Aran, his voice sharp. "They didn't ... I mean, nothing—"

Yosip gave him a small smile. "They're tired. They had to run a bit to get the raiders to follow them, and I don't think they'll want to do that again anytime soon. But—" the smile-wrinkles in the corners of his eyes deepened. "They're alright."

Aran closed his eyes, the tension in his shoulders releasing for the first time since he'd left Istvay here with the others.

"I won't be coming back with you," he said, turning back to Alba. "Istvay and I promised the raiders we'd go back, and—" he shrugged helplessly. "This is the best chance I have of finding that cure. But when we find it, we'll try to make our way to you."

Yosip's eyes were twinkling. "Thank you, Aran. For everything." He lifted a hand, giving Aran a questioning look. Aran nodded, and Yosip put his hand on Aran's shoulder.

"Good luck," the old man said with that kind, friendly smile. "To both of you."

Aran nodded, then took a deep breath and turned away.

Istvay was waiting for him.

He made his way back to the camp, ignoring the bustle around him. His heart was beating faster again, and he found his hands were shaking. Ani gave a questioning chirrup, and he smiled, leaning his head against the bulk of her on his shoulder.

"It's alright, Ani," he said, his words coming out strange. "It's just ... I ... I think, maybe ..."

He couldn't finish. Ani didn't seem to mind, though, just purred and clamped herself tighter against his shoulder.

When he reached the tent, Aran paused, closing his eyes for just a moment.

His heart was pounding, almost as fast as it had been back in the yibo compound.

Istvay had kissed him. And with that kiss, every wall that Aran had spent the last however many years of his life building up had crumbled into dust.

He loved them. And maybe, just maybe, somehow—

He couldn't let himself think farther than that, because his heart was beating too fast already, and he felt lightheaded and a little dizzy.

He took a deep breath, then pushed the tent flap aside and ducked inside.

It took a moment for his eyes to adjust to the darkness. Istvay's supplies pouch and their knapsack lay in a heap, their jacket tossed over it in the unconscious, comfortable way they had when they were resting after a long day.

And then he frowned.

Istvay wasn't there.

He crossed over to the back of the tent in two quick steps. He could still see the place where Istvay must have sat.

And beside it … a long, sharp gash cut through the tent wall.

He stared at it, feeling like someone had hit him in the stomach.

This couldn't be happening. Not now, not after everything.

Maybe he'd misinterpreted the signs. Maybe Istvay had stepped outside. Maybe they were playing a joke on him, or they'd gone for a drink of water, or … something.

He ducked through the slit opening, looking around desperately.

His lungs were having a hard time pulling in air, his hands shaking.

There, on the ground outside where the tent had been slit open— there'd been some sort of scuffle.

He dropped to one knee slowly, dazedly. His fingers ran along the ground in a practiced motion until they touched something wet.

He swallowed hard. His heart beat a sharp pain in his chest.

He rubbed the wet dirt between his fingers, then brought it to his nose. He could smell the sharp, iron tang of it even before he touched it to his tongue.

He spat out the bitter, metallic taste, and had to fight to keep from throwing up.

Blood.

Istvay had been here. And then something had cut through the tent, and there was a shape where a body had fallen—a human-sized body—and blood on the ground. Blood smeared in the place where the head would have landed.

And around it—

He forced himself to open his eyes, despite the screaming panic in his brain, forced himself to look.

Footsteps. Raider footsteps.

And then he couldn't hold it anymore, and he leaned over and vomited, again and again until his stomach was empty, his whole body shaking.

It was impossible. This couldn't have happened, it had to be a dream. He had to wake up, he had to stop this, Istvay couldn't be gone …

Ani was making plaintive sounds of distress, her tentacles tightening around his arms and brushing across his face, but he couldn't spare attention even for her, he couldn't breathe, he couldn't think—

"Aran. They said we might find you here. You and I have some things to talk about, I think."

He didn't even look up at the dangerous tone in Krevai's voice, just sat where he was, curled into a ball, shaking.

"Aran?" Dimly, he recognized Dessi's voice, heard her footsteps as she crossed over and crouched beside him. "Aran. Are you injured? We came here to find you and your Ani and your Istvay. Where's—"

She trailed off. Then she jumped to her feet with a curse and strode off.

Aran stayed where he was, trying to remind his lungs to breathe.

Trying to remind himself why it even mattered.

A moment later, he heard Krevai, behind him, cursing loudly and creatively. "Damn her!" he snarled. "You're sure she's the one who took our Aran's Istvay?"

"Come look," said Dessi. "This wasn't one of ours."

The raiders' footsteps crossed over to the tent, next to where Aran was sitting. Aran didn't even look up.

"That's her," said Krevai at last, his voice gruff. "She must have been watching for a time when they were alone." He swore again. "It's just like her. Take one of my humans, just to spite me. And then she'll think she can flaunt them around, like her prize of war—"

Aran wasn't listening, but something in the captain's words seeped through the dull emptiness in his brain.

He jerked his head up sharply. "Flaunt them around?" His voice was tight. "You mean—you mean she wouldn't have just killed them?"

Krevai turned to Aran, frowning. "No, I doubt she'd do that. She would have, before you were part of my crew, but if she knows the human's mine, she won't kill it right away. I can't promise you she won't eat it sooner or later, but generally speaking, if you capture an enemy's crew, you give it three or four days before you kill them. Give the other ship a chance to try to get them back. It's a show of strength, and she'll need that, now that the portal is gone."

Aran closed his eyes, sucking in a quick breath.

Something cold was hardening in the pit of his stomach. He rose to his feet, grabbing Istvay's knapsack and slinging it over his back. He strapped Istvay's supply pouch beside his, and turned grimly back in the direction that he and Istvay had left the stolen attack pod.

"Aran! Where are you going?" Dessi called.

Aran turned to face her. He felt completely calm, completely cold, and for the first time in his life, even the aching, unmistakable terror at the thought of what he was going to do couldn't penetrate the deathly calm. "I'm going to find Istvay. And I'm going to bring them back."

35

Epilogue

The first thing Istvay was aware of was the sharp pounding behind their eyes.

For a moment, they lay perfectly still, trying to remember what the hell had happened.

And then they remembered, and choked out a mumbled curse.

They'd been waiting in the tent, eyes closed, fighting back the exhaustion of their long run to attract the raiders' attention, get them to start towards the hill where the transmitters Alba and Yosip and Feliu were holding would bounce the signals back from the facility.

They'd pretended to be alright when Alba asked, but they hadn't been, really. They'd been so tired, almost too weary to put one foot in front of the other.

But it hadn't mattered.

Because they were waiting for Aran. They were waiting for him to come back, like he'd promised he would. And Aran wouldn't ever break his promise, not a promise he'd made to Istvay. He'd walk through hell and the Void and not even notice. Istvay had always known that.

And then—

Istvay groaned.

The raider captain. The knife slipped through the fabric tent walls. How Istvay had scrambled to their feet, too late, the hands grabbing at them, being dragged outside, shouts muffled.

The blow to their head.

Cautiously, they blinked their eyes open.

They were in a small, enclosed space. Their hands were bound behind their back, their feet tied together. Blood crusted across the side of their face and down over their lips and chin, and Istvay grimaced, trying to brush it away on their shoulder.

The movement sent a wave of pain through their head, and they had to close their eyes for a moment, waiting for it to subside.

There was something sick and heavy sitting in their stomach.

Aran would come back. Istvay had no doubt of that. Aran would come looking for them. And he'd find them gone. He'd find the marks in the ground, see the blood. And then he would—

Istvay squeezed their eyes shut, fighting back panic.

They'd seen the look on Aran's face, back when the two of them were children together and Istvay's mother had died. They'd seen what it had done to Aran. And seeing that blank hopelessness in his eyes had been—worse than anything. Worse than Istvay's own sadness, worse than their own despair.

They couldn't bear the thought of those bright, gentle eyes, that sensitive, sweet face, gone blank and empty and hopeless, ever again. They couldn't. Even as a ten-year-old, it had almost broken Istvay— seeing Aran in pain, and not being able to do anything to fix it. And now …

They took a deep breath.

They were still alive. There was that, at least.

The door creaked open, and the raider captain stepped inside. She looked Istvay over with a wide smile. The scar from a pulse pistol rippled across her face, angry and red, and there was vicious satisfaction in her expression.

"So," she said, crouching down in front of Istvay, her hands on her knees. "The human is awake." She smiled, showing her teeth, but there was sharp hatred in that smile. "Krevai added you to his crew, did he? Good. That only makes this more satisfying." She reached down, pulling a long butchering knife from her belt. "At first, I wanted to kill you out of revenge for this." She gestured to the bright scar across her face. "That would have been enough. And then you took down the portal, which is going to cause more bloodshed—the other raider crews were looking to me to lead us through it. And now I learn that Krevai took you and the other human on as part of his crew." She brought the knife up, the sharp blade of it pressing against Istvay's throat.

Istvay forced themself to keep their eyes on her face, instead of glancing down at the blade. Their heart was beating fast and uneven.

"Krevai may act stupid, but he's canny. He wouldn't have got where he was if he hadn't been. So there's a reason he took you." She paused. "I suspect the reason had more to do with your friend and his—whatever the hell that thing is." She shuddered, and Istvay bit back a grim smile.

"But I don't know that for certain. Either way, the two of you seemed close. And if I know anything about humans, I'm sure losing you will break the other one. So either way, I win." She drew the knife gently down Istvay's throat and across their shoulder. Istvay grimaced at the sharp flare of pain that followed the blade, the hot wet of blood dripping down after it, soaking through their filthy shirt.

"Tradition says I keep you alive for three days, since you're part of Krevai's crew. But this is too important. I'm facing challenges to my leadership, and I can't afford to be fighting Krevai in the meantime. Besides—" She raised an eyebrow suggestively. "It's been a long time since I've tasted human flesh. I miss it." She straightened, looking them over appraisingly, and drew back the knife.

Istvay gritted their teeth.

They couldn't die, not now, not like this. Not with Aran waiting for them back in the camp.

Not with everything they'd left unsaid.

"Wait!" they snapped.

The captain paused. "Yes?" she said, her tone amused. "Are you going to beg for your life? That could be entertaining."

"Wait," said Istvay again. Their breath was coming quick and unsteady. "I'm more useful than you think."

Her smile widened. "Really? Are you sure you're useful, not just afraid to die?"

Istvay had to fight back a slightly bitter smile.

Their whole life, that had always been the question. Aran was brilliant, Istvay knew it as well as anyone. And Istvay honestly didn't mind not taking any of the credit. For all he hated it, Aran deserved every bit of fame he had, every word of praise he received. Istvay— the former homeless child, the research assistant, whatever the hell people called them—Istvay was always the afterthought.

And Istvay had never minded, not as long as Aran was the one getting the credit. Because—well, dammit, because Aran *was* brilliant. Because Aran was everything.

Aran deserved the whole damn world. Istvay had known that, instinctually, since they were five years old and had crouched down beside the child crying in the street in the rain, and looked into the tear-streaked face of the most beautiful boy they'd ever seen.

But this once, this one time, Istvay had to convince someone they were worth something themself. On their own merits, not because of Aran or anyone else.

Istvay shook their head gingerly, wincing at the wave of pain the movement brought. "No," they muttered. "Listen. You're facing a leadership crisis? Fine. But I've watched you, this whole time you've been after us. Your crew may be good, but they're inefficient as hell. I study systems. I'd be willing to bet I could get your ship running twice as efficiently as it is now. Which gives you time to deal with whatever the hell the rest of the raiders will do to kick you off your throne." They paused. "And think what kind of pull that would give you—you have Krevai's former crew working for you. That has to mean something."

She quirked an eyebrow at them. "You'd help me? There's going to be a war for leadership. You'd have to renounce your loyalty to Krevai. But if you did that … like you say, it looks impressive, at least."

Istvay forced themself to meet her eyes.

There was a time, not too long ago, that the thought of a leadership war, whatever that meant, would have meant something to Istvay. When they might have told Aran, if he were here, that their own life wasn't that important. When they might have, in Aran's words, been a self-sacrificing idiot.

But … that had been before. Before Istvay had let themself realize how much they meant to Aran. How much losing them would hurt him. Before they'd realized to what lengths they'd go to keep Aran from being hurt.

Before they'd kissed Aran, and finally, finally admitted to themself how much, how desperately much, they wanted to live.

The raider captain studied Istvay for a few moments. "And I'm supposed to believe you."

They didn't drop her gaze. "Try me. If you find I'm not useful, you can kill me then."

At last she gave a brusque nod. "I suppose it won't hurt to try. I'll give you a chance. But best hope you can do what you promise." She shot them a toothy smile, then turned to leave. "I'll send someone in to cut your restraints, and you can get to work. But it might be a few hours. I have to make sure we're out of range of Krevai and his people first."

Then she was gone.

Istvay stared after her. Their stomach still churned with nausea, their head spinning, and pain throbbed in all the places they'd been injured.

They closed their eyes and leaned back against the wall, pushing back against the hopelessness.

It didn't matter. They were going to survive this, they had to. Somehow, they'd stay alive long enough to find a way to get back to Aran, no matter what it took.

Istvay could still feel Aran's lips against theirs, warm and soft, the way the sensation had jolted through their entire body. Aran's hands on their hips, his fingers tightening, pulling Istvay closer, Istvay's hands tangled in the warmth of Aran's hair. The way Aran's breath had quickened, the taste of him on Istvay's lips, the rough brush of his short beard against Istvay's skin, just like how Istvay had remembered, how they'd dreamed about every damn night for more years than they really wanted to admit. How close to unbearable it had been to pull back, finally, break off the kiss. The look on Aran's face when they had—his eyes wide and dark with a mixture of wonder and desire, that small, disbelieving smile tugging at the corners of his lips, something bright and light inside him that almost glowed through his skin. The way he'd looked at Istvay as if Istvay was every dream he'd ever had, finally come true.

They would find Aran. They would see that look again. And they'd finally damn well tell him—

Istvay blinked their eyes open again.

They'd promised. They'd promised Aran. And this was a promise they were damn well going to keep, even if it meant setting the whole system on fire.

Book four, Quantum Entanglement, available now!

You might also enjoy The Ungovernable series, also by R.M. Olson.

A mouthy ex-smuggler pilot, a grumpy demolitions expert, a tech genius and a hacker. They're pulling a job on the most dangerous weapons dealer in the System. They're stealing tech that could change the course of history. And every one of them has something to hide.
What could possibly go wrong?
"Spectacular and thrilling! Olson's debut novel is filled with compelling characters and endless excitement." -SD Simper, author of the Fallen Gods series

You can order book one, Zero Day Threat, on Amazon.

I also have a Patreon, where I post character art, short stories, sneak peaks, and other fun stuff. You can get in on it for only $3/month, so if you're interested, check it out here!
https://www.patreon.com/rmolson